RICHES and HONOR

ALSO BY TOM HYMAN

GIANT KILLER
THE RUSSIAN WOMAN

RICHES and HONOR

a novel by
TOM HYMAN

Viking

VIKING
Viking Penguin Inc., 40 West 23rd Street,
New York, New York 10010, U.S.A.
Penguin Books Ltd, Harmondsworth,
Middlesex, England
Penguin Books Australia Ltd, Ringwood,
Victoria, Australia
Penguin Books Canada Limited, 2801 John Street,
Markham, Ontario, Canada L3R 1B4
Penguin Books (N.Z.) Ltd, 182–190 Wairau Road,
Auckland 10, New Zealand

First published in 1985 by Viking Penguin Inc.
Published simultaneously in Canada

LIBRARY OF CONGRESS CATALOGING IN PUBLICATION DATA
Hyman, Vernon Tom.
  Riches and honor.
  I. Title.
PS3558.Y49R5 1985   813'.54   84-29917
ISBN 0-670-80508-4

Grateful acknowledgment is made to the following for permission to
reprint copyrighted material:

Essex Music Inc.: Portions of lyrics from "Those Were the Days,"
words and music by Gene Raskin. TRO—copyright © 1962 and 1968
by Essex Music, Inc., New York, N.Y. The rights to this song are
controlled by the Essex Music Company throughout the world.
*Silkie Music Publishers, A Division of Vanguard Recording Society,
Inc.:* Portions of lyrics from "Pack Up Your Sorrows," by Richard
Fariña and Pauline Marden. Copyright © 1964 (unp.), 1966, 1977,
1979, 1982 by Silkie Music Publishers.
Warner Bros. Music: Portions of lyrics from "Tomorrow Is a Long
Time," by Bob Dylan. Copyright © 1963 by Warner Bros. Inc. All
rights reserved.

Printed in the United States of America by
The Book Press, Brattleboro, Vermont
Set in Times Roman

To Dick Adler and Steve Gelman
for a lot of good deeds over a lot of years

Riches and honor are what men desire.

CONFUCIUS

PROLOGUE

Dachau Concentration Camp
April 29, 1945

Karl Koenig woke before dawn, surprised that he was still alive.

The windows at the far side of the ward were paling with the first warnings of the new day. Koenig hated the arrival of that desolate gray light. It came as a harbinger of dread, pulling him from the refuge of sleep into the terror and pain of the waking world.

He strained his eyes to focus on the uneven rows of wooden slats two feet above his head. They were creaking under the weight of the Russian, Karpov, in the bunk above.

The beds were three tiers high and jammed together in pairs so that three patients could be squeezed onto each level. The typhus epidemic that had raged through the camp all winter had abated finally, and the spaces were emptying fast, as recovery or death rapidly claimed their occupants.

The infirmary seemed unnaturally still. Had an entire night really passed? Koenig was no longer sure. He was losing track of the passage of time. He felt less feverish now, but much weaker. He doubted he would be able to get out of bed at all, even with help. This upset him, not so much because he knew it was a sign that he was dying, but because he would soil his bedding. The humiliation of such abject helplessness was more terrifying to him than the prospect of death itself.

Koenig closed his eyes again, and fragments of the dream he had just awakened from drifted back. Like most camp prisoners, he usually dreamed of food—intense imaginings of childhood and the family table back in Freiburg before the war, his mother bustling and cheerful in her bright dirndl skirts bringing in an endless procession of dishes: wurst and sauerkraut, schnitzel and potato pancakes, Christmas goose with bread-and-walnut stuffing.

But this morning's dream had been about flying. He had risen from his bed and floated right through the roof of the infirmary. And he had continued on upward, like a hot-air balloon, until he was high enough to see the entire camp compound—the long double row of prisoners' barracks, the Appellplatz and Jourhaus, the guard towers, the crematorium, workshop, laboratories, even the brick houses of the SS, with their neat courtyards and vegetable gardens.

No one tried to stop him. No fire came from the machine guns in the towers; none of the Dobermans barked. No one even looked up. It was serene, awesomely beautiful. The countryside around the camp looked green and warm. He could see trains moving far below, and cars on the road to Munich, ten miles to the east.

The dream had one obvious meaning, he supposed. It was telling him that he would soon leave Dachau the only way any prisoner ever left it—by dying.

But did the dream also mean that he would go to heaven? The possibility filled him with a mixture of yearning and anguish. He had left God and the Catholic Church behind in Freiburg when he was thirteen. He was a Communist now, and an atheist. Heaven, Marxism had taught him, was right here on earth, waiting only for the revolution to usher it in.

Koenig felt for Grunwald beside him. His blanket was pulled over his head. Fearfully, Koenig rolled it down and placed a hand on his cheek. It was rubbery and dry but still warm. Grunwald moved his head slightly under Koenig's hand. "Don't forget your promise, Herr Grunwald," Koenig whispered. "Please don't."

They had made a private pact, he and Grunwald, that they would not let each other die. Grunwald had introduced the idea several months ago, when six prisoners staged a mass suicide by flinging themselves against the electrified camp fence. They were wrong to do it, Grunwald had insisted. Survival was the moral obligation of every prisoner. They must survive to bear witness. That was what mattered most.

Grunwald had already survived the camp longer than anybody. Ten years. He was a Jew in his fifties and he had lost everything to the

Nazis—his furniture business, his house, his possessions, his family. They had murdered his wife and two daughters at Ravensbruck, and most of his relatives had met the same fate somewhere else. Before becoming so ill, he had treated Koenig like a son, and Koenig felt great affection for him, despite the man's stubborn beliefs in God and capitalism. Would Grunwald go to heaven? he wondered. Maybe the dream was really about him. Because if heaven did exist, Grunwald had earned his place there.

There was another explanation for his dream, Koenig thought. Rescue. There were many rumors, good and bad. The camp hummed with new ones every day: The Allied armies were across the Rhine. The collapse of the Third Reich was imminent. Some were saying that the SS planned to move all the prisoners to camps farther east. Many, in fact, had already been moved. Others swore that the Allies were only hours away. Just last night someone claimed to have seen flashes of artillery in the west. Yesterday, or the day before, Koenig's friend Gunter had told him there was much talk among the prisoners about Wolkenbrand, the Nazi plan to exterminate the concentration-camp population before the Allies could liberate them. Rumors. No one really knew.

Koenig felt a hand shaking him. He opened his eyes and saw the stick-thin figure of Gunter leaning over him.

"I brought you water, Karl." He held up a little glass medicine bottle. "Can you drink it?"

"I'll need help."

Gunter slipped a hand under Koenig's neck to prop up his head, then held the bottle to his lips. Koenig drank in slow, painful gulps.

"You feel less hot this morning," Gunter whispered. "You're going to get well!"

Koenig nodded. If he did survive, it would be because of Gunter. Koenig marveled at his friend's unquenchable optimism. Gunter had nursed him patiently through his illness, keeping up his spirits under conditions that had caused the strongest to despair. Gunter was nineteen, a year younger than Koenig, but he looked like a frail boy of twelve. Under the stenciled number on the prison pajamas was sewn the lavender triangle that identified him as a homosexual. He had been in the camp three years, working in the infirmary. Koenig was proud of him: He was the first person he had successfully converted to communism.

"It's quiet," Koenig said.

Gunter's eyes searched the dismal ward nervously. "Something's going on. They canceled all the work parties this morning. About an hour ago the morning guard hoisted a white flag over the Jourhaus. All the prisoners are out on the Appellplatz, just milling around, waiting to see what's going to happen."

"Maybe the Allies are coming," Koenig said.

"A lot of us think the flag is a trick. The guards are still in the towers. And we aren't getting any food today. That could start a riot. Just the excuse they'd need for Wolkenbrand."

Koenig closed his eyes. It was probably so. The prisoners knew that there had been many desertions in the SS ranks the past few days, and confusion in the camp's chain of command. If Wolkenbrand was more than a rumor, the SS would act soon. The prisoners' only hope was that the Allies got here before the slaughter started.

"I think Grunwald is dying," Koenig said.

Gunter nodded and made a despairing gesture with his hands. "I'm going back out on the Appellplatz. I'll come back if there's news."

Koenig drifted off to sleep. At midmorning he was awakened by a tumult of noise. He heard machine-gun fire, then shouts and screams and the pounding of running feet. The noise continued for a long time, alternately fading and then building again, sometimes to a frenzy and volume he could scarcely believe. The few patients still in the infirmary were sitting up, whispering to one another in fright. From a bunk nearby, Koenig heard heavy sobbing. Wolkenbrand had surely begun.

Suddenly Gunter burst into the ward, gasping for breath. He seemed transfixed and agitated, all at once. His eyes bulged from his thin face; his arms flapped at his sides. Tears streamed down his cheeks. "The Americans!" he cried, his voice cracking. "They're here, Karl! The Americans are here!"

Koenig lifted his head up, then let it fall back onto the bunk. The momentous news rolled over him like a tidal wave. He felt dizzy and on the edge of blacking out.

The other patients began to babble excitedly, filling the ward with their keening and sobbing as they marshaled their faded strength to embrace this miracle. Gunter danced by Koenig's bunk, his shabby hemp slippers slapping against the floor in frenzied joy. "We're free, Karl! God, we're free! You've got to live now, Karl! You've made it!"

Unable to contain his euphoria, Gunter hugged Koenig's blanketed form and then dashed back outside.

The afternoon passed. Several times Koenig managed to rouse Grunwald, only to have the older man sink immediately back into unconsciousness. Koenig rolled over onto his side and looked toward the windows on the far wall, hoping to see something—an American, perhaps. It was ironic that he was going to be saved by the Americans. The collapse of Nazi Germany was the beginning of the end for capitalism. The real winner of this war would be the Soviet Union, and the cause of international communism. If he lived, he could become a part of that new world. Thanks to the Americans. He could love them individually as soldiers, he decided, without having to love what they stood for. And this afternoon he could feel only pathetic gratitude.

Gunter returned later with a tin cup full of stew and a piece of freshly baked bread. The Americans had raided the SS stores, he explained, and were handing out everything. And they were coming to the infirmary soon, with doctors and medicine. Koenig let Gunter spoon some of the stew into his mouth.

"The Americans are shooting the SS guards," Gunter whispered, his hand trembling with emotion. "They lined them up against the wall near the Jourhaus and executed them."

"How many?"

"At least a hundred so far! We watched and cheered them on!"

"How did it happen?"

"The SS surrendered like the meekest cowards! They were so eager to please the Americans! Can you imagine, Karl, what it was like for us to see that? Can you imagine the joy? The SS cringing before their captors! The Americans didn't know what to do! Then they found the bodies stacked by the crematorium. They went crazy!" Gunter made an obscene gesture and laughed. "The SS are all *kaput!*"

Gunter left and Koenig drifted into a dreamlike stupor. Toward evening his temperature began to rise again, and he worried that he might not be strong enough to make it through another night. Grunwald beside him was still breathing, but his heartbeat was very faint. Could the Americans still save him? Did they really have doctors and medicine with them, as Gunter had promised? Where were they? Why didn't they hurry up?

At dusk he heard someone come into the infirmary.

"Gunter?" he whispered.

No answer.

The figure moved around to the other side of the three-tiered bunk, and in the fading light, Koenig noticed his uniform. An American soldier at last!

The soldier began examining Grunwald. Maybe he was a doctor. Koenig turned his head and strained to see in the dim light. He whispered that Grunwald was dying. The soldier looked up but didn't respond.

Even as Koenig was thinking that the soldier wouldn't understand German, he caught the faint outline of a skull and crossbones on his cap. He clenched his jaw to keep from crying out in terror. Impossible, he thought. The SS guards had never dared venture into the infirmary; they feared contagion from the sick prisoners. Why was he here? Where were the Americans?

The guard pulled the blanket from Grunwald's inert form and, to Koenig's astonishment, began undressing him. There were no gowns in this hospital, and Grunwald was wearing what he had come in with, the striped cotton pajamalike prison uniform with his identification number and yellow Star of David sewn over the heart. What could the guard want with it?

Gradually Koenig understood. He lay utterly still, barely daring to breathe. The guard slipped out of his own SS uniform, rolled it up tightly, and stuffed it under the empty straw mattress at the bottom of the next bunk over. He then dressed himself hurriedly in Grunwald's wrinkled, dirty prison clothes.

He planned to escape disguised as a prisoner. And in the confusion of the hour, he would probably get away with it.

Suddenly Grunwald stirred. He groaned and flopped his arms protectively over his thighs and stomach, as if protesting the indignity of his nakedness. Startled, the guard took the thin blanket, folded it to the size of a pillow, and pressed it down over Grunwald's face.

Koenig wanted to scream, to plead for his friend's life, but his lips were glued together, dry as paper. Reason told him that he was powerless to intervene, that he must save his own life by remaining absolutely still. But the shame of it, to do nothing! How his conscience ached to grab the guard's wrists and try, with whatever strength remained, to rescue his friend from death.

The guard held the blanket over Grunwald's face for a long time. Koenig saw him plainly now. He was young, about Koenig's age. They might have been in Gymnasium together. Or Hitler Youth. The cords of his neck bulged, and his lips were drawn back, exposing his teeth. Koenig realized that he, too, was afraid.

Tears started from Koenig's eyes. He was so dehydrated, he felt as if he was surrendering the last drops of moisture from his body. He closed his lids to hold them in, and imagined the horror of that coarse blanket pressed with the same hard finality over his own face.

Survive, Grunwald had told him. *Survive and bear witness.*

Finally the guard released his grip on the blanket and disappeared into the darkness. Koenig lay awake the rest of the night, clinging to

RICHES AND HONOR / 7

life with a new determination, his emaciated body nursing a fanatic new purpose.

Before dawn he tumbled from his bunk and managed, with a supreme effort of will, to crawl across the infirmary floor to the bunk where he had seen the guard hide his uniform. He groped under the straw mattress and found the discarded tunic. He pulled the neck up close to his eyes and searched for a laundry tag. The only identifying mark was a number: SS 43526.

Koenig repeated the number to himself, over and over, determined to remember it as long as he lived. An American army doctor found him on the floor an hour later, unconscious but alive, the tunic still clutched in his hands.

1

Nice, France
March 10, 1982

Brian Duffy was a hack writer.

Unreliable, untalented, and dishonest, he was the journalistic equiv-
alent of a stray dog, keeping himself alive by foraging for scraps in
the trash heaps of the day's news.

What he lacked in virtue he made up for in enterprise, and with
his network of paid informers and his skill in producing stories swiftly
from a hasty pudding of half-truths, rumors, innuendo, and gossip,
he had managed to maintain a debt-ridden free-lance existence on the
French Riviera for years by cranking out lurid features for tabloids
back in the United States.

He was checking into just such a story now, on the top floor of a
hospital near the Palais des Expositions in the old quarter of Nice.
The night before, an orderly from the hospital had confided to him,
while drunk in a local gay bar, an intriguing tale about a Vietnamese
refugee being treated secretly in a heavily guarded private ward. Duffy
had smelled something salable.

Predictably, the orderly had exaggerated his story. People always
exaggerated their stories, Duffy had discovered; it was one of the few
peculiarities of human nature that could be depended upon. Sneaking past the nurses' station, he found his subject stuck away in a
tiny, dark room at the end of a long corridor. The door was wide

open, there was no guard anywhere in sight, and the patient was alone.

Duffy slipped in, closed the door, cranked open the venetian blind to let in some light, and pulled a chair up next to the bed.

"I'm from the International *Herald Tribune,*" he lied in French. "Do you know the *Herald Tribune?*" He pulled out a copy of the newspaper and held it up.

The patient, a wiry, black-eyed male Vietnamese in his mid-thirties, appeared tired but otherwise healthy. He lay quietly on his back, with one arm outside the blanket, an intravenous needle taped to the wrist. Duffy's informant had said he was suffering from exposure and exhaustion.

Duffy unslung his cassette recorder from his shoulder and briskly cleared a space for it on the bedside table. "We intend to do a story on your escape from Vietnam," Duffy told him, punching down the RECORD button. "Do you speak French?"

The patient nodded. He didn't look to Duffy as if he was burning to communicate. "What's your name?" he demanded.

"Ngo Din Tran," the man replied.

Duffy pushed the recorder closer to the bed. "Okay, Tran, speak up, now. What made you decide to leave Vietnam? Was it your hatred of the Communist dictatorship? Did they torture you? What will happen to your family? Come on, I don't have all day."

An hour later Duffy's interview was interrupted by an angry nurse, who tried to confiscate his tape recorder. He managed to hold on to it, but the interview was clearly over. No amount of reassuring sweet talk on his part seemed to appease her. She became hysterical and threatened to call the police if he didn't leave immediately. He left.

Back in his apartment, Duffy poured himself a cognac and played back the tape. As the reels spun, Duffy's disappointment grew. The subject's command of French was poor, and he had repeatedly lapsed into Vietnamese during the interview. What little of his story Duffy could understand was confused and vague.

Duffy pulled out a notepad and jotted down the salient points: Ngo Din Tran was thirty-five years old and had once served as a sergeant in the South Vietnamese Army. Sometime after the Communist takeover of the south in 1975, he had been sent to a labor camp near the Laotian border. He had apparently just escaped from the camp and made his way across Laos to Thailand, where he was able to establish contact with relatives in France. They, in turn, had managed to bring him to Nice. None of this interested Duffy in the slightest. Refugee stories were as common as they were depressing.

What interested—and frustrated—Duffy were the references to an

American Marine POW named Billy Grunwald. According to Tran, the American was still alive over there, after twelve years. Duffy had heard of this Grunwald before. His father was William Grunwald, a big-shot businessman, very rich and very well connected politically. He had made headlines some years ago with a ransom offer to the Vietnamese government to free his son. And now he was up for an ambassadorial nomination.

Duffy had been able to extract from his Vietnamese subject the precise location of the camp where he claimed Grunwald was being kept. He had even sketched a map of the area on a piece of Duffy's notepaper. The camp was situated between the villages of Lang Vei and Khe Sanh, right on the Laotian border.

An American MIA from a prominent family turning up alive in Vietnam twelve years later was a dynamite piece of news, but Duffy had learned almost nothing from the patient beyond the location of the prison camp. The mere mention of Grunwald's name invariably caused Tran to abandon his French and jabber agitatedly in Vietnamese. *"Très dangereuse"* was the only explanation Duffy got. To whom it was dangerous and why, he had not been able to discover.

He considered his options. He could try to sneak back into the hospital and pry more of the story out of the man, or he could go with what he had. That wasn't much. He would have to make up most of it. He toyed with a number of possible leads and tried to visualize the story's headline. He liked "Millionaire's Son Kept Alive as Slave in Vietnam." That was a grabber. He could knock out a couple or three thousand words on that, describing in imaginative detail the ghastly conditions of his captivity—the horrible tortures, the starvation diet, the forced marches, the primitive bestiality of his captors, etcetera, etcetera. Maybe he should even introduce a sadistic woman guard. A little kinky sex never hurt a story.

The bottom line was two thousand dollars, he figured. That was the most he could get from any of the tabloids, and then only by selling them world rights. Maybe he could push it to two-five if he outdid himself.

He listened to the tape all the way through again and tried to think of someone he knew who might understand Vietnamese. The answer was no one. And why bother? A few more authentic details wouldn't increase the value of the article. He was working for a payday, not a Pulitzer.

Duffy uncovered his portable Olivetti, poured himself another brandy, and went to work. Two hours later he had completed a rough first draft. He stacked it on his desk and went out for a late supper at a café down the street.

Through the meal he kept revising the story in his mind. He wasn't happy with what he had written. It lacked feeling, verisimilitude. A few more authentic details were exactly what the piece needed, after all. Even the most cynical journalistic rip-off needed *some* facts to make it work. And all he had was the location of a prison camp in Vietnam. And the claim of a Vietnamese refugee that Billy Grunwald was there. Everything else in the piece, Duffy had manufactured.

The dread possibility of rejection loomed large. He decided he had better sound out the editor in New York by phone before he wasted any more time on the story. If the guy was interested, Duffy would find a way to get back into the hospital and squeeze more information out of the refugee.

He gulped a large mouthful of brandy, and as he swirled it noisily between his cheeks, he was seized with a bold inspiration. The blood rushed to his face, and he nearly cried out loud in delight. There was a much better way to capitalize on this story. A way that could net him far more than a couple of thousand dollars. And he wouldn't have to rewrite the damned piece at all.

He bolted down the rest of his meal and rushed back to his apartment, his head churning, making plans, assessing risks.

Duffy's idea, in a life that had been crowded with bad ideas, would turn out to be the worst one he would ever have.

2

New York City

William Grunwald, chairman of the board and principal owner of Grunwald Industries, took his seat at the head of the long conference table in the boardroom of his New York headquarters and tapped the polished teak surface gently with the edge of his metal-frame eyeglasses. Conversation in the high-ceilinged room faded as abruptly as if someone had turned down the volume of a radio. The twelve other executives seated around the table pulled themselves up in their leather armchairs and turned their attention toward their boss.

At fifty-six, Grunwald was the master of his sizable domain, and everything in his appearance and manner confirmed it. His deeply tanned face was wide and square, its corners framed by the receding edges of his thinning, sand-colored hair and the angles of his jawline. There was no hint of sag in his cheeks, no trace of a double chin. His eyes, coppery brown with flecks of gold, were set far apart and hooded beneath thick brows that slanted in a shallow V across his flat forehead. His nose was prominent, jutting out sharply at the bridge and then plunging vertically, in a perfectly straight line, to a squared-off tip. His mouth was wide, and stretched in a perpetual frown. Head on, he looked like a fierce owl.

He was dressed in dark-gray pinstripes, his habitual business costume. His tan contrasted sharply with the starched white of his collar and cuffs, and his blunt face, broad shoulders, and long torso made him appear taller and heavier than his six feet, 185 pounds. Despite the immaculate tailoring, his restless energy created an impression of discomfort, as if the wearer weren't quite civilized enough to accept the restraints of modern clothing.

Grunwald surveyed the twelve expectant male faces with the unhurried self-indulgence that comes with the exercise of great authority. These were all tough, experienced executives, each handpicked by him, each wielding considerable power within his own sphere. And each an individual of tested loyalty.

The organizational chart of the multi-billion-dollar international empire they ruled was a model of clarity, as elegantly simple an arrangement as the table and the men seated around it. A medieval monarch would have understood it immediately, and approved.

At its head, of course, stood Grunwald himself, chairman and first executive officer of the parent corporation, Grunwald Industries. It was the forty-second largest corporation in the world, and he owned eighty-six percent of its stock. He was the modern businessman-king, as much the absolute monarch in his nation-state of offices, factories, mines, and ships as a nineteenth-century Russian czar.

Flanking him were his ministers—on his left the corporation's treasurer, Charles Carlson; on his right, the corporation's chief counsel and executive secretary, James Safier. The ten remaining chairs were occupied by his barons—the presidents of the corporation's ten major divisions, a tightly integrated juggernaut that included giant industrial firms like Grunwald Arms, the manufacturers of military hardware, weapons, and ammunition; Grunwald Technologies, the makers of sophisticated electronic equipment; Grunwald Shipping, a Panamanian-registered company with a fleet of forty freighters and six supertankers; and Grunwald Mineral, a company heavily involved in the mining and production of strategic metals worldwide.

Grunwald opened the meeting without ceremony. "Let's start with the Brazilian offer," he said, his low voice still faintly thickened by the vestiges of a German accent. "Jim?"

James Safier nodded briskly and rose to his feet. He was tall with black, curly hair and a pug nose that gave him a vaguely Italian toughguy look, an impression not softened by his weakness for tight-fitting hand-tailored suits, high shirt collars, and bright ties. A bachelor lawyer in his mid-thirties who devoted all his energies to his work, he was Grunwald's most trusted and valuable assistant. As confidant, troubleshooter, hatchet man, advisor, Safier existed to protect and promote the cause of Grunwald Industries, to vanquish its enemies and turn its goals into reality. He was widely feared and respected, and considered, next to Grunwald himself, to be the most important individual in the corporation.

"I've Xeroxed maps of the Amazon Basin area," Safier began, in his clipped, formal manner, "which are before you in your folders, along with our geologists' report. As you can see, they show rich deposits of tin and copper in the Serra Do Cachimbo, and a vein of ore along the Madeira River, south of Manaus, with substantial concentrations of gold. Not traces but real nuggets of the stuff. Both these areas are remote from any highways and the development costs will be very high. Brazil wants us to buy out Ludwig's concession, which, as you know, he has decided to abandon. Brazil is desperate for cash, with the IMF breathing down its neck, and so our bargaining position is excellent. . . ."

Grunwald focused on Safier's profile as he addressed the board. His chief deputy was an orphan. Grunwald had found him, at the age of fifteen, working in a coal mine in West Virginia. Grunwald bought the mine, and the young Safier approached him with some suggestions on improving productivity that so impressed him he moved Safier to a job in the mailroom of his New York headquarters, where he might have a better chance to advance himself. The young adolescent proved to be so enterprising and intelligent that Grunwald took him completely under his wing, putting him through college and law school and watching him advance through the ranks of the corporation with the pride of a man who knows he has made an inspired investment.

Safier had been with Grunwald for twenty years, and his devotion to him was complete and unquestioned. He made himself available round the clock and the calendar, and appeared to have no life of his own outside the corporation. Grunwald had come, gradually, to think of him almost as an extension of himself. Almost like a son.

Grunwald forced his attention back to the matter at hand. Safier was holding up a big map and pointing to a spot somewhere in Brazil's Mato Grosso. "We'll inherit Ludwig's development, too," he said. "Roads, towns, water, some equipment—"

"Is that really worth anything?" a voice interrupted. It was Grayson Boyce, president of Grunwald Mineral. "Ludwig's development consists mostly of that paper mill of his that the Japs built for him and floated across the Pacific. It's a white elephant now. They've cut down thousands of acres around it. And you need the trees for both the paper and the fuel to run the mill. It'll have to be relocated, and that'll cost millions. . . ."

Grunwald turned his gaze to the tinted wall of glass behind Safier's back. The conference room was located on the forty-eighth floor and offered a magnificent view of New York Harbor and the two-mile-long span of the Verrazano Narrows Bridge beyond. Grunwald watched a ferry on its way to Staten Island, visible only as a square gray silhouette through the blanket of midmorning haze. Directly in front of him, poised in dignified splendor on a tiny rock outcropping in the middle of the busy harbor, stood the green copper monolith of the Statue of Liberty. Behind her, softened and miragelike in the haze, he could distinguish the abandoned red brick buildings of Ellis Island.

He remembered the view from another time and another perspective: A chilly morning in early November 1945. Friday the ninth. He had never consciously tried to remember that date, but it was branded in his memory. It was the day he had arrived at Ellis Island as a refugee from Germany. The day he had begun his new life.

He recalled the mixture of fear and excitement. He was twenty years old, without money, friends, or relatives. His English was poor and his knowledge of America nonexistent. Yet he was alive and healthy. And, most important of all, he was free. Free from Europe and the past. He was determined to take advantage of his luck.

The first year was lonely and difficult. There was so much to learn. He worked fourteen hours a day at menial jobs on the Lower East Side, slept in a run-down boardinghouse on St. Mark's Place, ate one meal a day, and spent his evenings teaching himself English. He could recall little from that grim period except the constant feeling of exhaustion. Exhaustion and anxiety. And frustration.

An old Orthodox Jew from Delancey Street named Weinstein gave him his first break. He worked as a busboy in Weinstein's dairy restaurant on Second Avenue, and the old man was so impressed with him that he bragged about him to a cousin, Martin Josephs, a prosperous Forty-seventh Street diamond wholesaler. Josephs offered to take Grunwald on and teach him the diamond trade.

Grunwald had barely begun his apprenticeship with Josephs when he met and fell in love with the widower's only daughter, Cornelia, and almost ended a great American success story before it even started. Cornelia was a beautiful, naive, seventeen-year-old virgin, and Grunwald won her affections too easily. Three months after they met, she discovered she was pregnant.

They married a month later, without Martin Josephs' blessing. Ironically, it was the birth of Billy, five months after the wedding, that won back Josephs' goodwill. He loved being a grandfather, and he went to his grave believing two improbable things: that his grandson Billy would one day be President of the United States, and that he had been born four months prematurely.

Meanwhile, Grunwald applied himself to the diamond trade with ferocious energy. By his twenty-sixth birthday, Cornelia had given birth to a daughter, Sarah, and a second son, Rob. By his twenty-seventh birthday, he had persuaded his father-in-law to let him take over the day-to-day operations of the business. By his twenty-eighth, he had doubled the firm's size and tripled its profits.

By the time he was thirty, he had founded a new company, Josephs and Grunwald Mineral, and branched out from the parochial diamond trade into platinum, gold, silver, and the fast-growing new area of strategic metals.

During Grunwald's thirty-third year, his father-in-law retired to Florida and turned all financial control of his business and his personal fortune over to him. With several more million dollars to play with, Grunwald blossomed as a capitalist. He bought and sold, wheeled and dealed, gambled and schemed, studied and planned, and started the building of an entrepreneurial legend that would come to be compared with Gould and Morgan, Rockefeller and Vanderbilt.

That bleak November day at Ellis Island, Grunwald had set a goal for himself: He would be a millionaire by his thirty-fifth birthday. When he finally reached that age, he was a millionaire seventy times over.

Now, at fifty-six, with a personal fortune of six hundred million dollars, he had done everything in the world of business that he could ever want or imagine. Those few peaks that remained worth scaling lay in other realms.

That ambassadorship, for example.

He rubbed his eyes a couple of times and turned back to the conference table. Safier was still talking. Grunwald picked up his eyeglasses and stood up, suddenly. Safier paused in mid-sentence and looked over at him inquiringly.

"Go on," Grunwald muttered. "You gentlemen just go right on with the discussion." He gripped the edge of the table and grinned at Safier reassuringly. "I must excuse myself for a second."

He hurried to his office next door and sank heavily into the soft folds of a large leather swivel chair, overcome by a sudden weakness. He pressed his palms over his eyes, feeling his heart beginning to race. He tried to slow his breathing but instead found himself panting for air, sucking it in and out of his lungs in quick, ragged gasps. He had experienced such attacks before, and had subjected himself to an exhaustive battery of medical tests, only to be told that there was nothing wrong with him. Simple anxiety, his doctor had declared, dispensing, along with a prescription for a tranquilizer, the shopworn advice to cut down his work load and avoid stress. Grunwald had laughed. He had thrived on stress all his life. No one built and ran one of the world's biggest business conglomerates by taking it easy.

The failure to find a physical cause only intensified Grunwald's fear of the attacks. Beyond the shame he felt—it was the kind of psychological weakness he so much despised in others—he sensed they might be a bad omen of some sort.

He wondered if the disorder might be related to his uncertainty over the ambassadorship. The President was to announce his nomination tomorrow, and there was no use pretending that he didn't covet the appointment desperately. It would be the crowning achievement of his career. He had worked many years toward this goal, backing conservative Republican candidates for office at every opportunity, pouring money into the campaign coffers of the Republican party in gigantic amounts. With the death in 1979 of his bitter enemy Nelson Rockefeller, Grunwald had become the most powerful force in New York Republican politics, and he had worked hard to swing the state to Reagan in 1980. The ambassadorship was to be his share of the spoils of the GOP victory. It was a reward he felt he had earned.

Securing that appointment, however, meant facing Senate confirmation hearings. His life would be subject to close public scrutiny and he would be vulnerable to his enemies. No man in his position could welcome the thought of having to defend every statement he had ever made, every action he had ever taken. In his battles for success, he had, like every powerful man before him, resorted to shortcuts, done things to protect himself which could be difficult to explain in a public forum, where facts could so easily be twisted and moral hypocrisy was the accepted standard of behavior.

Something might go wrong. The Press, in its thirst for the sensational, or the Democrats, eager to discredit the administration, might find some way to embarrass him. He had brooded about that possibility often recently and done what he could to prepare himself against it. Beyond that, the ambassadorship was in the hands of fate, a place Grunwald did not like to see things left.

He opened a desk drawer and retrieved the little plastic bottle of tranquilizers jammed in under a stack of notebooks in the back. Taking such medication was almost as humiliating to him as the attacks themselves, but he needed to do something to calm himself. The day's schedule was crowded with difficulties.

Grunwald examined one of the capsules with distaste, then popped it into his mouth and swallowed it without water. He glanced down at the day's neatly typed schedule Florence had placed on the blotter. An hour and a half had been allotted for the executive board's meeting, now in progress. At ten-thirty he was to meet a group of geologists just back from Canada's Northwest Territories. At eleven he was to review corporate budgets with Safier and Carlson. His lunch date uptown at the Metropolitan Club at twelve-thirty had been crossed out, and in its place Florence had penciled in the name "Mr. Brian Duffy."

He tapped the name hard with a forefinger. Here, surely, was a cause for anxiety. This Duffy was bringing him news about Billy.

Grunwald inhaled deeply. Still, after all this time, he felt the same sharp rush of anger and heartache. His eyes focused on the large photograph on the corner of his desk. It had remained in that identical spot for twelve years, carefully repositioned every night by the cleaning lady when she dusted his desk. It showed his son, Marine Lieutenant William Grunwald, Jr., in dress blues. He was a handsome, square-faced young man with bold, penetrating eyes and short, sandy hair just growing out of a crew cut. His smile radiated an unmistakable air of optimism and self-confidence. The photograph had been taken shortly before Billy left for Vietnam.

Billy meant more to Grunwald than anything else in his life. From the day of his birth, on a freezing January morning thirty-five years ago in Manhattan's Doctors Hospital, Grunwald vowed that his son would one day know greatness. He saw Billy as a continuation of himself, as the final vindication, consolidation, and triumph of the Grunwald family name.

And Billy had not disappointed him. He had covered himself with glory in the classroom, on the athletic field, and in the military. Physically attractive, forceful, quick-minded, and charismatic, he was that natural leader of men that his father had prayed he would turn out to be. He had married well, and he was possessed of the drive and ambition that could carry him as far as he wanted to go. With his father's resources behind him, nothing was beyond his reach—the governor's mansion, the U.S. Senate. Even, as his grandfather Martin Josephs had so confidently maintained, the presidency.

Grunwald stared at the photograph as if it were an icon that might contain the power to bring his son back to him.

With but a week remaining on his tour of duty, Billy's platoon was ambushed and decimated in a village in the Central Highlands in February of 1970. Billy and nineteen others were captured alive. The others were repatriated in 1973, but Billy was not among them. The U.S. Marines and the Department of State claimed that he had died in captivity. The North Vietnamese claimed that he had never been captured.

In the years following 1973, Grunwald mounted a superhuman effort to find Billy. And he persisted unrelentingly in the face of the most discouraging odds. He put pressure on the Pentagon and the State Department. He tried negotiating directly with the Vietnamese, offering them a multi-million-dollar ransom. He followed up every lead, offered—and frequently paid out—many rewards for information.

Over the decade, many tantalizing bits of evidence had surfaced to show that Billy was still alive. Most had turned out to be false or even fraudulent, but enough ambiguity still clouded Billy's fate to keep Grunwald from giving up hope. But, after all those years of effort, the situation had not yielded one inch to Grunwald's stubborn assault.

Billy was still missing.

Grunwald pushed himself up out of his chair and paced the wide expanse of carpet in front of his desk. His hyperventilating had stopped and his pulse was slowing to normal. He doubted that this man Duffy, judging by what he had learned about him, would bring him anything of value, but he dared not deny him an audience.

Grunwald stepped to the window. It offered the same magnificent panorama of New York Harbor as the conference room next door. Why should he suffer these ridiculous bouts of fear? He had fought his battles and taken his risks in life with a sense of determined exhilaration, with the optimistic conviction that he would always prevail. Why not now? Why not see these problems in the same light? This disquieting illness was just another test, another challenge to overcome. And he would triumph over it. As he had always triumphed.

The haze was lifting from the harbor, and the water sparkled now in the early spring sunlight. Even the crumbling bricks of the buildings on Ellis Island looked fresh and clean. . . .

His eyesight seemed to dim. He blinked several times to clear it, and saw to his terror that he was beginning to hallucinate. The brick buildings were swelling in size, looming out of the harbor and closing swiftly in on him. He shut his eyes.

The buildings remained, the hallucination penetrating past his eyelids to invade the dark within. A tall barbed-wire fence materialized, and in the long yard on the other side, endless rows of refugees stood silently at attention. They were dressed in rags and gaunt from starvation.

Grunwald opened his eyes again. Ellis Island had retreated back to its normal location, but the afterimage of the hallucination still flickered. A wave of dizziness overtook him. His legs buckled and he slipped down on one knee, clutching the deep window ledge for support. His pulse pounded in his neck. He opened his mouth for air.

He rested his face on the ledge, feeling the cold metal of the sill pressing against his forehead. He squeezed his eyes shut again, to wring the image from his mind. *"Grosse Gott,"* he gasped.

He repeated the phrase again and again, mumbling the words in a mindless incantation, like a chant to drive out the devil.

The buildings stayed with him, their grim presence flowering around him in a waking nightmare. The Jourhaus, the Appellplatz, the barracks, the guard towers, the crematorium.

Dachau. His coffin. His cradle.

A boy who had once existed was gone forever. No trace of him remained. No trace at all. Gone too was his family, his boyhood friends, his very childhood. He had blotted it all from his mind and invented a new past to take its place.

But it was still there, the knowledge of his lie, lurking in the shadows of his consciousness. One simple mistake—made a long time ago, when he was very young and very afraid. It had seemed so necessary then, and so innocent, amid the uncountable cruelties of that evil time. And it might once have been set straight—atoned for and forgotten. But, as the years passed and his wealth and power grew, the lie became something that could no longer be undone, a dread secret that he must keep at any cost. The very need to hide it had been the engine that had driven him through his life, piling achievement upon achievement, riches upon riches, as if finally to build a fortress strong enough to protect his vulnerability.

"Grosse Gott," he moaned. He had come so far, gained so much. But the lie remained. God help him if it was ever discovered. His fortune and good name—indeed, the entire edifice of his empire—could collapse overnight.

3

Belize City

Rob Grunwald studied the sea.

It was hot, as it always was in March, and the Caribbean lay flat and gray as an iron table under the harsh pressure of a high sun. Later in the afternoon, when the sun had settled in the soft hazes over the Maya Mountains in the west, the iron would dissolve into a magnificent rainbow of greens, blues, and purples, and the peeling wood frames and tin roofs of the town would take on a romantic amber softness. Grunwald had watched the process hundreds of times from the tiny second-story balcony of his room in the Bellevue, a weather-beaten hotel that overlooked the harbor from the southern corner of the town. Sometimes he watched all day, until the sun disappeared and the tropic night abruptly dropped its curtain on the show.

Boats creased the water's surface, their wakes intermingling in endlessly changing patterns. Cabin cruisers curved north toward the fishing banks off Ambergris Cay; old gaff-headed schooners raced on a broad reach southward toward the Turneffe Islands; and long, flat-bottomed barges shuttled cargo between the shallow harbor and the deep water out past the barrier reef, where a line of anchored freighters, their gray hulks like warships on the horizon, waited to be unloaded.

Rob Grunwald drained the last mouthful from a Carta Blanca and rested the empty bottle carefully on the top of the veranda railing. He was thin, with glossy dark hair and large deep-brown eyes that made him look sad, even when he was smiling. He wore baggy white cotton trousers and a white Mexican shirt with a pleated front and no arms. His face was shaded under the broad brim of a straw hat.

His eyes followed a blue smudge of smoke on the eastern horizon, and the squat silhouette of a boat that was growing beneath it. It was Lopez, in the *Santa María,* a rust bucket of a trawler that the Mexican managed, miraculously, to keep in operation year after year, through leaks, engine blowouts, broken propeller shafts, pirate harassment, hurricanes, and shakedowns by the governments of Colombia and Belize.

Lopez was on the last leg of a run to Barranquilla, on the Colombian coast, a thousand-mile haul around the hump of Honduras and Nicaragua that he made once every three months or so, depending on the weather, the state of his boat, and the availability of the right cargo at the right price. If Lopez had had a good trip, the trawler's hold would be bulging with cocaine, packed in inflatable life vests and buried beneath a ton or so of not very fresh fish.

Lopez was a wholesale distributor. He repackaged the coke and at night resold it out of his boat at dockside to smaller dealers who would take it on by plane and boat to Miami. He gave Rob Grunwald the same wholesale rate—eight Belizean dollars the gram. Last month's supply for himself and Yvonne, his French Creole girlfriend, had cost him two thousand dollars Belizean. That was a thousand dollars American. A great bargain, even in a country like Belize, where if something wasn't cheap it wasn't available.

But coke was like a worm in the brain. Each day it grew larger and required more food to keep it happy. It had already outgrown his ability to support it. He would have to increase his income somehow. And the prospects for that were dismal. But that was in the future, and the future had always looked dismal.

Rob propped his feet on the balcony railing, tipped his hat over his face, and dozed off, dreaming of Lopez and his boatload of happiness.

At four o'clock a soft pounding noise from somewhere inside the hotel brought him awake. Someone was methodically working his way down the second-floor corridor, knocking on all the doors. By the time the pounder reached Rob's door, he had already opened it for him.

A small, neat young man in a cream-colored Dacron wash-and-wear suit stared at him uncertainly. Streaks of sweat trickled down his neck, and broad circles of stain were spreading outward from the underarms of his jacket. He was carrying a leather attaché case and gripping it very hard. "Excuse me," he whispered, nervously. "I'm looking for a Mr. Robert Grunwald."

Rob stood aside and motioned for him to enter. The man hesitated inside the door, as if expecting an ambush. His eyes flickered over the cramped disorder of the room and Grunwald's disheveled appearance. "You're Mr. Grunwald?" he asked, squinting suspiciously up into Rob's heavy-lidded eyes.

"I'm Mr. Grunwald."

"My name is Jonathan Ordway." He produced a billfold from his coat pocket, opened it, and withdrew a laminated plastic card, which he placed in Rob's hand.

Rob looked down at the card, then up at Ordway, incredulous. "United States Department of Justice?"

Embarrassed, Ordway plucked the card back from Rob's hand. "Yes. I tried to set up an appointment with you, but you were impossible to reach."

Rob grinned. "The FBI," he said, pronouncing the letters slowly to savor the sensations they roused. "I haven't had a visit from the FBI in years. I thought you guys didn't like me anymore. Come out onto the deck. It's cooler there. I can offer you Mexican beer. Not very cold, but guaranteed wet."

"Yes. Thank you very much," Ordway said. "It's so damned hot here," he added, as if to justify his drinking during working hours.

"This is the cool season. You should try us in July."

Ordway settled self-consciously into a rattan chair, holding his case across his lap. "Nice view," he said, when Rob brought him the beer.

Rob laughed. "The only good view in Belize is looking away from it. 'If the world had any ends,' Huxley once said, 'British Honduras would certainly be one of them.' Hope you don't mind drinking this from the bottle."

Ordway shook his head and tipped the bottle daintily to his lips. Rob slouched into the chair next to him, spread his arms upward, and yawned.

"The town has open sewers," Ordway said, as if accusing it of a sexual perversion. "How do you stand it here?"

"You learn to ignore it. After a while the place just goes away."

"I expected it to be like Cozumel. The Fort George is the only first-class hotel in town. And the air conditioner in my room doesn't work."

"I'm sorry to hear that," Rob replied, amused by Ordway's fussiness. "Why don't you take off your jacket, unbutton your shirt?"

Ordway shook his head firmly. "You no doubt realize why I'm here," he said.

"As a matter of fact, I don't have the faintest notion. I was expecting an art dealer and I thought that's who you were. You don't exactly fit the G-man mold."

Ordway sniffed. "I'm not that sort of agent. I'm a special investigator attached to the attorney general's office."

"Have you arrested someone I know?"

"It's about your father."

The mention of his father caused a painful pressure against Rob Grunwald's chest. "What's he done?"

"When a man is nominated for an ambassadorship, we naturally have to check his background carefully."

"Ambassadorship?"

"Yes. Israel. You hadn't heard?"

Rob stared at the agent's sweaty pink face. "We're not very close," he replied.

Ordway nodded as if he already knew. He withdrew a thick folder from his attaché case and poised over it with a silver pen. "Would you tell me what you do for a living, Mr. Grunwald?"

"This and that," Rob replied. "I get by."

Ordway produced a damp handkerchief from his back trouser pocket and used it to wipe the moisture from his chin. "Of course, your cooperation is voluntary," he said, sounding bored.

Rob tasted his beer and thought about it. "What the hell," he muttered. He went inside, retrieved a suitcase from beneath the bed, and carried it out onto the balcony.

"My ambition once was to become an archaeologist," he said, resting the suitcase carefully on the small balcony floor. "The mysteries of the ancient past fascinated me. Unlike the mysteries of the present, they have a nice way of holding still while you decipher them."

He snapped the brass clasps back with a quick flick of his fingers. "Watch closely," he commanded. From a wad of crumpled newspapers he withdrew a small cylindrical clay jar with a flared rim, broken in several places. He handed it to Ordway, who examined it briefly and handed it back.

"Not worth very much," Rob said. "Little better than pottery fragments. Dime a dozen."

"What is it supposed to be?"

"A ceremonial vase. The Maya had an unfortunate religious practice of breaking their pottery. That makes the undamaged ones worth a lot of money." Rob placed the piece on the floor and withdrew another object, identical to the first but flawless.

Ordway turned the jar over cautiously. "I don't know much about archaeology. Where did you get it?"

"In a limestone cave near Belmopan."

"You sell these things?"

"When I can."

"What is this one worth?"

"Whatever I can get from a dealer. Probably a thousand dollars. Of course, he can sell it in New York or Europe for much more."

"It's against the law, isn't it?"

Rob smiled indulgently. "Not necessarily." He produced a much larger bundle from the suitcase and undid the layers of newspaper slowly and deliberately. The last page came away to reveal a round, intricately carved stone head, seven inches in diameter. Ordway sat motionless, eyes popping, as Grunwald held the object aloft and rotated it slowly in his hands, his fingers caressing the cool polished surface reverentially. The gleaming green head, grotesque and bloated, would have struck anyone as supremely menacing but for the curiously comic effect of its eyes, the pupils of which were carved close to its fat nose, making it cross-eyed.

"Just about the ugliest thing you ever saw, isn't it?"

"Is it jade?" Ordway whispered, awestruck.

"The archaeologist David Pendergast found it in 1968 at Altun Ha, just north of here," Rob explained. "It's the Mayan sun-god, Kinich Ahau, and it's the biggest Mayan jade carving in captivity. It's worth over half a million dollars. Here—catch."

Rob tossed the ten-pound stone into the agent's lap. Ordway uttered a shrill gasp and clutched for it as it thunked onto his attaché case, denting the top. Ordway fell back against the rattan chair, his entire body wet with perspiration. "You'll give me a heart attack," he protested, when he could speak. "How could you have obtained such a valuable thing?"

"My circumstances make me enterprising."

"You stole it?" Ordway asked, his face paling with shock.

Rob laughed. "It's a fake. Everything I've shown you is a forgery. That jade head is polished granite. It was carved and dyed green by a Carib Indian who lives out in Orange Walk. I paid him fifty dollars to make it, and twenty for the two pottery vases. I'll sell them to a shady art dealer for several thousand."

Ordway removed the sun-god impostor from his case and placed it on the balcony deck. "That's reprehensible," he murmured.

"I con the con men, that's all," Rob said. "I convince them that the artifacts are hot, and greed does the rest. Even if they suspect a forgery—and some of the smarter ones can spot even expert work—they usually buy anyway, because they have customers who won't be able to tell the difference. Like Robin Hood, I steal from the rich and give to the poor."

"What poor?"

"Me."

"Your father is one of the wealthiest men in the world."

"I support myself," Rob snapped.

Ordway picked up his pen and sighed as if in pain. "I'll put you down as a dealer in artistic reproductions."

Rob offered his guest another Carta Blanca. Ordway refused. "We have a lot of questions to cover," he said, cracking open the folder. "I understand that you were a member of the Students for a Democratic Society?"

Rob propped his feet back up on the balcony rail. "Not just a member. I was president of it for two years."

"You were arrested in June 1966 in a sit-in demonstration in San Francisco?"

"Yes. That was a wonderful week. I fell in love with a girl named Pamela. She was from Berkeley. A real flower child."

"And you were arrested three times in antiwar demonstrations in 1967—in Boston, New York, and Washington, D.C.?"

"Sounds right."

"And arrested at Columbia University on May tenth, 1968?"

"We closed the college that year. Heady stuff."

"Arrested during the Democratic National Convention in Chicago in July 1968?"

"After I was clubbed unconscious outside the lobby of the Hilton Hotel."

"Arrested November eighth, 1968, in front of the White House?"

"That must have been the draft-card burning."

"Arrested at the gate of your father's munitions plant in Westfield, Massachusetts, in October 1969?"

"How many more of these do you have?"

"That's all the arrests," Ordway said. "You went to Canada sometime in March 1970 to avoid the draft?"

"March thirteenth. A Friday."

Ordway paused to write down Rob's answer. "You lived in Toronto from March 1970 to April 1973?" he continued.

"And I wasn't arrested once."

"What did you do for a living during those years?"

"I worked at odd jobs."

Ordway wrote that down. "Then you moved to Montreal for the period of May 1973 to March 1977. What did you do there?"

"Odd jobs."

"Can you be more specific?"

Rob shrugged.

"Then you moved to Amsterdam?"

"I also spent time in Paris, London, Rome, Athens, Monaco, Cap d'Antibes, Capri, Juan-les-Pins, Mallorca, Geneva, Madrid, Marrakesh, Alexandria, Jerusalem, and a few other locales I can't recall at the moment."

"What were you doing in all those places?"

"Living off the land."

"You came here in 1979?"

"Yes."

"Why?"

"I took a job crewing on a French yacht. The owner wanted to sail around the world. The boat went aground during a storm off the Quintana Roo. I came here to await repairs. The owner changed his mind and went back home. I stayed on."

"How do you spell 'Quintana Roo'?"

Rob told him.

"Why didn't you come home when President Carter offered the amnesty to draft resisters?"

"I did. For about a month in 1977."

"Then you left again?"

"Yes."

"Why?"

"I was unhappy. Home wasn't home to me anymore."

"Are you a member of any political party or group that advocates the violent overthrow of the United States government?"

Disgusted, Rob dropped his feet back onto the deck. "Let me ask you a few questions," he said. "You look about my age. Where the hell were you during the sixties? Didn't you ever march for civil rights or protest the war?"

Ordway shook his head violently. "No. I hated what you radicals were doing. I was a scholarship student at Holy Cross. My family was working class. I considered it a privilege to go to college."

"What about Vietnam?"

Ordway looked out across the water. "I couldn't serve my country," he whispered.

"Why not?"

"Medical reasons."

"What reasons?"

"That's really none of your business."

Rob pursued the point: "A history of asthma? Bed-wetting? Homo-sexuality?"

Ordway flushed deeply at the last word.

Rob sighed. "If you wanted to serve your country so badly, why didn't you lie and say you were straight?"

"I have only a few more questions, Mr. Grunwald," the agent said, his voice now brittle with hostility.

"I have a few more to ask you," Rob replied. "Since my father has already been nominated, and since you already seem to know all about me, what's the point of this interview?"

Ordway cleared his throat. "We would have interviewed you earlier, but I told you, we had a hard time finding you."

"Then why did you bother?"

"Your behavior has been a source of concern to your father in the past. Now it is a potential source of concern to the President. The ambassadorship to Israel is an especially sensitive post. We have to assess your potential to embarrass the administration."

Rob stood up and walked back inside, suddenly impatient to get this man out of his sight. He picked up a small earthenware figurine from the top of a dresser and returned with it to the balcony. "A small going-away present," he said, handing the statue to Ordway. The surprised agent murmured a thank-you, examined the gift critically for a moment, then slipped it into his attaché case, along with his questionnaire.

Rob walked him to the door. "Is it genuine?" Ordway asked hope-fully. "The figurine?"

Rob smiled. "Of course." He held the door open and watched Ordway retreat down the hotel corridor. "It does have a curse on it, though," he added, just as his visitor reached the stairwell at the far end. Before Ordway could react, Rob slammed the door and went back inside.

He returned to his balcony and leaned against the rail. The day's heat was lifting, and the streets were crowded with Belizeans lingering out of doors between work and supper to catch the first stirrings of an evening breeze. Loud voices mingled with the music of transistor radios and the smell of cooking food in the stalls along Haulover Creek.

Ordway had gotten to him, dragging in the past like a witness for the prosecution, ticking off the milestones of his life like items on the rap sheet of a petty thief. He had fended him off with a show of casual disdain, but in truth the fussy little homosexual had kicked Rob's fragile self-esteem to pieces.

Rob felt the panic beginning to mount. The bastard had ruined the day, he thought. Maybe the entire week. He tried to focus his mind back on the narrow line of the immediate present, like a circus performer, concentrating only on keeping his balance for the next few seconds, the next minute.

He summoned up an image of Yvonne—her resilient copper body, her greedy sexual smile. She'd be back late, lying about where she had been all day, diverting his questions with imaginative lewd displays that never failed to arouse him. Or she'd be whiny and petulant, forcing him to coax her into a better mood.

Whatever her mood, she'd certainly be back. If not for him, then for the coke.

The coke. The third partner in their mysterious ménage. Their teacher, their lover, their best friend. Experience itself. It expanded the present and swallowed the past and future up inside it. With coke they escaped time altogether.

Wonderful stuff, cocaine. It saved him from having to face the mess he had made out of his life.

His life. It pained him, scared him. At the age of thirty-one, he was little better off than a cornered rat. Out of moves. Out of time. Out of hope. Out of possibilities.

Increasingly, in those depressing valleys between the coke's euphoric highs, he felt the panic building, telling him to run, to change, to struggle. Before it was too late. But it *was* too late. There wasn't enough willpower left in the entire universe to pull him out of that corner.

"Dead end," he said aloud, looking down at a drunken Belizean trying to negotiate a straight path along the sidewalk below.

Dead end. Well, the hell with it. Let it be. Get some coke and let it be.

At six o'clock he left his room and walked to the Water Street dock. Lopez was standing in the open hatchway to the bridge of his trawler, smoking a black cheroot. His deck lights were on and the bow hatch cover was off. The stench of fish was overpowering.

"Cómo está," Rob called, as he approached the boarding plank. *"Es bueno, esta noche?"*

Lopez nodded, but he looked uncharacteristically subdued. *"No es bueno,"* he whispered.

Rob's preoccupation with Ordway's disturbing visit made him careless. He totally missed the significance of the deck lights. Lopez never left them on when he was selling. And, worse, he didn't even hear Lopez's warning, when he still had time to turn away. He stepped across the greasy plank and hopped down onto the deck, landing amid the Mexican's usual hazardous clutter of buckets, tarps, ropes, tools, and boxes.

Men materialized from behind the deckhouse and from the darkened bridge, moving in unison, cautiously, fanning out around him. Lopez remained stationary, leaning against the deckhouse bulkhead, staring at his boots. One man, large and black, gestured toward Rob with an index finger, grinning malevolently with a mouthful of gold teeth. He was barely six feet away, his huge hand smothering the small revolver it contained. Rob saw no uniforms. Was it a raid or a robbery? The big black pointed the short barrel of his pistol at Rob's head and wagged it slightly, gesturing for him to move under the deck light.

Dead end.

Rob's fingers tingled from a surge of adrenaline. He sucked in a lungful of air, charged five strides across the rear deck, and leaped over the transom gunwale into the water.

He popped to the surface half a minute later, barely thirty feet from the boat. He had once been an excellent swimmer, but years of neglect had left him badly deconditioned. He gasped for air, his lungs choking on the taste of oil and salt, and tried to swim in the direction of one of the winking red buoys at the mouth of the harbor. Over his pounding heart he could hear the yelling of voices from the boat and along the dock. A searchlight swept back and forth over the black surface of the water and finally pinned him in its harsh white glare.

They began shooting. Explosions echoed off the tin warehouses along the waterfront. Rob thrashed the water violently, fighting to escape from the pitiless net of light. A bullet stabbed his upper arm. He felt the jolt more than the pain, but the limb went instantly dead. He continued beating the water with his good arm and kicked his feet furiously to propel himself forward. Energy drained from him rapidly, and before he could swim another thirty feet, his movements slowed and his feet sank downward, until he was floating vertically, submerged to his chin. He tilted his head back to pull in a last gulp of air, then closed his eyes and drifted into unconsciousness.

They pulled him out of the water and pumped his lungs and eventually brought him round. He had lost a lot of blood, and after they bandaged him up, they took him to a Catholic missionary hospital. He spent three days there, under guard, recuperating. On the third day the police officially charged him with conspiracy to traffic in illegal drugs and removed him to the Belize City jail.

4

New York City

William Grunwald began sizing Duffy up the instant he appeared in the doorway of his office, looking for the soft spots that might give him an advantage in dealing with him. The writer was small and pallid, with hooded eyes and soft, pursed red lips that looked rather ugly against his white skin and heavy shadow of beard. He was dressed in a hand-stitched beige suede sports jacket, matching cavalry twill slacks, and Italian shoes that looked as thin and supple as a pair of gloves. *He likes to indulge himself,* Grunwald thought. And clothing stores along the Côte d'Azur weren't the only places holding his tab. According to what quick intelligence Grunwald had been able to gather on the man, he had accumulated car-rental and restaurant bills all through southern France and northern Italy, and serious gambling debts at Nice's Municipal Casino and at Monte Carlo. A pathological big spender. The thought comforted Grunwald. He had always been able to handle people with a weakness for money.

Safier ushered Duffy into the room, introduced him, and motioned him to the narrow straight-backed chair in front of Grunwald's massive desk. Duffy placed the thin calfskin briefcase he was carrying on the edge of the desk and came immediately to the point.

"I have information that will interest you, Mr. Grunwald," he began.

"It concerns your son Billy. I must warn you, however, that the information comes with a high price tag attached to it."

Grunwald felt the same rush of hope and excitement he had experienced before whenever news of Billy seemed imminent. But he had learned through many past disappointments to suppress those feelings ruthlessly. He said nothing. Instead he laced his hands together across his lap, tilted back in his chair, and focused his most intimidating stare on his visitor, a wordless warning to Duffy that he was in the presence of a man who could not be made a fool of easily.

Duffy cleared his throat pompously. "I'm acting as an intermediary for an important Vietnamese refugee. I met him doing research on another subject. He has defected to the West and now lives in the south of France. I'm selling this information on his behalf, to finance his resettlement."

Grunwald exchanged glances with Safier, who was sitting on a sofa behind Duffy. Safier was there to put additional pressure on their visitor. It was a strategy Grunwald used frequently in difficult business confrontations.

"What's the name of this refugee?" Safier asked.

Duffy craned his head around. "Obviously I can't tell you that."

"Why doesn't he take his information to a Western government?" Safier demanded.

Duffy fingered the corner of his briefcase and glanced from Safier to Grunwald and then back to Safier again. Being double-teamed clearly made him nervous. "He's got plenty of other stuff to tell them. But they won't pay anything for it. He selected this bit of intelligence out just to—as I said—finance his resettlement."

Grunwald spoke for the first time: "Let me see what you have."

Duffy pulled a cassette tape from his case and placed it on the desk. "This is the recording of the interview I had with this official two days ago. It was conducted at a villa in Nice, in French and Vietnamese."

Duffy produced a scarlet-red file folder from the case and laid it beside the cassette. "This is a transcript of the tape, with an English translation. Your son is being held in the same prison my informant escaped from. He has identified him completely—name, description, and so on. He's in good health. He has given me the precise location of that camp and details about its security arrangements."

Grunwald appraised Duffy carefully. He was damned if this sleazy hustler was going to extort money from him. But beneath the chemical blanket of the tranquilizer he had taken earlier, he felt the smothered fears of the morning still smoldering. If there was even a remote chance that this journalist's information would help bring Billy back, then he must have it. He must outwit this opportunist, not crush him.

"What do you want for your information?" Safier asked, from behind.

"My source thinks that in return for helping you find your son, you would be willing to assist him in starting a new life in the West. He's a sick man, with few friends or prospects. He needs help badly. And he thinks this information is very valuable."

"How valuable?" Grunwald demanded.

"I've advised him to ask you for fifty thousand dollars."

Grunwald nodded calmly. "Of course, I will have to speak to the man personally, to verify everything."

Duffy pursed his vermilion lips in distaste. "That's not possible. He's agreed to let me represent him. I'm the only one he will talk to."

"I see." Grunwald pulled open a drawer of his desk and withdrew a checkbook and opened it. "What is this man's name?"

"I repeat, I can't tell you that," Duffy insisted. "I'm sworn to respect his wishes for anonymity. He has reason to believe that the Vietnamese government will take reprisals against his family in Vietnam. And he fears for his own life, as well."

"I suppose you expect me to make the check out to you, then?"

"No. We want cash," Duffy declared.

Grunwald leveled his eyes at Duffy. He knew he was dealing with a simple case of greed, but something in the situation frightened him. He felt threatened, and he didn't know why. He tried to shrug off the feeling. *My God,* he thought, *I'm making myself paranoid.*

For a while no one spoke. Grunwald swiveled his chair around and looked out the window, pretending to consider Duffy's demands. Ellis Island was still there. As soon as this parasite was dispensed with, he decided, he would tell Safier to have both his suite of offices and the adjacent conference room moved to the north side of the building.

After a long, tense interval, Grunwald turned back to the open checkbook on his desk and wrote out a check payable to Brian Duffy for ten thousand dollars, tore it from the book, and pushed it across to him.

The writer picked it up hesitantly, as if it might burn his fingers, and stared at it for nearly half a minute. "What's this for?"

"That's what I'm going to pay you," Grunwald said, "for the truth— the name and address of the man you claim to have interviewed, and the tape and transcript from that interview. If you give us those, then you'll be able to cash the check. If you don't, I will call the police and have you arrested for attempted extortion."

Duffy's face seemed to redden and swell, as if he were inflating it from the inside. He started to protest, but only managed to get out a prolonged stutter.

"If you have something genuine to sell me," Grunwald continued, glaring at him, "all you have to do is let me verify it. What do you have to lose? You need that ten thousand dollars badly, and this is the only way you're going to get it—not by making up preposterous stories about how you are acting on the behalf of some important Vietnamese official."

Duffy found his voice and repeated his demands, but it was an empty performance, designed to save face. Bit by bit, Grunwald and Safier stripped away the fictitious trappings from his story. He surrendered the name of his Vietnamese refugee, and Safier was able to reach the hospital in Nice by telephone, find someone there who spoke English, and verify that Ngo Din Tran was in fact their patient. Then Safier produced a cassette recorder and played Duffy's tape all the way through. Neither he nor Grunwald understood much French, let alone Vietnamese, but they satisfied themselves that the tape did at least contain an interview of some kind.

Duffy, feeling more violated than vindicated, sat through the ordeal chain-smoking Gauloises and sulking.

Grunwald thumbed through the transcript. The information was not as detailed and precise as Duffy had claimed, but it was clear to him that this Tran, whoever he was, knew Billy. Pretending disinterest, Grunwald closed the transcript and shoved it into a desk drawer, along with the cassette tape. "I guess that's all, Mr. Duffy. I think we're satisfied now that we have all we're going to get from you."

Duffy waved the check in front of him. "I want you to call your bank," he demanded, "and tell them that I'm coming over to cash this."

Grunwald accommodated him. He looked up a number in a small black leather book, dialed it, and explained to the party on the other end that a Mr. Brian Duffy was on his way over to cash a check from him and that he should approve it without delay.

Satisfied, Duffy tucked the check in his wallet and stood up. "This information I'm giving you for free," he said, pulling a folded piece of paper from his shirt pocket and dropping it disdainfully on Grunwald's desk. "I was at the *Post* this morning, and I came across this little item on the AP wire. It's about your other son, Rob. He's in jail in Central America. Belize City. For trafficking in drugs."

The reporter snatched up his attaché case with a flourish and saun-
tered triumphantly across Grunwald's thick blue carpet and out the
door.

"The little son of a bitch," Safier said.

Grunwald nodded. "Check that out about Rob," he said. "But first
call Sam Frick at Irving Trust and tell him to put a stop order on
Duffy's check."

Safier's eyes widened. "You just told him to okay it, didn't you?"

Grunwald snorted impatiently. "Of course not. I dialed my study
at home. I was talking to my answering machine."

5

Belize City

Captain Godfrey Price of the Belize Constabulary selected a large metal key from the ring at his waist, inserted it into its slot in the heavy metal door of the cell, and twisted it energetically. Rob Grunwald, curled up like a fetus on the narrow cot in the corner of his cell, raised his head and blinked against the sudden invasion of light from the corridor.

"Good morning, Mr. Grunwald," Price rumbled, in his baritone cadence. "We have some surprise for you dis morning. Come right dis way, please."

Grunwald stumbled to his feet and stood, hunched over, groaning softly. He had swallowed the last of the painkiller pills the hospital had given him the day before, and the bullet wound in his upper left arm was throbbing powerfully. He was also suffering the effects of a forced five-day withdrawal from cocaine, an ordeal that left him weak and shivering, even in the stale ninety-degree heat of the jail. Price, a black Creole with enormous biceps and a narrow waist, slammed the steel door open with a bang against the wall, and Rob followed him down the corridor to the desk where they had booked him after his release from the hospital.

Two other policemen were there, uniformed in wilted white shirts and shorts and maroon knee socks. One leaned against the far wall

chewing gum and swatting at an occasional fly with the aimless bore-
dom of a teenager hanging out in a drugstore. The other, behind the
desk, pecked away patiently on an old Royal typewriter. The walls
of the big room, like those of the entire police station, were constructed of cement block and painted pea green. Two large ceiling
fans stirred the hot air in unpleasant gusts against the face. A faded
black-and-white photograph of Queen Elizabeth II, a legacy from the
recent colonial past, still hung on the back wall.

In the center of the room, to Rob's astonishment, stood his sister,
Sarah, with hands planted on her hips, chin cocked at an arrogant
angle, and a toe tapping impatiently on the dirty tile floor. She was
dressed for New York in winter, in a chic gray-wool-pinstripe pantsuit
and a salmon-colored silk blouse. Indignation radiated from her like
heat from a boiler. From the policemen's sullen demeanor, Rob guessed
that she had been berating them in her best courtroom manner.

At the sight of her brother, stooped and haggard, his arm bandaged
and hanging in a sling, her eyes widened in horror. "My God," she
cried. "You've been beating him!"

Captain Price chuckled deferentially. "Just a li'l bullet hole in him,
ma'am. He be good as new soon now."

Sarah enfolded Rob in her arms and hugged him strenuously, tears
running down her cheeks. The policemen watched them with bald
curiosity, as if the reunion was being staged for their enjoyment. Sarah
pushed Rob out at arm's length. "My poor brother," she wailed. "You
look absolutely awful!"

He managed a feeble grin. "What the hell are you doing here,
anyway?"

"Everything's already arranged. You're free. I've booked seats on
the next flight out."

"Flight out to where?"

"New York. Via Miami."

Rob shook his head slowly. "I'm not going to New York. I'm staying
here."

"You have no choice in the matter," she said. "They're kicking you
out of the country."

On board the flight to Miami, Rob swallowed a tranquilizer and tried
to escape into sleep, but his sister was determined that he explain
himself. "It upsets me so much," she said. "Seeing you like this."

Rob yawned. "It's not as bad as it looks," he mumbled. "Nothing
serious."

"I see. Just another American tourist happily rotting away in a Central American prison with gunshot wounds and a cocaine habit."

"The wound is almost healed. And I've sweated out the coke problem. You always exaggerate."

"Well, I'm not exaggerating when I tell you that the Belize authorities wanted to make an example of you. They were willing to drop the cocaine charge on lack of evidence, but they were going to get you on archaeological theft. The prosecutor was planning to ask for ten years. We had to bribe them."

"How much?"

"A hundred thousand dollars," she said. "A discreet donation to the archaeological commissioner's office."

Rob groaned loudly, attracting the stare of a middle-aged woman passenger across the aisle. "You were suckered. The archaeological commissioner's the biggest thief in Belize. They could never have pinned that kind of theft on me. I dealt only in fakes. They knew that. They ripped you off."

"You treat the whole thing like a joke."

"It *is* a joke," Rob replied. "Who told you I was in jail?"

"Some reporter told Father."

Rob shook his head. "You should have left me there."

Sarah sighed. "I considered it."

Rob let his head fall sideways on the cushion and gazed at his sister's profile. She was thirty-two. Ten months older than he. Tiny cracks of age had appeared around her eyes and mouth since he had last seen her in 1977. She had hunted him down in Montreal that year and begged him to take advantage of the amnesty and come home. She had finished law school and was full of plans; a career and marriage were both just beginning. He realized with a stab of remorse that he didn't know what law firm she worked for, whether she had any children, or even if she was still married.

Sarah was staring at him accusingly. "What the hell have you been doing?" she demanded. "No one has had a word for years. Mother worries about you all the time. It's been hell for her, with both you and Billy gone."

Rob nodded.

"You have nothing to say?"

"There's nothing to tell."

"Tell me anyway."

Rob shifted uncomfortably in his seat. "I went back to Montreal after you dragged me to New York in 1977. But it wasn't the same. The atmosphere had changed. Most of my friends had returned to the

States by then, and I never really felt comfortable in Canada, anyway. It was an artificial situation. The Canadians are very polite, but I didn't make many friends. So I went to Europe. Later, in Morocco, I met a Frenchman who owned a yacht and I crewed on it for a while. We crossed the Atlantic and sailed down the Quintana Roo from Isla Mujeres and ran afoul of the barrier reef during a storm. That's how I ended up in Belize. When the boat was repaired and ready to leave, I decided to stay."

Sarah wrinkled her nose in distaste. "You actually liked it in Belize?"

Rob shrugged. "It's unpretentious—I'll say that for it."

"What have you done for money?"

"You're interrogating me."

"I'm your sister," she replied firmly. "I have a right to interrogate you. I'm concerned about you."

"We went through this same routine in Montreal, Sarah. Let's not argue about it. I'm tired as hell."

Rob closed his eyes and slept until the stewardesses served dinner.

"I'm divorced now," Sarah announced, when the plastic plates and glasses had been cleared away.

Rob racked his brain trying to recall something about her husband. All that came to him was the vague recollection that their father had disapproved of the match. "I'm sorry," he said.

"I'm glad to be rid of him."

"What went wrong?"

"Everything. He made a mess of his own career and he resented mine. I think he resented the family money, too. Especially when he learned he couldn't get his hands on any of it."

"Why did he want it?"

"Why does anybody want money? He planned to run for Congress and he wanted me to finance it. Can you imagine? Fired from two law firms and he wanted to run for Congress."

"Your luck with the opposite sex was never good."

Sarah agreed. "Neither was yours. What happened to that awful female revolutionary you were living with in Montreal? What was her name?"

Rob grinned at the memory. "Margaret. All Canadian women are named Anne or Margaret."

"She was scandalous."

"Whatever she was, she kicked me out when the feminist movement hit Canada. She lives with a woman in Winnipeg now and sells real estate. Some Marxist."

"I'm seeing Jim Safier now," Sarah announced.

Rob's mouth fell open.

His sister crossed her arms and settled heavily against the seat back, her expression defiant. "We're going to be married in June."

"This must be the old man's doing."

"Father has nothing to do with it. I've known Jim ever since I was little. He's practically a member of the family. He asked me out when I was going through the divorce. He's been very considerate."

"I always thought he was gay."

"He's not gay!" Sarah retorted angrily.

"I'll take your word for it. But the guy's thirty-four, and you're the first female I've ever heard him show an interest in. There must be something wrong with him."

"You don't know anything about his life."

"The guy's in love with power. That's why he and the old man get along so well."

"You're jealous of his success."

Rob swore under his breath. He despised Jim Safier, and the thought of him marrying his sister appalled him. He was sure that it was a carefully calculated move on Safier's part to consolidate his claim on the Grunwald fortune. He was maneuvering to succeed their father as the head of Grunwald Industries. With Billy missing and probably dead in Vietnam, and Rob disinherited, Safier saw the vacuum and was rushing to fill it. The man was a usurper. Why didn't Sarah see that?

"Are you in love with him?"

"Yes."

"Then I'll keep my mouth shut."

"How about just wishing us well?"

"Don't push your luck."

Sarah changed the subject. "Father is up for an ambassadorship. Israel."

"I know."

"How did you hear?"

"An FBI agent came to see me last week. Part of the routine background check, he told me. Wanted to make sure I wasn't doing anything that might embarrass the future diplomat."

Sarah lapsed into an uncharacteristic silence—a sure sign that she was hiding something from him.

"It's pretty transparent," Rob said. "He bailed me out of Belize because he thought I might jeopardize his appointment."

"That's true," she admitted. "He doesn't expect you to be grateful."

"That's a relief. What *does* he expect? That I'll pay him back the hundred-grand bribe?"

"He hopes that you'll stay out of trouble at least until the Senate confirmation hearings are over. They start next week."

"How is he going to do that? Lock me up in the cellar at Green-wood?"

Sarah hesitated, then looked her brother square in the face. "Father wants a reconciliation."

"You're joking."

She shook her head. "I talked with Mother yesterday afternoon. Father is just back from Washington. He'll be at Greenwood until Monday. You can stay with me tonight in Manhattan and take the train up there tomorrow."

"What are you talking about?"

"You've got to go see him. You've got to come to terms with him."

Rob stared at her in disbelief. "That's crazy."

"It's not. You've got to go up there and try. Father is ready to listen to you. You must go."

Rob wrapped his arms tightly across his chest. "I can't do it."

"You must."

"Why? In return for bribing me out of jail? I didn't ask him to. The hell with him. I'm not going to humiliate myself."

"You can stand a little humiliation."

"What's the point? He'll just use the occasion to crucify me again. I can live without that."

"You're wrong," Sarah said. "I think you can get your trust back."

Rob pressed his fingers against his temples and massaged them to relieve the pain. "Fuck the trust."

"I notice how well you're doing without it."

"Maybe not well, but I'm doing it. If I've succeeded at one thing in my life, it's been to get out from under the old man's control. And I'm not going to be put back in his debt again for anything."

Sarah's face reddened with anger. "Damn you, Robbie! Mother hasn't seen you in five years. You're going back to Greenwood to-morrow if I have to take you there at gunpoint. What you and Father do is beyond my control, but this romantic-exile pose of yours has to end sometime. You can't wait around for society to become perfect before you condescend to participate in it. You have to compromise and get on with your life. Stop pretending to be some character out of Graham Greene."

Rob tried to outflank her: "You've never read anything by Graham Greene in your life."

"I have so."

"Name one book."

" 'The Man from Havana,' " she declared, triumphantly.

"It was *Our Man in Havana*. And you didn't read it. You saw the movie."

"I hate it when you nitpick."

Rob slumped back into the seat. "He just wants to buy me off."

"Then take advantage of it," Sarah snapped. "Stop playing the misunderstood victim and get back what belongs to you. You have real leverage with him. Now's your chance."

"I just can't do it."

Sarah reached across the seat and took Rob's hand in her own. "Your palm is sweaty," she said.

"Fear of flying," he muttered.

"Fear of living, I think."

Rob stared at the blank underside of the tray folded up into the seat back in front of him. She was right, of course. This *was* his chance. His father, for the first time in his life, was suddenly vulnerable. He needed Rob's cooperation, and he was obviously prepared to pay for it. Rob wondered how much it was worth. And he wondered if there was really anything in the world he wanted from his father. His understanding? His respect? His love? Not anymore. It was too late for that.

All he really wanted was revenge.

Alexandria, Virginia

A black Chrysler limousine with heavily tinted side and rear windows cruised into a shopping center off the Shirley Highway, parked beside a Datsun sedan near the back of the plaza, and switched off its lights. The driver stepped out, glanced briefly at the smaller car, then walked away from both vehicles and took up a position a hundred feet distant, in the shadows of the tall bushes that bordered the edge of the plaza.

Captain Henry Short, a squat, brown-haired man with ball-bearing eyes, small ears, and thin lips, stepped from the Datsun and hurried over to the Chrysler, a briefcase clutched tightly under his arm.

He opened the front passenger-side door and climbed in. The front seat was empty, and the opaque glass partition that separated it from the back seat was closed.

After a pause, a flat, bored voice greeted him over an intercom speaker just behind his head. Short undid the two leather straps on his briefcase and pulled out a manila envelope. The partition glass hummed down a couple of inches, and Short fed the envelope into

the opening. A hand pulled it away, and the glass hummed closed
again.

A small hooded lamp blinked on in the back, spilling light into a
man's lap. Short turned sideways in the seat and watched through the
tinted glass of the partition, hoping to catch a glimpse of the mysterious
individual known to him only as "Mr. Walker." He saw the man's
hands withdraw the report from the envelope and rest it carefully on
his knees. The hands were long-fingered and manicured, and they
turned the pages slowly, as if the file was a rare manuscript. In a sense,
Short thought, it was. Finally, Walker's lethargic voice vibrated the
intercom. "This concerns one of our operations. Monarch Eagle."

"Yessir."

"Where did you get it?"

Short cleared his throat. "This Duffy tried to sell it to one of those
schlock tabloids. The editor called someone at the Pentagon to verify
the story. A DIA contact intercepted it and passed it on to us."

"What's the status of the information?"

"We've persuaded the tabloid that it's phony. So they won't print
anything. Duffy's another matter. According to the editor, he thinks
he has a valuable property."

"Has he approached anyone else?"

"We don't know yet."

"Find out."

"Do you want us to buy him out?"

"There's no point. He'll still know the information, no matter what
we pay him. The damage is done."

"What then?"

"Get rid of him."

Short nodded. In the pool of light, Walker's hands shuffled the
pages of the file with a lazy motion. "Did you hear me?" he demanded.

"Yessir."

The cone of light embracing Walker's lap went out. Short sat and
waited, staring alternately at the now black surface of the bulletproof
glass that walled him off from his host, and across the deserted expanse
of the shopping plaza. He could just make out the dim blot of Walker's
driver, standing patiently on lookout, shifting his weight from foot to
foot.

"There's also the problem of the refugee, Ngo Din Tran," Walker
muttered. "Get rid of him, too."

Short waited for further elaboration. None came. He saw the driver
walking back toward the limousine and realized that the meeting was
over. Walker must have instructed him to allow just so many minutes.

It was spooky, though, the way the driver suddenly came walking back, as if under telepathic control.

Short got back into his Datsun and drove out of the plaza without looking back. The word "spooky" kept rolling around in his head and he smiled to himself. How perfectly it fit this Walker. Arrogant, condescending, obsessed with secrecy. A spooky spook. The sort of thing Short might have expected from a CIA type. The boys at Langley were always prone to put on airs. But Walker wasn't from CIA. Short didn't know where he came from. He barely knew anything about the group he headed, even though he was working for it. It was called the "Army Intelligence Support Activity." A stupid name. And talk about secrecy. Even its acronym was top secret. He sometimes wondered if it really existed at all. Normally Short remained quite happy in his ignorance. His work was demanding enough without his being burdened by the political and moral justifications for it.

Not that he minded the killing. That was his profession, and he was good at it. Some people were doctors or lawyers; others ran businesses or practiced a trade. He killed for a living. It was challenging, hazardous work, and enough of it to keep him employed full-time. There were a surprising number of people in the world who needed killing.

He looked upon himself as a simple instrument of government, and his occupation as a simple extension of policy—a kind of hardball diplomacy. He realized, too, that his work was also an ideal outlet for his aggression. He thought he was probably the least frustrated man in the U.S. government. Outside the practice of his forbidden craft, he was a middle-class, law-abiding suburban husband and father who loved his wife and two girls and got along with his neighbors.

But this Monarch Eagle was beginning to bug him. It wasn't like Walker, or any of the other intelligence-community honchos, for that matter, to so quickly order people killed. And just to silence them, at that.

And why the hell were they so worried about this Lieutenant Grunwald? He was a prisoner in Vietnam. Possibly dead by now. Why did they want to keep him a secret? Did he have something on them? How could he? He couldn't even know that they existed.

Usually Short could assemble in his mind a rough picture of the workings of an operation, and usually it made some kind of sense. But this one didn't make any sense at all. He thought Walker might be operating out of desperation, trying to hide something that had gotten out of hand.

Short didn't like to kill people in that kind of environment. Results were unpredictable.

6

Rhinebeck, New York

Rob Grunwald climbed the long stairs from the train platform of the Rhinecliff station, ducking his face from the gusts of March wind swirling off the Hudson River. Little had changed in five years, and the sensation of walking back into his own past overwhelmed him suddenly. He thought of the hundreds of times, coming home from so many places for so many years, he had mounted these same steps. And he remembered the last time. The spring of 1977. He had come with Sarah and left before his father's return from a South American business trip. Three days. How his mother had lectured him on family responsibility! It was so out of character for her. Every word must have pained her enormously.

What a coward he had been, he thought. Not to have dared face his father then. But what would have been gained? Another ugly scene. Certainly no hope of reconciliation.

He hadn't seen his father since that snowy, cold day in 1970, one week after word had come that Billy was missing in action. Full of smug defiance, Rob had come home to confront the old man with the news that he was exiling himself to Canada to avoid the draft. *Exiling*. He remembered what a fury the word had ignited in him.

He walked through the echoing nineteenth-century white brick waiting room and out to the parking lot and glanced around, half expecting to see the same old Buick station wagon with the discreet GREENWOOD lettering on the side door. He searched among the parked autos for the familiar black face of Herbert, the family chauffeur, but he couldn't find that, either.

A fur-coated arm waved at him from a nearby Mercedes sedan. He hesitated for a second, then walked over. The window hummed down a few more inches and a gloved hand reached out and touched his coat. He bent down slightly for a better view of the occupant. A smiling blonde. He had to think for a moment before he realized that it was his brother's wife, Caroline.

"Don't stand there looking so disappointed," she said. "Get in! That wind is freezing!"

Rob jumped in and Caroline threw the car in gear. "Herbert had to take your mother to Albany," she said, smiling at him nervously. She squealed the tires turning out of the parking lot and accelerated rapidly up the street. "And one of the horses stepped on Angelo's foot in the stable yesterday. So I was delegated to chauffeur you home."

Rob fumbled for the seat belt and snapped the buckle into place. "Don't rush on my account. How is old Herbert, anyway? He must be near eighty by now. Can he still drive?"

Caroline shrugged and glanced across at him, taking her eyes completely off the road. "I was terrified that I wouldn't recognize you. Or maybe that you wouldn't recognize me. I guess that's why I didn't come down to the platform to greet you. I'm a silly coward. Sorry."

She looked tired, he thought—sleepy and heavy-lidded, like someone who hadn't really gotten into gear for the day. He remembered Sarah telling him that Caroline was a chronic insomniac. He saw the left turn onto River Road looming just ahead of them and felt a sharp spasm in his stomach. It was only ten minutes from that corner to Greenwood. He wasn't ready to confront it yet. "Let's drive through Rhinebeck first," he said. "I haven't seen it in a long time."

Caroline obliged and zipped on past the turnoff. "What did you do to your arm?" she inquired.

"The police in Belize shot me."

"Really?" She didn't inquire any further. He supposed she didn't believe him. He had caught the fragrance of alcohol on her breath when she had opened the window to greet him. And she drove the Mercedes as if intent on suicide. She was unhappy, he realized, but, in typical Wasp fashion, was determined to hide it.

"I didn't see you when you were here last," she said. "When was it—1977?"

"Not many people did. How's life in Boston?"

"Marblehead," she corrected. "Very dull. Not like your life, I'm sure."

"Last time I saw you, you were just a bouncy young deb."

She laughed, and he felt a sudden thrill of recognition. He had forgotten that incredible laugh. It was throaty and insinuatingly familiar, at once warm and helpless, suggestive of shared little secrets and pleasures. Its timbre and effect were so different from her voice that it seemed to come from another personality altogether. Rob smiled to himself, recalling the powerful aphrodisiac effect it used to have on him.

"And you were still Billy's bratty little brother," she was saying.

"Is that how you saw me?"

"Pretty much. The two of you were always fighting. Do you remember the night you let the air out of all the tires on Billy's new MG? We were going to a big party on Long Island. I thought he was going to kill you for that."

"I guess I was jealous of him in those days."

"Everybody was jealous of Billy," Caroline said.

"I meant because of you."

Caroline looked surprised. "You had a crush on me?"

"Blondes with long tanned legs in white tennis skirts used to drive me wild."

"I would never have guessed."

"No? Why?"

"You went out of your way to be rude to me, ignore me, and contradict me."

He smiled. "Just my way of showing interest."

She arched an eyebrow. "Come to think of it, I was terrified of you. No wonder I was afraid to meet you at the train today."

Caroline had a delicate ski-slope nose and small ears. Some fat had collected under her chin in the twelve years since Rob had last seen her, and her straight blond hair, pulled back at the moment and pinned at the nape of her neck, had darkened. Under the short fur coat, she was wearing a silk blouse, cream-colored slacks, and open-toed shoes. Some thin gold chains dangled from her neck. A little overdressed for the country in March, he thought. Despite her blueblood New England pedigree, where dowdiness was considered good manners, Caroline loved to be well turned out. He remembered that she was a sports nut, and always wore the last word in swimsuits, ski clothes, tennis wear, riding habit, and hunting gear. She was also obsessively clean. Billy had once confided to him, shortly after their marriage, that she took two baths a day and changed the sheets every other night. Rob had assumed that this was Billy's way of bragging to him that they were doing a great deal of fucking.

When Billy first met her at an Assembly ball, she was ripe and blond and pretty and so spoiled that she made it seem sexy. Rob remembered the first time Billy brought her home to meet the family. Rob was seventeen, feeling anarchistic and obsessed with sex. He was fascinated by her, and spent most of the weekend conjuring up lurid fantasies about her. He imagined that behind the snooty upper-class façade lurked a fiercely intelligent and recklessly passionate girl who would soon tire of Billy and run off with him. He was always wishing people were better than they were.

What their father had admired about her was her bloodline. Centuries of Angles, Saxons, Scots, Danes, Picts, Jutes, Normans, and Visigoths had fought, copulated, and died to produce this creature, and by the mid-1900s, the line had become an endangered species. Caroline's mother had died young of some blood disease, and her father, Hugh Appleton, who justified his existence by raising cockatoos at their estate in Marblehead, Massachusetts, was an alcoholic with no money in the bank and a two-hundred-year-old house on the National Registry that was collapsing around his inebriated head.

Caroline and Billy made a powerful marital combination. There was something for everybody. Caroline got a handsome young hero—captain of the Harvard football team, editor of the *Crimson,* near the top of his class at Harvard Law, and in line to inherit part of an enormous fortune. Billy got a healthy, well-bred beauty from Boston's oldest, bluest stock. The Appletons got money; the Grunwalds got blood.

William Grunwald, Sr., was ecstatic over the match. He even paid for the wedding, a nondenominational affair held, at his insistence, at Greenwood. That was thirteen years ago. Then Billy joined the Marines, went off to war, and never came back.

What had she been doing all these years that his brother was missing? Did she just sit all day in that twenty-room house in Marblehead? His sister Sarah had told him that she had had several affairs. That hardly surprised Rob. No one would have expected her to remain celibate all that time, and divorcing Billy to marry someone else presented some problems. She was living on Billy's trust fund, which amounted to over a hundred thousand dollars a year. And her father was living on Grunwald largesse as well. Grunwald had established a special foundation to preserve the Appleton estate, and had set up Caroline's father as its director, at a salary that kept him comfortably in his favorite scotch and pipe tobacco. Grunwald had effectively absorbed the entire Appleton family and all its possessions into his domain.

"Historic Rhinebeck," Caroline said, bringing the car to a halt under the traffic light at the town's main intersection.

"My hometown," Rob murmured, gazing around. "Funny, I grew up in the privileged class, and I used to envy the hell out of the local high school kids."

"Why?"

"I don't know. They seemed to have such a snug, secure world. Families, friends, and futures they all knew and understood. No pressures. They seemed happy to me. I envied their normal existence, I guess."

Caroline turned onto Montgomery Street.

"How is Mother?" Rob asked.

"A nervous wreck at the moment, with you coming home. She tells everybody that she hears from you regularly. Does she?"

"Occasionally," he lied. "There never seemed to be much to communicate."

"You'd better be prepared to make up for it. There's a big party tonight. Your mother's annual spring ball for the Arts Council."

Rob groaned. "My God, does she still do that? I'll have to hide out in the guesthouse."

"You can't. It's occupied. And obviously your mother expects you to put in an appearance."

"It's a dress-up affair. I don't have any clothes."

"You're not getting out of it that easily. We've already found one of Billy's old blazers for you to wear."

"I'll be miserable around those people."

"There are a few new faces since you were here last," Caroline said. She swung the Mercedes off the highway onto River Road and continued north, past a succession of walled estates. "Were you seeing anyone in wherever-it-was-you-were?" she inquired suddenly.

"Belize. Someone named Yvonne."

"What did Yvonne do?"

Rob expelled a short laugh. "She claimed she was a model."

"I remember a procession of scruffy little secretary types you used to bring up from New York. And a few tough ones with no bras or makeup. I never saw you with anyone terrific."

"Traveling in cheap company has its advantages," he replied. "It's like penny-ante poker. You can't get hurt much."

"What a cynic you've become," Caroline said. "You used to be filled with intimidating lectures on morality and commitment, among other things."

"I was probably a young fool."

Caroline took her eyes from the road again, looking at him with surprise. "I think you made other people feel foolish. I imagined how superficial and silly I must have sounded to you. You were such an angry person."

"That's the emotion I remember best," Rob admitted.

They drove in silence for nearly a mile. The spasms in Rob's stomach were increasing.

"What's Mother say about the ambassadorship?" he asked.

"She says she's looking forward to Israel."

"She never admits her real feelings. He's not going to ask her opinion, anyway. This is his big dream. He thinks it'll make him respectable."

"I've never understood your bitterness."

Rob slumped down in the seat. "That's an essay question. Sometime when you have a month free, I'll explain."

"You're more like your father than you realize," she continued, taking her eyes off the road again. "You and Billy both."

"How is that?"

"You're all so determined to have your way."

"Most people would say we're pretty different."

"It's only what's happened with your lives that's so different."

Caroline's remark disappointed him. Perhaps she was right about Billy, but she didn't know him, or understand how profound was the gulf that divided him from his father.

"What are you doing at Greenwood, anyway?" Rob asked, trying to move off the defensive. "Shouldn't you be organizing Junior League benefits or something back home in Marblehead?"

"There's news about Billy," she replied.

Rob felt his stomach tighten again. He wasn't sure he wanted to hear what it was. She told him anyway.

"A writer came to your father with a tape and transcript of an interview with a Vietnamese refugee who claims he met Billy in a prison camp near the Laotian border two months ago." Caroline pressed her lips together tightly, as if holding in some powerful emotions.

"You don't look very happy about it."

"I'm not," she admitted. "There've been so many false leads in the past, I don't dare get my hopes up anymore. Your father's become a regular target for con men and swindlers. They know he'll pay for information about Billy. I don't know who is hurt the most—your mother, your father, or me. But each time it happens, it's horrible. A year or so passes, and I begin to accept that Billy is probably dead. Then something like this comes along again and revives all my anxiety. I'm not divorced, I'm not widowed, I'm not anything. I'm a married woman who hasn't seen her husband in twelve years."

Caroline stepped on the accelerator angrily, sending the car sweeping around a corner and onto the shoulder. She regained the road and eased her foot off the gas pedal. "It's cruel," she said. "It's really very cruel."

As the Mercedes topped a gentle rise, the high stone wall that surrounded part of Greenwood's eight hundred acres came into view. Rob could see the south orchard, its neat rows of bare-branched apple trees looking as desolate as an army of skeletons in the snow-streaked brown fields. Some distance to the north, on a bluff overlooking the Hudson, the main house loomed, the rows of dormers in its steep Norman roof like eyes watching over the wide aprons of lawn.

The car approached the main gate, with its towering stone portals and the enormous arch with the letter *G* filigreed into a wrought-iron pattern of leaves and trees. The gate itself was open, and Rob could see, tucked in just behind it, the gray slate roof and brick walls of the small gatehouse where the gardener and his wife had lived when he was a boy. Beyond the cottage the long driveway, bordered with tall elms, snaked its long, familiar way up through the acres of meadows and lawns.

"Stop the car," he gasped.

Caroline slammed on the brakes and brought the heavy vehicle to a rocking halt just outside the entrance. Rob jumped out, rushed to the edge of the road, and vomited in the gravel.

When the spasms subsided he sat back and fumbled weakly in his pocket for a handkerchief. Caroline knelt beside him and handed him a towel. He wiped his mouth and the sweat from his face and then felt her cool hand gently massaging the nape of his neck.

Back in the car she produced a silver flask from the glove compartment, unscrewed the cover, and handed it to him. "It'll make you feel better," she said. "I know from experience."

East Berlin

At the Platz der Akademie, Dieter Rheinhart slowed his step and glanced around, astonished. He had traveled to East Berlin dozens of times over the past ten years, but his eyes had never seen so desolate a sight.

It was a warm, sunny day in March, and he was only two blocks from Unter den Linden, East Berlin's busiest thoroughfare. Yet here the square and the streets that fed into it were deserted and silent. The stillness was remarkable. The rumbles and whines of the great city had vanished utterly, and nothing moved. Directly before him towered the derelict remains of an enormous church. A collapsed eighteenth-century wedding cake of brick, steel, and stone, it dominated the square like a ruined colossus, its jagged late-afternoon shadow swallowing the street around him in its gloom. He stared at the portico of broken pillars and statuary that framed its entrance and wondered if he had misunderstood his directions. The windows and doors were bricked up, and there were no signs that anyone had disturbed its bleak slumber for many years.

He prowled hesitantly among the weeds and the piles of toppled statuary heaped in the front courtyard, then spied the small doorway cut into a boarded-up side entrance.

Stepping cautiously, he ducked through the doorway and picked a path through the rubble, pausing frequently to gape at the scene around him. The walls, pocked and eroded like those of an ancient ruin, teemed with crumbling bas-relief and broken statues. Overhead, a once massive dome had been replaced by the blue Berlin sky. Decades of sun and rain had invaded the interior and fostered a jungle of plants, which rose from the decay like bacteria on a mold. The place smelled sharply of carth and plaster dust. He jumped when a voice, raspy and uneven, croaked at him from out of nowhere, "Welcome to the Französischer Dom."

Rheinhart jerked his head around and found the source—an old man in a gray suit sitting in a low niche near the back of the cathedral. The figure stood up very straight and walked slowly toward him.

"A church for French Huguenots," the old man continued, his tone conversational, disinterested. "Built in the first decade of the eighteenth century by Cayart and Quesnay. Von Gontard added a dome to it in 1780. It was one of Berlin's great landmarks. What took eighty years to build was destroyed in two nights—April fourth and fifth, 1945, by American bombs."

"Why haven't you bulldozed it away?"

The man stopped five feet from Rheinhart and looked him over speculatively, as if checking him against a mental file. "We intend to restore it," he said. "Meanwhile it serves a useful function. A history lesson of sorts."

A thin smile cracked his lips. Rheinhart was intimidated by the sheer decrepitude of the man. His pallid features were scarred and cratered, as ruined as the statuary around him. And he was cadaverously thin, an armature of bones and eroded flesh in a fastidiously tailored wool suit. He moved with the slow economy of the chronically ill, and his eyes seemed clouded with pain. Rheinhart suspected that some terrible disease ravaged him, and like most healthy people, he was frightened by the thought that it might be contagious. The man's voice, however, was hard and sharp, resonant with authority. "I am Karl Koenig," he said. "I will be your control from now on."

Rheinhart felt suddenly faint. Karl Koenig was the name of the head of East Germany's Secret Police. Could it possibly be the same man? But, my God, he thought, what could be so important as to bring the director himself out into an operation? It was unheard of. He studied Koenig with a new attention. He was very expensively dressed. The suit was hand-tailored, the shoes handmade, both probably Hungarian. The wristwatch was thin and gold, probably Czech. Nothing from the West. That was unusual. Such single-minded resistance to the consumer luxuries of the capitalist world indicated a man of uncompromising ideology. The dedicated Communist, the true believer. The last of a dying breed.

"How did you come over, Herr Rheinhart?"

"Friedrichstrasse," Rheinhart replied, fighting down the butterflies in his gut. "The U-Bahn. It took an hour. That's why I'm late."

Koenig's thin lips stretched across his teeth in a sardonic grin. "You know our customs procedures are thorough. You must make sure you allow enough time. Don't be late again."

Rheinhart nodded eagerly.

"There is an American writer who lives in Nice," Koenig said. "His name is Duffy. An unsavory character. He claims to have interviewed a Vietnamese refugee on the subject of a U.S. Marine Lieutenant named William Grunwald, Junior, who was taken prisoner in Vietnam in 1970. You must approach this man at once. He is greedy for money and you should be able to buy his information from him. Find out as well the name and address of this refugee, so we can confirm it."

"Yes, sir."

"Hanoi will be very eager about this," Koenig said in a low voice, thinking aloud. He grimaced slightly, as if disturbed by an unpleasant memory, then gazed up at the gaping ruins of the roof. A skeletal network of rafters still remained in place over a section of it. The sky beyond had deepened to the hazy purple of early twilight. Rheinhart suddenly noticed that it had grown quite dark inside the church. When Koenig lowered his gaze again, Rheinhart was astonished to see that the man's face had taken on an almost demonic expression. The corners of his mouth twitched up in a hard, secretive smile.

"This is of the highest importance, Herr Rheinhart," he said. "It is extremely important that you act at once. Do you understand?"

"I understand."

"This Grunwald is not a prisoner," Koenig continued, the words escaping his thin lips with a fierce intensity. "Not at all. He is something evil. Quite evil."

Rheinhart fidgeted uncomfortably in the path of the director's burning stare. "Do you know this man personally, Herr Koenig?"

Koenig displayed his decayed teeth in a sudden grin. "Yes. I know him." He paused and stared up through the wreckage of the church's dome at the darkening patch of evening sky as if he saw this nemesis looming over them in the clouds. "He comes from bad blood."

7

Rhinebeck, New York

Rob awoke late from a nap in his old room on the third floor and took a long bath, filling the ancient claw-footed tub in the hall bathroom up to the overflow and sitting, submerged to his neck, for nearly an hour.

The homecoming had been intense, painful, and exhausting. His mother was overwhelmed, and had cried much of the afternoon. Even Herbert, the chauffeur, and Katherine, the housekeeper, the only members of the staff who were around the last time he had been home, were moved to tears. He had finally cried himself, awash in a confusing emotional tide of nostalgia and regret. He was grateful that his father had not been there.

He dressed slowly, lethargically, picking among the clothes Katherine had laid out on the bed like an unenthusiastic shopper at a rummage sale. He shrugged finally into Billy's old blue blazer and stared at his image in the floor-length mirror. The jacket appeared a trifle shiny at the elbows, and one of the three brass buttons on the right cuff was missing, but, to his surprise, it fit him perfectly. Years of being the younger brother had left him convinced that he was smaller than Billy.

He fiddled uncomfortably with the French cuffs on the shirt, and loosened the tie around his throat. He saw himself in this same room at the age of eight, with Gerta, their nanny, tying his bow tie and scolding him for getting dirt on his cuffs, and his brother Billy stealing the laces from his polished black dress shoes. Years of balls and parties and teas and dinners and stuffy weekends in Beverly, Southampton, Dark Harbor, and New York City lay between himself and that little boy of eight, and he could barely remember details from any of them. They seemed to have taken place in another lifetime. During his junior year at Columbia he had thrown out his entire wardrobe and replaced it with work shirts and blue jeans.

He jammed his hands into the blazer's side pockets and pulled out some residue from past wearings—some wadded bits of Kleenex and a folded scrap of paper—and carried it to a wastebasket. The folded paper missed the basket. He bent down, picked it up, and then, on an impulse, unfolded it. The paper was of a cheap quality and brittle with age. The printing on it had faded badly, and he carried it over to the window to read it in better light. Gradually he began to decipher the words. He felt goose bumps race along his flesh. He stared at the small rectangle of paper a while longer, then refolded it carefully and tucked it into an inner pocket of his wallet.

His mother appeared in the doorway just as he slipped the billfold back into his rear pocket. He smiled at her absently, still preoccupied with the words on the piece of paper.

"My prodigal son," she murmured, straightening the blazer lapels and brushing stray bits of lint from his shoulders. "It's so good to have you back again."

When he had first left home, in 1970, she was a beautiful woman, barely past forty. Now in her early fifties, she was still remarkably attractive, her figure slim and graceful; but her once luxurious black hair had grayed dramatically, and the porcelain-white skin of her face looked dry and fragile.

Rob's devotion to her was complicated. She had always seemed to him more like an older sister than a mother. Like many rich and beautiful women, she had preferred to delegate the intimate chores of motherhood to others. His growing up had largely been entrusted to a series of governesses, who exercised the real maternal commitment and authority in his life. When his mother came to the nursery, it was only to visit. As a child he had been utterly in awe of her. She was this magnificent, benevolent creature, usually seen from afar, at the center of some admiring circle of other adults. She was always hugging him hello and kissing him good-bye as she came and went on the rounds of her mysterious and wonderful life—a life that rarely included children.

When Rob was older he began to see her flaws. Behind her culti-vated wit and charm she was insecure and weak-willed, content to live in her husband's shadow. She was cut in the mold of a martyr, not a champion, and she had survived the strong and clashing egos of her husband and three children by either giving in to them or avoiding them. Her angers and frustrations she turned inward, ab-sorbing everything, confronting nothing. Only once in his life could Rob recall her actually displaying her temper, and that was at one of the maids for breaking an expensive Chinese vase.

Poor Mother. Sarah told him that she had become addicted to tranquilizers. He wasn't surprised. People who spent much time under the sway of William Grunwald invariably seemed to develop nervous afflictions, almost as if he gave off, in the domineering manner in which he took control of everyone and everything around him, some kind of radiation that corroded one's health.

When she had first met his father, she was young and naive, the overly protected daughter of a rich Jewish merchant family. His fath-er's intense courtship of her, from the bits and pieces of gossip and confessions Rob had picked up over the years, indicated that he had not so much persuaded as bullied her into marriage. She was afraid of him, but he was the strong authority figure she apparently wanted— the one who would take charge and make all the decisions. And relieve her of responsibilities.

Rob kissed her lightly on the cheek. "Where's Father?"

"He had to run into the city for something or other. He won't be back until late."

"Years ago he was talking about installing a heliport on the lawn by the river. What happened to it?"

She furrowed her brow, trying to remember. The tranquilizers gave her a slightly unfocused manner. "I think the town board wouldn't allow it," she replied. "Too much noise."

"When did he ever let a town board stop him?"

"Melissa Stahl is coming tonight," she said. "You remember her, don't you?"

Abrupt subject changes were an old habit of hers, Rob remembered, a device she used to evade arguments, explanations, and unpleasant subjects generally. He pressed a fist to his chin and pretended to think hard. "Let's see. Foxcroft, Wellesley. Plays awful tennis and terrible backgammon. Fat thighs and poor conversational habits. That the one?"

"That was a very long time ago, darling. She's been in the Peace

Corps, and she's writing a book. She's a very impressive woman. And she's dying to see you again."

"What's her book about?"

"Oh, I can never remember the subject. A history of something, I think. You must ask her to describe it."

Rob cupped his mother's cheeks in his hands and stared at her with mock severity. "You're not trying to fix me up, are you?"

Cornelia Grunwald laughed with embarrassment and pushed his hands away. "You can't blame me for trying, darling. You've always had appalling luck with women."

"That seems to be the consensus."

His mother frowned suddenly. "Have you decided what you're going to do?"

"No."

She hugged him to her. He felt her tremble. "I'm so afraid that you're just going to take off again somewhere and it'll be years before I see you again."

"I need some time to think about things."

"Of course you do," she replied. "You can live here, you know, if you like. Until you decide. We'll need someone to run the house while we're in Israel."

Rob shook his head. "I couldn't do that."

"Please don't make up your mind now. Wait and see what your father has to say."

"He won't like the idea any more than I do."

"Your father wants to bring the family together again. Please promise me that you'll at least listen to him. If you both really want a reconciliation, I know you can bring it about."

Rob patted his mother on the arm to reassure her. Of what, he wasn't sure.

"Promise me you'll try."

"I promise."

She pulled his head toward her and kissed him hard on the cheek. "I must get back downstairs. Come down whenever you're ready. People will start arriving around eight. And don't drink too much." She paused by the door. "I'm so happy you're here," she whispered.

"What's the news about Billy?" he asked.

"Your father will explain it."

"Is he optimistic?"

"Neither of us has ever lost hope."

Rob wished he could say something positive to her, but nothing came to mind. He thought that Billy was probably dead.

"I've always loved you the most, you know," she said, following her own peculiar train of thought.

He looked at her, surprised. "And I've always thought I was a hell of a nuisance to you."

She smiled. "Sometimes you were. You were much more demanding and difficult than Billy or Sarah. But I think that's why I loved you so much. You needed me more than they did. You missed me more when I wasn't around. You had the capacity to make me happy or sad." She paused, as if she had just remembered something important. "Billy's absence has been hard for me to bear, but yours has been harder. It was so unnecessary."

Rob stared at the floor, suddenly overwhelmed with sadness. So far, every human connection in his life had failed, he realized. Even with his own mother. "I'm just a different kind of casualty than Billy," he said.

The party was in what was informally called the "Josephine Room." It was a two-story-high ballroom on the west side of the mansion with a long row of French doors that opened onto acres of lawn and a spectacular view of the Hudson River. The room had earned its name from the two black marble columns that flanked the huge fireplace at one end. They were said to have once guarded an entrance to the Château Malmaison, Napoleon's palace outside Paris. At the end opposite the fireplace, the ballroom floor was raised three steps, like a shallow stage, and a string quartet was ensconced there, struggling to keep the notes of a Brahms piece afloat in the heavy tide of conversation and laughter.

Rob stopped at one of the bars, set up in the wide hall just outside the ballroom, ordered a vodka on the rocks, and surveyed the scene. Several hundred guests—the usual local gentry plus twenty or thirty imports from New York City—were shoving their way around, forming and reforming in tight clusters and keeping the decibel level growing with the consumption of drink. The New York people were his mother's idea. Some were society, but most were in the arts—museum types, gallery owners, a few musicians, writers, and actors. "Seasoning," his mother called them. She was a famous party-giver, part of her strategy for gaining acceptance among the local establishment, a campaign she had waged tirelessly in the face of three decades of social snubs and gossip. The Grunwalds were still deeply resented by the old guard—for their money, their influence, and their Jewishness, but they were just too powerful a force in the community to be ignored.

Rob had always despised society. It was complacent, insular, and openly anti-Semitic. It used to embarrass him intensely, the extent to which his family—his mother particularly—seemed willing to go to ingratiate itself with such hopeless Gentile snobs. He had gone through a period, during his late teens, of defiantly flaunting his Jewishness, and he had taken a lot of criticism from the family because of it. Now he hardly cared. People were anti-Semitic everywhere, he had discovered, and Jews were often no less arrogantly prejudiced in their own social attitudes. What he was up against, he realized, was human nature, not racism.

Surveying the dense herd of glittering clothes and polished faces, he felt a moment of panic. Most were people he had never met, and those he had once known had aged past recognition. He groped through his memory for some names. There was Charles Suttenfield, but who was his wife? And there were the Farrells. He couldn't remember either of their names. Mrs. Van Schuyler? Or was it Van Schoon? No. Schoonmaker? He craned his neck around in search of someone safe.

He spotted Caroline, started off in her direction, but then slowed down. She was bent in conversation with a man who looked vaguely Latin. Caroline was sizing him up, flirting with him. The man suddenly moved his face close, and she smiled and patted his arm. To his surprise, Rob felt a sharp sting of jealousy.

Caroline always created a kind of sexual undertow around her—an invisible current of sensuality that pulled people off balance. There was something of the tease about her, he thought. An aura of restlessness and unscratched itches. She liked to touch when she talked, he noticed, and she held eye contact too long. And of course she dressed to kill. Tonight she was wearing a beige pajamalike costume that looked very easy to slip in and out of. He imagined she also went in for expensive underwear—silk bras and camisoles, and panties trimmed with lace. He heard that subtle, pagan laugh of hers float through the noise of the crowd and bit his lip.

An engulfing cloud of cigarette smoke made him turn. A middle-aged man in an out-of-date tuxedo was baring his teeth at him like a nervous hyena at a water hole. "Rob, old boy! I don't believe it! Back from Timbuktu! You remember Millie!"

Rob glanced at the man's wife, a mousy woman in a shapeless brocaded gown. Who were they? "Of course," he heard himself saying. "How are you, Millie?"

She started to answer but was cut off by her husband. "So what are you up to, old boy?" The man's bloodshot eyes were swiveling the room like twin radar dishes, scanning for important faces.

Rob remembered. He was a local banker. Rutledge. Howell Rutledge. He had once blackballed the Grunwalds from the country club. The Grunwalds now owned the bank he worked for. Several other voices were shouting hellos around them, and Rutledge exchanged a couple of hearty greetings and handshakes while Millie stared at Rob.

"So what are you up to, old boy?" Rutledge repeated, not listening to himself.

Rob forced his mouth into a grin. "Just fresh out of jail, as a matter of fact."

"That's wonderful. Wonderful! Glad to hear it." Rutledge looked past Rob's shoulder and called to someone he knew. "Keep up the good work, old boy!" he said, and pulled his wife, now gawking wide-eyed at Rob, along behind him.

A muscular hand squeezed his shoulder and spun him around. This face he remembered. Fred Livingston, an old friend of Billy's. Livingston had accumulated a layer of fat over the years, but the arrogant energy was still there.

"You've been missing almost as long as your brother," he brayed. "What the hell have you been up to?"

Rob shrugged. "Foreign intrigues."

"I'm at the same old stand," Livingston replied, as if Rob had asked. He sounded pleased with his modesty. "Money gets better every year, though."

Rob had no idea what Livingston did. Something on Wall Street, probably. "Is it dangerous work?" he asked, keeping a solemn face.

"I'm a vice-president now," Livingston countered.

"How many vice-presidents do they have?"

Livingston changed the subject. "I still miss your brother's tennis game," he said.

"He used to beat the hell out of you."

"That's just it," Livingston persisted, determined to remain jovial. "I finally get good enough to beat him and he has to go and get lost in the mysterious East. I miss the son of a gun. Billy and I were pretty close, you know."

Rob watched Livingston take a heavy swig from his drink. The party was about two hours old and he was half drunk.

"Buddies! That's what we were," Livingston insisted. "But always competing. See who was best. Right through prep school, college. Girls, tennis, skiing, sailing, honors club, debating. We were always right up there, fighting it out for top dog. Billy always liked a challenge, and so did I. We had some times together, Robbie. We did it all. I miss the son of a gun."

Rob remembered. Fred had been a fixture at Greenwood for years, a kind of one-man fan club who had followed Billy around like a personal servant. Rob had always disliked him: Billy was different when he was around, always playing a role for his benefit, acting tough and sadistic.

Rob recalled that Livingston had tried to enlist in the Marines with Billy but had been rejected for some reason. Obviously it had hurt him. And now, incredibly, he seemed to envy Billy's MIA status, as if somehow his old buddy had one-upped him by never coming home and facing the tedious realities of family and career.

"He was tough and smart," Livingston continued. "He wouldn't let any of those little gook bastards kill him. He's alive over there somewhere, the son of a gun. I can feel it. He'll be back. He's a winner. First class all the way. Nobody's going to kill him. I'd sure like to beat his ass at tennis, though." Livingston turned away suddenly, apparently overcome with sentiment, and pushed toward the bar.

Rob wandered around, avoiding conversation, his eye nervously searching the crowd for his father. He caught a glimpse of Caroline again. She was surrounded by three men now, including Fred Livingston. He wanted to ask her about the piece of paper he had discovered in Billy's blazer. He consumed another vodka, refilled the glass a third time, and decided to retreat upstairs, where he could compose himself in private for his impending confrontation with his father.

A female voice stopped him. "Aren't you going to say hello?"

The perfectly round face, small nose, and short, fluffy hairdo were instantly familiar, but she appeared shorter and thinner, and the big breasts that he had once salivated over when she was dating his brother were smaller than he remembered. She emanated a cheery, wholesome blandness that unnerved him almost immediately.

"Hello, Melissa."

"It's been years, hasn't it," she declared in a hearty voice, overcoming the din of the party.

"I guess it has been."

"Are you still a revolutionary?"

"No. I'm just a bum now."

"I've been married and divorced," she pronounced solemnly, as if those accomplishments might impress him.

"No kidding."

"We're still friends, though."

"Who?"

She tossed her head impatiently. "Geoffrey. My former husband."

"Oh."

"Are you married?"

"No."

"You look sad."

Rob bared his teeth in a mock grin. "What gave you that idea?"

"I plan to get drunk tonight," she confided, in a stage whisper. "I've already had three drinks. Do you want to get drunk together?"

"I better not."

She giggled coyly. "You're not afraid of me, are you?"

Rob nodded emphatically, which seemed to please her. There was something about Melissa's trying to be a sophisticated flirt that disturbed him. She was stepping dangerously out of character. At least the character he remembered. He put an arm around her waist and guided her to the bar in the hall. They refilled their glasses and stood awkwardly facing each other.

"You used to be very funny," she said. "Every time your brother brought me to Greenwood, there you'd be, saying the most outrageous things. You used to make me laugh all the time and it made Billy mad. He said the family thought you were crazy and they were going to have you put away. Sent to the 'funny farm,' he called it."

Rob nodded. "That's where I've been all these years. They just let me out."

A stray elbow from a passing guest caught Melissa's arm and dumped her vodka and ice cubes down the front of her dress. She gasped and dropped the glass. Amid the flurry of apologies and paper towels that followed, Rob took her hand and led her up the stairs to an empty guest bedroom on the second floor. She lost her balance by the doorway and fell against him. He caught her and tried to set her upright, but she leaned into him. He kissed her playfully on the neck, and then, feeling her wet gown soaking his shirtfront, he pushed her away and into the bedroom.

"I'll find some clothes for you," he said.

"Just bring me a drink," she commanded, flopping heavily onto the big canopied bed.

Rob enlisted one of the maids to hunt up some dresses and took the back stairs down to the ground floor. Nearly midnight, he thought, and still no sign of his father. The stairs terminated in the long corridor that ran from the kitchen pantry back through the servants' wing. The hallway was unlit, and he fumbled around momentarily, feeling for the light switch. His hands touched someone's arm.

He found the switch and clicked it on. A low-wattage, unshaded bulb illuminated the narrow corridor in a pallid incandescent glow. The dark-haired man was there, one hand pressed against the wall. Trapped between him and the wallpaper, her arm draped casually over his shoulder, was Caroline.

She saw Rob and removed her arm.

"Excuse me," Rob said. He pushed through the door into the pantry and strode angrily across the mansion to the bar at the bottom of the main stairs.

The hell with it, he decided. It was impossible to stay sober tonight. To the consternation of the bartender, he grabbed a plastic bucket half full of ice, stuffed a bottle of vodka and a couple of glasses inside, and retreated back upstairs.

Melissa was sitting on the bed, holding a towel across her lap. She had removed all her clothes except a half-slip. The maid had already returned and left a couple of dresses for her, neatly folded over the back of the chair. Rob set the plastic bucket on the nightstand and sat down beside her. He gazed down at the pile of gown, panty hose, bra, and underpants on the floor, then at her. Her breasts, pink from the towel scrubbing, were still quite large after all.

She stared at him defiantly. "You like them?" she asked.

"You're drunk, Melissa."

"I'm going to get drunker. Don't try to stop me, either."

"I don't plan to." He pulled the two glasses from the bucket, filled them with ice, and poured vodka over the cubes.

"You going to get drunk with me, then?"

"Why not."

She giggled conspiratorially, like a schoolgirl on a prank. "Let's get crazy drunk," she whispered. "I haven't been really crazy drunk in years. Maybe never, come to think of it." She rested her glass on the night table and fell back on the bed, gazing up at the rose-colored canopy. "I'm tired of being proper. That's all I ever am—damned proper Melissa." She groped for his hand and placed it on her breast. "Make love to me, Robbie."

Rob didn't need further coaxing. He yanked off his clothes, slid down beside her, and quickly applied his tongue to the nipples of her breasts. Melissa reached down and grasped his penis. "My God," she whispered, "you're really ready, aren't you!"

She began to climax the moment he entered her. She thrashed about wildly, and bit into his shoulder in a violent orgasm that lasted about a minute and ended in a shuddering moan. Rob paused for a few seconds, then began moving again, drawing out and plunging against her in long, hard, rhythmic strokes that made her cry out. He kept up the same unvaried pace for fifteen minutes, seeing her through another orgasm and on her way to a third. Finally he came inside her in a violent eruption that caused her to burst into tears.

He withdrew and fell flat on his back beside her, soaked with sweat and gasping for breath.

"Jesus Christ," she said, her voice shaking. "I think you bruised me."

"I'm sorry."

"Don't apologize. I loved it!"

Rob reached for the vodka on the night table. His arm trembled with weakness. It was the first sex he'd had without cocaine in a long time. He was relieved to know that it was still possible.

"Who were you making love to?" Melissa asked, when she had recovered enough to sit up.

Rob was perplexed. "When?"

"Just now, silly."

"Melissa Stahl."

Melissa picked up her vodka glass and studied it. "No, you weren't. Your eyes were closed tight. You were thinking of somebody else, weren't you?"

There were some things you always lied about, he thought, no matter what. "Of course not."

"It doesn't matter," she said. "You were terrific. My God, I was so excited I thought I was going to faint. Geoffrey never did that to me."

"Geoffrey?"

"My husband."

"Oh."

"I always wanted to make love with you," she said. "Even when I was going with your brother. Of course, I was just a silly virgin, but I fantasized that you would make a wonderful lover. I thought about you a lot. I knew that Billy never really liked me."

"Of course he did."

Melissa shook her head firmly. "No. I was just another girl he wanted to screw. He was very selfish. I know I shouldn't talk this way about him, because of what happened to him, but I'm not a member of your brother's fan club, like everybody else around here. He was very cruel to me."

"What did he do to you?"

Melissa hesitated, then took a swallow from her vodka glass. "I'll tell you because I'm drunk," she said. "And because I trust you. I've never told anybody else."

Rob waited, wondering how big a bombshell Melissa was capable of dropping.

"Your brother raped me."

"Come on."

"Yes he did," she hissed, her expression fierce. "Right in this room. The day he married Caroline. He was drunk and he caught me coming out of the bathroom. I guess I flirted with him a bit. I was a little tipsy myself. Billy and I had only gone out a few times. I was too old-fashioned for him. He dropped me as soon as he realized I wasn't going to jump into bed with him. He asked me if I was jealous of Caroline. Like an idiot, I said yes. I was just trying to be nice. It was his wedding day, after all. I didn't want to say I thought she was a tramp—which is what I do think. Anyway, he told me this was my last chance to go to bed with him. I thought he was just teasing me, but he wasn't. I was horrified. Caroline and the guests were all downstairs. He grabbed me, pushed me down on the bed, and held me there, saying dirty things to me. After a while I just gave in. What else could I do? I didn't dare scream. I was as terrified of someone walking in on us as I was of what he was doing to me. Of course I never told anyone. How could I? I would've been blamed."

Melissa picked her gown up from the floor and covered herself with it, as if suddenly aware of her nudity. "It would've been better to have been raped by a stranger. At least my feelings would've been spared. Your brother's really selfish and mean. He's not the hero everyone thinks he is."

Between frequent sips of vodka, Melissa struggled back into her clothes. Her impatient ardor of only minutes before had given way to a sullen sadness. Had she done this to get back at his brother? Rob wondered. She pulled on her gown and glared at it in the mirror. It was wrinkled and still damp. She made several fruitless attempts to smooth it out, then gave up.

"You're not mad at me, are you?" she asked. "For talking about Billy?"

"No. I'm sorry about what happened to you."

"Don't tell anyone."

"Of course not."

"I'd better go home," Melissa said. "I feel sick."

"Do you want a ride?"

"I drove over myself."

"I'd better drive you."

She shook her head. "You're drunker than I am. I'll be all right."
She hugged him and kissed him on his neck. "You're the best Grunwald, Robbie. No matter what anyone else says." Before he could
answer, she had opened the bedroom door and disappeared down the
hall.

Rob stumbled into the bathroom and splashed cold water on his
face, thinking about what Melissa had said. He wondered if she had
twisted the incident around in her mind to make it seem like rape.
Would his brother really have acted in such a brutish fashion? She
had also called Caroline a tramp, he remembered.

She must just be jealous, he decided. But, jealous or not, her
accusations could still be true.

Rob pulled on his pants and shirt, noting with an amused detach-
ment that they looked as wrinkled as Melissa's gown.

He was in the process of putting on his socks when he felt the weight
of footsteps on the carpet behind him. He turned, to see a man in a
dark business suit standing just inside the doorway.

His father.

8

Rhinebeck, New York

William Grunwald stood in the doorway, his hands braced against the jambs, looking at the disheveled blankets, the strewn pillows, and the two half empty glasses beside the vodka bottle on the night table. A mixture of embarrassment and curiosity played across his features.

Rob pulled on his shoes in nervous haste and stood up. The awkwardness of the situation paralyzed him. It was like a confrontation of lifetime political enemies mortified to be caught in each other's company.

His father seemed shorter, grayer—a diminished version of the one he remembered. Had he exaggerated his size and ferocity in his mind to fit the magnitude of his dislike for him?

"What are you doing?"

"Getting ready for bed," Rob lied.

"Are you drunk?"

"I'm coherent."

Grunwald gestured in the direction of his study, down the hall, and Rob followed him there. The study was part of a small suite that included a dressing room, bedroom, and bath. William Grunwald had had it installed years ago as a private retreat where he could work and sleep undisturbed. By unspoken mutual agreement, he had abandoned the master bedroom down the hall to his wife, and he seldom visited it.

Grunwald settled into a chair by his desk and directed his son to a sofa against the wall. Rob dropped onto it heavily. He had rehearsed in his head whole paragraphs in preparation for this moment, but in his father's presence they all fled. Some acknowledgment of the bitter twelve-year separation they were now ending was needed, but neither man seemed willing or able to find the right words.

"Your sister," his father began, his voice stiff, almost formal, "has filled me in on the details of your circumstances in Central America."

"Oh?"

"She told me that you have a drug habit."

"I got over it the hard way. In jail."

Grunwald nodded skeptically. "Your long absence has hurt your mother deeply, you know."

As if you cared, Rob thought. "I've talked to her," he said.

"I won't pretend that I've missed you very much. You've caused me a lot of problems over the years."

Rob said nothing.

"I think we should try to put the past behind us," his father said.

Rob nodded mutely. Words of conciliation simply wouldn't form on his lips.

His father's tone hardened: "It cost me a lot of money to get you out of Belize."

"I didn't ask you to bail me out."

"Would you have preferred ten years in a Belize prison?"

"I'd have served every day before I'd have come to you for help." He marveled at how easily the unpleasant words leaped to his tongue.

The elder Grunwald flushed angrily. "Yes, you probably would have." He extracted a pair of half-frames and a small leather-bound notebook from his inside suit pocket. Rob watched him as he slipped the glasses over his ears and began thumbing the pages.

"You were in jail before," he said, glancing up from the notebook. "In Zurich, in 1978. For some kind of bank fraud."

"A simple misunderstanding. I was released in a week."

"You were arrested in Monaco in 1979 for trying to cheat the casino. And arrested in Venice the same year for involvement in some kind of art forgery."

"You have good spies."

"I have to protect the family. You still bear the family name."

"You do it for the same reason you do everything," Rob retorted. "To protect yourself. The hell with the family name."

Grunwald placed the notebook on the desk behind him and removed his glasses. The muscles around his eyes and mouth tightened in bitterness. "I've never understood you," he said. "But it beggars belief that you would become a criminal."

"None of the arrests stuck."

"Don't be a wise guy. The pattern is obvious."

"Well, you should be proud of me. I've shown initiative, daring, and entrepreneurial skill. And I've survived without the help of a nickel's worth of your money."

Grunwald rose from his chair and paced the room. "I found an old letter the other day, from the headmaster of Exeter. Maybe you remember it. You were a mathematical genius, he said. He wanted to create a special program to help develop your abilities. You had a great future, he said. A month later, of course, you got yourself expelled. Anybody who's ever tried to do anything for you, you've turned around and kicked them in the teeth."

Rob folded his arms across his chest and slid down in the chair. "I was no math genius. He was just buttering you up for a new science building."

"He sent me your test scores," Grunwald replied.

"What did you hope for? That I'd end up an accountant for Grunwald Industries?"

"I didn't think you'd go to Columbia and major in art history, for chrissake! I hoped for more than that!"

Grunwald paused by the far wall and began straightening the rows of framed photographs there. Rob was familiar with many of them, but he saw that the collection had been augmented substantially over the past twelve years. They covered the entire wall, a gallery of documented associations, many of them autographed: Grunwald with John F. Kennedy, with Richard Nixon, Barry Goldwater, John Glenn, John Wayne, Ronald Reagan, H. L. Hunt, J. P. Getty, William Westmoreland, Sukarno, Menachem Begin, Madame Chiang Kai-shek— a voluminous collection of the world's movers and shakers over the past thirty-plus years. It was a harmless enough vanity, Rob supposed, but he had often imagined that, if analyzed properly, the pictures would reveal some truth about his father beyond the simple need to be counted among the great.

"You were brought up with every privilege it's possible to have," Grunwald said, his finger pushing against the corner of a gold frame to bring it exactly level. "Privileges I couldn't even have dreamed of as a kid. You were our youngest and I suppose we indulged you too much. But that hardly accounts for your contempt for your family and for civilized values."

Rob shook his head. "You gave this same speech twelve years ago, before I went to Canada."

"When you dodged your responsibilities to your country!"

"The war was immoral and stupid. Everyone admits that now."

"It was not the place of a nineteen-year-old to decide on the morality of his government's policies."

"He had a right if his life was on the line . . . and if he was willing to accept the consequences. I accepted the consequences. And I have no apologies and no regrets."

Grunwald's eyes burned with wounded fury. "You brought shame to this family. You dishonored Billy's sacrifice."

"I don't mean to sound like a smart ass, but I thought the Holocaust put the idea of unquestioned obedience to authority in disrepute once and for all."

William Grunwald pressed the palms of his hands over his eyes, as if overcome by fatigue. When he took them away, his face looked ashen and sick. "I promised myself I would not become angry with you. But it's impossible. Your contempt, your ingratitude, is monumental."

"What do I have to be grateful for? What you're really unhappy about is that I was born with a will of my own. That I've refused to let you call the shots in my life, the way you did Sarah's and Billy's. You never respected our desires or our opinions. And I'm not talking about just what kinds of careers we could pursue. We never had any choices about anything—what schools we wanted to go to, who we wanted as friends, where we could spend the summers, how much money we could have, what kinds of clothes we could wear, what kind of haircuts we could have. There was never any way but your way! You interfered in every goddamn petty little corner of our lives! You manipulated us like puppets."

Rob's tirade seemed to stun Grunwald. "A father has an obligation to raise his children," he answered, retreating behind a pedantic, self-justifying sermon. "To protect them from their own mistakes until they are old enough and wise enough to protect themselves. If that father is also the head of a rich and prominent family, he bears a special obligation, both to his children and to society. I don't pretend to be perfect—"

"You *do* pretend to be perfect, damn it!" Rob interrupted. "That's why growing up under you was so goddamn painful. Can you recall for me one moment in your whole life when you ever admitted being wrong about anything? Just one?"

Grunwald straightened another photograph on the wall. "You are a spoiled weakling," he said. "You can't tolerate discipline. I can assure you, my childhood was far tougher than yours. In Germany before the war you learned to obey your elders—without question. And you accepted, without question, what they taught you—until you were old enough to decide for yourself what was right and what was wrong. And mistakes were costly. They were evidence of weakness, and weakness could be fatal. I don't defend the world I grew up in, but it taught me to be strong. It taught me to hide my mistakes and take advantage of the mistakes of others. And that's a lesson I still believe in."

"Are you admitting that you actually made mistakes in your past?"

"Of course. Everybody does."

"Tell me one that you made."

Grunwald stared at the rows of photographs. No more remained to be straightened. "I can't recall one right off hand. . . ."

"See? You're afraid to admit that you're human. That you're fallible."

Grunwald turned to his son, his face livid. "What would be gained? Why don't you accept my admission at face value? Why do you need evidence? You want to have something on me—is that it? Or do you just want to see me make a fool of myself, as you have done? To wear my mistakes, as you do, like a badge to signify that I'm a clown, a silly weakling? I'm not like you, damn it! And I'm not going to pretend to be to make you feel better. You've made enough mistakes for all of us—for the whole damned family!"

Rob let his chin fall to his chest and stared at the floor, overwhelmed by the same sense of injustice he remembered so well from his childhood.

Grunwald paced the room silently for a long time, then sat down heavily in his chair. "I asked you here to make you an offer, not to exhume the past," he said, his voice deflated of emotion. "Making amends is obviously not possible. Let's put it aside."

"What kind of offer?"

"A truce."

"What does that mean?"

"I've gotten you out of a serious jam. All I want in return is a promise that you'll stay out of trouble in the future. To make it easier for you, I'll restore your trust. You'll have money to live on."

Rob shook his head. "Money's your answer to everything, isn't it. You punished me by taking it away, and now you hold it out to me as a bribe. What do I have to do to convince you that you can't buy me like that?"

"Don't talk such moralistic crap, Robbie. I'm making you a straightforward business proposition. Don't pretend you don't need money. You do. Don't insult my intelligence."

"Don't insult mine by pretending to be magnanimous. You're only offering me something that you stole from me. The trust is rightfully mine."

"Do you think you could prove it in a court of law?"

"Against your battery of lawyers, probably not. If you want to talk straightforward business, as you put it, let's make sure we understand what we're talking about. You're worried about your ambassadorship. You bailed me out to straighten things up before the Senate confirmation hearings begin."

"I won't deny that that's a major reason. But I'm also doing it for your mother's sake."

"The Senate might find better reasons to deny you the nomination than having a son in jail in Central America."

"What are you accusing me of now?"

"The SEC and the Federal Trade Commission have investigated you several times. You must have a few things to hide."

Grunwald laughed contemptuously. "Nobody makes over half a billion dollars without attracting some attention from the regulatory agencies. Don't start in on me with that anticapitalist bullshit again. You know even less about business than you do about politics. I've made you an offer. I can't force you to take it. But you damned well owe it to yourself to consider it."

"I've considered it and I reject it."

Grunwald sighed impatiently. He rolled his chair up to the desk and picked up his glasses, signaling that their conversation was over. "Think about it tomorrow," he said. "When you're sober."

"Not necessary. I have a counteroffer to make."

Grunwald's eyes widened in surprise. He replaced his glasses on the desk and laced his fingers across his chest. "Well, what is it?"

"I want to go find Billy."

Grunwald cocked his head to one side, as if he hadn't heard him correctly. "What?"

"I want to find Billy. Caroline said you have evidence that he's alive."

His father narrowed his eyes in disbelief. "Don't joke about such things."

"I'm not joking. If Billy's alive, I'll find him and I'll bring him home. For the hundred thousand I owe you for Belize. Plus expenses. Plus returning my trust to me. You foot the cost of the expedition and I'll do the rest."

Grunwald tilted back in the chair. "Why would you want to go after Billy? You two never got along."

"You want Billy home, don't you?"

"Of course I do."

"Then I'm asking you to pay me to bring him home, that's all. From your point of view, it ought to sound like a hell of a good deal. You'll get something for your money. Even if I fail, at least you won't have to worry about what I'm up to."

"And what's in it for you?"

"Maybe I just want to do a good deed."

"I don't believe it."

"Okay, I'll give you the real reasons. I'd like to see Billy home. Because he's my brother and he's suffered. But I'm also tired of hearing about what a hero he is. Let him come home and pick up with Caroline, drive a station wagon, have a few kids, join the country club, finish law school, and run for Congress. Let him settle into the privileged upper-class routines that you groomed him for. Let him become familiar, aging, and ordinary, like everyone else. Maybe, when he becomes a mere mortal again, we could even become friends."

"You can't do it," Grunwald said. "It's absurd."

"Then call my bluff. What do you have to lose? You're already out the hundred grand. I deserve the chance to earn it. To get out of your debt."

"You'll end up in jail again. Or worse."

"I didn't say I would do it all by myself. I'll hire the best men your money can buy—mercenaries, Green Berets, whatever is needed. I'll recruit the men and get them trained. If your new information is any good, it seems that this is your best chance of getting Billy back again. Maybe your only chance."

Grunwald just sat there, staring at him. Rob had thrown out the idea as a dramatic challenge—to put his father on the defensive. But the instant the words had left his tongue, they took on a life and power of their own. However foolhardy or impossible, the idea tugged at him powerfully. It really was something worth doing, he realized, something that might break the self-defeating cycle of his life. *Bring Billy back. Why not, damn it, why not?*

Grunwald, the most decisive of men, seemed unable to make up his mind. He fiddled with his glasses, holding them by the earpieces and swinging them in quick, impatient arcs.

"What better way to keep me out of trouble?" Rob prodded.

Grunwald nodded. "If I wanted to hire a team, I could do it without you."

"Of course you could. But you'd still need to put someone in charge."

"It wouldn't be you, Robbie."

"Well, that's my offer," Rob said, enjoying the sensation of having his father over a barrel. "Take it or leave it."

Grunwald laughed. "And what if I told you to go to hell?"

"I probably would. That's one thing I'm good at—going to hell. I might even take that ambassadorship of yours with me."

Rob watched his father stroke his chin. It was an eerie feeling, dealing with him like this. What made it all the more unnerving was that he could see that his father took a perverse pleasure in it. A Darwinian capitalist in every cell of his body, he really enjoyed and trusted only this kind of human relationship—an adversarial one, force against force, wit against wit, maneuvering for advantage.

"Let me sleep on it," his father said, finally. "I'll give you my answer in the morning."

"Fair enough," Rob replied. He stood up to leave.

"You'd better sleep on it, too," his father warned. "You've made a proposal that has a lot less chance of success than you think. You better decide whether or not you mean it."

Nice, France

On the plane from New York to the Nice–Côte d'Azur airport, Brian Duffy reflected on what a good day he had just concluded. He had managed to interest two separate parties in what he was now calling "the Grunwald MIA Secrets." One party was the same sleazy tabloid he had sold so many stories to in the past. It had offered only a thousand dollars, and he would have to flesh the transcript out into an article, with all the usual manufactured hyperbole and lies, but it was bread and butter. The second party, a German magazine, was far more promising. It had found out about the story and actually come to him. It was so interested, in fact, that it was sending a man to Nice to listen to the tape and negotiate a deal. He had never published anything in a German magazine before. And they were eager! He would squeeze them for a handsome bundle of deutsche marks.

Maybe he should hire an agent, he thought, to sell syndication rights worldwide. If the Germans would bite, why not the French, the Italians, the English? The story might yet be sold to dozens of magazines and newspapers all over the world, Duffy calculated, and he might make real money out of it. He might teach that arrogant, check-canceling son-of-a-bitch William Grunwald a lesson after all.

An hour after his arrival in Nice, Duffy was having thoughts of an entirely different kind.

His apartment had been burglarized during his trip, and the locked metal strongbox that he kept at the bottom of a clothes hamper in the bedroom closet was missing. The box contained, along with two thousand francs of emergency cash, the duplicate tape that he had had the foresight to make of his interview with the Vietnamese refugee, Ngo Din Tran. He still possessed copies of the transcript, but without the actual taped interview to back it up, he was in trouble.

As he paced through the vandalized disorder of his three small rooms, agonizing over a course of action, he concluded that his only hope was to sneak back into the hospital and interview the refugee all over again.

He telephoned his contact, the hospital orderly, and talked fast: "Listen, René. It's a long story which I cannot go into now, but I need to get back in to see that Vietnamese patient on the fifth floor. There's a lot of interest in his story and I have to flesh it out, ask him some more questions. Won't take that long. But I need your help. Some bitch of a nurse threw me out last time, just when we were really rolling, too. Can you get me in? You know, late at night if necessary."

René said nothing.

"Look. I don't want to get you in trouble. I'll be careful as hell, I promise. I can even cut you into some of the action on this. As soon as I collect my first payment. How does five hundred francs sound? All you have to do is get me up there and past the nurses' station. That shouldn't be too hard. Hey, René, are you listening to me?"

"He's dead," René said.

"What did you say?"

"He's dead."

Duffy drew in his breath and held it. "Who?"

"The refugee. Tran." René's voice sounded frightened.

"He didn't look that sick to me. What happened to him?"

"I don't know. The hospital's investigating. If they find out I told you about this guy, I'll lose my job. Don't call me anymore."

"Jesus Christ!" Duffy swore in English. "Listen, I—"

Duffy stopped and lowered the receiver from his ear. René had hung up on him.

9

Rhinebeck, New York

William Grunwald arose early after a sleepless night and walked across the acres of north lawn, enjoying the feeling of the chill morning air and the crisp sound of the frozen grass beneath his riding boots. At the stables, he saddled up his favorite horse, Araby, a gift from the Aga Khan, and took him off on a brisk canter across the fields. Grunwald was an athletic man, but he found the traditional executive sports—tennis, golf, and squash—both boring and time-consuming. Horseback riding was his passion. He loved the masculine tradition of it, the wealth of legend, from cavalry to cowboy, and the solitary exhilaration, the feel of the union between himself and the powerful beast beneath him, moving to his commands.

Araby had a bad habit that made him unsafe in the company of other horses. He always pushed his way into the lead, even if it meant bumping other horses and riders out of the way, and no amount of shouted whoas and pulling on the reins would deter him. No one had ever been able to correct him of this stubborn flaw, and Grunwald admired the animal deeply because of it.

He brought Araby to a halt on a bluff overlooking the Hudson. The sun was rising in a clear sky and a strong wind was blowing down the river, rippling the surface with small whitecaps. He remembered what a good horseman Billy was. What a pleasure it would be, he thought, to have him here now, riding with him across Greenwood on this blustery March morning.

He had decided to back Rob's rescue mission. There were many reasons not to—the slim chances for success paramount among them—but the opportunity to keep Rob both busy and out of trouble was irresistible. And besides, Grunwald had himself many times considered doing exactly what Rob was proposing. A rescue party was plausible. The Pentagon had actually launched a number of such secret missions to rescue other POWs. They had all failed, apparently, which certainly didn't make the odds look very good for Rob. On the other hand, he could learn from their mistakes. And Rob had one thing going for him the government missions did not have—motivation. Grunwald had seen it burning in his eyes. His prodigal son was suddenly eager to accomplish something, do something to atone for his misspent years. He needed a big success, and needed it desperately.

It was a bad gamble, but Grunwald just plain liked the idea of it. If Rob pulled it off, the benefits would go beyond just having Billy back home again. It would make the whole family look good. And the experience could be a crucible for Rob, transforming him, redeeming him. Grunwald imagined himself being proud of this son for the first time in his life.

And if Rob failed? What would be lost? By then the Senate confirmation hearings would be over, and he and Cornelia would be on their way to Israel.

Grunwald shifted uncomfortably in his saddle, pained suddenly by the raw truth of his feelings. God help me, he thought. If Rob fails, it would be better if he never came back—dead or alive.

Grunwald punched Araby's belly hard with the heels of his boots, and took him on a fast gallop down along the river.

Rob walked into the dining room at ten o'clock, hung over and tired. Caroline was sitting alone at the long table, drinking a cup of coffee. She was dressed in silk cravat, hacking jacket, and jodhpurs, and her blond hair was pinned up to fit under her riding cap, which lay on the table, alongside a sleek leather crop.

Rob blinked his eyes a few times, surveying the table for fresh place settings. Only one remained. So he was the last to show up for breakfast. No surprise. He had abandoned breakfast years ago in favor of staying in bed. He fell clumsily into the chair and groped for the coffee urn.

"Hello," Caroline said.

"Have a good time last night?" he asked, crooking the corner of his mouth up into a comical half-grin. The picture of her in the back hall, her arm over the shoulder of the dark-haired man, still lingered vividly in his mind.

She smiled back brightly. "Not as good as you, apparently."

He filled his cup too full and opened the urn to pour some back. "What are you talking about? I had a terrible time."

"Not according to the gossip in the kitchen this morning," Caroline replied, fixing her eyes on him knowingly. "The maids are very good with circumstantial evidence: wet clothes, vodka glasses, messy sheets—that kind of thing."

Rob blushed intensely. It surprised him. He didn't embarrass easily. He dumped two spoonfuls of sugar and a heavy dollop of cream into his coffee and stirred it lethargically. "That doesn't mean I had a good time," he answered lamely.

Caroline laughed her sensuous little laugh. It felt like a feather teasing his ear.

"Have you seen the old man?" he said, changing the subject.

"He went into town. He'll be back at noon. Why don't you come riding with me?"

Rob tasted the coffee and shivered. "Horses make me sneeze, I'm afraid."

"Poor baby. Don't you want something besides that coffee?"

Rob shook his head. "I won't be able to keep anything down until after I talk with him."

"Why?"

Instead of answering, Rob fished his wallet from his back pocket and pulled out a folded piece of paper. "I found this in Billy's blazer last night," he said, handing it to her across the table. "I wanted to ask you about it at the party, but the crowd of men around you was too thick to penetrate. Does it mean anything to you?"

Caroline carefully unfolded the brittle piece of paper and held it up. "Not a thing. What is it?"

"A trolley ticket."

"Is there something important about it?"

"I don't know. It was issued by the Municipal Transport Authority of Karl-Marx-Stadt. Did you ever go there with Billy?"

"No. I've never even heard of it. Where is it?"

"In East Germany."

Caroline's eyes widened in surprise. "Why would Billy have gone there?"

"Good question."

"Is there a date on it?"

Rob tipped the thin square of paper to catch the light from the window. "I think it says June fourteenth, 1969."

Caroline wrapped the palms of her hands around her coffee cup and concentrated. She looked up, suddenly. "That would have been right after our honeymoon. We stayed a week in Venice, then drove north through the Alps. Eventually we ended up in Munich. We were supposed to go to visit an aunt of mine who lived in Ulm, about an hour's drive away. But Billy begged off, saying he had some friends in Hannover he wanted to see. He left me in Ulm and picked me up there a week later. He could have gone to East Germany then, I suppose. If he did, he never mentioned it. Perhaps he went with his friends in Hannover, on an impulse."

Rob refolded the paper and slipped it back into his wallet. "No. He must have planned it. He'd have needed a visa, and that would have taken time."

"Why are you so intrigued by it?"

Rob propped his elbows on the table and rested his chin on his hands. "Our father grew up in that city. At least that's what he's told us. I thought it might have something to do with him."

Caroline folded back the white cloth covering the tray of toast and removed a slice. "Billy never said a word about it," she said. "I'm sure I would have remembered."

Rob watched her spread butter on the toast. Her hands, manipulating the knife, looked larger and stronger than he had remembered them. "I told the old man last night that I want to go look for Billy," he said.

Caroline stopped the knife halfway across the slice of toast. "Go to Vietnam?"

"Yes."

She put the knife down and stared at him in open astonishment. "My God," she murmured.

"I have the feeling he's going to agree."

"What are you going to do?"

"I'm going to go."

"You aren't serious, are you?"

"I haven't thought about anything else all night."

Caroline looked at the half-buttered toast, then dropped it on her plate. "You really are extraordinary," she said, half in a whisper.

"You mean dumb?"

"That's pretty close," she admitted. "Certainly wildly romantic."

"Why are you so disturbed about it? Don't you want the matter settled, finally, one way or the other?"

"Yes. But I can't believe you're the one to do it."

Rob smiled. "I want to try."

"Why? Just to impress your father?"

"I don't care about impressing him."

"I don't believe you. I think you want to prove to him that he's underestimated you."

Rob tasted the coffee before replying. "Maybe," he admitted. "But to do that I'd have to outperform Moses himself, and show a profit into the bargain."

"You should be thinking of yourself," Caroline said.

"What do you mean?"

"Getting your life in order. Getting a job . . ."

He stared at her incredulously.

"Starting a career," she continued, suddenly impatient. "You do intend to do something with the rest of your life, don't you?"

Rob placed the coffee cup back quietly in its saucer and narrowed his eyes at her. What had he expected—applause? He should never have brought the subject up. Still, her condescending attitude infuriated him, especially because he suspected she was right. "Yes, god damn it, I do," he replied, in a wounded tone. "And I'm going to start by finding Billy."

10

New York City

"You're completely out of your mind," Sarah said. "One hundred percent completely."

Rob bit into an English muffin and stared out the window of her apartment kitchen on East Seventy-first Street. A tugboat was hauling a string of barges down the East River. It was a gray, gusty morning and the gulls tailing the barges were riding the air currents like gliders, slipping back and forth across the dirty expanse of water. "I had to come up with something."

"You didn't have to come up with anything. Father made you a perfectly simple offer to get you out of debt. You could just have swallowed your pride and accepted it."

"I have to pay him back."

"It's totally crazy. He can't honestly expect you to go through with it."

"We made a bargain."

"You didn't make a bargain. You made a foolish boast, that's all. And he called your bluff. You were probably drunk."

"I'm going to do it, Sarah. I'm seeing Safier at eleven to get the information on Billy and set up the money arrangements."

Sarah placed her coffee cup carefully in its saucer and looked across at her brother with a wistful frown. "Mother is against it. And so am I. Will you reconsider for our sakes?"

"I don't understand your attitude. Billy's our brother. Why shouldn't I try to rescue him?"

"We'd all love to see Billy home again, but you can't just go over there and free him from a Vietnamese prison. It's completely unrealistic!"

"I'm not claiming it'll be a piece of cake. But I have nothing to lose. And after twelve years over there, I don't think Billy does, either."

Sarah began clearing the breakfast dishes from the table. "It's crazy," she repeated, yanking open the dishwasher and banging the cups and plates onto the racks inside.

Rob watched the last barge on the tug's line disappear from view under the Fifty-ninth Street bridge. "Did I ever tell you that I went to Dachau?" he asked.

Sarah straightened up. "No. When would you have told me?"

"Well, I did. About three years ago, when I was living in Europe. It's been preserved, most of it, and turned into a kind of Holocaust museum. They don't exactly advertise it as a tourist attraction, but that's what it is. The day I went, the parking lot was jammed. People from everywhere."

"What on earth made you want to visit it?"

"I was curious. I thought it might give me some insight into the old man—seeing the place with my own eyes."

"I think it's morbid."

"Maybe. Anyway, I didn't get any insights. The place was as tidy as a cemetery—the buildings painted, the grass cut, every pebble of gravel in place. It was impossible to imagine, even after walking through the main building, where they have all the photographs and relics, the true horror of the place. All the prisoners' barracks had been torn down except two, and they had almost nothing in them. Only the fence and the guard towers seemed real."

"What did you expect, for heaven's sake—piles of corpses lying around?"

"They shouldn't have sanitized it so much. I've felt more authentic emotion walking through Roman ruins."

Sarah glanced at her wristwatch. "Does this have a point? I'm going to be late for work."

"The point is that we don't know anything about the old man's past in Germany."

"Well, how much of a past could he have had? He was only twenty when he emigrated. And if you had lost your entire family to the Holocaust, you wouldn't talk much about it, either."

"I also checked the camp's records. No one named 'William Grunwald' was ever a prisoner there. There were other Grunwalds, but no 'William.' "

"For God's sake, Robbie! It was a chaotic time. Files must have been lost. Maybe Father was never even properly recorded. How do you know?"

"The Nazis were compulsive record keepers. If a William Grunwald had been at Dachau, they'd have a record of him."

"How do you know you saw all the records?"

"Over the years I've looked in a lot of places. Israel's Holocaust Archives at Yad Vashem, for example. I found fourteen William Grunwalds, but none of them had been in Dachau."

"What are you suggesting? That Father was never there?"

Rob stuck his hands in his pockets and slumped down in the chair. "I think he must have changed his name."

"Why would he do that?"

"Possibly because he had something to hide under his real name. Maybe he collaborated with the Nazis. Some prisoners did that, in return for preferential treatment. Maybe that's how he survived when so many others died."

"What's gotten into you? What does this have to do with finding Billy?"

"Billy went to East Germany back in 1969. I found a trolley ticket in his old blazer pocket from Karl-Marx-Stadt. That's Chemnitz— Father's hometown. Billy must have gone there to look for relatives, to see if he could discover anything about our family."

"Is that why you want to find Billy?" Sarah demanded, her voice heavy with sarcasm. "To ask him if he ran into any of our cousins in Chemnitz?"

"Damn it, Sarah, I think the old man is hiding something from us. Something important."

"That's absurd. You just want to get something on him. It's time for you to call off your war against Father. He's trying to make peace with you, and you're already plotting against him."

"His trying to make peace with me is what makes me so suspicious. For the first time I can remember, he's suddenly nervous as hell about being in the limelight. He's scared of something. His change of attitude toward me confirms it. He's always disliked me, and he's always been among the world's least forgiving human beings. He holds lifetime grudges."

Sarah jumped up from the table, angry. "I don't want to hear any more of this poison. I have to go." She snatched up her attaché case and stormed out of the kitchen.

Rob heard the door bang shut and then the drone of the elevator climbing to the penthouse floor. He poured himself another cup of coffee and went back to watching the river traffic.

Maybe he was wrong about Dachau. Maybe everything had happened the way his father always claimed. But his instincts told him otherwise. His evidence was weak, but it was there—not just in Billy's trip to East Germany or in his own failure to find a record of his father's existence at the camp. It lurked in a dozen little episodes remembered from his childhood, incidents that in themselves were meaningless but, when added up, pointed to something, some private torment his father lived with—either about the concentration camp or about his life in Germany before. It was there; Rob knew it. He had inherited the torment. It lived in his blood.

His eyes fell on the small reproduction of Picasso's *Guernica* on the kitchen wall, and a sudden flood of long-suppressed memories overwhelmed him. Billy's war games. Much of Rob's childhood, he recalled, had been spent inside Billy's military fantasies.

The whole idea had come to Billy from a picture book about World War II. Later there would be other books, but the picture book was the one Rob remembered best. The games started as simple tag and hide-and-seek affairs, but, as Billy grew older and read more, he created little set pieces, scenarios with the action and the lines rehearsed, as complete as one-act plays. He sometimes enlisted other playmates in the performances, but often it was just he and Rob.

There was "Normandy Invasion," played with rowboats down by the dockhouse on the Hudson; "Battle of the Bulge," played in the woods north of the main house; "Afrika Korps," staged on the beach at Southampton during the summers; "Hitler's Bunker," played out in the gloomy expanses of cellar under Greenwood. Billy always took the role of the hero for himself, and the little dramas always ended the same way: Rob, the villain, was either captured or shot.

Rob came to hate the games. They were a ritualized form of bullying, and the less enthusiastically he played his part, the more violently Billy would play his.

Billy's favorite game was "Freeing the Jews"—probably because it gave him the chance to imagine that he was avenging their father.

The stables served as the concentration camp. Billy was the American general leading his troops to the liberation. Sarah was locked in one of the empty box stalls, playing the prisoner's role. And Rob, of course, was the camp commandant, destined to be captured and sentenced to death for his crimes.

One day the game got out of hand. Following his role, Rob ran up into the hayloft in an attempt to "escape." Billy cornered him up there, demanding he surrender. But Rob departed from the script and resisted capture. Enraged, Billy smashed him in the face with the stock of his play rifle. With blood gushing from his nose, and his eyes flooded with tears, Rob ran, lost his balance, and fell out of the loft. He landed on the stable floor fifteen feet below, unconscious, with a broken nose and collarbone.

Their father reacted to the accident the way he always reacted to their fights: He accepted Billy's self-serving version of the incident and did nothing to punish him. Instead of sympathy, Rob got lectures. "The world is a tough place for weaklings," his father told him when he returned from the hospital. "The sooner you learn that, the better."

During their prep-school and college years, Rob saw less and less of his brother. Summers and vacations were periods of truce, and Billy seemed to forget the antagonisms of their childhood. But Rob nursed bitter frustrations, and he converted their old physical rivalry into a verbal one. He put himself at odds with his brother on every matter.

He last saw Billy when he was twenty-two years old, just back from boot camp at Parris Island. He remembered the peculiar mixture of awe, envy, and disapproval he had felt, seeing his brother in his crisp dress blues, hardened for real war.

If he was still alive over there, he would be thirty-five years old now. What had he endured, Rob wondered, during those dozen years of captivity? What would be left of him?

What kind of a man would he be?

James Safier's outer office bristled with corporate pretense. The walls were wood-paneled and exuded an oiled satiny glow so rich one could almost smell the teak forests from which they came. Expensively framed works of art were hung at intervals, each with its own portrait light and brass plaque. The floor was buried under a large, ornate Oriental rug in vivid blues and reds. Tall, wiry-looking plants lurked in the corners, their presence, like the paintings, highlighted by tiny spotlights. Rob sat on the edge of a polished leather sofa and flipped through the available literature on the table—a copy of Grunwald

Industries' Annual Report for 1981, a few copies of *Fortune* and *Business Week,* and a stack of glossy brochures crammed with propaganda about Grunwald Industries.

Safier's secretary, a sleek young woman in a white blouse and pink bow tie, kept sneaking glances at him between her typing and answering the phone. After a ten-minute wait, she ushered him into her boss's inner sanctum, a large corner room decorated by the same overpriced hand that had done the outer office.

Safier came out from behind his desk and clasped Rob's hand briefly. "Sorry to have kept you waiting," he murmured. "It's been a busy day." He gestured toward a chair. "Please."

Rob's strongest memories of Safier were from years before—when he was still a young man on the make. Once, when Rob was home on vacation from school, his father had brought Safier to Greenwood to spend the weekend. He and his father's new employee were about the same age, and Rob had resented his presence, feeling that his father was forcing him to entertain someone with whom he had nothing in common. Safier was clearly intimidated by Greenwood and its huge staff of servants, and he suffered through the stuffy cocktail hours and dinners with an awkward, doglike servility that Rob found contemptible. Rob had done his best to add to the young man's discomfort, deflecting his efforts to be friendly with a cool and arrogant manner that, thinking back on it, must have been pretty contemptible, too.

He was not happy that his father had put Safier in charge of handling the money arrangements for the rescue mission, but he was determined to be businesslike and cooperative.

Safier opened the right-hand top drawer of his big desk and pulled out a folder. "I've set up a bank account for you," he began. He held up a large, office-style checkbook, opened it to reveal the pages of checks inside, and then set it down alongside the folder. "It contains a balance of three hundred thousand dollars. No strings are attached as to how it's spent, other than that you provide me, from time to time, with an accurate account of your outlays. If more money is needed, you'll have to request it directly from me personally."

"What's to prevent me from writing out a check for three hundred grand, cashing it, and fleeing to Rio?"

Safier displayed a wintry smile. "I've set you up as an independent subsidiary of Grunwald Industries. You're the president; your sister is treasurer. She countersigns all checks."

"Good thinking," Rob said. He watched Safier's nimble hands shuffle through the stack of documents from the folder, and felt a sudden perverse admiration for the man. His movements were practiced and quick, like a cardsharp working a hustle. Safier had traveled far and long to become somebody, and his years of striving had left their stamp. He would never relax and trust his success, never lose that lean and predatory look. No matter how many kills, Rob thought, James Safier would always be hungry.

Safier pushed up out of his big swivel chair and strode across to a small safe built into a low credenza against the back wall. He knelt before it, spun the dials, pulled open the steel door, and withdrew a thick leather case. Returning to his chair, he squared the case on his desk, opened it, and turned it so that Rob could see its contents—a pile of dog-eared folders. "Your father has instructed me to turn this over to you."

"Billy's file?"

"Yes. It includes the transcript of the taped interview with the Vietnamese refugee, Tran, and the tape itself. The rest is everything from press clippings about MIAs to detailed records of all the information we've collected about Billy over the past twelve years." Safier threw the checkbook in on top of the pile, closed the case, and pushed it toward Rob. "You'll find that most of it is completely useless. But at least you'll see what's been done. And see what you're up against."

Rob pulled the battered case onto his lap, surprised at its considerable weight. "Is that it?"

"There's one thing more: You must keep this matter an absolute secret. Publicity and money bring creatures out of the woodwork. Opportunists, ax grinders, con artists, screwballs, you name it. I've dealt with all of them in the years since your brother's disappearance. If word gets out that you're planning a rescue mission, you'll be sunk before you get started. And it happens to be against the law for an American citizen to enter Laos or Vietnam with an armed search party. If you don't keep it quiet, you'll be stopped cold. Or worse, stopped dead."

"Thanks for the advice."

"Don't thank me. I'm just carrying out your father's wishes. In my opinion, you'll be stopped anyway, whatever you do."

"It sounds like you're counting on it."

Safier studied the backs of his hands for a moment, as if rehearsing his reply. "My personal view, for what it's worth, is that your brother is dead. What you're doing is a waste of time . . . not to mention Grunwald money."

"You may be right. But if I only prove him dead, that at least would end the uncertainty."

Safier crossed his arms and sat up very straight. "You'll be lucky to get that far."

"You're not impressed with the new evidence from this Vietnamese, then?"

"I'd be more impressed if the man hadn't died yesterday. Now he can't be questioned about it."

"What did he die from?"

"Exposure. Malnutrition. He was in a hospital in Nice. The individual who brought us the story is a hack journalist with no moral regard for anything—certainly not the truth. I suspect he made the whole thing up."

"But you have the tape, don't you? With the Vietnamese talking on it?"

Safier shrugged. "The tape could be a hoax. You better confront the writer, Duffy, before you do anything else. His phone number and address are in the files."

Rob stood up and hefted the case. "I'll do that."

"You realize," Safier said, as he escorted Rob to the door, "that it would probably be better for everybody if Billy never came home."

Rob stopped. The remark stunned him. "Why?"

"Because if he's still alive he's either a collaborator or the Vietnamese have done something to him that they don't want the world to know about." Safier looked down, as if embarrassed, and brushed some imaginary flecks of dust from his sleeve. "This may sound odd to you, but I've given it some thought. Nothing else can justify a twelve-year absence. His coming home could be destructive—to his family, his wife, his friends. And to Billy himself."

Rob had a sudden insight. "And to you?"

"Me?"

"You don't *want* him to come back, do you."

"Why shouldn't I?"

"Because you'll lose your standing with our father. As long as Billy stays missing, you're the number-one son around here—by default. Especially after you marry my sister."

"That doesn't deserve a reply."

"It doesn't need one. Forgive me for being so blunt. Just promise me that you won't try to obstruct the mission."

"I'm confident it will self-destruct without any help from me," Safier replied angrily. "You don't have the first clue as to how to go about finding your brother. You're doing this because you're jealous of Billy, because he always outshone you. You have some fantasy that you'll make yourself a hero and even the score. You're grandstanding, and frankly, I feel sorry for you. Now, if you'll excuse me, I have a great deal of work to do."

Safier shut the door in Rob's face. Rob stared at the oiled wood surface for a moment, then glanced over at the secretary. She had obviously been eavesdropping, because her face turned red the instant their eyes met.

He mustered his warmest smile. "You want to wish me good luck?"

11

Wilmington, Vermont

Seven miles down a narrow dirt road, north of the village of Wilmington, Vermont, Rob Grunwald found what he was looking for.
He pulled his rented car onto a barely passable driveway and inched
slowly along, dodging large rocks and fording foot-deep stretches of
mud that sucked at the tires and pulled at the steering wheel. About
a mile in, the trail terminated in a wide uphill meadow protected by
a heavy ring of pine and hemlock trees.

At the back edge of the field was a new two-story log cabin with a
long front porch. A beat-up van and a pickup truck were parked near
it, along with an aluminum canoe, an outboard motorboat with a hole
punched through the bottom, and a large stack of firewood, partially
collapsed at one end. It was a clear, chilly day in early April and the
entire yard was a soup of melting snow and mud, scarred with deep
tire ruts and potholed by boot prints.

Rob picked a zigzag path across the yard, climbed onto the porch,
and knocked. No one answered. He tried the door, finally, found it
unlocked, and stepped inside. He was greeted by a large, overheated
room, two stories high, with a second-floor balcony across the back.
A black Labrador retriever, who had been napping on a rug in front
of a large woodstove, stood up, stretched, and came over to sniff at
his pants legs. From a bench against the rear wall, a tiny rectangle of

flashing green light from a computer screen winked at him. Near the bench, collapsed on a big lounge chair, was the inert form of a large man. He was bearded, bald-headed, and barefoot—and snoring loudly.

Rob scratched the dog's ear, then snatched up a pillow from a nearby sofa and tossed it in the direction of the lounge chair. It landed on the bald head and slid to the floor. Rob tossed another pillow. Still no reaction. He sat down at a trestle table in the center of the room and noticed a book and a pair of eyeglasses resting near the edge. He picked up the book and thumbed through it.

The Lab padded over to the lounge chair, grasped the shirt sleeve on one of the man's dangling arms, and tugged it forcefully. The figure stirred, rubbed his eyes, and sighed deeply.

" 'By the old Moulmein Pagoda, lookin' eastward to the sea,' " Rob intoned in a stentorian voice, " 'there's a Burma girl asettin' and I know she thinks o' me. . . .' "

The occupant of the chair jumped up as if stung in the seat by a bullwhip and spun around, almost losing his balance. "Who the hell?!" he yelled. He scrabbled about blindly, searching for his eyeglasses.

Rob held them out. "Is this what you're looking for, Howie?"

Howard Gilmore lurched forward, snatched the glasses from Rob's outstretched palm and hooked them hastily over his ears. Sight restored, he peered at Rob for several seconds, his expression sliding rapidly from indignation to incredulity. He laughed, lunged forward, and batted Rob affectionately on top of his head. "Son of a bitch! It must be that Humboldt County grass. I'm hallucinating!"

Rob patted the book. "A student of Plutarch and Thucydides reading Kipling? Your mind has deteriorated."

Gilmore's bald white pate reddened with embarrassment. "Just getting ready for my boy. He likes Kipling. He's coming up for the weekend. He's ten now. You oughta see him. What a kid!"

Rob swallowed hard. "I guess I didn't even know you were married," he said lamely.

"I guess you didn't," Howard replied, still grinning at him. "And I'm not, anymore. Been divorced six years."

"I feel like Rip van Winkle. Should I be sorry?"

"Nah. It's okay. Got a great son out of it, if nothing else. Just don't see him as often as I'd like. But hell, it's good to see you! Where have you been?"

" 'I traveled among unknown men, in lands beyond the sea.' "

"Wordsworth," Gilmore guessed.

"Right. Basically, I went to Canada."

Gilmore smacked his big fists together. "I thought you did. You were smart. I should have done the same." He bustled around, talking excitedly, trying to put the place in order. The Lab, bored, returned to the rug by the stove and went back to sleep. "All I got is beer," Gilmore said, hauling out a handful of unfamiliar bottles. "But it's Anchor Steam. Seven bucks a six-pack. Best there is." He popped the tops off two bottles and banged the cupboards in search of clean glasses. "Hey. It's great to see you!" he repeated. "How did you find me? Why the hell are you here—I mean so suddenly, after all these years?"

"Wanted to see an old friend, that's all."

Gilmore set the bottles and glasses on the table and pulled up a chair across from Rob. "Robert Grunwald never did anything unless he had at least three reasons to do it. What are the other two?"

"And you never had any patience. Fill in some yawning gaps for me, first."

"Let's see," Gilmore began, stroking his beard thoughtfully. "After we got kicked out of Columbia I was drafted and went to Vietnam. Did my tour. Got slightly wounded. Went back to school for my B.A. and M.S., married Sally, taught at George Washington University for a few years. After the divorce, I moved up here. I run my own engineering consulting business—just me and Sam." He pointed across the room to the computer. "That's Sam, my acronym for Stand-Alone Microprocessor."

"What does Sam do?"

"Damned near everything but cook dinner. I'll show you later. But it's your turn now, you revolutionary old bastard. I'd hate to admit how much time I've spent over the past decade or so thinking about you, wondering what black hole it was that swallowed you up."

Rob was reluctant to discuss his past. "It's not a hell of a pretty picture, Howard."

"Now you're just whetting my curiosity. I don't give a fuck how pretty it is. You can confess anything to your old buddy Howard."

Rob shrugged. "*Confess* is the word, I guess. Mostly I've been a hustler of one kind or another."

Gilmore's jaw dropped. "You? You're putting me on."

Rob sighed. "No. I slipped into it gradually. In Montreal, when I was completely broke and desperate, I met a guy. 'Danny,' he called himself. He was an Egyptian. I don't know what his real name was. We got along, and he took me under his wing, taught me his con games and swindles. We became partners. He was very smooth, very erudite. He could ingratiate himself with anybody. He preyed on the European rich, and he was so damned good at it that most of his victims never knew he had taken them. He swindled some of the same people half a dozen times. Anyway, with my background and mathematical skills, we made a good team. We traveled all over the Continent, following the seasons. In winter it was Mallorca, Málaga, and Marbella—and the ski resorts, usually Gstaad and St. Moritz. In summer it was the Costa Brava, Estoril, the French Riviera, Monaco, Costa Smeralda, Capri. Spring and fall we jumped around to wherever the action was—the races in Paris, the bullfights in Madrid. Wherever the rich liked to play, we were there, picking up the loose change."

Gilmore struck his forehead with the heel of his palm. "Christ, Rob, you of all people. Committed to serious things."

Rob nodded. "Yeah, I know. It's hard to explain. I could never get a decent job anywhere because of my citizenship status. I was forced underground to survive. Or at least that's what I told myself. I was marking time. I didn't intend to get into it permanently. I never saw myself as a criminal. But the funny thing was . . . I liked it. And I was good at it. It was exciting. I was living by my wits. I enjoyed conning those people out of their money. I justified it in all kinds of ways. I was taking from people who had far more than they needed, and I thought they deserved it. I was still fighting the Establishment, I told myself. Redistributing the wealth."

"What kinds of cons did you run?"

"Stock swindles, mostly—South African diamond and gold mines, things like that. And fake masterpieces, that was fun. At one time we had three painters busy round the clock turning out 'Renaissance' works of art. Their efforts hang today in some of the best homes in Europe. I liked the cons because the people we suckered were not innocents. We weren't stealing from widows and orphans. It wasn't even like burglary. Those people were rich and greedy. They had a lot and they wanted a lot more. The secret to a successful con is appealing to that greed, persuading the target that he's the one taking advantage of you. Greed makes people stupid. And it's truly astonishing how greedy some people are. I guess it's fair to say that Danny undid my college idealism for me. Not that I blame him for it. He only brought out something that was there all along. He helped show me who I really was."

Gilmore combed his beard, pulling his big fingers through it in long, hard tugs. "I'm utterly astonished, old buddy. Utterly astonished. Didn't you hate yourself? I mean, ethics and morality aside, you were wasting your life."

"Sure. But there was always the need for money. You'd think we'd have piled up a fortune, but somehow it got spent as fast as it got made. And I didn't want to let Danny down. He had done a lot for me. He was my mentor and friend. I really liked the guy."

"You never got caught?"

"I was arrested twice. But the nearest anyone ever came to really nailing us was the last time, in Baden-Baden. We had a rich German count on the hook. But he got onto us, somehow, and tipped the police. They wired him, set up a trap for us. Fortunately, the count was an extraordinarily clumsy man. The tape recorder they had strapped to his leg actually fell off. He bumped something, I guess, and it just dropped right onto the floor of the hotel room where we were meeting. You should have seen his face. You should have seen *our* faces. I would have fallen over laughing if I wasn't so scared. We just got the hell out. We were lucky, but this time the police had a good description of us, and once that went out to Interpol, our act was in trouble. We split up. I moved to Central America and went into selling fake artifacts."

Rob twisted the cap off the last bottle of beer and studied it thoughtfully. "I really went downhill there. I got hooked on coke, for one thing. I knew I was running my string out, but I couldn't break the cycle. Hell, I didn't *want* to break it." Rob tasted the beer. "Then I got help from an unexpected quarter. Stupidly, I let myself get caught in a drug bust. I tried to run, and they shot me." Rob opened his shirt and showed Gilmore the still healing blue welt between his chest and shoulder. "The hospital and the jail got me off the coke, and my sister Sarah got me out of Belize. That about covers it."

Gilmore regarded him suspiciously across a crowd of empty Anchor Steam bottles. "Except for one thing."

"What's that?"

"Why you came to see me."

Rob laughed. "That's a whole other story."

"You wouldn't try to con an old friend, would you?"

"I do have a little proposal, as a matter of fact. . . ."

Rob explained in detail the true purpose for his visit. When he finished, Gilmore's mood was bleak.

"You're out of your fucking gourd, Robbie," he murmured. "And I say that with love. I mean, it's crazy."

"That's what my sister keeps saying. Can't you do better?"

"She's right. The bottom line is that it's insane."

"You're my best friend, Howie—"

"*Was* your best friend," Gilmore corrected, a hurt look creasing his big face. "I haven't seen you for twelve years."

"If it makes you feel any better, *nobody* has seen me in twelve years."

"Still . . ."

"You really think I'm trying to con you?"

"I *know* you're trying to con me. You always were a persuasive son of a bitch. Or maybe it was just relentless. You never gave up until you got your way."

"I'm going to do it, Howie. And I need your help."

"No way."

Rob sighed and tipped an empty beer bottle upside down over his glass. "It's not just that you're my friend and I trust you. You've got the skills for it. I don't."

"We're out of beer," Howard said, staring morosely at the army of dead soldiers on the table. "And what skills are you talking about, anyway?"

"You've been there, for one thing."

Howard laughed and ran his big hands over his bald scalp. "I've been there, that's right. And I'm sure as hell not going back!"

"You're tough. Resourceful. Dependable. I can't do it without you."

"Flattery won't work, old buddy. I'd do anything for you, honestly. But this idea is just foolhardy. Vietnam is a military dictatorship— the Sparta of the twentieth century, forged by over forty years of warfare and suffering. It occupies Cambodia on one side and is in a state of open hostility with China on the other. And it hates Americans as a matter of official policy. 'Yankee' is a big numbah ten. You can't just go waltzing into a place like that and say 'Hey, where's my brother?' "

"I don't intend to. We'll devise a plan, together. Something that will work."

Howard Gilmore shook his head violently. "There's no plan that will work. They've all been tried. I've been a member of everything from the Viet Vets Against the War to the VFW. I've been in touch with dozens of MIA families and I've tracked this subject for years. The government has sent in rescue groups nine times that I know of, and there have been a couple of privately financed efforts as well. All spectacular failures. Not one MIA has ever been found, let alone brought out. Going in there is a complete waste of time, not to mention hazardous to your health."

"This is different. We know where my brother is. He's in a camp near Khe Sanh, close to the Laotian border. We have a very precise location. And according to this Vietnamese who was there with him, it's not heavily guarded."

"Since this Vietnamese escaped from the camp, it's a good bet that your brother isn't there anymore," Gilmore argued. "Whenever the Vietcong released a prisoner—there weren't many escapes—they always moved the rest somewhere else. They assumed the camp's location was no longer a secret and therefore no longer safe from an American raid. That's why we could never free anybody. By the time our patrols got to a site, it was abandoned."

"There was a war going on then, Howie. We had five hundred thousand soldiers over there, and a whole damned air force."

"You don't think the Vietnamese today would be nervous about that camp's location if somebody escaped and told people in the West that they're still keeping an American prisoner there?"

"Not nervous enough to abandon a prison camp, no. They're not Vietcong guerrillas in hiding. They're running the country now. They can do what they damned please."

"Do you have any idea what the terrain is like?" Gilmore persisted. "What the weather is like? Not to mention that a Caucasian stands out in Indochina like Paul Bunyan at a dwarf convention? And how are you going to get across Laos? Walk? Assuming you can even get across Thailand first. There's one road in the area—Route 9. Patrolled during the day by the Pathet Lao and at night by bandits. You'd need a Marine division. With air cover. At least."

"We can hire mercenaries, Special Forces types. Buy jeeps, weapons. I've got the funds."

"If you try to raise an army, word will get out and Uncle Sam will grab your ass before you can get it on a plane for Asia."

Rob looked his old friend in the eye. "Howie, these are just obstacles to be overcome. Of course it won't be easy. But don't tell me it's not possible before we've even tried."

Gilmore stroked his beard with agitation. "That's exactly what I'm telling you."

"I'm disappointed in you. You've grown middle-aged and timid. I'm not talking to the same Howie Gilmore who brought Columbia University to its knees in 1968."

Gilmore burst out laughing. "You sure aren't. I was an asshole kid then. And so were you."

"We had ideals and we acted on them. Nothing wrong with that."

Howard sighed. "In retrospect, I'd rather have graduated."

"I'm not asking you to do it for free. I'll pay you, you know."

"I didn't even think you liked your brother," Howard said.

"I didn't like what he was doing, joining the Marines. But that was a long time ago. He's my brother. He's suffering. Of course I want to get him out."

Howard picked up an empty beer bottle and examined it. "We can run down to Mike's, in town, and get some more brew."

"At least tell me you'll think about it," Rob persisted. "It'll be a few months' work. Whatever happens, we'll have a hell of an adventure. . . ."

Howard raised his hand. "No. You don't understand," he said, his tone turning apologetic. "You weren't there. You don't know how much that place fucked me up. I still get nightmares from what I saw. Cold sweats in the middle of the night. Crying jags that come on right out of nowhere. It drove Sally away from me. It really freaked her out, you know, seeing me get so scared, so depressed. I still go to a shrink in Bennington once a week. PTSD—Post Traumatic Stress Disorder. That's the fancy name for it. And that's not all Vietnam did for me."

Gilmore rolled up his pants leg and showed Rob the network of scar tissue that covered his leg. "I thought I was smart, getting into Army Intelligence. Must have been the dumbest thing I ever did. I was sent out on more patrols than Audie Murphy. Finally I stepped on a booby trap. A pull-release bouncing Betty, the kind that pops up and explodes shrapnel all over you when you take your weight off it. I knew instantly that I'd stepped on it. I could feel it click under my weight, like someone cocking a trigger. I'd seen another guy blown apart by one. The damned things hit you right in the testicles and go on up through your ass and your intestines. The only thing worse than being killed by one is surviving it. I froze. I knew I was as good as dead, but I was going to get time to think about it. Some feeling, man, standing there knowing that the next move I made would kill me. I begged for somebody to do something. I stood there for half an hour, sweat running off me so fast I thought I might melt before I was blown away.

"Obviously I lived to tell about it. The other guys on the patrol risked their lives to save me. They piled trees, ponchos, ammo boxes, tarps, everything they could find, in a net around me to suppress the blast. Inch by inch I angled my body out and away. When I finally lifted my foot off the release, I was almost lying on the ground. I escaped with a shattered leg and foot. And a decade's worth of nightmares. I'm scarred in more ways than one. And my medical and shrink bills run me three hundred a month. The fucking VA is no help at all."

The dog, whose name was Hank, wandered over and licked the back of Gilmore's hand, as if to console him.

After a long silence, Rob spoke: "Let me make one more argument, then I'll shut up. I may not find Billy. I may not get him out. But I'm going to try. And even if I fail, I expect at the least to bring everyone out alive. And no matter what happens—success or failure—you'll still get paid, and paid well. You need the money, Howard. I'll pay you fifty thousand dollars. More, if you insist hard enough. It's my father's money, and I intend to spend as much of it as I possibly can get away with. Come with me. And put an end to worrying about medical bills."

"You know what you're doing, don't you," Gilmore replied. "Just what you always hated your father for. You're using money to make people do what you want."

The remark stung Rob deeply. "That's not fair."

Howard shook his head sadly. "I'm sorry. Forget it. Let's go get some more beer."

Rob and Howard piled into Howard's four-wheel-drive pickup, with Hank wedged in between them, and bounced and splashed their way back out the driveway and down the road. It was dark and surprisingly cold for April. Rob remembered how winter always dragged its heels in New England. He wished he had brought a coat.

"You know, everybody envied the hell out of you at Columbia. The other guys in SDS, anyway," Gilmore said.

"Why?"

"I guess because you were rich and good-looking. You had some charisma going for you. I think it pissed a lot of them off that you had all that and still wanted to carry water for the downtrodden."

"You weren't envious of me, were you?" Rob asked.

Gilmore shifted his big bulk uncomfortably. "I knew you too well to envy you. I guess I always thought of you as being tragic, somehow."

"Tragic? Come on!"

"I thought the movement meant something different to you than it did to the rest of us," he confessed. "You needed something from it that I didn't think you'd ever get. A lot of what we were all doing was just raising hell, let's face it. We were young and it was the thing to do. Protesting, demonstrations, sit-ins—confrontation was in and we were having a ball. I suppose we accomplished a few things, but basically we weren't doing anything more earthshaking than growing up. But you were different. I used to imagine that you were born in the wrong circumstances. You really believed in that revolution. You really wanted to overthrow the Establishment. I was afraid that when it didn't happen, you wouldn't know what to do with your life, you'd end up trapped in your romantic dream. Based on what you've told me tonight, I guess I was right. At least partly right. Do you remember how you used to go on all the time about Che Guevara and Ho Chi Minh?"

"Christ, we all did. They were our heroes."

"Yeah, but you were jealous of them. You wanted your own country to overthrow. The problem was your father, I guess. You used to talk about him a lot. Boy, you really had it in for him. He was the Establishment you really wanted to overthrow." Howard paused, suddenly embarrassed. "I apologize for practicing psychiatry without a license."

They arrived at the store. Rob sat and waited in the truck with the dog. After what seemed a long time, Gilmore returned, bearing two heavy bags of groceries. He loaded them in the back and jumped behind the wheel, grinning like a boy on Christmas morning.

"You like steak with your beer?" he asked.

"Steak?"

"Sure. I got some groceries. Figured you'd want to stay for dinner."

"Of course I would. But let me contribute something."

"No way. This dinner is in your honor."

"I'll drink to that."

"You ever learn to play the guitar?"

Rob laughed. "No, but I'm still trying."

"You really are a stubborn son of a bitch. I told you years ago that rich boys can never play the guitar. It's just not in their genes."

"Well, now that I'm cut off from the family fortune, maybe I'll develop some musical talent."

"I'll tell you what," Gilmore said. "After dinner I'll get out my guitar and teach you a few chords. We'll drink some more Anchor Steam, smoke some of my Humboldt County grass, and do the whole sixties songbook. Dylan, the Beatles . . . The whole nostalgic trip."

"That reminds me," Rob said. "You still have that disconcerting habit of breaking into song for no good reason?"

Howard answered by breaking into song, his rich baritone vibrating in the small cab of the pickup:

" 'Those were the days, my friend,
  We thought they'd never end,
  We'd sing and dance forever and a day;
  We'd live the life we choose, we'd fight and never lose.
  For we were young and sure to have our way-y-y!' "©

Hank the dog crooned off-key with his master. Rob closed his eyes and relaxed. He felt better than he had in months.

"And tomorrow," Gilmore concluded, "after we get out from under a truly revolutionary hangover, we'll sit down and see if we can figure out how the hell we're going to get your brother out of Vietnam."

12

Washington, D.C.

The Caucus Room of the Old Senate Office Building, the famous setting for the Watergate hearings nine years earlier, fell to a hush as the chairman of the committee, Republican Senator Carl Landers, gaveled the session to order. The business at hand: a public hearing to determine, under Article II, Section II, of the Constitution of the United States, how the Senate should advise, and whether it should consent, to the President's nomination of William Frederick Grunwald as ambassador to Israel.

All nine members of the committee were on hand, five Republicans and four Democrats, seated in a row behind their microphones and pitchers of water on the raised dais that ran most of the length of the front end of the large chamber. Facing them, from a cluster of oak tables and hard-backed chairs, sat William Grunwald and his counsel, two attorneys from the prestigious New York firm of Cravath, Swaine, and Moore. Immediately behind them sat Grunwald's chief business associate, James Safier, and his personal secretary, Florence Weld. No members of Grunwald's family were present. The rows of seats reserved for the Press and the public were all filled, and an extra fifty standing spectators jammed the narrow aisle at the back of the hall. The word was out that the hearing might produce some fireworks.

Grunwald was aware of that possibility, too. He had pushed Safier and a team of lawyers and researchers into overtime for days to anticipate any awkward lines of questioning. He felt completely prepared to turn back even the most ruthless probing; nevertheless, he was nervous. The hot, bright glare of the television lights, and the dozens of still photographers kneeling expectantly on the floor space between his table and the senators' dais left him in no doubt of the nature or importance of this hearing. He was in the arena, and the crowd, as always, was hoping for blood.

The chairman opened the session with a long-winded speech, extolling Grunwald's virtues in the most glowing terms, painting a picture of him as the classic American success story—the immigrant, the victim of foreign oppression, who seeks refuge "in the land of opportunity," makes his fortune, and now desires to serve the country that gave him that opportunity. According to Landers, no finer example of what America was all about could be found anywhere. Landers capped his speech on a strong emotional note, reminding his listeners of the great sacrifice William Grunwald had already made to his adoptive country by losing his eldest son to the war in Vietnam. The senator was heavily involved in the MIA issue and exploited this chance to score a few patriotic points on the subject.

Landers then led off the questioning, interrogating Grunwald much as a defense attorney would, giving the nominee the chance to present himself before the committee and the cameras in the best possible light. Grunwald handled this part of the hearing with considerable aplomb, mixing humility and pride, humor and seriousness, in an expertly balanced performance.

The questioning continued on through the morning, the Republicans playing up Grunwald's strengths, some Democrats only wondering aloud whether his lack of diplomatic experience would make it difficult for him to represent the country effectively in such a sensitive post. He fielded their questions about foreign policy with ease and in the kind of detail that impressed everyone in the room.

When the hearing broke for lunch, it looked as if his nomination was secure. But Grunwald knew he hadn't yet faced any real opposition. That would come, he was certain, in the person of Samuel Glass, senior senator from New York State. Glass was a liberal Democrat from Brooklyn, a former district attorney, a muckraking consumer advocate, and a bitter enemy of Grunwald and everything he stood for. Twice Grunwald had tried to unseat him, pouring heavy doses of money and influence into the campaigns of his Republican opponents. Each time, Glass had squeaked through a winner.

At three o'clock that afternoon, Glass's turn finally came. He began with a brief rhetorical flourish, assuring the chairman that he shared everyone's respect for and awe of William Grunwald. "I have read many accounts of your achievements, sir," he said, in his pronounced Brooklyn accent. "In the *Wall Street Journal, Business Week, Fortune.* Even," he continued, pausing for effect, "in that bulwark of liberal anticapitalism, the *New York Times.*" Some titters from the audience. Grunwald permitted himself a wry smile.

"Fortunately for me," Glass intoned, scanning the rows of seated reporters with a sly grin, "there seems to be at least one area in your brilliant career where you have so far failed quite completely."

Grunwald tensed immediately. "And that," Glass continued, "has been in your efforts to remove me from the United States Senate."

Loud and prolonged laughter. Their antagonism was well known to the public, and Glass scored with the spectators by making a joke of it. Grunwald forced out a chuckle, intensely conscious of the photographers in front of him, popping up from the floor like jack-in-the-boxes to snap his picture. The chairman gaveled for quiet.

"Stay on your toes," one of his lawyers whispered. Grunwald nodded curtly. He hardly needed to be told.

Senator Glass opened a very thick folder in front of him and paused dramatically to study a particular page. *Another one of his phony courtroom tricks,* Grunwald guessed, *bringing in a thick folder to frighten the opponent into thinking you've got something on him.*

"How much are you worth, Mr. Grunwald?"

"In whose estimation, Senator?" This drew a small laugh.

Glass frowned in disapproval. "You understand my meaning, Mr. Grunwald. How much money do you have?"

"I have provided the committee with a detailed disclosure statement, Senator—"

"Yes, yes, I am aware of that. But, for the sake of our discussion, just give us an approximate figure."

Grunwald turned to the lawyer sitting next to him. The man shrugged. "It's very difficult to answer that question accurately and simply, Senator. To begin with—"

"Just a ballpark figure," Glass persisted. "Round it off to the nearest million."

Grunwald squirmed in his seat, thinking of the vast audience who would see and hear him on the evening news. "About six hundred and fifty million," he muttered.

An audible gasp vibrated through the chamber. Glass sat up straight and peered over the rims of his spectacles. "Six hundred and fifty million dollars," he said, pronouncing each word slowly and carefully, to make sure no one missed the amount. "Would you say that made you the richest man in America?"

"Hardly."

"*Hardly,* you say?"

"That's right."

"There are men richer than you?"

"The Senator has heard of the Rockefellers and the Duponts."

Glass smiled. "But that's family wealth, Mr. Grunwald. I'm talking about individual wealth."

"I share my good fortune with my family, Senator."

This brought a big laugh, and Grunwald felt pleased with himself. Glass ignored the remark. "Well, would you admit to being one of the richest men in the country, then?"

Grunwald nodded impatiently.

"Would you put yourself in the top ten?"

Grunwald threw out his hands in a gesture of surrender. "Will the Senator be satisfied if I can only make the top one hundred?"

"Would you say all of that immense wealth has been acquired honestly, Mr. Grunwald?"

Grunwald flushed with anger. "That's a rhetorical question, Senator, and I resent the implication behind it. I can assure you my wealth has been acquired without breaking the law."

Glass was unmoved. "Well, I ask it, sir," he said, "only because my files here indicate that you have been investigated by the SEC on seven different occasions, from charges ranging from trading on insider information to stock fraud."

The son of a bitch, Grunwald thought. *He's going to try to smear me in public.* "I run a very large and active company," he replied, his voice even. "Most successful businessmen have run afoul of the SEC at one time or another, Senator, as you well know. The laws that govern business are so complicated they require companies like mine to retain a whole department of lawyers just to sort them out— and to keep up with the new ones you people in Congress never seem to tire of passing."

"Nevertheless—"

"And I might point out, in my defense," Grunwald continued, "that all of those investigations were subsequently dropped. No charges, no indictments have ever been sustained against me in my long career in American business. I have, in fact, appeared in court only once in my life, Senator, and that was in 1957 to answer a speeding ticket. I pled guilty with an excuse. I was on my way to the hospital to see my son, Billy. The judge let me off with a warning."

Grunwald glanced behind him. He could feel the crowd in the packed chamber coming around to his side. James Safier and Florence Weld were both grinning at him proudly. Senator Glass was studying the folder in front of him, his face an impassive mask. Grunwald was beginning to enjoy himself.

"Well, of course you're not on trial here," Glass said, finally, trying to win back the offensive. "I raise these matters merely to assist the committee in reaching its judgment on your fitness to represent the country abroad. Sometimes reputation alone, whether deserved or not, can weigh against a candidate and his effectiveness in carrying out a mission that requires the host country to have the utmost confidence and trust in him. The appearance of dishonesty can be as crippling, sometimes, as the real thing."

The thrust and parry continued through the afternoon. Glass pressed his offensive relentlessly. He delved at length into the charges leveled in the seven SEC investigations, and brought up details of several other business deals from Grunwald's past that, if not illegal, he was certainly able to make sound unethical. But Grunwald was as well prepared as Glass, and he deflected each fresh attack skillfully and persuasively. As they played out each round, it was hard to say who was scoring more points.

By four o'clock, Glass seemed to have spent himself. He slouched back in his chair, as if admitting defeat. "Do you speak Hebrew, Mr. Grunwald?" Glass's tone was offhand and casual.

"I'm afraid I do not, Senator."

Glass nodded. "That could place you at a disadvantage, sir. The Israelis, as you know, are both tough and thin-skinned at the same time. Great tact and delicacy are required in diplomatic dealings with them. Understanding their culture and language is important."

"I agree with the Senator completely. I have undertaken the study of Hebrew. But I would point out that it's a rare government official in Israel who doesn't understand English."

Glass smiled broadly, revealing rows of rather crooked teeth. "And an even rarer American one who can speak Hebrew," he replied.

Grunwald joined in the general laughter.

"At least you're Jewish," Glass added, his voice almost jovial. "That can't hurt."

Grunwald nodded slowly. Did he detect a trace of mockery?

"Where was your family from?"

Grunwald had been anticipating this line of questioning. He was confident that he could handle it without difficulty. Still, Glass's sudden move into this dangerous zone made him uneasy. "In Germany, you mean?"

"Yes."

"A small city in Saxony—Chemnitz."

"That's in East Germany, isn't it?"

"Yes. It's called Karl-Marx-Stadt now."

"What did your father do there, before the war?"

"He was a businessman. In textiles."

"You had brothers? Sisters?"

"One sister."

"And what became of her?"

"She was killed during the war."

"And your parents?"

"They were killed, too."

"In concentration camps?"

"I believe so, yes."

"Do you know which ones?"

"No. I was taken away first, Senator. To Dachau. I don't know where they were taken."

"Did you return home after the war?"

"No. It was occupied by the Russians."

"But weren't you anxious to find out what had happened to your family?"

"Of course. There were terrible stories of raping and looting coming from the Russian-occupied areas."

"And yet you didn't return home?"

"No."

"You were afraid of the Russians, then?"

"Yes."

"Why?"

"Because they would take reprisals—"

Grunwald stopped in mid-sentence, suddenly confused. Glass and the other senators were staring at him, perplexed. He realized that he had started to say the wrong thing. The Jewish past that he had fabricated for himself long ago and refined in every detail over the years was so familiar to him that he half believed it was real himself. It was a perfect history—a plausible, carefully researched, and brilliant blend of verifiable facts and completely unverifiable lies. In thirty-five years, no one, not even his wife or children, had ever questioned any part of it. And yet here this Senator Glass had suddenly punched a hole in it. Beads of sweat popped out on Grunwald's forehead. The nightmarish fear of being identified, of being found out, was beginning to take hold of him. Did this Glass know, somehow? No, no, it was impossible. He mustn't panic. It was just a coincidence. Glass couldn't know anything. Grunwald had just made a little slip. He had told Glass the truth: he had not returned to Chemnitz because the Russians were hunting down SS members and shooting them. But, for Grunwald the Jew, there had to be a different reason. He must find it quickly. How could he have never thought of this, after all these years? He groped frantically for the persuasive answer.

"I didn't want to live under communism," he said finally.

Senator Glass nodded. "How, then, did you ascertain that they were dead?"

Grunwald stared at Glass without replying. He hadn't even heard the question. Glass repeated it. "From records," Grunwald snapped.

"What records?"

"The records!" Grunwald was conscious that he had raised his voice. "The international committees," he added, almost in a whisper.

"The International Jewish Refugee Center?"

"I believe that was it. Yes."

" 'Grunwald' is a common name in Germany. Were you absolutely satisfied that they were dead?"

"Senator, I don't understand the reason for these questions, but I can assure you they are painful. Yes. I was quite certain that they were dead."

Glass raised an eyebrow skeptically. "I only ask, Mr. Grunwald, because there are so few details available in the public record concerning your background. I, too, lost relatives in the Holocaust, and appreciate the pain you must feel. I am merely trying to fill in some of the gaps in your biography. Since the post for which you have been nominated is Israel, I think your family background in Germany is relevant to the public record."

Grunwald said nothing. He felt a shortness of breath coming on. He readjusted his position in his chair to hide his sudden gasping for air.

Glass continued his probing. "What year did the Nazis come and take you away?"

"Nineteen-forty-four."

"How long were you in Dachau?"

"Nearly a year . . . until the Americans liberated the camp."

"What were you doing before you were sent to Dachau?"

"What do you mean?"

"Well, you were about eighteen years of age at the time. Hitler's persecution of the Jews had been going on for years. I assume you weren't in the army. What were you doing?"

Grunwald wiped a trickle of sweat from the corner of one eye. Like a victim of stage fright, he had suddenly forgotten all his lines. His carefully memorized past had now completely deserted him. Flustered, he glanced at his lawyers as if seeking help. They stared back at him, puzzled by his deteriorating composure. "I suppose I was helping my father, Senator."

"Your father was still in business? In 1944?"

"No. I mean I was just helping the family survive."

"Did you go into hiding?"

"No, no . . . Yes. For a while."

"Which is it?"

"It's hard to remember exactly."

"Do you feel guilty about those days?"

"I beg your pardon?"

"Many survivors of the Holocaust suffer from guilt feelings, as you probably are well aware. The feeling that they didn't do enough to resist the Nazis, perhaps. The feeling that they didn't deserve to survive when so many others died. It's a common reaction, I understand. Do you feel that way?"

Grunwald didn't reply. His face was drained white, and his chest was heaving rapidly.

Senator Landers interrupted in his behalf: "May I ask the distinguished Senator from New York if he feels it necessary to pursue this line of questioning? It seems to me that it serves no function other than to arouse the most painful of memories for the nominee."

"I apologize to the committee and to the nominee for any pain I have inflicted. I am merely trying, to the best of my ability, to ascertain the nominee's fitness to serve in a difficult and sensitive foreign post. His attitude toward Germany, Israel, and the Soviet Union may have been affected by his past experiences in such a way as to seriously impair his judgment. In which case—"

"I think you are harassing the nominee unnecessarily, Senator," Landers cut in.

Glass sat back and tilted his face toward the ceiling in a gesture of frustration, then turned to face Landers, seated three chairs away. "Then I have no more questions at this time, Mr. Chairman," he said.

Landers nodded with a perceptible look of relief, and banged his gavel. "This committee stands adjourned until ten o'clock tomorrow morning."

The photographers were standing now, a crowd of about twenty, their cameras snapping like a forest of crickets. Grunwald spun around in his chair, looking for Safier and Weld. Sweat was pouring from his forehead and down his cheeks. Several reporters and a camera crew had already made their way to his table, questions spilling from them in an excited jumble.

He rose unsteadily to his feet, waving his arms, his features contorted in panic. The TV cameraman, sensing something dramatic, switched his camera back on and held it on Grunwald as he tried to fight his way through the crowd. Safier edged over to his side and grabbed his arm to slow him down.

"Get me out of here," Grunwald gasped. "Get me out of here!"

13

Shawnee, Oklahoma

A crowd of several thousand, drawn from Tulsa and Norman and Oklahoma City and small towns all across the state, squinted in hushed silence up into the April sky, shielding their eyes from the late-afternoon sunshine with the flats of their hands and the clutched pages of their programs.

Their attention was riveted on two small objects circling several thousand feet above the flat expanse of Oklahoma prairie. One was a World War I vintage French Nieuport, the other a Fokker DVII biplane with Iron Crosses painted on its wings—one of the aircraft once flown, as their programs pointed out, by the legendary German ace of World War I, Baron Manfred von Richthofen. For half an hour the spectators had watched with open-mouthed awe as the two pilots re-created a dogfight, running through a repertory of classic maneuvers, from simple loops and slow rolls to elegant and demanding chandelles, Cuban eights, and Immelmann turns.

The climax of the performance was now at hand, and the crowd tensed in anticipation. The script dictated that the German plane always lose the dogfight, so the pilot of the DVII was permitted only one variation—the manner in which he plunged to his make-believe death. Veterans of the show claimed he never did it the same way twice.

As all eyes fastened on the tiny kitelike craft overhead, the voice on the PA system fell silent, suspending its cornball patter in deference to the drama about to unfold. In the tense stillness, the only sound was the faraway whine of the planes' engines as they bent around in a tightening circle, positioning themselves for the grand finale.

Rob Grunwald, standing near a corner of the main bleacher, craned his neck upward with the rest of the crowd. The Nieuport eventually gained the advantage, moving in behind the Fokker until it seemed to be riding on its tail. Several thin cracks of gunfire punctuated the drone of the engines, and a cloud of cottony white smoke billowed out from the rear of the German craft.

The Fokker dipped downward suddenly in an inside roll, then climbed out behind the Nieuport in a belated evasive maneuver, smoke still pouring from its tail. The Nieuport, its part in the drama over, straightened out into a long and gradual circuit away from the field, leaving the center stage to the DVII and its pilot.

The Fokker began climbing now. Rob could hear clearly the strain of its small rotary engine as it scaled the heavens on an almost vertical incline. After nearly a minute of steady ascent, the DVII had become a tiny smudge against the deep blue, its shape no longer identifiable. Rob guessed the pilot to be at about ten thousand feet and wondered how much higher he could take the open-cockpit aircraft.

The noise of the plane's engine abruptly died, chasing its echo across the prairie. A communal gasp from the crowd filled the sudden stillness. The biplane paused motionless in the sky, standing on its tail for several seconds, then began to slip rapidly backward, like a climber who has lost his footing on a sheer rockface. The backward plunge grew quickly into a crazy series of somersaults as the craft flipped over on its back and began to tumble down through the afternoon, growing larger and closer as it twisted out of control.

The crowd moaned softly. Rob jammed a thumbnail between his teeth and bit down on it.

The Fokker wrenched free of its tumble only to plummet into a straight nosedive. Again the crowd gasped. The plane hurtled earthward like a kamikaze locked on its target, accelerating rapidly under the pull of gravity, its plume of smoke stretched out like a thin white paper streamer behind it. It seemed to be aimed straight for the stand of bleachers, and the crowd began to move out of the way in panic.

Rob waited for the screaming force of the wind to rip the machine's wings from its sides, but at a thousand feet from the hard-packed Oklahoma soil, when it seemed that the fragile strut-and-canvas structure could not bear another ounce of stress, the plane popped out of its nosedive and bounced upward, still with the engine off, using the momentum of its dive and the available air current to propel it in a long, soaring glide back into the heavens. The crowd exploded in frenzied applause. The PA system blared out a few banalities, then quickly fell silent.

In seeming defiance of gravity, the pilot managed to keep the craft airborne for several more minutes, guiding it through a graceful series of turns and glides, sometimes swooping so low over the heads of the spectators that they could hear the rush of air through the wing struts. Rob ducked with the rest of them, overwhelmed by a heady mixture of fear and excitement. The pilot—out of either contempt or insane recklessness—appeared to be risking the lives of the crowd along with his own.

In a final, dazzling flourish, he brought the plane to a perfect dead-stick landing about thirty feet in front of the bleachers. The crowd erupted into a wild cheer that went on, undiminished, for several minutes. No sports star or opera singer, Rob thought, had ever received a more intense ovation. Rob watched the pilot pull himself from the DVII's cockpit and wave self-consciously to the people swarming around the plane. A master performer, he was uncomfortable in the role of celebrity.

Rob lingered patiently on the outskirts of the crowd. The pilot's act had climaxed the day's show, and hundreds of people were fighting to get his autograph or just to shake his hand. Finally Rob saw him break loose and trot toward the airport office, a small prefab building next to the field's lone hangar. Rob hurried over and intercepted him at the door.

"Nice flying, Mr. McWhirter," he said, holding out his hand. "My name is Rob Grunwald."

Harris McWhirter glanced at the hand, then shook it reluctantly.

"Could I have a few words with you in private?"

The pilot cocked an eyebrow. "You a bill collector or a bounty hunter?"

Grunwald grinned. "Neither. I want to offer you a job."

"You own better planes than these?"

"Your performance was impressive as hell, but I'm not interested in your flying skills. . . ." Rob left the sentence for McWhirter to fill in himself.

The man appraised him suspiciously. "Who told you where I was at?"

Rob gave him some names. McWhirter nodded. "Lemme change

and shower. There's a place about a mile from here down Route 43 called the Broadway Café. I'll meet you there in half an hour."

The Broadway Café was a run-down wood-frame roadhouse with a panel busted out of its front door and a clientele that would have thrown a scare into Wyatt Earp. Rob waited at the end of the bar closest to the exit, hunched over a glass of beer, practicing his tunnel vision. It was barely five o'clock on a Saturday afternoon and everyone in the joint appeared drunk. Four Indians in one booth were arm-wrestling one another in grim silence punctuated by the occasional crash of arms against beer bottles. In the booth behind, three men were sitting with one woman. She was tall and raw-boned and she kept jabbing the man beside her with her finger, accusing him, in her twangy voice, of a wide variety of shameful acts. The other two men were wheezing with laughter. Rob caught the phrase "He ate my pussy in the Cadillac Hotel!" just as Harris McWhirter appeared, half an hour late, and slid onto the stool next to him.

"Welcome to Fistfight City," the pilot said. "Not much class, but it's the best entertainment in the whole miserable state."

McWhirter had changed out of his World War I German flying-ace uniform into a tight green T-shirt and khaki trousers. He was small, no more than five-seven, and slight of build, but every pound of him was as tough as tanned horsehide. His biceps and forearms were large, and the definition of his chest and stomach muscles showed through the T-shirt. His movements were fluid and powerful. He looked as if he could spring over a ten-foot wall—and do it from a standing start.

The pilot's face harbored contradictions: His nose and ears were small and undistinguished, and his lips were thin and spent a lot of time stretched tightly across his teeth in a kind of perpetual Humphrey Bogart grimace. But his eyes, revealed to Rob finally when he removed his sunglasses in the dim light of the bar, were large and soft—the vulnerable eyes of a woman. Rob understood at once his fondness for the shades.

His hair was dirty blond and sparse on top, and what little remained was cut short. There was nothing extra or unnecessary about him. He exuded an air of extraordinary self-possession—of not needing or wanting anything. Or caring about anything.

"That was an impressive show you put on out there this afternoon," Rob said. "Where did you learn that kind of flying?"

"Air America," McWhirter replied, in his laconic manner.

"I've never heard of it."

"It was a CIA cover. I was a contract pilot for them. Spent four years in Laos."

"Doing what?"

"Everything. We had a secret war going on there all through the sixties. We were backing Meo tribesmen against the Pathet Lao. We supplied them by air, relocated them by air, and moved their opium to market for them by air. That's where I learned what flying was all about."

McWhirter sipped his beer and stared at the bar mirror. Just when Rob was convinced he wasn't going to volunteer anything further on the subject, he started talking again:

"Laos is a shitty place for almost anything," he said. "But especially airplanes—monsoon rains, heat, high altitude, mist, jungles, and mountains as steep as the side of this building. Real shitty. But the CIA found us these incredible planes—Helio Couriers. They look just like your average weekend pilot's Cessna 180, but they were something awesome. They had fat wings and an outsized prop that was geared way down. They were tricky bitches to fly, but you could do things with those beauties that can't be done with anything else in the sky, except sometimes a helicopter."

McWhirter held his hand out flat over the bar and moved it slowly in a horizonal direction. "You could fly them so slow—under thirty knots—that you could let off passengers without landing. And when you did land, you could do it in a bumpy field about twice the length of this barroom." He brought his palm down toward the bar at a steep angle, then flared his fingers, touched the heel of his hand gently to the polished-wood surface, and slid it along for about a foot, gradually bringing it to a stop. "There was this one landing strip that was cut into the side of a mountain. When there was a stiff breeze blowing, which was most of the time, I could take off in a Helio straight up, just like an elevator." He demonstrated again with his hand. "We flew other stuff—Pilatus Porters, C-130s—but the Helio was my baby. There was nothing that sweetheart couldn't do. It even knew how to crash. I walked away from eight of them."

"Eight? That's unbelievable. How many missions did you fly?"

The pilot shook his head. "Who the hell knows? Thousands. We got paid by the trip. And most runs were only about half an hour. Sometimes less. I flew thirty-three in one day once. Rice drops. We used to ferry thousands of bags of rice to the tribesmen. We dropped so many the wild pigs caught on to us. They used to wait at the edge of the drop zone, and when the bags started falling, there'd be a hell of a race between Meo and pig. The pigs usually won." McWhirter smiled at his reflection in the bar mirror. "One day we loaded the wrong cargo by mistake. The kicker in back was busy pushing the bags out, when suddenly I heard him yelling at me. I looked down and saw these big white circles on the ground. The bags were all busting and scattering what looked like white flour all over the place. We ripped open a sack and discovered it was full of cocaine crystals. We must have dumped several million dollars' worth of coke on that spot. The pigs wouldn't touch it, but the Meo stayed high for months."

McWhirter checked himself, and an embarrassed look crossed his face. "I can get pretty flap-jawed on the subject of flying," he said. "But I don't think that's what you're here for."

Rob nodded. He signaled the bartender to bring them another round of beer. "I want you to help me rescue my brother."

McWhirter studied Rob's reflection in the bar mirror. "He in the slammer or something?"

"He's in Vietnam."

Rob waited for some sort of response, but McWhirter remained silent. Rob went on: "He was captured twelve years ago. I have evidence that shows that he's still alive—and where he's being held."

"And you're goin' in to get him out."

"That's my plan." Rob braced himself for a scornful laugh. It didn't come.

"How big a team are you puttin' together?"

"Besides myself, I've recruited only one other member so far. How many do I need?"

McWhirter shrugged. "Four to six is ideal for a cadre. Then you flesh it out with about a dozen IPs."

Rob blinked in bafflement. "Eye peas?"

" 'Indigenous Personnel.' That's Special Forces jargon for 'natives.' "

Rob nodded uncertainly.

"Sounds to me," the pilot said, his tone sincere, "like you don't know what the fuck you're doing."

Rob swallowed his annoyance and concentrated on his goal. "That's why I want to hire you, McWhirter. You're the expert. I need you to train the mission and develop a plan—how we get in, who and what we take with us, how we get out. From what I've heard about you, you have the skills, the contacts, and the experience."

McWhirter took a long, thoughtful swig from the bottle of beer. "Your brother must be real important to you, Mr. Grunwald."

"He is."

The pilot bared his teeth in a tight grin. "And you must have a lot of money to play with."

"I do."

McWhirter caught the eye of the bartender and traced a quick circle with his forefinger over their empty beer glasses. "I did that once, about five years ago."

"What happened?"

"We were ripped off by the same ratty-assed IPs we hired to take us in," he said, his tone bored, as if he had tired of telling the story years ago. "They helped themselves to our jeep, our clothes, food, weapons, radios. It was a real embarrassment."

"How many of you were there?"

"Four Caucasians. The IPs that turned on us were Sek tribesmen. Bandits is what they were. I should've known better."

"You all make it out okay?"

McWhirter shook his head. "Just me."

Rob swallowed hard and hoisted the beer glass to his lips. Through the mirror, he saw that two of the men at the table with the uncouth woman had stood up and squared off against each other. The bartender was lumbering over to intercede.

McWhirter glanced over at them with the same bored look. "Those guys couldn't go a round with my dead grandmother. Wait'll those Indians get cranked up, though. Those suckers'll fight to the death."

"You get involved in these brawls?"

"Me?" McWhirter grinned, incredulous. "Nah. They leave me alone."

Rob supposed that he had probably *persuaded* them to leave him alone. McWhirter fished a handful of peanuts from a ncarby bowl, popped several in his mouth, and chewed on them thoughtfully. "I can't say as how I'd look forward to going again. Especially Vietnam. Laos is bad enough. Nam, though. Those bastards there are too organized."

"What do you mean?"

"Laos is just a jungle full of warlords. Little yellow guys with their own armies. It's like a big slum full of street gangs. It's outlaw heaven. Each gang protects its own turf and everything else is up for grabs. The government in Vientiane is just a stage show. It can't do anything. It certainly can't patrol its borders. But Vietnam is different." He paused and munched another handful of nuts. "Those bastards are in charge over there. They know what's happening. Hard to get away with anything."

"That's why I need you," Rob said. "You have the best references."

For the first time he heard McWhirter laugh out loud. It was a dry, scornful chuckle. "You're talking just like a big shot, Mr. Grunwald," he said. "What branch of the service were you in?"

"No branch," Rob replied.

"No branch?"

"I dodged," Rob explained, careful not to choke on his words. "Went to Canada."

McWhirter froze, his fist poised with a peanut in front of his open mouth. "Are you making fun of me?"

"I wouldn't dream of it."

The pilot seemed genuinely stunned. "You were a peace creep?"

"I guess that's what you'd have called me."

McWhirter rolled his eyes in disbelief. "And now you want to be some kind of jerk-off hero and go rescue your brother?"

Rob said nothing.

"Christ Almighty," McWhirter muttered, sounding genuinely disappointed. "A peace creep. And a New York Jew, to boot. I hate everything you stand for. And you probably hate everything I stand for. And yet you're here in this bar asking me to go to Vietnam with you." McWhirter dropped the peanuts back in the bowl and glanced around the room in disgust. "You know that every redneck son of a bitch in this room would probably stand in line just for the chance to kick the shit out of you—me included?"

Rob laughed, in spite of the fluttering sensations in his intestines. "I'm sure you could do it, too."

McWhirter scowled menacingly. "You don't seem very worried about it."

Rob pulled a five-dollar bill from his wallet and laid it on the bar. "Opposing the war doesn't mean I'm a sissy. It usually takes more guts to stand up for what you believe in than it does to go along with the crowd."

"Bullshit."

Rob studied the ornery man beside him for a moment, then decided that if he was ever going to close a deal with him, now was the moment to do it. "You consider yourself a man of the world, Mr. McWhirter?" he asked.

"You're damned right."

"Well, your mouth is telling me you're nothing more than a local redneck. And probably a liar, too. I guess you're not the man I'm looking for after all."

McWhirter's face took on a deep purple hue.

Rob stood up to leave. "Thanks for the air show, anyway."

McWhirter grunted noncommittally. "You running away?"

Rob knew he had him hooked. Now to haul him in. "There's a late flight from Oklahoma City. I think I can still catch it."

"You want me that bad," the pilot said, looking disappointed, "you'd think you'd be willing to beg me a little."

"I don't want you at all now," Rob insisted.

"I was just testing your seriousness. I can see you're a proud son of a bitch."

Rob sat down again. "It's just not in my nature to beg."

McWhirter relented a little: "The kind of things I can do, after all, they require more than a college degree. You know what I mean?"

"Spell it out for me."

The pilot looked at himself in the bar mirror. "As an old cowboy I once knew used to say, 'I can ride any man's horse and do a lot of other goddamn things.' "

"I don't doubt it."

"My services don't come cheap."

"I didn't expect they would."

Rob waited. McWhirter glanced around the room again, as if hoping that some distraction might be in the offing. "You have a figure in mind to pay me?"

"I'd rather just pay you what you want. Within reason."

"Within reason to me is five thousand a week."

"That sounds reasonable."

"Plus expenses."

"Of course."

"And a bonus if the job is a success."

"How much of a bonus?"

"I'll leave that to your generosity."

"Why don't we negotiate the details on that plane back to New York tonight?"

McWhirter hesitated, caught off guard. "You're in one son-of-a-bitch of a hurry, aren't you!"

Rob shrugged. "Think it over for a day, then. I'll call you from New York tomorrow."

McWhirter slapped his hand down on the table and slid off the bar-stool. "I've never needed a day to think anything over in my life. I don't want to start now. Let me go back to my motel and pack."

Nice, France

Brian Duffy was nothing if not resourceful.

He opened the French doors onto the small balcony on the top floor of the Negresco and looked out across the broad Promenade des

Anglais, noisy with evening traffic, to the purple Mediterranean beyond and the long, graceful crescent of lights twinkling in the dusk across the Bay of Angels. Renting this opulent space in Nice's most luxurious resort hotel was part of his new plan. He needed to impress a certain magazine editor.

The death of the Vietnamese refugee had thrown him, but now it was clear that it had actually opened up new avenues of opportunity. Now he, Brian Duffy, was the only living source for the story. And that one tape still remained to verify the story's truth—the one he had left with William Grunwald.

So Duffy had concocted a scheme for revenge. What he would do, he decided, was include in the article he was writing a description of how Grunwald had used a cheap trick to cheat him out of information about his son Billy. Then he would cap that with an interpretative account of how the Vietnamese Ngo Din Tran had met his end. He would be skirting the laws of libel, but he was sure he could contrive a narrative that would implicate Grunwald in the refugee's death. And who knows, maybe Grunwald did have him killed, Duffy told himself. Stranger things had happened. In any case, Grunwald could hardly afford publicity of this kind, not while trying to nail down an ambassadorship.

The key to success, Duffy realized, lay in selling the story to this German magazine. He knew that Grunwald could easily intimidate or bribe the wretched tabloid in the States that had already commissioned the article. But Germany was different. Grunwald wouldn't be able to touch them. So he would have to come to Duffy.

He had the hook-nosed bastard now, right by his circumcised cock and balls. And the price this time was not going to be a lousy fifty thousand dollars; it was going to be a million. And Duffy would never have to write another article again, as long as he lived.

He surveyed the expensive elegance of the suite with satisfaction. It was done in the extravagant style of the Empire period, and the ornate decadence of it pleased Duffy enormously. It was his style, he decided, and he expected soon to be able to afford a lot more of it. He glanced at the Piaget on his wrist: the German representative was due to arrive any minute. Duffy wondered if he could clinch the sale by letting the German have the article cheap. He'd play it by ear, he decided.

The same low comedy of errors that had defined Duffy's life marked its end as well.

At the sound of the door buzzer, he walked swiftly from the balcony to the small vestibule. He had already opened the door when it occurred to him that his guest should have called him on the house telephone before coming up.

The next minute was a violent blur. Two men shoved their way swiftly through the doorway, grabbed Duffy, threw him face down on the bed, and tied his wrists together behind his back. When they let him up, he saw that they had tied another length of cord around the ceiling post that held the room's chandelier. They stood him on a small chair beneath the chandelier and attached the rope above to the one around his wrists. He began to tremble. One of the men, a tall, muscular thug with a bad acne problem, reached up and slapped him hard across the face.

"We have a few simple questions to ask you, Duffy," he said in an American accent. "Let's have quick, complete answers. If we have to pull this chair out from under you, you won't be able to use your arms for a long time. You understand?"

"Yes," Duffy gasped. "Oh God, please don't hurt me!"

"Good. We want the names of everybody who has heard or read any of the information on that Grunwald tape, and everybody who knows of the tape's existence."

Duffy shook his head. "It's hard to remember—"

The tall man with the acne clapped his big hands with tremendous force against Duffy's ears, nearly collapsing his eardrums. His head roared with pain and his knees buckled. "That help your memory any?"

Duffy, his voice shaking from fright, spilled out the answers in such detail that his inquisitor had to slap him twice more to keep him to the point.

"We want all copies of any transcripts," the tall man demanded, when he was satisfied that Duffy had no more to tell him.

"They're in my case," Duffy whimpered. "On the desk."

The man who had been standing behind him walked over to check. He was short, with sandy hair and freckles, and sported a white Lacoste T-shirt. He seemed to be in charge. "Okay. They're here," he said.

"Anything else we ought to know?" the tall one asked Duffy.

Duffy shook his head vehemently. "I've told you everything. Everything! I swear to God I've told you everything!"

The thug kicked the chair back and watched Duffy's bound arms snap up behind him, ripping muscle and tendons as the weight of his body pulled them from his shoulder sockets. Duffy screamed. The man behind him clapped his hands over his mouth to muffle the noise.

"That jog your memory?" the tall one asked. Duffy, his eyes popping from the horrible pain, continued to scream into the other man's hands. The tall one righted the chair and pulled Duffy's feet onto it again. Duffy moaned and gargled incoherently.

"I think we pumped him dry," the tall one said, laughing at the stain of urine spreading across Duffy's Pierre Cardin trousers.

The short man nodded, turned, walked over to the open balcony, and peered down. "Shit," he muttered, "we're only five floors up."

"You forgot the *rez-de-chaussée*," the tall one answered, in an execrable French accent. "They count the ground floor extra here. We're six floors up."

"What the fuck difference does that make?" the short one retorted. "I'm looking out the window and it only looks about five stories high."

"That's high enough."

"He might only break a leg."

"It's at least seventy feet," the tall one argued. "And it's pavement down there. It'll kill him for sure."

The short one shook his head skeptically. "I wish I had your optimism."

"What are we gonna do? Carry him to a higher building?"

"I'm thinking about shooting him."

"It's supposed to be an accident!"

"We could smother him, then."

"Fuck it. Let's stick with the plan."

"If it doesn't kill him," the other said, "I'm on record advising against it."

"I'll give you ten to one it kills him."

"Give me twenty to one and you're on."

"How much?"

"A hundred bucks."

"You got a bet."

Duffy passed out. The tall one held him while the short one untied the rope around his wrists. They carried him to the balcony, balanced him for a moment on the wrought-iron railing, and then shoved him off.

Dieter Rheinhart was dialing Duffy's room from a phone in the front lobby at the precise moment Duffy made his unexpected rendezvous with the pavement outside.

Rheinhart stayed in the lobby for nearly an hour, watching the screaming guests and pedestrians, the hysteria of the doormen and the night manager, the arrival of the police, the ambulance, and the

Press. Finally, when things had quieted down, he approached the clerk at the desk and asked him who the gentleman was they had found on the sidewalk.

"His name was Brian Duffy," the clerk whispered. "I hope you weren't waiting for him?"

Rheinhart shook his head. "No," he said. "Fortunately not."

14

Columbus, South Carolina

Captain Blood came out of his corner at the Apex Arena in downtown Columbus and was met with a loud chorus of boos and catcalls. He danced around the center of the ring, shaking his fists at the crowd with exaggerated menace, stirring their derision even further.

He was large and ugly, with curly black hair and an olive complexion, and he walked with muscle-bound deliberation, flexing his elaborate chest and forearm tattoos like a bodybuilder. His chin was dimpled and his nose broad and fleshy over a luxuriant black mustache. A disfiguring purple scar, thick as a bead of welding, started just above his right eyebrow, disappeared under a black eye patch, and reappeared to continue on down his cheek to the edge of his mouth. Along with the scar, a rivulet of red blood also ran out from under the bottom edge of his eye patch and onto his neck and shoulder. The scar was real; the blood was red dye.

His crimson-and-blue cloak was emblazoned with the Marine Corps emblem, and over his wrestling trunks he had strapped a belt laden with mock hand grenades. He unhooked one of the grenades, made a big fuss of pulling the pin, and then tossed it out in the direction of some of his more vocal hecklers. It landed on the T-shirt of a fat woman many rows back and burst across her big breasts, splattering them with red-dyed water. The crowd roared with outraged delight.

Captain Blood's opponent climbed into the ring—a sullen young Elvis Presley look-alike with slick black hair and bulging biceps. The crowd cheered him lustily as he pranced before it in a gaudy purple-and-gold costume.

More antics followed, with Captain Blood baiting his opponent, the referee, the ring announcer, and the broadcast commentator, each in turn. Rob Grunwald sat patiently watching in the back row of the seedy, dimly lit arena, wedged between a pock-faced teenaged boy with body odor and a skinny old farmer chewing Red Dog tobacco and spitting it into a paper cup.

After Captain Blood's theatrics, the wrestling match itself was an anticlimax. Like the bouts that had preceded it earlier in the evening, it was transparently phony, choreographed in a simple-minded fashion that allowed each wrestler to take his turn appearing to do great bodily damage to the other. They bounced off the ropes, flipped each other over their shoulders, gouged, squeezed, pulled hair, twisted, grabbed, punched, howled in agony, hopped in rage, fell out of the ring, threatened the referee, and finally settled the pseudo-event in a predictable manner: the villain, Captain Blood, was disqualified for "unsportsmanlike conduct."

Following the match, Rob found his way to Captain Blood's dressing room—a sweat-smelling, overheated space with a training table, a sink, and a couple of folding chairs—and introduced himself.

"Frank Wyler," Captain Blood said, shaking Rob's hand lethargically. "Glad to meet ya." He motioned toward one of the folding chairs and Rob sat down. Wyler wiped the perspiration from his chest, then draped the towel around his neck and slid onto the edge of the training table, alongside a large pizza and a six-pack of beer someone had just delivered.

"Want a brew?" he asked, popping the top on one of the cans.

"Thanks." Rob reached across and took the can from Wyler's big paw. "That's some show you put on."

"Yeah," Wyler admitted. "I used to wrestle in the Corps. Not that you'd know it, watching this. All I get to do in this business is act. Professional wrestling is all bullshit. You'd think everybody'd know that by now, but people take it seriously. I get about a hundred letters every week—fifty-fifty hate mail and fan mail: 'Dear Captain Blood, I hope you squeeze the head off The Hulk next week in Indianapolis.' 'Dear Captain Blood, I hope that you get cancer and die a horrible, painful slow death, because people like you don't deserve to live.' That kind of shit." Wyler took a long swig of beer and mopped his face with the towel. "Showmanship, that's what it's all about. You have to have a gimmick that'll stir up the crowd. For you or against you, it don't matter. It's all gimmicks. The guy with the best gimmick makes the most money. It's not a bad life. Nobody ever gets hurt, except by accident."

"Harris McWhirter recommended you," Rob said. "He said he talked to you and you told him you were interested in what we're doing."

Wyler pulled open the top of the pizza box and ripped off a slice. "That's true."

"Tell me about yourself."

"I was in the Marines," Wyler said. He tapped his eye patch. "I lost this during the Tet offensive."

"McWhirter said you were a POW."

Captain Blood nodded, his one watery blue eye squinting at Rob knowingly. "This guy you're going after—it's your brother, isn't it."

"McWhirter tell you that?"

"No. I figured it out for myself. I know your old man's been trying to find him for years. Word gets around about things like that."

"Why do you want to go? Looks like you've got a good thing here. Why leave it for something as risky as a rescue mission?"

"Excitement. It gets in your blood."

Rob considered the remark. A lot of men would go for just that reason, but he wasn't sure that Wyler was one of them. "I'm leery of hiring volunteers," he admitted.

Wyler's eye widened in surprise. "What are you going to do? Draft some guys to go with you?"

"I don't want adventurers on this trip. I don't trust people motivated by the thrill of danger."

The big wrestler nodded slowly. "You got a point," he admitted, tearing off another slice of pizza. "Maybe 'excitement' isn't exactly the right word. But something gets in your blood. As bad as it was in Nam, and that was pretty fucking bad, it never leaves you, because it was the most intense experience you ever had. After what you've been through, home can be a big comedown. You understand what I'm saying?"

"Sounds like you're romanticizing it after the fact. You wouldn't want to be a POW again, would you?"

"I didn't say I'd want to do it all over again," Wyler countered. "What I'm saying is that important things happen to you. You find out your limits—what you're capable of. You find out who you are."

"Why was coming home such a big letdown, then?"

Wyler cracked his knuckles on the edge of the training table. "It was pretty hard to readjust. Suddenly you didn't have to live on the edge anymore. Somehow you expected something when you got home that wasn't there. You know, some kind of reward, some kind of gratitude for what you went through. But we were treated like shit. It was hard to take."

"You seem to have survived it all right," Rob said.

"Some scars don't show," Wyler replied. "That doesn't mean they're not real. The day I got off the bus in Madison, Wisconsin—that's where I grew up—I was so goddamn glad to be home and still be alive that my insides hurt, just from the sheer fucking joy of it. I walked down Main Street, still in my uniform. I felt like a real hero. I imagined they'd have a parade for me, make speeches, that kind of thing. They never did." Wyler took another slice of pizza. "You know what happened instead? This college girl walks up to me and spits in my face and screams these fuckin' obscenities at me. She calls me a killer. Me, a POW, for chrissake! It made me physically sick. It freaked me out for days. I couldn't understand the hate. It was so fucking unjust. That was nine years ago, and I can still hear that broad's voice in my head."

Rob focused on the can of beer in his hand. He imagined he might have done the same thing as that college girl, and he felt a secret embarrassment.

Wyler chewed on the pizza thoughtfully. "Anyway," he admitted, exhaling a deep sigh as if to expel the bitter memory, "it turns out I have a better reason for wanting to join you."

Rob waited for him to tell him what it was, but Wyler seemed to want to keep him in suspense. He gazed at the remaining slice left in the pizza box, apparently trying to decide how to best present his case.

"I knew your brother," he said, finally. "I served with him. Fifth Marines, Second Battalion, Charlie Company. We were captured together. I was even in the same POW camp with him for a while."

When Rob had recovered from his astonishment he leaned forward in the metal chair, anxious to hear more. "Do you know what happened to him?"

"No. They separated him from the rest of us after a few months. I never saw him again."

"Did you hear anything about him?"

"From time to time. Not much, though."

"What did you hear?"

"Different things. Some said he was collaborating. That's why he didn't come home with the rest of us. Some said he was tortured to death because he wouldn't be brainwashed. There were a lot of stories."

"You think he's alive?"

"Oh yeah."

"What makes you so sure?"

"They'd never kill him."

"Why not?"

"Too valuable."

"What do you mean?"

"It was your brother's own theory, come to think of it. He knew a lot about Indochina. All about Ho Chi Minh, the war against the French, and all that. He said they wouldn't kill him, because he was worth too much to them alive. What the gooks always did, he said, was hold hostages for ransom. They did it with the French. He told me they even held the corpse of General de Gaulle's own grandson for years. I checked that out later, when I got back. He was right. Anyway, Grunwald sensed, before anybody else, that America was getting out of the war. Most of us would be repatriated, he said. But some of us they'd hold for ransom, and he knew he'd be one because of who his father was. His money and all. They'd use him as a bargaining chip. Cash him in years later, maybe. Or maybe never. But they'd never let him go for nothing."

"My father *did* try to buy him back, several years ago. He went to the Vietnamese government and offered them millions. They refused it."

"Just goes to show you how smart they were to hold your brother. Maybe your old man didn't offer enough. Maybe they figure if they hold out, the price will go up." Wyler took the last slice of pizza and gulped it down. "But money isn't the only reason they'd hold him," he continued. "There's worse reasons."

"What are they?"

"They might be afraid to release him."

"Why?"

"You never read about it anywhere, but of all five hundred and ninety-one of us POWs repatriated in 1973, not one of us was suffering from any injuries. Not one of us."

"So?"

"It kind of defies the law of averages, don't it? I saw guys beat to death in camp. I knew two or three who were permanently crippled by torture. None of those guys came back. The North Vietnamese kept them. They didn't want the world to see what they'd done to them."

"You think they tortured Billy?"

"I never saw them actually hurt him when he was with us, but I think eventually they must have. He was a prime candidate for it."

"Why?"

Wyler, still sweating heavily, mopped his chest and forearms with the towel again. "You don't know your brother very well, do you."

"I thought I did. But I'm beginning to wonder."

"Billy Grunwald was what you'd call a natural leader. Every man in his outfit was sort of fanatical about him."

"Fanatical?"

Wyler scratched his brow in search of the right words. "Devoted to him. They'd die for him."

"Would *you* have died for him?"

"I almost did. Twice."

Rob waited for him to explain.

"He was only a lieutenant," Wyler said, his voice suddenly a little shaky with emotion. "Young rich kid from Harvard, at that. Most of us grunts would chew guys like that to shit in no time. But he was different. He had a way about him. He knew what to do. How to act. How to survive. He set a standard and made the rest of us live up to it. So we looked to him to call the shots. You understand what I'm saying?"

Rob tried to digest Wyler's statement. It seemed incredible that his brother could have inspired such devotion. "How did you get captured?"

"They ambushed our patrol at a place called Long Ba, in the Central Highlands. We moved into the ville one morning because we'd been getting a lot of trouble from it—booby traps, land mines, snipers. We knew Charlie was holed up in there, but it took us weeks to get permission to go in and pacify it. So we hit it hard and fast, grabbed some prisoners and a big cache of weapons. But we walked into a goddamn trap. A whole division of NVA regulars surrounded the place and cut us off. They laid down a sheet of fire so thick we couldn't even get choppers in. They slaughtered us—and they wiped out most of the population of the village as well. Twenty of us survived and they marched us for about a week. All the way into North fucking Vietnam. Some of us would never have made it, but Billy held us together, kept up our morale."

Wyler finished another beer and threw the can into the wastebasket behind him. "Of course, the gooks zeroed in on your brother right away," he continued. "They wanted to break his spirit, humiliate him, degrade him. They figured that if they could get to him, the rest of

132 / TOM HYMAN

us would cave in, too. They tried everything. They gave him extra privileges, extra food. He refused them. They put him in solitary—a hole in the ground filled with water and rats—and he came out just as tough as he went in. They took away his food, his clothes, tied him up, did everything but kick the shit out of him. They didn't want to torture him, because they were trying to show us what humane, forgiving gooks they were. But it all backfired. It was something, the way he held out against them. Remember that guy in *The Bridge on the River Kwai*—what was his name?"

"Alec Guinness?"

"Right. He was like him. He made a fool out of them. When they realized that, they just removed him from the scene. I don't know what happened to him after that. We never saw him again."

Rob watched Wyler's one good eye shift its focus nervously about the room. He seemed agitated, almost frightened. Finally, the burly wrestler held his beer can up in front of him as if about to offer a toast. "You love your brother, don't you?" he asked. "Isn't that the reason you want to find him?"

Rob hesitated, then said yes.

"Well, he saved my life—twice," Wyler said, shaking his fist. "During that battle at the ville and then again later, on that march. So I owe him twice. I want to find him just as much as you do."

Rob took a sip from his can of beer. It had grown warm in his hand. Clearly, Wyler seemed like an excellent candidate for the mission. He was obviously tough and experienced, had the necessary military skills, and, according to McWhirter, had been decorated twice for bravery. And he knew Billy. He was an obvious choice.

But Rob's gut instinct about him was negative. Years of living by his wits in Canada and Europe had taught Rob how to read people, and he suspected that Wyler was hiding something important from him. The man's Captain Blood routine, as he himself had confessed only moments ago, demonstrated nothing so much as his acting ability, his skill at creating illusion. So his story was persuasive. But Rob didn't believe that Wyler had any affection for his brother Billy at all.

Rob should have trusted his instinct, but he didn't. "I'll take you on," he said.

15

New York City

William Grunwald inhaled and exhaled in short, strenuous gasps. His arm muscles tensed and quivered, and the veins in his neck bulged. James Safier sat watching him, tapping a pen impatiently against the top of a black leather notebook.

"That's enough!" Grunwald exclaimed, letting the Nautilus weights clank back down into place. He grabbed a towel from the bench beside him and wiped the sweat from his face and upper torso. Grunwald believed in keeping fit. He exercised in his private gym next to his office every day and, when he had time, swam laps in the Olympic-sized swimming pool he had installed, along with a large gym, for his employees, in the basement of the office building. Fitness for Grunwald possessed an importance that went beyond his concern for health. It was an atavistic obsession. Like a superstitious tribal chieftain, he felt it a vital component of his managerial power. Staying strong physically meant staying on top. "What time is it?" he demanded.

"Nine-twenty," Safier replied, straightening his vest. "The Florida bankers are already here."

"Keep them waiting for a while. What else?"

"The Dutch shipping firm makes its presentation at ten."

"What are they selling?"

"Air-cargo containers. And at eleven you've got the Brazilians again."

"What's their mood?"

"I think they're about to crack. They know that if they don't make a deal on the Ludwig holdings soon, they'll be in trouble. They owe the IMF five hundred million by the end of the month, and we know they're looking everywhere for cash."

"Let's lower our offer, then. Fifteen million. Including the paper mills."

Safier penned a notation in his book. "Lunch is downtown," he continued. "The Sachs investment group. At three we're flying to Chicago. The stamping plant there is facing a strike. We're meeting with management for dinner at six. They want your okay on some compromises."

"Can't we do that over the phone?"

"It's pretty sensitive. They were hoping you'd meet with the union heads informally."

"Hell," Grunwald muttered. "What a way to end the day. Any more reactions to the hearings?"

"It's looking good," Safier said, smiling broadly. "*Time* magazine says you're a shoo-in. It thinks Glass's interrogation of you backfired." He glanced down at a clipping he had pulled out of the notebook. "I'll read it to you: 'William Grunwald stepped into the arena of public scrutiny for the first time last week, under the glare of more than TV lights. Liberal Democrat Senator Samuel Glass, out to convict him before the world as a corrupt and unfeeling capitalist, ended up looking and sounding more like Torquemada than the champion of the working classes. Grunwald parried Glass brilliantly in the early rounds, easily deflecting the senator's intimations of shady business ethics. Glass, unwilling to quit when he was behind, then turned his hostile questioning to Grunwald's past in Germany. The Jewish industrialist, who immigrated to the U.S. in 1945, the sole family survivor of the Nazi death camps, squirmed in obvious discomfort under Glass's surprisingly tasteless attack. Many who had opposed Grunwald's nomination because of his arch-conservative background and his lack of diplomatic experience and skill came away from the hearings feeling sympathetic toward him. It seemed that Glass had accomplished what even the most persuasive arm-twisters in the White House were having a hard time doing—making William Grunwald popular. Glass, himself a Jew, admitted to one close colleague that he had overplayed his hand. Observers on the Hill now believe Grunwald's confirmation to be all but certain.' "

Grunwald grinned in obvious enjoyment. "I hope to hell they're right, Jim."

Safier tucked the clipping back inside the notebook. "The consensus is you'll have no problem."

Grunwald shook his head wonderingly. "It's funny what can happen, isn't it? It turns out that my little panic there at the end of the hearing was the best thing I could have done."

"It was more than a little panic," Safier said. "It was an anxiety attack. You've been having a lot of them lately."

Grunwald scoffed. "You're making too much of them. Next you'll be telling me I should see a shrink."

Safier shrugged and let the matter drop.

Grunwald wondered if his assistant really did care about his health or if he was just playing politics. He wished desperately that he could tell Safier the truth about the attacks. It would be such an enormous relief to share the burden with someone he trusted. But there were some things that could never be trusted to anyone. Who could possibly understand and forgive, after all these years? No one. No one in the world. "What about Rob?" he asked. "And the rescue mission?"

"He seems to be working quite hard. He's run up ten thousand in airplane fares in the past two weeks, chasing down prospects."

"Is he getting anywhere?"

"He's hired three men."

"How long do you think he'll last?"

"He seems determined," Safier answered carefully. "I warned him about spending too much, but other than that . . . He does seem determined."

Grunwald threw the towel down on the bench and stood up. "I'm afraid it'll come to nothing," he said. "If he was half the man Billy is, I'd believe it possible." He removed his trunks and stood unselfconsciously nude in the middle of the small gym. "But I have to give him his chance."

"I'm worried about word of the mission getting out," Safier said. "It could do you harm."

Grunwald scratched his cheek. "I've thought about that. It could embarrass the administration, I suppose, but the larger effect should be positive. If it comes to light, it'll look good to the public. A family working together, taking risks to rescue one of its own. And if by some miracle Robbie succeeds, then we'll have a family full of heroes. It'll be the best damned war story since Kennedy's PT-109."

Safier nodded glumly.

"I'd better get into the shower," Grunwald said. "Anything else?"

"I'm still disturbed about this rescue mission," Safier repeated. "Some ominous things are happening."

"You mean the Vietnamese refugee? I thought you accepted the hospital's explanation."

"There's another death now. That two-bit hustler who was in here last week with the tape and the transcript. Brian Duffy. He committed suicide. Jumped from a hotel balcony in Nice."

"Any reason?"

"None we know of."

"A coincidence, Jim. A con artist like Duffy was bound to self-destruct sooner or later. No surprise there."

"You've told me many times," Safier replied, "never to believe in coincidences."

"Assume the worst, then," Grunwald said. "That both of them were murdered for that tape and transcript. I don't believe it, but let's assume it. What's the motive?"

"Well . . . either to get the information from them or to prevent them from spreading it."

"That's right. And it would almost certainly be someone who wanted it to sell it. Who would be concerned enough about the information spreading to kill two people?"

"How about the Vietnamese government?" Safier suggested. "It could embarrass them."

Grunwald shook his head. "They don't embarrass easily."

"Still assuming the worst," Safier persisted. "If someone really is after the material, then we're the next logical targets. You, me, Rob. We have the stuff."

Grunwald laughed. "What point would be served by taking the tape back from us? Even if it were the Vietnamese, as you suggest, what good would it do them? For all they know, we may have shared this information with hundreds of people. We may have taken it to the U.S. government. How many people are they going to try to kill? If the Vietnamese were worried about Billy being rescued—and I don't for a minute believe they are—all they'd have to do to prevent it would be to move him somewhere else."

Safier nodded. "Should I tell your son about Duffy's death?"

"No. Let's not give him any excuses to quit. I'm sure he's not in any danger. Just keep a check on it yourself. If something more comes up, we'll decide what to do then."

"Okay."

"That it?"

Safier cleared his throat. "There is another matter I'd like to discuss with you, but it can wait until later."

Grunwald detected Safier's discomfort. "What is it, Jim?"

"Well, with your appointment virtually assured, we ought to start laying out the ground rules for how Grunwald Industries will be run during your absence. You know that officially you'll have to resign all your positions and have your stock put in a blind trust."

Grunwald smiled. "You're my man, Jim. You know that. You'll be in charge. We'll work out the details of how you report to me and when and so forth. But I intend to turn over the day-to-day operations of the company to you. And, as far as I know, this will have the solid support of all the division presidents."

"Thank you," Safier said, "for your confidence in me."

"Hell, what did you expect I'd do?" Grunwald chided him, heading toward the shower in the next room. "And to my future son-in-law, at that?"

Safier followed a few steps behind and watched as Grunwald twisted the shower control until he was obscured behind a heavy downpour of steaming hot water. "But suppose Billy comes home," he said, barely loud enough to be heard over the noise of the spray.

"That would be one hell of a day, wouldn't it?" Grunwald shouted back.

"What I mean is, if Rob does find him and he comes home, what happens? I mean, what sort of place will he have in the company?"

Grunwald let the water splash on his face. "That'd be up to him, of course," he replied, his voice muffled behind his hands. "He'd need some time to orient himself, I imagine. Decide what he wanted to do with his life. . . ." Grunwald found the soap and began scrubbing himself with it. "But as far as I'm concerned, if Billy comes home, he can have whatever the hell he wants."

"That's what I figured," Safier whispered.

16

Wilmington, Vermont

Howard Gilmore offered Rob his log cabin and its sixty surrounding acres of field and woodlands as a camp to train the rescue mission. The remote location made it ideal, and Rob accepted happily. He moved in on Monday, April 12, and while Gilmore rearranged the cabin for its new role, he shuttled the pickup back and forth over Hogback Mountain to Brattleboro, forty miles to the east, buying food, sleeping bags, boots, work clothes, and a large supply of Howard's Anchor Steam beer.

The other members of the team arrived later in the week—Harris McWhirter on Thursday, Frank Wyler on Friday. Saturday and Sunday were spent getting settled in and adjusting to one another's company in the cramped quarters of the cabin.

Sunday night Rob convened the first formal meeting round the cabin's stone fireplace. "You all know what we're here for," he said, coming directly to the point. "From this moment on, Harris McWhirter is in charge. It'll be his responsibility to train us for the mission."

McWhirter stood up and opened a dog-eared notebook he had been scribbling in for the past few hours, then launched into the program he had worked out, biting off his thoughts in a string of short sentences.

"We've been talking about all this over the past couple of days," he said. "So you have some idea of what's coming. The goal of the mission is to make a prisoner snatch. All rescue missions are difficult. This one will be more difficult than most. In fact, it'll be a real bitch. We'll have to operate deep inside enemy territory—without outside support and with no certainty about the status of our target. We'll have to work out the best possible plan of attack, then get ourselves in shape to carry it out."

McWhirter paused and glanced down at his notebook. "We'll divide the day into three parts. The mornings, from six to noon, we'll spend getting in shape. This'll consist of endurance training, weapons practice, and tracking and survival techniques. All of you will have a lot to learn in a short time. Wyler and Gilmore, you're going to have to unlearn half of what you think you know. And you, Grunwald, are going to spend the next weeks wishing you were never born.

"The afternoons, let's say one to six, we'll use to work on the specific details of the mission—gathering intelligence, evaluating it, getting our supplies together, arranging our timetable, and so on. The evenings we'll save for sweating out the plan itself. There'll be a thousand details to worry about. I'm assigning each of you special areas of responsibility."

McWhirter pointed a finger at Frank Wyler, sitting on the sofa with a bored look on his face. "Frank, you'll be in charge of the endurance training program. Put us through the standard Parris Island boot camp, minus the drill instructor and the marching bullshit."

Wyler nodded.

"Howard, you'll be responsible for intelligence gathering. We have to pull together a lot of information to make this mission go, and some of it will be hard to get."

Gilmore scratched his beard and nodded.

"Rob, you're the sucker with the bank account, so you'll have to handle the logistics. We'll need a lot of stuff—special clothes, food, and equipment. I'll give you some lists later. It'll be up to you to assemble what we need."

Rob nodded.

"As for me," McWhirter said, "I'll be giving a lot of lectures. Attendance will be compulsory." He turned a page in his notebook. "We'll rotate the cooking, shopping, and cleanup chores. We'll be on a seven-day schedule with no time off. Wyler and Gilmore, you both ought to try to lose about ten, fifteen pounds. Grunwald, you ought to gain that much. I don't care what's on the menu, but let's keep the drinking down to a few beers at night. If we stick to that piss Gilmore buys, that should be no problem."

McWhirter got the expected laugh.

"That's about it," he concluded, closing the notebook and tossing it onto a chair. "All we need now is a target date. I say thirty days from tonight. That's optimum. Any shorter and we might not be ready. Any longer and we'll be overtrained and flat. We can adjust it later if we have to, but let's try to be ready then. Tomorrow morning will be D-day minus thirty."

At five-thirty on D-day minus thirty, Grunwald, Gilmore, and Wyler sat down to breakfast. McWhirter was nowhere to be found.

Gilmore picked up a note from the table and read it aloud: " 'I borrowed the van,' he says. 'See you all tonight.' "

"We're off to a great start," Rob muttered. "What the hell is he up to?"

Gilmore put down the note and adjusted his glasses on his nose. "We'll find out tonight, I guess. Meanwhile, we can devote the whole day to calisthenics. Right, Frank?"

Wyler fixed his one eye on Gilmore and snarled.

McWhirter finally appeared at breakfast on the following morning.

"When did you get back?" Rob demanded.

"A couple of hours ago. I got nailed in Massachusetts for speeding."

"In my van!" Gilmore moaned.

"You mind telling us what's going on?"

"After breakfast," he replied, mysteriously.

At six o'clock McWhirter led the others out to Gilmore's van, pulled open the rear door, and unveiled, beneath a heavy green plastic tarpaulin, a stack of rifles, several big boxes of ammunition, and an assortment of pistols, grenades, and mines.

"Can't do any weapons training without the weapons," he said, a big grin lighting his face.

Rob stared at the cache, bug-eyed. "Where the hell did you get all this?"

"You don't ask," McWhirter replied.

"And you got stopped for speeding in Massachusetts?" Gilmore asked, his deep voice trembling. "In my van? With this in the back?"

McWhirter nodded.

"They have a mandatory one-year jail sentence for possession of firearms," Gilmore said, still white-faced with shock. "What'd you have done if that cop had searched the van?"

McWhirter hauled out three of the rifles and handed them around. "Probably shot him on the spot," he replied. "It was late at night. No witnesses."

"Jesus Christ!" Gilmore bellowed.

"He's pulling your leg, Howard," Rob said.

"But still . . ."

McWhirter grabbed a box of shells from the van and hefted it onto his shoulder. "Come on, you assholes. Help me unload this stuff. We've got a long day ahead of us."

New York City

James Safier poured himself a bourbon and leaned against the parapet of the large wraparound terrace of his Sutton Place penthouse. Sarah wanted him to give up the apartment after they were married. She had her mind set on buying a huge co-op duplex on Fifth Avenue in the Seventies. The asking price was insane—two million dollars. And the maintenance was three thousand a month. Even with their combined six-figure incomes, it would be a strain meeting the payments. But she was right. Neither this bachelor pad nor her little place on East Seventy-first Street would be adequate for the two of them together. They needed something that would accurately reflect their professional and social status. Something that anticipated the future.

The future.

Safier tasted the bourbon. It was his fifth of the day. Or was it number six? He was beginning to drink too much. A sure sign of stress. He looked southwest across Manhattan Island at the tower of the Empire State Building, its top floors bathed in white light from the banks of spots on the eighty-sixth floor. Suddenly the lights blinked out. Midnight, Safier thought, and checked his watch. Yes. They always went out at midnight. A new calendar day had begun.

The only cloud on the golden horizon of that future was so small as to be almost invisible. But it was there, and it threatened to grow bigger. Safier looked west, over Manhattan, to the glittering pattern of lights made by the wall of high-rise apartments across the Hudson River. In his mind's eye he traveled far past them, across the continent, over the vast global curve of the Pacific Ocean to the distant shores of Indochina, where the new day was already into its afternoon.

If Billy Grunwald was still alive, he would be somewhere in that afternoon.

It had been a long time since he had seen Billy, but Safier still remembered the intense sense of intimidation he had always felt in his presence. Would he feel that way today, he wondered, if Billy came home? In twelve years, after all, he had risen far in the world, while Billy had languished, presumably, in some savage prison, his once promising future crumbling with the passage of time.

Billy's coming home was so damned unlikely, but even the thought of it made a knot in Safier's stomach. If Billy came home, he would get it all, everything Safier had spent his life struggling for. Grunwald wouldn't admit it in so many words, but Safier could read the old man's emotions better than the old man himself: Billy was his weakness. And if he came home, he would get it all and Safier would be shouldered aside. Even his marriage to Sarah would not save him.

It was so unfair. He, Safier, was the real son, the dutiful son. Had not Grunwald picked him himself? Taken him from his anonymous childhood and made him into a true son? Billy and Rob were mere accidents of birth, the haphazard commingling of genes in the middle of the night. But he was picked, consciously chosen. And in return for that extraordinary elevation, he had devoted his life to building Grunwald's empire, while Billy and Rob had played no role. No role at all.

In a couple of months Grunwald would be in Israel, he and Sarah would be married, and the control of Grunwald Industries would effectively be his. He was so close to fulfillment.

Safier rattled the cubes of ice in the bourbon and pressed the cold rim of the glass to his lips. Grunwald himself had taught him: never leave to chance what you yourself can do. And all he had to do to assure his future was derail Rob Grunwald's rescue mission. No mission, no Billy. It was as simple as that.

He would have to proceed carefully. If he got caught at it, he would be in serious trouble. And he didn't underestimate Rob Grunwald. He despised him, but he didn't let his feelings color his objective assessment of the man. Rob was misdirected, even self-destructive, but he was a Grunwald and he possessed the classic Grunwald trait— that fanatic, stubborn willfulness.

Rob Grunwald had misspent his life tragically, but he had done it out of an excess of rebelliousness and pride, not weakness. Safier had considered it carefully. The same energy and willpower, the same determination that had propelled William Grunwald to the top were evident in his son Rob, albeit perverted by their context. Rob had chosen to live life the hard way, constantly skirting the edge of ruin. He was a smart, resourceful outlaw, with an outlaw's mentality. Not one to be taken lightly.

He had watched Rob put together his rescue team with growing apprehension. What he had initially dismissed as a fantasy was fast becoming a reality. Rob Grunwald seemed poised to make a credible attempt to bring Billy home.

Bring Billy home and dash all of Safier's dreams.

The chill night air made him shiver. He drank the remainder of the bourbon and went inside to his bedroom and sat on the edge of the bed, thinking.

Finally, he picked up the telephone and dialed a number in Alexandria, Virginia. It rang five times before a sleepy male voice answered.

"Hello?"

"Joel?"

"Yes?"

"It's Jim Safier."

"Hi, Jim. What's up? Kinda late for you to be calling, isn't it?"

"I have an important favor to ask of you."

"Business or personal?"

"A little of both. I have a problem and I'm kind of groping for the right thing to do. You know the bureaucracy down there, and I need you to put me in touch with the right party."

Wilmington, Vermont

Harris McWhirter laid the rifles out on the grass in a neat row, like giant matchsticks, and invited the others to kneel down beside him. "We'll be picking up our real weapons in Southeast Asia," he said. "I don't know yet what they'll be. Depends on what's available, but it'll be one of these you see in front of you. So, before the month is out, you want to be familiar with everything here."

McWhirter touched the barrel of the first rifle with his index finger. "The M-16," he said. "Made by Colt. Standard issue for the army and the Marines. There are five million of them floating around. We left at least a million of them behind in Vietnam. Like most American products these days, the M-16 is basically a piece of shit. The army hates it; the Marines hate it. More men were killed by Charlie while trying to unjam this son of a bitch than are buried at Arlington National Cemetery. If the Winchester won the West, the M-16 lost Vietnam."

McWhirter's finger moved to the next rifle. "Grunwald Arms GA-15. I'll say one thing for your old man, Rob. He makes a good lightweight submachine gun. But he charges too much for it. We might run into these, though, because the Thai army uses them."

His finger moved on: "This is the nine-millimeter Israeli Uzi. Very compact, good safety features and balance. Cheaply manufactured with stampings and plastic parts, but still a popular gun. Our Secret Service uses them.

"This is the nine-millimeter Mark V British Sten Gun. Been around since the forties, so they're apt to turn up anywhere. It's reliable, rugged, and easy to maintain.

"Here's another nine-millimeter, the Swedish Carl Gustaf. This fires a special high-velocity armor-piercing cartridge. It's one of the strongest, best-designed submachine guns made.

"This is the French MAT-49. Also nine-millimeter. Has a couple of unique features—a grip safety and a folding magazine housing. Especially good weapon for airborne troops. The French left a lot of these behind in Algeria and Vietnam."

McWhirter reached for the last rifle in the row and picked it up. "But this is the champ," he said, cradling the weapon in his hands. "The Russian Kalashnikov. Its correct designation is the 'AK Assault Rifle.' It's gas-operated, the barrel is chrome-lined, and it's much more accurate than any of these other weapons because it fires 7.62-millimeter rifle rounds. The others use pistol ammunition. It's also much better made. No stampings in this baby. All the parts are machined. With any luck, this is the one we'll be carrying on the mission."

McWhirter stood up, demonstrated how the metal stock unfolded, then placed it against his hip. "Right here," he continued, gesturing with a finger, "above the trigger guard, is the safety lever. It has three settings. All the way up is 'safe.' Halfway down is full automatic. All the way down, semiautomatic."

McWhirter pulled a loaded magazine out of the pocket of his pants and slid it into place. "When you load it," he said, "push the safety up to 'safe.' Draw the bolt handle back, like this, and then release it. The bolt will move forward and chamber a round." He brought the rifle up to his shoulder and aimed it at the target he had set up across the field—a bale of hay propped on end with a white sheet tied to its side. On the sheet he had drawn the outline of a figure. "Select full or semi"—he clicked the lever to the mid-position—"and let 'er rip."

A series of rapid concussions, so close together that they sounded like one stuttering explosion, rent the bucolic Vermont air and put to flight a screaming crowd of crows from the nearby woods.

In the ringing silence that followed, the four men trudged across the field to examine the target. From a distance of a hundred yards, McWhirter had sewn a neat seam of bullet holes across the sheet, bisecting the painted figure diagonally across its chest. Wyler uttered a low whistle of appreciation. Gilmore tugged at his beard. Rob shook his head.

As they walked back across the field, McWhirter handed the Kalashnikov to Rob. "You try it now," he said.

"Let someone else go first."

"No," McWhirter insisted. "You're going to need the most practice."

Rob accepted the weapon reluctantly. It felt heavy and dangerous in his hands. Back at the spot from which McWhirter had first fired, he hefted it awkwardly to his shoulder.

"Try semiautomatic first," McWhirter instructed.

Rob nodded and pressed the safety lever all the way down. He closed one eye and squinted along the top of the barrel with his other. He brought the sight in line with the figure on the sheet. It seemed an enormous distance away. He hesitated. The alarming boom of his father's Purdy 12-gauge shotgun sounded in his memory. He had always felt sorry for the birds his father shot, the poor blasted bundles of beautiful feathers, the sagging necks and the closed eyes. To his father's disgust, Rob could never eat them.

He squeezed the trigger. The recoil kicked the barrel toward the sky and jolted his shoulder as if someone had punched him.

"Don't let it kick," McWhirter said. "Hold it down."

Rob tried again, with the same result. After half a dozen shots, he clicked the safety up to full automatic and, in frustration, pulled the trigger back and sprayed a blizzard of bullets in the general direction of the bale of hay, wrestling to hold the rifle on the target as it bucked in his arms like a live animal.

"You're firing over the target. Hold it down," McWhirter said, in his maddeningly casual tone.

"I'll probably never hit the goddamned target," Rob cursed, his ears ringing from the explosions.

"As soon as you hold the weapon the way I told you to, you will."

"And if you'd painted a bull's-eye on that sheet," Rob yelled back, "the way I asked you to, instead of a human being, I wouldn't have any problem!"

McWhirter produced a tight-lipped grin. "You're not going to be shooting at bull's-eyes in Vietnam."

Rob glared at McWhirter and then at the recalcitrant rifle in his hands, and felt an insane hatred for it welling up inside him. "I'm not going to be shooting at people, either, for chrissake!" He threw the rifle on the ground and stood there, cursing under his breath. He squeezed his eyes shut and bunched his fists, digging his nails into the palms of his hands, fighting to choke down the rage. In the wake of the racketing gunfire, the sudden tense stillness seemed eerie. McWhirter folded his arms. Gilmore and Wyler stood to the side, watching in awkward silence.

"Let me put it to you like this, Mr. Grunwald," McWhirter said, biting his words out like shards of ice. "I don't intend to spend one fucking minute in the middle of Indochina with some millionaire's son who thinks he can liberate a prison without even knowing how to defend himself, let alone protect his buddies. If you want somebody else to do your shooting for you, I suggest you stay home and hire somebody to go in your place. Otherwise, you better pick up that rifle and try again. If you don't, I'm walking out of here."

Half a minute ticked by. The angry flock of crows cawed in the distance. Rob finally bent down and picked up the rifle. The barrel, still hot to the touch, was coated with mud and grass. He wiped it off slowly, using the tail of his shirt.

He saw the others watching him and felt suddenly ashamed of himself. "Okay," he repeated, in a low voice. "Show me how to hold it again."

Washington, D.C.

It was late at night, and Mr. Alvin Payne Walker, director of the officially nonexistent military-intelligence service AISA, lay awake in his bed—a big, canopied antique that he had inherited from his mother many years ago. The five rooms of his apartment on a high floor in the Watergate were all dark. The blinds were tightly shut and heavy drapes were drawn across them to cut out even the least leak of illumination from the streets and nearby buildings. A twenty-four-hour guard was posted outside his front door, and the exterior walls of the apartment were protected by a highly sophisticated security system—sealed, in effect, behind an electronic envelope that could detect and intercept any eavesdropping or intrusion.

Walker's head was propped up by several pillows, and his eyes were focused on a six-foot-high television screen on the wall across from the foot of the bed. The surface of the screen flickered and changed rapidly as a series of high-altitude photographs, taken from space by an S-70 satellite, paraded swiftly past. At a certain point, Walker stopped the parade, backed it up several frames, then settled on one particular image. It showed a two-mile-wide area of hilly Vermont countryside, just north of the town of Wilmington. Walker punched in the number of the grid he wanted enlarged, and watched as a one-inch-square segment of the photograph gradually expanded until it filled the entire screen.

Now he could see a two-story log cabin situated at the edge of a large field. Two vehicles were parked near it, and out in the middle of the field, four human shadows, stretched long and thin by the late-afternoon sun, were clearly visible. Walker pushed his tongue against the inside of his cheek and stared at the figures for a long time, thinking.

Walker's enormous screen was the figurative center of a vast and unique electronics espionage web, a one-of-a-kind technological marvel that had been secretly designed, built, and installed in his apartment at considerable taxpayer expense. From a computer-control panel at the side of the bed, he could call up almost anything, from the most obscure library reference to the most secret government document; from any TV broadcast anywhere in the world to the most highly restricted data banks of the National Security Agency and the CIA.

This extraordinary apparatus served Walker as a kind of compensation for his handicaps. He was possessed of a morose, uncongenial disposition, and his frail, lethargic physical constitution was the victim of a collection of disorders, including chronic asthma, gross obesity, and severe heliophobia—a sensitivity to sunlight so extreme that he was forced to spend most of his waking hours the same way he spent his sleeping ones, in the dark.

He maintained a suite of offices and a staff in a sub-basement level of the Pentagon, but he was rarely ever seen there anymore. He directed his secret little bureaucracy entirely from the glassed-off back seat of his limousine and the private recesses of this plush cave in the Watergate complex.

He had physically withdrawn from the world, but through his electronic web he was still in constant touch with its every breath and whisper. He thought of himself as a kind of omniscient ghost, an immaterial being who could transport himself, invisibly, anywhere upon the face of the earth, without leaving the womblike protection of his apartment. Of course, his desire for anonymity suited his position perfectly. Increasingly, as he grew in stature and power within the ranks of the intelligence services, he allowed himself to be seen by fewer and fewer people, thus turning his infirmities to his advantage. By shrouding his very existence in mystery, he had enhanced his freedom of action and his control over others.

Walker punched another series of instructions into his bedside console, and the four shadows in the field disappeared, to be replaced by green phosphorescent lines of text. Walker scrolled the text rapidly, letting screenfuls of it flicker by, then stopping, reading briefly, and scrolling further. Finally he found a section that interested him, and he read it slowly, scrolling it up one line at a time:

The goal of the mission is to make a prisoner snatch. All rescue missions are difficult. This one will be more difficult than most. In fact, it'll be a real bitch. We'll have to operate deep inside enemy territory— without outside support and with no certainty about the status of our target. We'll have to work out the best possible plan of attack, then get ourselves in shape to carry it out.

Walker scrolled further, then stopped again:

But this is the champ. The Russian Kalashnikov. Its correct designation is the "AK Assault Rifle." It's gas-operated, the barrel is chrome-lined, and it's much more accurate than any of these other weapons because it fires 7.62-millimeter rifle rounds. The others use pistol ammunition. It's also much better made. No stampings in this baby. All the parts are machined. With any luck, this is the one we'll be carrying on the mission.

Walker had read enough. He snorted in derision and punched the control panel forcefully with his fat index finger. The words disappeared and the screen faded to black.

Walker lay in the dark, his hands folded across his large belly, and concentrated his mental energies. He must do something quickly. The crowning achievement of his exceptional career, one of the boldest covert operations in the history of modern espionage, stood in great jeopardy.

It was too late to prevent the spread of the information in Brian Duffy's interview. Too many people already shared it. And he couldn't ask Short to just go on killing people. It would serve no useful purpose. What he must do now, he realized, was discredit that information.

17

Wilmington, Vermont

"How about going in from the South China Sea?" Rob suggested. "It'll save us a lot of travel."

"Can't be done," McWhirter replied, pushing aside his dinner plate to make room on the table for his notebook. "Unless you're the U.S. Navy. The coastline is watched. We'd never make it onto the beach. And even if we did, we'd sure as hell never make it across to the Laos border. And that's where your brother is."

"Why not lease helicopters in northeast Thailand?" Wyler said. "They have a shitload at Udorn. From there it's only about two hundred miles across Laos to the Khe Sanh area. We could do the whole snatch from the choppers. Be in and out in a few hours."

"That won't work, either," McWhirter responded. "Helicopters attract too much attention. And we need time to study the prison-camp area up close. If we blunder in with whirlybirds, they'll hear us coming all the way from Thailand. We won't even have time to pick out a landing zone, never mind recon the target."

"What does that leave us?" Rob asked.

"We have to do a walk-in through Laos. There's no other way. And we need the Laotians, anyway. The four of us can't attack a POW compound and expect to get anything except killed."

"I thought we'd be hiring Thais," Gilmore said.

"No good. Only the Laotians can get us across Laos. And even that's not certain. We'll hire men from an anti-Pathet Lao tribe. Either the Meo or the Souei."

"How are we going to find them?" Wyler demanded.

"I have the contacts. I'll have to make a separate trip over there first and scout the Thai–Laotian border, anyway."

"What about weapons?" Rob asked. "Will we have to supply theirs, too?"

"Hell, no. They'll be supplying us. We can't bring guns through Thailand. That's another mistake the earlier missions made. Thai customs will search us head to toe, mouth to asshole. We have to be clean."

"What about radios, then?" Wyler wanted to know. "We'd better get looking for them. The good ones are hard to come by."

"We'll take HT-1s. That's all."

"Shit, those are just walkie-talkies, with a mile range," Wyler complained. "How the hell do we communicate with the outside world?"

"We don't. If we get in trouble, we'll have to get ourselves out. Nobody's going to swoop in to rescue us, anyway. MACV and his Jolly Green Giants left Nam years ago."

"I don't understand," Rob said, joining the argument. "If we aren't able to get out, our only chance of telling the world what we've found will be by radio. There may be other MIAs in there with Billy. We've got to be able to let people in the West know."

McWhirter shrugged. "It would be nice, but we can't risk it. If they find anything bigger on us than an HT-1, the Thais will toss us in the slammer. That's what happened to Bo Gritz. Even the five-mile-range FM radios, like the AN/PRC-25s, will get us in trouble. And any kind of special shortwave device, like a burst transceiver, is as bad as being caught with a box of hand grenades."

"I don't know," Gilmore said, adjusting his glasses on his nose. "I tend to agree with them. Some kind of radio seems essential, even if only for an emergency. Surely we can figure out a way to hide one?"

McWhirter shook his head patiently. "You can't hide from Big Ears."

"Big Ears?"

"If we use a radio in there, Russian spy satellites will pick us up. And so will Vietnamese ground stations. They'll home in on our signal. And then come and get us."

"You're beginning to convince me," Rob admitted. "What about the prison camp itself? How do we recognize it when we get there?"

"If our source has his location right, it's a remote spot," McWhirter answered. "It'll most likely be the only thing around. But that's not what you ought to be worrying about."

"No?"

"We don't know anything about conditions at the camp. How many guards, how many prisoners, the layout of the compound, which hooch they're keeping your brother in—that kind of stuff. I've listened to that tape ten times. The refugee, what's-his-name, doesn't give us any of that. In fact, I picked up some Vietnamese on the tape that wasn't in the transcript. He seemed to be saying that the camp is some kind of big secret. You ought to go talk to him—see if you can pry some more information out of him."

Rob picked up his empty coffee cup and stared into it. "I thought of that. Jim Safier, one of my father's executives, was supposed to fly over to see him in Nice, to verify the tape's authenticity. The guy died, he told me."

McWhirter's eyes narrowed. "Accidentally?"

"He was already seriously ill when this writer Duffy interviewed him. The hospital assured Safier it was natural causes."

"What about this Duffy, then?" Gilmore suggested. "Maybe he can remember a few things not on the tape."

Rob set the coffee mug back on the table and shook his head slowly. "Don't tell us he's dead, too?"

"I called Safier yesterday. He told me Duffy jumped out a hotel window two days ago."

McWhirter laughed. "This information must have a curse on it."

"Seems that way," Rob admitted. "I didn't say anything because I didn't want to scare off the rest of you the way I know Safier's trying to scare me. He'd derail this mission himself if he could do it without getting caught at it."

McWhirter scoffed. "A little bad luck, that's all. We'll just work around it."

New York City

James Safier met him at lunchtime in the reptile house at the Central Park Zoo. He was a short, freckled man with small ears and mouth and small, agatelike eyes set close together, giving him the attentive look of a hungry ferret.

"Captain Henry Short," he said, taking Safier's hand and squeezing it brutally. "I'm pleased to meet you." The reptile house was empty of people, and his words reverberated loudly off the concrete walls.

"You a friend of Joel's?" Safier asked.

"Not really. Your material was bumped over to us, for appraisal."

"Us?"

"That's right. We're a special support group for Defense Intelligence. We do analysis, mainly." Short grinned self-deprecatingly. "The plodding, painstaking part of intelligence you never hear much about. Slaving over hot computers all day is what it amounts to."

Somehow Safier couldn't picture Short behind a computer terminal. Over his shoulder he saw a huge anaconda winding its way up a tree trunk that had been placed in its cage. Short thumped the edge of the attaché case he was carrying with a callused thumb. "Have some bad news for you, I'm afraid."

"What's that?"

"We've run a thorough check on this Vietnamese refugee, Tran. Seems he was a Vietnamese plant."

"I don't follow you."

"He was working for Vietnamese intelligence. His defection was a phony."

It was more than Safier could have hoped for. "Are you sure?"

"Positive. I have documents right here with me to prove it."

"So his story about Billy Grunwald—"

"Phony," Short said. "Completely phony."

"My employer, William Grunwald, will be sorry to hear that."

"Well, of course," Short agreed. "But Mr. Grunwald will just have to face up to the probability that his son is no longer alive."

"That's always been my view."

Short rested an arm on the railing and looked into the snake cage. The anaconda had stretched out its head in Short's direction and was testing the air with its tongue. "Mr. Grunwald has to understand that the Defense Department has done everything in its power to find out what happened to his son. But without the cooperation of the Vietnamese government, it's a hell of a difficult task."

"Why would they send this Tran individual out to plant such a story about Billy Grunwald being alive?"

Short shook his head, his eyes fastened on the anaconda. "That's a tough one, Mr. Safier. Our best guess is that the Vietnamese are just trying to stir up a little trouble. We don't think that Tran was sent to the West just for this purpose. That would be a waste of a valuable asset. His real mission was to keep tabs on the Vietnamese refugee population in France. This phony story about Mr. Grunwald's son was what we call 'disinformation.' They want to sow some doubt about the true nature of the MIA situation. Maybe they imagined Mr. Grunwald might make the information public, and embarrass our government. There are a lot of possibilities, Mr. Safier, and these bastards are hard to figure sometimes."

Safier nodded. There was nothing about Short—his facial expressions, his body language, his tone of voice—that inspired the least degree of trust, but Safier wanted so much to believe what he was hearing that he was reluctant to challenge him.

"And by the way," Short said, his voice straining to sound casual, "the fact that this guy's information is phony doesn't mean you should talk about it. If it got back to the Vietnamese that we were on to an agent of theirs, it would compromise some pretty highly classified stuff about how we operate. You follow my meaning?"

"I think so."

"So we'd advise you to keep it quiet. Pretend you never heard about it. You'll have to break this to your boss, and get his promise of secrecy as well."

"Is that it?"

The snake weaved its head slowly from side to side, its forked tongue flicking the air, sensing Short's presence. Short fastened his eyes on the serpent and moved his own head in unison with it, as if mocking it. "Well," he said, "I guess you better let those boys up in Vermont in on the fact that they're wasting their precious time—training to go rescue somebody who isn't even there."

Safier flushed. This Captain Short was well informed. "Yes, of course," he replied. "Anything else?"

"There is one more thing. We determined that the documents you gave us had been photocopied. You'd better turn over all the copies you made to us."

"I'll see that they're destroyed."

Short grinned unpleasantly. "No, you'd better turn them over to us. We have secure methods of disposing of that kind of material. You'd be surprised who might go through your garbage. You follow my meaning?"

Safier nodded.

"I'll be in town for a while," Short said. "Why don't I stop by tomorrow and pick them up from you?"

"Whatever you say."

"Good. I'll be in your office at noon, sharp." Short inflicted another bruising squeeze to Safier's right hand, and departed. Safier watched him leave. A woman with two young children was coming through the entrance just as Short was going out. Instead of stepping aside to let them pass, he pushed one of the children out of his way.

Returning downtown, Safier reflected on how he would handle Short's demands. He would turn over to him several photocopies of the transcript and the tape. But he still intended to keep one photocopy. Short would never know. And as for warning William Grunwald that the material was phony—that was out of the question. He could not tell Grunwald anything. He had gone behind his back to pass Duffy's transcript on to the Pentagon in the first place.

Fortunately, it wasn't necessary to tell him anything. Or his son Rob, either, for that matter. Let the damned mission go forward. He no longer needed to worry about Rob's bringing Billy home. Instead, he could look forward—with considerable pleasure—to Rob's certain failure.

Unless, of course, Short was lying to him for some reason. Safier prayed that he wasn't.

Wilmington, Vermont

The days of the first week melted into one another in a crucible of pain and fatigue unlike anything Rob had ever experienced. Awakened roughly at daybreak, joints and muscles so stiff that he had to roll out of the bunk on his side, he stumbled through a seemingly endless gauntlet of torture, both mental and physical. Sandwiched between his frantic day-long efforts to locate and order the never-ending lists of needed supplies, he endured calisthenics, hikes, obstacle courses, martial-arts lessons, rifle practice, and McWhirter's field trips.

"Today," McWhirter said, leading them along a trail that wound through the woods behind Gilmore's cabin, "we talk about the use of your senses to keep you alive in enemy territory. In the jungle you sometimes won't be able to see three feet in front of you, so the senses of smell, touch, and hearing take on added importance. With smell you can detect the enemy before he detects you. If the wind is right, cigarette smoke can be smelled a quarter of a mile away. So can cooked foods. Different kinds of wood are burned in Vietnam for different reasons. If you know the wood, and the direction the smell is coming from, you may know whether you're close to an encampment of soldiers or just a peasant village. Conversely, the enemy might smell you if you're wearing insect repellent, scented soap, or after-shave lotion. So anything the locals don't use, you don't use, either. Many an ambush has been sniffed out by a smart nose."

McWhirter paused to snap off a small branch from a sapling alongside the trail and continued on: "To use the sense of touch to identify something, you consider four things—temperature, texture, shape, and moisture. Your skill in using your touch can save your life. Example: recognizing the feeling of a trip wire against your exposed forearm. Or holding a fine branch out in front of you and recognizing the pressure of a trip wire against it."

McWhirter stopped abruptly. The others came up beside him, wondering what was wrong. He nodded at the branch in his hand. It was bent downward by the pressure of a thin, nearly invisible wire he had strung across the trail earlier. "If there was a grenade hooked to one end of this," he said, plucking the wire like a guitar string, causing it to twang faintly, "the branch would just have saved our lives."

Rob nodded. Wyler snorted. Gilmore turned pale.

"During the Korean War," McWhirter continued, removing the wire from the path, "the Turks used touch in a clever way. On night patrols they removed all their clothes. If they rubbed against another body in the dark and it had clothes on, they killed it."

The group came to a small clearing and McWhirter stopped again. "Sounds can tell you even more," he said. "But you have to master the vocabulary. You have to recognize animal and bird warnings and distress calls. Sometimes it may be the sudden sound of a bird's flight, or the sudden silence of animal noises, that signals the presence of an enemy. You know the sounds of a man's voice, but you have to know the sound of a man crawling, or a man running, as well. If you hear a weapon fire, you should be able to figure the distance, the direction, and the type. And in order to hear these things, you have to learn to make less noise than the enemy."

He told the three of them to turn and face away from him. They did. "Now, just listen to sounds," he directed. "Try to identify everything you hear. If you hear something you think poses a threat to you, drop to the ground."

Rob stood between Wyler and Gilmore and looked at the trees. He heard a bird twitter and a dog barking far away. Nothing else. A minute passed. Then two. He glanced sideways at his colleagues. They shook their heads. Nobody dropped to the ground.

Disgusted, McWhirter ordered them to turn around again. He held up a rifle and clicked the safety catch back and forth impatiently.

"You dumb bastards better learn to recognize the sound of a safety catch being released. I could have shot you all." He put down the rifle and picked up a grenade and yanked the pin. "And the sound of the striker of a hand grenade coming off." He tossed the grenade at the three of them. Wyler and Gilmore dove to the side and buried their faces in the leaves. Rob caught the grenade in midair and tossed it as hard as he could into the woods.

It didn't explode. McWhirter grinned. "Think you'd have gotten away with that if it was alive?"

"Seven seconds is seven seconds," Rob replied, still shaking. "I caught it on three."

"Yeah, you did," McWhirter admitted. He stared at Rob and scratched his chin speculatively.

Each night after dinner and the daily mission-planning session, Rob invariably fell asleep at the table, usually in the middle of Gilmore's guitar playing.

On the fourth day of training, Rob humiliated himself spectacularly. While disassembling the Kalashnikov rifle, he accidentally discharged a round. The bullet traveled clean through Howard Gilmore's clothes closet, puncturing his entire wardrobe of suits, coats, jackets, and pants as neatly as if someone had run a giant shish-kebab skewer through them. McWhirter, when he was able to stop laughing, said he knew of a tailor in Texas who specialized in repairing bullet holes, but Rob insisted on buying his dumbfounded friend a new wardrobe.

"Let's start with footprints," McWhirter said, once more leading his three students over a path behind Gilmore's cabin. It was a chilly day and a steady drizzle soaked their clothes. "Footprints can tell you a lot. The number of people in a party, their sex, direction of movement, and what kinds of loads they may be carrying. Deep toe prints, for example, usually means a heavy load. Footprints, like fingerprints, are unique to their wearer. Tread patterns, the amount and type of heel or toe wear, cuts or irregularities can all be read in a print and recognized if you see them again. The elements also play a role." McWhirter stopped and pointed to a set of boot prints in a patch of mud in front of him. "What do these tell you?"

His three students bent down and studied them.

"Well, they're your boots," Gilmore said. "I know that much."

"And they're headed north," Wyler added.

McWhirter rolled his eyes skyward in despair.

"The prints were made about an hour ago," Rob said.

"How do you know?" McWhirter challenged.

"The water in them has had time to settle. If they were more recent, the water would still be muddy. If they were much older, the drizzle would have eroded them more."

McWhirter nodded. "Now we're getting somewhere. A light rain will round off prints and make them look old. A heavy rain will erase them. Fresh prints will either have muddy water in them or a ridge of moist dirt pushed up around them. Sunlight will dry older ones, causing that ridge to crumble. Wind may blow grass and leaves and other litter into footprints. It may be important to remember when the wind was last blowing."

McWhirter stepped off through a patch of heavy grass growing in a cleared area alongside the path. "There are many other signs you should know how to read," he said, pointing to the grass he had just walked through. "Vegetation, for example. When it's stepped on, moved, or broken, the lighter underside will show. Grass is bent toward the direction of movement." He kicked the top of a rotting log beside him. "If bark on a log or root is scuffed, the lighter inner wood will show." He led them through a heavy stand of undergrowth, then turned around and took them back through it again. "The jungle is hard on clothes," he said, picking from a thorny branch a tiny strand of thread from one of their shirts and holding it up. "If someone is in a hurry, he'll leave threads and bits of clothing hanging in the underbrush."

They walked on. "An enemy may be dumb or careless enough to leave litter behind," McWhirter continued. "And you should be able to take advantage of it if he does. Learn to look for cigarette butts, scraps of paper, cloth, sticks, cans, equipment. Even human shit. Rain will flatten paper and cloth. If you remember the time of the last rain, you'll know how old the litter is. Sunlight bleaches and discolors both paper and cloth in well-defined stages. After one night, yellow spots form; after a longer period, the exposed material turns completely yellow; and eventually it will turn white." McWhirter bent down and picked up a soft-drink can someone had discarded on the trail. "In twelve hours or less," he said, "rust will begin to form on any exposed metal, like the rim of a ration can where it has been opened. If a metal can isn't rusty, like this one, it hasn't been here long."

"That can's aluminum," Rob said.

McWhirter glanced at it. "So what?"

"Aluminum doesn't rust."

McWhirter threw the can into the woods and gave Rob a nasty look. "I'm just making the point," he muttered.

On the morning of the eighth day, Rob rolled out of bed and discovered, to his great joy, that his muscles no longer screamed with pain.

On the afternoon of the ninth day, Rob suddenly found that he could hit the target on the bale of hay.

On the morning of the tenth day, Rob woke from a nightmare. He was firing the Kalashnikov, and the silhouette on the bale of hay changed suddenly into his brother Billy.

"Today," McWhirter said, standing before his class on the lawn in front of the cabin, "we learn patrolling techniques. First, you have to know where the hell you are. So you start a patrol by studying a map of the area. If there *is* a map of the area. On short patrols, you memorize the whole route. On long patrols, you memorize selected terrain features."

He knelt down and pointed to the objects arranged on the grass in front of him. "Before you venture out, you consider the special equipment you might need. Gloves, flashlights, flares, ponchos, binoculars, cameras, what kind of grenade you might need, that kind of thing." He picked up a small hunting knife. "And you *always* carry a knife. Not just any knife. A *sharp* knife." He demonstrated by taking a fast whack at a nearby weed. The decapitated top of the plant dropped to the earth without even disturbing the stem. "A dull knife is as useless as tits on a bull."

He picked up the Kalashnikov rifle and fired a single shot into the air. "You test-fire your weapon before the patrol and then leave it alone. No cleaning, no disassembling. If you take it apart, you can't be sure it's working without firing it again. And you can't do something dumb like that on a patrol." He picked up three rolls of tape and tossed them to the others. "You also want to remove the rifle's sling swivels and put tape over the bore to keep out dirt. You also tape the hand guard and dust cover to prevent any rattles or metallic clicks. And tape the stock as well, to break the outline of the weapon. The tape will come in handy for other things—gagging prisoners, repairing rips in clothes, and so on."

They taped their rifles, gathered their gear, and followed McWhirter into the woods. "You always carry your weapon pointed in the direction you're looking," he told them. "If you don't, the split second you lose moving it into position may cost you your life.

"On a patrol you have to learn to travel the hard way. Always expect an ambush. Avoid roads, trails, and streams as much as possible. They're the obvious way to travel, and the enemy knows that as well as you. If you have memorized the terrain, you won't have to rely on them. Avoid any human habitation. Avoid abandoned huts—they may be booby-trapped. The best time to travel is during bad weather. Don't establish patterns. Never return over the same route.

"Silence is an art—and it has to be practiced. Coughs and sneezes can be deadly. If necessary, carry medications—cough syrup, antihistamines, whatever will keep you quiet. Your footgear will be canvas jungle boots. They don't squeak when they're wet. But you still have to learn to walk the right way. On hard ground it's toe to heel; on soft ground, the entire foot.

"If you have trouble staying awake during a stop, kneel, don't sit. At night, sleep close enough to touch each other. If you snore, put a handkerchief around your mouth. Never remove your equipment while sleeping.

"In sudden engagements, fire low. A ricochet is better than no hit at all."

As the lessons progressed, they spent more and more of their time practicing their newly acquired skills. McWhirter would define an objective—laying an ambush, evading pursuers, tracking a target—and they would compete in carrying it out. Part of their training became an elaborate game of hide-and-seek, as each player took turns trying to avoid capture while the other three tried to hunt him down.

Rob, to everyone's surprise, not only developed into an expert tracker; he was himself impossible to track. In over a dozen trials, none of the other three, not even McWhirter, was able to find him within the time limit of the exercise. Wyler, who was always the easiest to track, accused him of cheating by hiding outside the agreed-upon boundaries of the game, but Rob was able to prove him wrong.

Rob's success lay in his cleverness at deceptions—his ability to create traps, diversions, and false trails. McWhirter became obsessed with catching him.

The last game they played, McWhirter correctly anticipated his tactic. To obscure his own trail, Rob had followed a deer path through a heavy stand of evergreens, and McWhirter spotted him on a low, flat rock in the middle of a grove of hemlocks. He approached with infinite caution, patiently checking his surroundings for any evidence of a trap. Satisfied at last, he swiftly parted the hemlock branches with the barrel of his rifle and stepped through.

"Gotcha this time, you elusive bastard," he gloated, grinning triumphantly.

Rob was sitting on the rock, twenty feet away, leaning back on his hands. "You sure?" he asked.

Hidden behind Rob's back was a length of rope. One end was anchored to a tree trunk, and the other end, following a couple of bends around other trunks, was tied to a strong, whippy length of cut sapling wedged horizontally between two other saplings and bent around like a bow to its maximum tension. Rob pressed down on the rope with his knife, severing it instantly. The sapling whistled forward and caught McWhirter just above the ankles, sweeping him clean off his feet.

Cursing, the pilot raised himself to a sitting position and massaged his shins. Rob was rocking back and forth, clutching his sides, helpless with laughter.

Wyler raised a finger to his jugular vein and measured the pulse in his neck as he ran. He counted twenty-two beats in ten seconds and multiplied by six: 132. Too low. He picked up his pace a little. He wanted his pulse at 140—the rate he judged would give him the highest training effect.

In two weeks, Wyler had dropped ten pounds. And he was determined to shed at least five more. He intended to be in top shape. He was training, after all, for the most important fight of his life.

He looked at the scattered figures of Grunwald, Gilmore, and McWhirter running up the narrow, twisting trail ahead of him, rucksacks bouncing on their backs. *Nam,* he thought. *It's beginning to look and feel like Nam again.*

He clenched his teeth and forced the air from his lungs in loud hisses. He saw Billy now. Felt him. Billy's fist was right there in front of his face again, holding the grenade under his nose. Wyler could see the tiny holes in the striker plate where Billy had pulled out the cotter pin.

Wyler shivered. All the bodies around him. The smell of gunpowder and blood and dirt burning his nostrils in the thick air. God, how he had needed understanding at that moment. Someone to put his arm around him, to tell him that it was all right. That it wasn't his fault.

That it just had to happen. Someone to share the awful moment with him, to ease the unbearable remorse.

He felt the sting of Billy's fist, weighted with the live grenade, as it pounded against his cheek. It struck him again and again. He was on his knees, spent of energy, terrified, powerless, begging.

The memory produced a film of tears over Wyler's one good eye. The fear was still so real. Would Billy Grunwald haunt him all his life?

The bastard, he thought. *The arrogant bastard!* How Wyler hated him! And now his brother wanted to bring him back alive!

The thought sent a thrill of fright through Wyler's sweating body. *Never,* he swore. *Never!* He would see to that. The only way Billy Grunwald was coming home was in a body bag.

18

Wilmington, Vermont

After dinner on day twenty-one the four men gathered on the chairs and sofa around the woodstove to listen to McWhirter make the first formal presentation of what they all referred to simply as "the Plan."

Rob reflected on how far they had all come in such a brief time. The three weeks of intense training had worked a physical and mental metamorphosis on them. They had not only survived one another's company; they were beginning to look and act like a team.

McWhirter slouched back against the sofa and cracked open a black loose-leaf notebook. "Okay," he said, in his usual deadpan manner, "the first leg of the expedition is New York to Bangkok, Thailand. Two of us—Frank and myself—will fly over first, a week ahead, to begin setting things up at that end. Frank will stay in Bangkok to collect and assemble the supplies you'll be shipping him from this end. I'll go on to the Laotian border to arrange our escort and buy our weapons. The Souei tribesmen in the area are our best bet. They've worked for the CIA in the past and they hate the Pathet Lao the way the Armenians hate the Turks. I'll hire a dozen of them to convoy us across Laos and into Vietnam. They'll have their own weapons and they're tough, reliable fighters. I don't expect any problem with them.

"We'll all rendezvous in Bangkok for the second leg, to the Laotian border. We've decided the best way to do it is to disguise ourselves as a documentary-film crew. Rob and Howard will bring the cameras, film, and sound equipment with them from New York. Frank will rent two jeeps for us in Bangkok."

McWhirter stepped over to the large map of Southeast Asia he had pinned to the wall. "It's four hundred miles from Bangkok to the Laotian border," he said. "And thanks to the American taxpayer, the roads are good all the way." He traced his finger along a red-inked line that ran in a crooked diagonal across Thailand. "I've marked the best route, taking into account what we know about areas of the countryside where guerrillas might be active. We'll take Route 5 north to Sara Buri—that's all rice flatlands. From Sara Buri, Route 21 to Khon Kaen, then 25 to Sakon Nakhon. We'll be in the mountains by then, and in tough country. Route 118 will take us from there right to the border. We'll pick up 27, which parallels the Mekong River, and head south to our border crossing. I figure if we drive nonstop and nothing delays us, we can do it in a day. But let's allow two."

He tapped the map at the Mekong River. "Where we cross, I won't know exactly until I can recon the area and work it out with the men we hire, but it'll be somewhere around the town of Mukdahan. Right across the river from there is Savannakhet and the beginning of Laotian Highway 9. We'll pick up our weapons in Mukdahan, hide our jeeps there, and sneak across by boat at night. We'll take our basic kit with us, plus food rations, extra clothes, and weapons. The Souei will supply the transportation.

"It's only about a hundred and seventy miles across Laos along Highway 9, but they'll be hard miles. How fast we move will depend on a lot of things—our transport, the condition of the roads, the weather, and who we meet along the way. If we're lucky as hell, we'll zip across in a couple of days. Most likely we'll have a few setbacks. Figure four days.

"The last fifty miles across Laos will be the worst—the terrain gets mountainous as hell. Highway 9 continues right into Vietnam near Khe Sanh. When we get to the border, we'll have to play it by ear. It may be heavily guarded; it may not. We'll probably have to lay up in the mountains for a day and watch it. Maybe send out a patrol. In any case, we'll have to plan to leave our vehicles behind in Laos and cross into Vietnam on foot, and off the highway, as well."

McWhirter returned to the sofa. In front of him, on a huge slab of polished oak that served as Gilmore's coffee table, he had painstakingly constructed a scale-model replica of their destination. With geologic survey maps and satellite photographs that he had bribed out of a CIA contact in Langley's National Photographic Interpretation Center as his guides, he had reproduced the terrain of the border area, shaping dirt, rocks, moss, and small weeds into a rough semblance of jungle and mountains; and fashioning the houses and huts of small villages out of matches and cardboard.

He picked up a pencil and pointed its tip at a strip of blue ribbon that wound through the moss along the left edge of the model. "This is the Sepone River. It comes in from Laos, just below Highway 9 and more or less parallel to it. At this point it veers south and forms the border between the two countries." He moved the pencil point to the right and brought it to rest on a cluster of cardboard huts. "This is the village of Lang Vei, two miles in from the river. In the late sixties there was a Special Forces camp here." He ran the pencil again, along a path he had made in the dirt, until it ran off the edge of his model. "Three miles farther down Highway 9 is the village of Khe Sanh, and north of it, the site of the old Marine combat base."

He brought the pencil point back across to the blue ribbon. "Right here," he said, "about a mile southwest of Lang Vei, the river detours briefly in a sharp eastward bulge. This is where we'll cross." He moved the pencil point diagonally to the southeast, across a dense patch of lawn grass until it touched a three-by-four-inch rectangle of matchsticks stuck side by side in the dirt to form a miniature bamboo stockade. Inside the fence he had placed six little green wood houses borrowed from Gilmore's Monopoly set. "Here is our target—the camp where they're holding Billy. In one way we're lucky. It's only two miles into Vietnam. The satellite photos and the maps don't show any roads, but you can be sure that there are plenty of trails around, hidden under the tree cover."

McWhirter tapped a large square rock he had placed just to the right of the matchstick stockade. "The camp is protected on the east by a steep hill. The other three sides are all triple-canopy rain forest. Once across the river, we'll cut straight through the jungle and bivouac about half a mile from the camp. From there we'll send out recon patrols. We'll need to observe it for two full days and nights, to learn the camp's routines—guard changes, meals, and so on. Once we've eyeballed the target and know the conditions, we can design the details of the raid itself. In the meantime, we'll rehearse alternate scenarios, so that when we get there we'll know what to do. I'll give us one day to get across the border and pick a bivouac, and three days to plan and execute the raid. If we hang around any longer, we'll be spotted."

McWhirter sat back on the sofa and picked up his notebook. "Getting out might be faster, since we know the way," he continued. "But it might be slower, too, if Billy's not in good shape. Allowing for that, and unanticipated fuck-ups, let's plan two days back to the border and four days across Laos. Once we're in Thailand, we're pretty much home free. We'll have our jeeps back and our cover as a film crew. Figure one day to drive to Bangkok, one day's rest, and then we're on the plane to New York. Throw in an extra day for delays. Total days for the return, nine. Total days round trip Bangkok and back, twenty. We might make it in fifteen or sixteen. But, to be on the safe side, we'll take provisions for a month." McWhirter closed the notebook. "You never know how many flat tires we may have to change."

No one laughed.

"Can't we get across Laos legally?" Gilmore asked. "Using the same documentary-film-crew cover? It would save us a lot of extra risk."

"We might," McWhirter admitted. "They've let in some journalists in the past. But if you go through the government in Vientiane, it might take months to get clearance. And they'll never let us out of their sight once we're there."

"What about our wheels in Laos?" Wyler wanted to know. "What kind of ox carts are these tribesmen of yours driving these days?"

McWhirter smiled. "They have a few beat-up trucks and jeeps, and they have a hard time keeping them running. No spare parts, no tires, no gasoline. I'll check out their vehicles when I meet up with them. In an emergency, we can probably float our own jeeps across the Mckong and usc thcm."

"Two jeeps won't carry us, all our equipment, plus a dozen Souei tribesmen," Rob said.

"We'll make the bastards walk, in that case," McWhirter replied.

"Are you serious?" Gilmore asked.

"Not completely. But on those roads, walking is almost as fast as driving."

"You think we'll be ready on schedule?" Rob asked.

"No point overrehearsing," McWhirter replied. "Today's D-day minus seven. Another week should do it. Then Frank and I should leave for Bangkok. You and Howard wind up things on this end and meet us in Thailand two weeks from tonight."

A silence fell. McWhirter's casual setting of the dates gave the expedition a reality it hadn't yet possessed. They would begin counting the hours now. Preparations would take on a new urgency.

"We know no rescue mission has ever worked," Rob said, addressing McWhirter but fastening his eyes on the miniature rectangle of matchstick fencing surrounding the six little green houses. "And none of them has ever even tried to get into Vietnam. We've been training three weeks now. You know us pretty well. What's your opinion of our chances?"

McWhirter shrugged. "We profit from their failures. We won't make their mistakes."

"We'll make our own mistakes," Gilmore said.

"I think we can make it in," McWhirter declared. "And I think we can make it out."

"What's in doubt, then?"

McWhirter shifted on the couch and cast his soft eyes toward the cabin's far wall, as if he could see the future of their rescue party projected on it. "The evidence about your brother is thin." He pointed his pencil at the Monopoly houses. "If he's not right here in this compound, where he's supposed to be, we probably won't find him. And even if he is in there, we may not be able to get him out."

Wyler adjusted his eye patch impatiently. "Why the hell not?"

McWhirter shrugged. "He's been in Vietnam for twelve years. Maybe he doesn't want to come home."

"Why wouldn't he want to?" Rob demanded.

"Shit, you were in the slammer in Belize and you told me *you* didn't want to come home. Maybe your brother's just as perverse as you are."

"That's no answer."

McWhirter sighed and offered another of his maddening shrugs. "Nobody goes through what he's gone through without big changes. You can be sure he isn't the same brother you knew a dozen years ago." He stood up from the sofa, stretched his arms out and yawned. "But there's no use wondering about it. We'll find out when we get there. One way or another."

East Berlin

Karl Koenig paced agitatedly back and forth across the wide central atrium of the Französischer Dom, his boots crunching pieces of debris into the dusty stone floor. Dieter Rheinhart stood at a respectful distance, listening to the hollow tock of the older man's heels on the ancient marble and the sibilant wheeze of his breath. The midday sun slanted through the gaping bomb hole in the roof, its light converted into visible pale-yellow shafts by the millions of motes of dust floating in the church's stale air. It was chilly and Rheinhart shivered, waiting for Koenig's fury to abate.

He had expected the director to be disappointed in him, of course. Disappointed that he had failed to get to either the Vietnamese refugee or the writer Brian Duffy before they were killed. But there were mitigating circumstances. In the world of espionage, success was only a sometime thing, and he assumed that Koenig understood this.

So he had not expected the volcanic explosion of anger and the stream of obscenities from the man. Koenig's decrepit face had metamorphosed into a quaking mask of rage, and for an instant the younger German felt a pall of terror.

Koenig interrupted his pacing and stared up through the blasted dome at the large patch of sky. Rheinhart pulled himself to attention and held his breath. The older man's sharp voice echoed against the eroded stone walls: "You must operate more effectively, Rheinhart. Do you understand?"

"Yes, sir," he replied.

"It is essential," Koenig rasped, pounding his fist into his palm. "You must succeed in this matter." He advanced toward Rheinhart, shaking a finger at him. "Your career is at stake."

Rheinhart swallowed. "Yes, Herr Koenig."

"I have a plan," Koenig said. "It will entail risk, and it will require effort. Daring." The director glared challengingly into Rheinhart's eyes, the sheer intimidating force of his countenance causing Rheinhart to edge backward.

"We will kidnap the arrogant pig," Koenig whispered.

Rheinhart shook his head. "Kidnap who?"

"William Grunwald!" Koenig cried. "He has the answers. So we will kidnap him!"

The implications of Koenig's proposal stunned Rheinhart. He thought of a thousand reasons to object, but he held his tongue.

Koenig flashed his rotted teeth in a cold smile. "You fear the difficulties?"

Rheinhart said nothing.

To the younger man's astonishment, Koenig patted him on the shoulder in a fatherly manner. "You needn't worry. You will succeed and you will be a hero for it. And I will show you exactly how you will do it."

19

Wilmington, Vermont

"Sit down, Frank," McWhirter warned, trying to thread a cleaning rod into a rifle barrel. "You're rocking the floorboards."

"I can't sit down."

"Then lie down."

"I'm not tired."

"Well, go *do* something, for chrissake. You're making me nervous."

Wyler ignored him, but he stopped pacing in favor of staring out the window by the front door. A heavy rain was beating against the glass, and everyone was cooped up inside the cabin, Gilmore clicking the keys of his computer, Rob sorting through lists of supplies, and McWhirter cleaning weapons. He and Wyler, as the advance team, were departing for Bangkok the next day, starting the rescue mission in earnest, and the mood in the cabin was tense.

"Anybody know a blonde who drives a Mercedes 450 SL?" Wyler asked suddenly.

Rob looked up from a clipboard. "What's that?"

"Take a look here."

He joined Wyler at the window. A white Mercedes sedan, barely visible through the sheets of rain, was mired in mud up to its rocker panels about a hundred yards from the cabin. McWhirter went over to see for himself. "How the hell do you know there's a blonde in there?" he demanded. "I have *two* good eyes and I can barely see the car."

"Only a woman would spin the wheels like that," Wyler replied. "The blonde part is just wishful thinking."

Rob grabbed a heavy yellow slicker from a coatrack and slipped it on. "Frank's right," he muttered. "It's female and blond. Excuse me, gentlemen."

Rob slogged across the muddy expanse of Gilmore's front yard, his boots sinking into muck up to his ankles, and reached the side of the Mercedes just as Caroline managed to pop the heavy sedan out of its hole, amid a roaring of engine and tires and a gusher of mud and rocks. Rob waited until the car had stopped moving, then yanked open the passenger-side door and jumped in.

Caroline sighed with relief and turned off the engine. "You certainly picked a remote spot. Between the rain and these dirt roads, I didn't think I'd ever find you."

She was wearing beige corduroy slacks and a matching sweater, and her hair was pulled back and tied with a designer scarf. Rob felt the same rush of excitement her presence always evoked. "How did you even know where to look?"

"Your sister Sarah told me."

"Blabbermouth," Rob muttered. "Well, come on in and meet the team."

"I'd like to talk, first," Caroline said.

"What's on your mind?"

She hesitated. "I'd better tell you over a drink. In town."

Rob looked at her, mystified. She toyed nervously with the end of her scarf. "Why not?" he said. "Leave your car here. We can take Howard's pickup. Do you have a raincoat?"

"There's an umbrella in the trunk."

"I'll get you a raincoat inside. And some boots. I'll be back."

In the restaurant, a skiers' hangout on a Wilmington side street, Caroline sat in awkward silence while Rob ordered half a carafe of white wine.

When the wine arrived, Rob poured it into their glasses. "Thank God I get to drink something besides beer again. Howard Gilmore is fixated on this brand called Anchor Steam. It's terrible stuff, and we kid him about it. I think it's the only pretension the guy has."

Caroline twisted the stem of her wineglass between her fingers and thumb, rotating the base in a series of wet rings across the wood of the table. She drew in her breath. "I want to go with you," she said.

Rob gazed at her quizzically. He had heard her, but he wasn't sure she really meant it.

"I'm serious," she said.

"Caroline, it's ridiculous."

"Is it any more ridiculous than you going?"

"Of course it is."

"Billy's my husband," she insisted. "I have a right to go."

"You have a right to do what you want. But that doesn't earn you a place on this mission."

"I can make myself useful."

"How?"

She had obviously rehearsed some answers. "I can cook," she said. "Be responsible for the food and drink."

Rob smiled. "We don't need a cook. This isn't a Lindblad cruise. We'll be eating out of cans and pouches."

"I can also handle the medical detail. None of you knows anything about medicine."

"How do you know? And when did you acquire an M.D. degree?"

"Very funny. I studied practical nursing at Peter Bent Brigham in Boston for two years. I can administer emergency first aid."

"Is that it?"

"I can also drive."

"That's open to debate."

Caroline refused to be goaded. "And I can speak French. The Vietnamese speak French. You'll need someone to interpret."

"We already have somebody—Harris McWhirter. He speaks Vietnamese, Thai, and three or four Laotian tribal dialects. And my French is passable."

"Still . . ."

Rob dug in mentally to resist her. "Look at it this way. You hate dirt on your hands. You don't like wrinkled clothes. You can't stand to be uncomfortable. You don't like the heat. Or the cold. Or the bugs. This isn't one of those luxury safaris where some native presses your underwear every day. You'll be a liability. The mission is risky enough as it is. If you really care about Billy, you'll just stay home and pray for us instead."

"You're being a chauvinist."

"You're not prepared for this kind of thing."

"You underestimate me."

"There's no room for you, anyway," he countered. "We've calculated this right down to the last freeze-dried packet of beef stew.

McWhirter and Wyler leave tomorrow for Bangkok. Gilmore and I will be following next week. We've all put in a month of hard training and planning. Even if we wanted to take you, we couldn't break in a new member on such short notice."

"Now you're just making excuses."

"Even if I agreed to it—which I don't—the others would never go along with it."

"Whose expedition is it? Theirs or yours?"

"The others have to have a say. Your presence would create problems."

"Why are you being so negative?"

"Because what you're asking for is absurd. You'd hate every minute of it. The trip will be difficult and dangerous. There'll be accidents, delays, confrontations, and probably a lot of unpleasantness. You could end up in a Thai jail, a prisoner of Laotian bandits, or just plain dead. Those are real possibilities."

"I accept that."

Rob was disturbed by her persistence. He didn't want to offend her—in fact, he wanted very much to please her. But she was making it impossible. He tried another tack: "If you want to go because you feel guilty about Billy and want to punish yourself, that's a very bad reason."

"That may be true," she admitted. "But it's only part of the reason."

"What's the rest of it?"

"I want to end twelve years of living in limbo. If Billy is alive, I want to know if we still have a marriage. I want to know if I still love him. Or if he loves me. And if he's dead, I want to know that, too. I want to be able to remarry."

"Can't you settle that when he gets back? You've waited all this time. What will a few more weeks matter?"

"You're overlooking the most likely result of the search."

"What?"

"That you won't bring back anything. That you won't find Billy at all—dead *or* alive."

"How will your going with us affect that?"

"It won't. But I want to see for myself. I want to satisfy myself that everything possible has been done. The outcome of this trip is more important to me than anyone. My future depends on it. I want to be there when my future is decided."

Rob poured more wine from the carafe into their glasses. It gave him an excuse to avert her gaze. He understood her argument, but he was afraid to take her. It wasn't just the idea of having an untrained individual along on a dangerous and illegal paramilitary adventure. It was the idea of Caroline. She was too attractive, too sexually provoking. He hated the thought of her being thrown in with Gilmore, McWhirter, and Wyler on a mission where almost anything might happen. And he feared they might resent her presence. And his own relationship with her was ambiguous. If she came along, he was apt to become too protective of her—too possessive. On their drive into town, he kept thinking that he hadn't had sex with a woman since Melissa at the party at Greenwood, over a month ago. And even then it was Caroline he had wanted, not Melissa. "I understand your feelings," he tried, "but—"

"It means a lot to me," she interrupted.

"No!" he replied, angrily. "No. No way. Forget it. You'll make everything more difficult. I just can't be responsible for you."

A heavy silence descended. Caroline sipped her wine with awkward deliberation. Rob thought he saw tears brimming in her eyes, but none fell.

"You don't have to take the responsibility for me, you bastard," she replied, her voice harsher than he had ever heard it. "I know how you see me. As a lazy socialite who can't even pick up after herself. I'm aware of my shortcomings. I wonder if you're aware of yours? I wonder if you realize how absurd it looks to me that you're the one going looking for my husband?"

"Wait a minute, Caroline—"

"What qualifies you?" she continued. "What have you accomplished in your thirty-one years that makes you so damned qualified? Your life is a mess, and has been as long as I've known you. You have no money, no marriage, no children, no college degree, no career, no skills, no prospects. What you do have is a drug habit, a tendency toward antisocial behavior, and a police record. And you have no excuse for it. None. Except to complain about how mean your father has been to you!"

Rob placed his hand on top of hers to placate her. She withdrew it roughly. "You have less right to make this trip than I do," she said. "It's just a damned stunt to you, that's all. You're doing it to rescue your pride and self-esteem, as much as to find Billy. Prove youself a hero. You're reckless and self-destructive. I wouldn't dream of having you be responsible for me. You've never shown that you can be responsible for anything. You infuriate me, with your maddeningly superior attitude!"

"Look, I'm sorry—"

"The truth is, you're afraid to take me. I might upset your smug little appraisal of me. I might embarrass you in front of your macho buddies."

She concluded her outburst by rising from the table and walking out of the restaurant. Rob watched her pass by the front window, heading in the opposite direction from Gilmore's pickup. It was still raining and she had left the slicker he had loaned her draped over the back of the chair. He paid the bill, grabbed the raincoats, and went out to find her.

She hadn't gone far. A block down the deserted sidewalk he could see her, head held high, long legs striding rapidly, impervious to the gusting sheets of rain that slashed at her clothes. He caught up with her quickly and draped the slicker over her shoulders.

"I'm just as tired of my life as you are of yours," she said, her voice calm, her eyes fixed straight ahead. "We're both looking for more than Billy."

"What are you looking for?"

"Purpose. I'm trapped and about to explode. I was brought up to be a rich man's wife—and for twelve years even that has been taken away from me." She clutched the raincoat collar with both hands and pulled it round her neck. "And I'm tired. I'm tired of charity work, of music lessons, of extension courses in art history, of classes in pottery and weaving and antique restoration. I'm tired of being the extra woman at dinner parties. I've got Pouilly-Fuissé and medallions of chicken coming out of my ears. I'm tired of concerts, gallery openings, museum gatherings, poetry readings, string quartets, and fundraising events. I'm tired of tennis and sailing and chic outings to anywhere. I'm tired of dating divorced stockbrokers looking for a quick lay. I'm tired of marking time. I'll be an alcoholic before I'm forty. I have to break out of all this before I suffocate. You must take me with you. I don't give a damn about the risk. Whatever happens will happen. But you must take me. I'm begging you."

Her hair clung to her neck in long, drenched strands, and raindrops were running down her cheeks. Rob wanted to embrace her. "I'll take you as far as Bangkok," he said. "That's all I can promise."

"I can get on a plane and fly to Bangkok myself."

"There's a difference."

"I'll take it," she replied. "But I'm not giving up on going the rest of the way."

"Let's leave the question of the rest of the way open," he said.

174 / TOM HYMAN

She squinted against the rain and smiled at him. He noticed tiny fans of wrinkles at the corners of her eyes. "I'm sorry if I insulted you, back in the restaurant."

174 / TOM HYMAN

She squinted against the rain and smiled at him. He noticed tiny fans of wrinkles at the corners of her eyes. "I'm sorry if I insulted you, back in the restaurant."

He shrugged. "I deserved it."

"I'll work out, Rob," she said. "I'll surprise you."

"You've already surprised me. Let's get out of the rain."

20

New York City

The cool female voice wafted through the cavernous recesses of the airport terminal: "Would Mr. Harris McWhirter please come to the Pam Am ticket counter. Mr. Harris McWhirter, please."

The voice repeated the message several times before McWhirter, waiting in a bar with Wyler just off the departure lounge, heard it. He muttered a short curse, threw a ten-dollar bill onto the bar, and stood up. "Go on ahead," he said to Wyler. "I'll meet you on the plane."

McWhirter found the ticket counter and pushed his boarding pass under the eyes of a clerk. "What's the problem?" he demanded.

"No problem, Mr. McWhirter. The gentleman over there wants a word with you." The woman pointed past his shoulder. He turned and saw a stocky male in sunglasses and a baggy gray suit advancing toward him. He stopped about fifteen feet away. His jaws, which had been working energetically on a wad of gum, slowed down to make way for some words. "Follow me, please," he ordered.

"Why the hell should I?"

"Mr. Walker," the man in sunglasses replied, grinning broadly. "He wants to speak to you."

McWhirter hesitated, then followed the sunglasses outside and across the terminal's approach ramps, jammed with buses and taxis, to a nearby parking lot. His escort led him to a black limousine and opened the front passenger-side door for him.

Walker's voice greeted him from behind the opaque glass partition. "Bangkok's awfully hot this time of year."

"It's hot there any time of year."

"You have a good reason for going?"

"Have to make a living."

"I thought you were doing quite well on the county-fair circuit. Has risking your life in those old motorized kites begun to bore you?"

"I wish you guys would stop following me around. You're wasting taxpayers' money."

A wheezy laugh rumbled from the back seat. McWhirter sighed. He glanced at the side window. Walker's chauffeur-bodyguard was standing by his door, in effect blocking his exit. It irritated him. What the hell did they expect? That he might try to run away? He heard Walker flipping pages in the back seat. Walker was too fond of shrouding himself in mystery, McWhirter thought. The whole production— the limo with the shrouded rear windows, the disembodied voice over the intercom—was pathetic. It grated on his nerves, the way the bastard tried to hide behind this fog of fear. And the bastard was succeeding, too: McWhirter's pulse was racing.

"I don't want you to miss your plane," Walker said.

McWhirter waited.

"I have a simple favor to ask," Walker continued, drawing his voice out in measured tones. "Really extremely simple."

"What is it?" McWhirter demanded, letting his irritation show.

"We don't want you to find Billy Grunwald."

McWhirter was stunned. He had guessed Walker would only be fishing for a little on-the-spot intelligence reporting from Laos and Vietnam. Suddenly the deaths of the journalist and the Vietnamese refugee took on added meaning. The guilty party was almost certainly sitting in the back seat of this limousine. "Why not?" he asked.

Walker chose not to answer the question. "The chances are pretty fair that you won't find him, anyway," he went on. "But we need to be sure. All I want you to do is make sure for us. You don't have to do anything ugly. Just throw the game, so to speak. The opportunities should be plentiful. One little well-timed accident should do it. Just see to it that you come back empty-handed."

"That kind of takes the fun out of the trip."

"I wouldn't ask you to do it if it wasn't important."

"What if I say no?"

"That's a very tiresome question, McWhirter."

"So I'm a tiresome guy."

"We'll pay you."

"More than Grunwald?"

"In addition to, not more than. Obviously I expect you to keep Grunwald's money."

"I'll tell you the truth, Mr. Walker: I don't want to do it."

Walker laughed. "Have you ever been asked for anything easier?"

McWhirter hated rhetorical questions. "A friend at Fort Bragg once asked me to fuck his wife. That was pretty easy."

Walker ignored the insult. "What is it?" he asked. "Were you looking forward to becoming a celebrity? Being interviewed on television?"

The thought had crossed McWhirter's mind, but he would certainly never admit it.

"Some moral problem, then," Walker continued, putting an ironic stress on the world *moral.*

McWhirter surprised himself by his answer: "I like the guy."

"I beg your pardon?"

"I don't want to double-cross him."

"If you do it correctly, he'll never know."

"I want to retire from this kind of shit."

"Look," Walker said, a trace of impatience creeping into his voice, "we'll stop the mission whether you agree or not. We'll just tip off the Thai police. You won't get past Bangkok customs. But we'd rather not do that. We'd rather that this little rescue party of yours not come to light. Let Grunwald look for his brother and just not find him. He'll get over the disappointment. You'll all get back safely, get your money, and that'll be the end of it. You stand to come out of it handsomely. The other way, you all end up in a Thai prison. Or worse."

McWhirter didn't need to think about it. There was simply no choice to be made. So there was no point making an ass of himself. He knew he could sabotage the mission easily and painlessly. It might even sabotage itself, in which case he wouldn't even have to feel bad about it. And if Walker was going to sink them anyway, it would be better if the time and the manner were under McWhirter's control. "How do I know you won't double-cross me and have us picked up?"

"You don't," Walker admitted. "But I have good reasons for not doing it. Except as a last resort, of course."

"What's this Billy Grunwald done that you don't want him found?"

"As you should know, that's none of your business. You'd better run and catch your plane. Your colleague, Mr. Wyler, will be wondering about you."

McWhirter found Wyler several minutes later and boarded the plane with him. Before the flight—Pan American 1 to Hawaii, Tokyo, and Bangkok—had even cleared New York airspace, McWhirter was fast asleep.

Wilmington, Vermont

Rob sat in the middle of a jumbled disorder of boxes, backpacks, cans, and equipment scattered across the cabin floor, clipboard in one hand, pencil in the other. "I can't remember," he said, looking up from his list at Howard Gilmore, who was patiently assembling the supplies for five medical kits on the dining table. "Why do we have four canteens and twelve canteen covers?"

"McWhirter's idea," Gilmore replied. "The eight extra covers we use as ammo pouches."

"Oh yeah."

"You'd better get another canteen, though," Gilmore said.

"Not necessary. Caroline gets off at Bangkok."

Gilmore chuckled. "You better get one. Just in case."

"What do you think?" Rob asked.

"About Caroline?"

"The whole thing. Is it going to work?"

Gilmore picked up a bottle of snake antivenin and squinted at the label. "Back in April I thought the idea was insane. But after a month of McWhirter's Green Beret boot camp, the mission itself will be a welcome relief."

"McWhirter did a good job," Rob said.

"I'm forced to agree," Gilmore sighed. "I lost ten pounds and you look a far cry from the pallid ghost of six weeks ago."

"You really notice a difference?"

"When you first showed up on my doorstep, I wasn't sure whether you had come to beg for food or to haunt me."

"I feel healthier," Rob admitted.

"Then the mission is already a success."

"I have faith in us. I think we'll make it."

"That reminds me," Gilmore said. "My background checking has finally turned up some semibad news." He got up from the dining table, stepped across to his computer, and picked up a couple of pages of printout. "It's about Wyler. I was saving it, hoping I could check it out more thoroughly, but it looks like this is all I'm going to get."

"What is it?"

"Wyler has a police record that he didn't tell you about. Juvenile-delinquency stuff. In 1965 he was given the choice of jail or the Marines. The Corps seems to have straightened him out. He re-upped in 1968 and again in 1970, shortly before he was captured. But he lied to you about his discharge in 1973. He got a general discharge, not an honorable."

"What do you think it means?"

"Hard to say. He was a POW, and a lot of POWs collaborated with their captors, in one way or another. The Marine Corps agonized over how to handle the matter when the POWs were released in 1973. It finally decided to sweep the issue under the rug. It granted amnesty to everybody. The worst any POW got was a general discharge. No one was tried. Except Robert Garwood, of course. But he came home years later, and wasn't protected by the amnesty of 1973."

"You think Wyler was a collaborator?"

"I don't know. I couldn't find any charges or testimony against him. No other POWs accused him of collaborating. But that's not what worries me. I came up with this notation from his debriefing hearings in 1973." Gilmore held the printout up in front of him and adjusted his glasses: " 'Sergeant Frank Wyler involved in Long Ba incident prior to capture.' I've spent hours doing keyword searches through all the data bases I can access for more on Long Ba, and all I can find is this, an excerpt from a newspaper account written by a reporter in the area at the time: 'There is controversy over what happened to the village of Long Ba on February 24, 1970. According to U.S. military spokesmen both at MACV in Saigon and Marine headquarters at Da Nang, units of a North Vietnamese division ambushed a company of Marines on a routine patrol through the village, killed or captured the entire unit, then set fire to the village and massacred its inhabitants. According to some of the villagers who survived, however, the Marines themselves may have been responsible for the slaughter.' "

"Another My Lai?" Rob asked.

"It's possible."

"I've always thought Wyler was hiding something from us. Maybe that's it. Some serious black mark on his record. You think I made a mistake taking him on?"

"No. Everybody's got something to hide, after all. That's part of the human condition. And it's irrelevant. He's worked hard training for the mission. Whatever he might have done—and we don't know that he's done anything—I don't see how it can affect our trying to rescue Billy."

"Billy was in command of that company at Long Ba. Wyler could know something about my brother that he's not telling us."

Gilmore scratched his beard thoughtfully. "That doesn't really change anything, does it?"

"No," Rob replied. "But I hate unpleasant surprises."

Rhinebeck, New York

The Josephine Room at Greenwood was festooned with balloons and flowers. The French doors were open, letting in the cool sweet breezes of a late-May evening, and the several hundred guests were in a boisterous springtime mood. Up on the low stage at the far end, a six-piece band was playing an old Bing Crosby favorite—"When the Blue of the Night Meets the Gold of the Day." Overhead a wide banner spanned the width of the two-story ballroom, with the words "Congratulations, Mr. Ambassador!" spelled out in large gold letters.

The band stopped in mid-song and the drummer began a slow, building drumroll. The crowd hushed and all eyes turned to the ballroom's main entrance. William and Cornelia Grunwald appeared, arm in arm, and paused for a moment at the top of the steps leading down onto the main floor. Grunwald, his face beaming with delight, clasped his wife's hand firmly in his and raised their arms together over their heads. The guests broke into loud applause. Shouts of "Hear! Hear!" filled the large chamber, and the band, on cue, broke into a spirited rendition of "Hava Nagila," sending a loud ripple of laughter across the room.

Cornelia Grunwald looked out at the throng of guests and, through her smile, felt tears welling up. All week she had been thinking about this very moment, anticipating it. Now it was happening, and her heart was full beyond expectation.

She measured her life by events, not years, and she could recall each significant hour in detail, from her first birthday party at the Josephs' mansion on Riverside Drive when she was five, and all the other firsts in her life—first date, first dance, first trip on an ocean liner; through all the momentous occasions she had shared with her husband—their wedding, the birth of their three children, the day they had moved into Greenwood, the important parties they had given there, the famous guests they had entertained, Billy and Caroline's wedding . . . The list of happy events was long.

And it was those happy events that had given her the strength to endure the many dark days in her life—the years of infidelity and estrangement their marriage had suffered, the endless anguish over Billy's cruel fate, and the long history of trouble between Rob and his father.

The happy events were her green islands in the sea of her miseries. And tonight's event, she knew, was the greenest. It marked a moment of double triumph—a professional one for her husband, a social one for her. The ambassadorship represented the pinnacle of respectability. Tonight the Grunwalds had become, by anybody's measure, a part of the country's history. Beyond cavil or criticism, they were now, officially, a prominent American family.

The band began playing "Red Sails in the Sunset," their favorite song. She looked at William and he smiled at her in a way she had not seen him smile in years. He offered her his hand.

"Madame?" he said.

"Your Excellency," she replied.

They moved onto the floor of the ballroom and the band shifted smoothly into a Strauss waltz. Amid snapping flashbulbs and applause, they began a slow and stately dance across the room. Optimism danced in Cornelia's head with the music. She dared look at the future with new hope. In Israel, she thought, they would spend more time together than they had in years. Soon Sarah and Jim Safier would marry. And Rob was back, confident that he would soon find Billy and bring him home.

There were many green islands yet to see. Perhaps life would work out, after all. But whatever happened, Cornelia knew, this night, of all the nights of her life, would be the happiest.

21

Bangkok, Thailand

McWhirter met them at the customs control barrier at Bangkok's Don Muang Airport. It was mid-morning and the arrivals area had the bustling atmosphere of an open-air market. Caroline, Howard Gilmore, and Rob walked, bleary-eyed and stiff-legged, through the raucous din of visitors and peddlers who jostled and swarmed through the cavernous spaces in crowds that vastly outnumbered the travelers. Despite the exhausting seventeen-hour flight, Rob felt a light-headed, almost manic euphoria.

"Everything's set," McWhirter assured him. "You got my cables, didn't you?"

"Yes. What about the jeeps?"

"Frank's rented them," McWhirter replied. "We're ready to go. We can start out the day after tomorrow."

Rob stacked their luggage on a baggage cart and waited for Gilmore, trailing behind with the cartload of camera equipment, to catch up. "Why not go tomorrow?" he asked.

McWhirter laughed. "That would be fine for me and Frank, but you're going to need twenty-four hours to acclimate."

"A good night's sleep should do it."

McWhirter shook his head. "I'm not talking jet lag. I'm talking culture and climate shock."

Rob soon understood what he meant. McWhirter had thoughtfully rented an air-conditioned limousine to take them to their hotel, but the air conditioner wasn't working, and the trip from the airport to the Oriental Hotel gave him his first taste of travel in Southeast Asia. Their chauffeur, a small Thai wearing a white dress shirt over a bathing suit, required an hour and a half of muscle-wrenching and horn-blowing to shoehorn the big limo through the congested traffic of downtown Bangkok. The noise level on the streets rivaled that of an overcrowded discotheque, and the temperature already boiled at 102 degrees, with the humidity not far behind.

"I knew it was a warm climate," Gilmore said, wiping the beads of sweat from his bald head. "But this is unreal."

"Cheer up," Caroline shouted over the cacophony. "The monsoons begin in about a week."

Rob absorbed the unfolding drama around them. Motorcycles roared past, threading their way through the impacted traffic. Motorized pedicabs, trishaws, and bicycles plodded along at a slower pace. The sidewalks were as jammed as the streets, but the mood seemed more festive than hectic. Saffron-robed Buddhist monks mingled with white-shirted office workers and street vendors, young girls in school uniforms skipped around old women in broad straw hats, adolescent boys zipped through the crowd, balancing trays on their heads. Beautiful women in bright sarongs strolled along with shopping bags. Radios, blaring out Western music, competed with the steady din of racing engines and auto horns for the highest decibel level. Over the potent cloud of exhaust fumes and humidity, the air carried other, more exotic smells—pungent cooking odors and the aroma of flowers, fruit, and incense.

Over the jumbled warrens of tin and wood and concrete block, Rob caught occasional glimpses of soaring temple roofs and gold spires, incredible relics of the vanished pomp and dignity of the old monarchies of Siam, still gleaming tranquilly, as unreal as a mirage amid the rampant disorder of the twentieth century.

A small boy lost in a khaki army shirt many sizes too big for him trotted up to Rob's window while they were stalled in traffic. On his head he balanced a wide straw tray of garlands made of jasmine blossoms. The boy surprised him by addressing him in English: "You want to buy good luck, *farang?*"

"How much?"

"Sip baht," the boy replied. "Ten baht."

"You sure they're good luck?"

"Yes, yes! Very best good luck!"

Rob reached into a trouser pocket and pulled out the wad of bills he had just purchased at the airport currency exchange. He peeled off several hundred-baht notes and handed them to the boy. "Let's have all of them," he said.

The boy, incredulous at first, squealed with pleasure and tipped the tray toward the window so Rob could brush the entire pile of garlands onto his lap. Rob scooped them up, inhaled their sweet fragrance, then gleefully tossed them about the back of the limousine, until they had settled on everyone's lap.

That day and most of the next passed in a rapid kaleidoscope of short naps, quick meals, and endless errands and conferences as Rob, in a tireless display of energy, checked the status of the mission. He reviewed every aspect of their plan, peered repeatedly into every box and case, corrected and altered details by the dozen, and generally drove the other four crazy in his obsession to assure himself that everything was ready and in place.

Caroline caught up to him outside the hotel late in the afternoon of the second day, and linked her arm through his. "Let me show you Bangkok," she said.

He started to protest, but she held him firmly. "You've done everything that can be done. And done it twice. Now you need to relax."

"What about the others?"

"Harris and Frank are going to show Howard some of the lurid nightlife on Petchburi Road," she replied.

"Maybe I'd like to sample some of that lurid nightlife myself."

Caroline affected a mock coyness. "You prefer a few transient thrills with some empty-headed pleasure girl to an evening of my company?"

Rob laughed. "What sorts of wholesome delights are you offering?"

"I should drag you through the Grand Palace and the Wat Phra Keo to see the Emerald Buddha, but there isn't time. You may have to settle for a lecture on the Chakri kings at dinner. But first let's visit the klongs."

"Are these Klongs friends of yours?"

"I never know when you're serious," Caroline complained, tugging at his arm. "Let's go."

They rented a water taxi at a dock on the Chao Phraya, the muddy serpentine river that divides Bangkok, and, like a pair of tourists on a holiday, spent the afternoon exploring the canals in the Thon Buri district, on the river's west bank, and then walked around the city's old sector, gawking at the Buddhist monasteries, the royal palaces, and the historical monuments built by past centuries of Thai monarchs.

On Rajadamnoen Avenue, Bangkok's fanciest thoroughfare, they gazed at the Kremlin-like expanse of crenellated walls and the soaring fairy-tale jumble of roofs and spires of the Grand Palace, gleaming gold and amber in the last rays of the afternoon sun.

"I have the feeling that that's where Anna met the king of Siam," Rob said.

"You're absolutely right," Caroline replied. "Anna Leonowens. She was here in the 1860s. Her memoirs slandered King Mongkut terribly, depicting him as a barbarian. In fact, he was a very enlightened man."

"Why did she slander him?"

"She was a busybody. She caused so much trouble at the court that the king finally fired her. She wrote her books to get revenge. Then someone turned them into a novel, and of course the novel inspired the musical. Her books were inaccurate enough, but the novel and musical are silly romantic fantasy."

"You mean they didn't have a love affair?"

"Hardly."

"Another illusion shattered. What's next on the tour?"

"An adventure in *haute cuisine*," she replied. "Siamese style."

By Memorial Bridge they found an old rice barge that had been converted into a floating restaurant, and under Caroline's guidance, they sampled *paw pia tod*—a crisp pancake appetizer wrapped around a mixture of pork, crabmeat, and bean sprouts; *tom yam*—a pungent hot-and-sour soup containing tiny green chili peppers with the fiery bite of a bee sting: *hor mok pla*—a fish curry with vegetables and coconut milk served in banana leaves; *kao nah gai*—a chicken dish with onions, bamboo shoots, and rice; and *gaeng mud-sa-man*—a spicy beef curry that tasted of peanuts. To salve their scorched taste buds, they downed copious quantities of a strong, creamy, beerlike liquid called a "palm toddy."

"The food is wonderful," Rob admitted, "but my mouth feels like a jet exhaust. I bet if I exhaled hard I could set fire to your blouse."

"You'd better not. We'll have fruit for dessert. *Somo* and *sup-pa-rod*. Grapefruit and pineapple. They'll put out the fire."

"I want to try *durian*. It's the great Thai delicacy, I understand."

Caroline warned him against it, but he insisted. The waiter brought an opened section of the fruit, a spiky monster with bits of custardlike material tucked in its inner recesses. The smell of it, even before it reached their table, appalled him. The world's most potent cheese could not have touched it. Its rank effluvium sent groans up from a group of American tourists seated nearby, and others in the restaurant began to laugh. Rob held his nose closed with one hand and scooped a bit into his mouth with the other. The Thais in the restaurant, including the waiters and the owner, applauded and cheered.

"It's an acquired taste," Rob gasped, fighting hard not to gag. He snatched a full glass of palm toddy and drained it in a gulp, then pushed his chair away from the table as if about to bolt for the door. A mingled roar of approval and amusement echoed through the room. Caroline pressed her napkin over her mouth to stifle her laughter.

McWhirter's eyes scanned the gloom of the Seventh Heaven Bar and caught something that interested him. He jumped up, nearly knocking over the table-load of drinks. "Have to take a piss," he muttered. Gilmore and Wyler, bar girls clinging to their necks, paid no attention.

He cut through the noisy haze of inebriated tourists, go-go dancers, and seminude hostesses to a narrow corridor that led back about ten feet to the rest rooms. He tried the handle on the men's-room door and found it locked. He waited, his eyes riveted like a cat's on the knob.

A few moments later he saw it begin to turn. He hit the door quickly. It flew inward and caught the occupant in the chest, knocking him back against the sink. McWhirter clamped a choke hold around his neck and pressed his thumbs under his jaw. His captive went limp almost immediately.

McWhirter reached back to lock the door. It nearly cost him his life. Far from unconscious, his opponent was up and pressing the attack with the ferocity of an enraged ape. McWhirter absorbed a flurry of blows to the head and a kick to the stomach. He crashed against a towel dispenser. It burst open, and a roll of brown paper unwound across the floor. McWhirter dodged desperately from side to side trying to avoid the blows. A kick aimed at his head hit the mirror over the washbasin and caught him in a spray of glass shards. Another kick struck his kidneys and he wobbled on the edge of blacking out.

The cramped space of the rest room saved McWhirter from annihilation. His opponent lacked the room he needed to wind up for a finishing blow. McWhirter bulled forward, striking the man in the stomach with his head, and drove him into the wall, knocking the wind out of him. Before he could recover, McWhirter planted an old-fashioned right fist to the chin. His victim folded onto the floor like a puppet with its strings cut.

McWhirter sat him on the toilet and examined him. He was Oriental, barely five feet tall, and clad in jeans, boots, and a dirty white cowboy hat that had rolled under the sink. McWhirter lifted open an eyelid. The pupil was dilated. Drugs. Speedballing, he guessed. A cheap plastic billfold in the back pocket of the jeans contained a handful of American dollars and baht notes and nothing else. No identification, no photographs. Just money. He threw it aside and went through the man's clothes, checking pockets and seams. Nothing.

He tucked the bills into his own pocket and tried to think the situation through. This Oriental cowboy had been tailing him for the past several days. He could try to beat the reason why out of him, but the men's toilet of a topless bar wasn't the ideal setting for an interrogation. He considered killing him, but discarded the idea. They'd just put someone else on the job.

It must be Walker's doing, he decided. Making sure that he was following through on his assignment. The bastard would never leave him alone, he realized. What had begun as a simple bit of free-lance dirty work in Southeast Asia years ago when he was hard up for money, Walker had converted into a lifelong obligation. He didn't call on McWhirter often, but every time he did, McWhirter felt the humiliation cut a little deeper. As long as Walker lived, he could never be his own man.

He hauled the still-inert figure off the toilet and picked up his cowboy hat and jammed it down tight around his ears. Then he lifted the toilet seat, shoved his victim's head face-first into the bowl, flushed the toilet, and left.

Rob and Caroline stopped in the lounge of the Oriental and ordered a nightcap. He clinked his brandy glass against hers. "To the mission," he said.

Caroline raised her eyebrows questioningly. "Do I get to go on it?"

Rob swirled the brandy in the snifter, watching the sparks of candlelight reflected in the caramel-colored liquid. "I've talked to McWhirter about it," he admitted.

"And what does he think?"

"He's against it," Rob said.

"Of course he would be."

"He has a lot of arguments on his side."

"I don't intend to sit here in Bangkok for two or three weeks worrying about what's happening to you all."

"I know. I want to compromise. We'll take you as far as the Laotian border. McWhirter has a place you can stay there. You'll be a lot closer, but you'll still be safe."

Caroline regarded him with a skeptical smile. "You retreat, but you never give in."

Rob threw out his hands. "I'm trying my best to accommodate you. And the truth is, we need someone to stay behind. To keep a watch on the jeeps and the equipment we'll have to leave there. And if we're in bad shape on our way out, we'll need your driving and medical skills."

"If that's all I can get, I'll take it," she replied.

"You're getting quite a bit. A few days ago, you'll recall, I was dead set against you even coming this far."

"Are you sorry I did?"

"No."

"I'm still not giving up on going the rest of the way."

"You that anxious to see Billy again?"

"I don't know," Caroline admitted. "I try not to think about it too much. If I do, my imagination starts conjuring up all sorts of frightening possibilities."

"Do you still love him?"

"I don't know if I ever loved him. It's hard even to remember how I felt about him the last time I saw him. I was a naive girl twelve years ago. I was in awe of him. He was the campus hero, and all my girlfriends were jealous of me. But I didn't really know him. And before I had a chance to find out very much, he was gone." Caroline lowered her eyes to the lighted candle on the table between them. "The first year that he was listed as missing in action I was miserable. I felt so sorry for myself. I couldn't think of anything except how the whole meaning of my life had been put in limbo. It's hard for me to believe it now, but I missed Billy so intensely I felt I would go crazy. I loved him so much when I couldn't have him, I forgot that we really hadn't gotten along very well during those few months we had together as husband and wife. Finally, I just wore my feelings out. After four or five years there wasn't any anguish anymore. I thought of it as something terrible that had happened to me that I had gotten over. I doubted that I would ever see Billy again, and it no longer mattered that much."

"Didn't you ever think of remarrying?"

"Yes. About four years ago. I was going to have Billy declared legally dead. You can do that after seven years."

"What stopped you?"

Caroline sipped her brandy and looked away from the table. The lounge was empty except for the bartender, an enormous Thai with a bald head, who was energetically wiping glasses with a sparkling white dish towel. "Your father," she replied.

"How?"

"He didn't want Billy declared legally dead and he didn't want me to divorce him, either."

"How could he prevent it?"

"The man I wanted to marry was an instructor at MIT. We lived together for a year. He had very little money. He had been married before and he was paying alimony and child support. Of course, I was getting Billy's trust fund—over a hundred thousand a year. And if Billy were declared dead, I would get his inheritance. I didn't think it right to take it all. What I wanted was to be free to marry again. So I asked your father for a settlement. I said I would be happy to continue getting the same amount I had been receiving, and in return for having Billy declared legally dead, I'd renounce my rights to everything else. He refused. He knew I had been living with someone, and he told me that he would use that against me in court if I pursued my plan."

"He controls us all with his dollars," Rob muttered.

Caroline shook her head angrily. "I should have gone ahead with it anyway. I was a damned coward. My fiancé didn't care about the money. I did. I was spoiled. I couldn't imagine living without that income. So I gave up a wonderful man—someone who really cared about me—just for that damned money. I'm ashamed of myself."

"You can still give up the money," Rob said.

"What would I live on? I don't have any experience working. Who would hire me?"

"What about starting a new life with Billy?"

"I don't really think about that. Who knows what kind of a man he has become. It will be like meeting a stranger. A stranger I happen to be married to. It scares me." Suddenly Caroline was crying. She took the cocktail napkin and dabbed under her eyes, but it failed to stop the flow. She sniffled once, then covered her face with her hands and began sobbing in earnest.

"What's the matter?" Rob asked, alarmed.

She shook her head and said something he couldn't hear. He waited, feeling helpless and confused. Gradually she recovered her composure. She fished a handkerchief from her purse and dried her eyes. "I'm sorry. I guess I'm under more strain than I realized."

The conversation came to a sudden halt, as if it had run into an invisible barrier that it couldn't find its way around. Caroline held her wrist up close to her eyes so that she could read the dial on her tiny gold watch. "It's past our ten o'clock curfew," she said. "And tomorrow's a big day."

Rob didn't want their conversation to end. The alcohol and the excitement of the last hours were rapidly eroding Caroline's Wasp veneer, and he wanted to see behind it. "Let's have one last brandy."

"We've had too much to drink already."

Rob persuaded her. When the drinks arrived, he tried again. "Tell me about you and Billy."

"I've told you enough."

"Not yet you haven't."

Caroline slouched back against the lounge cushions and looked at Rob defiantly. "The truth is, we never had much of a marriage. Through the years of waiting, I refused to let myself believe this, but it's true. I can face it now. Things went bad right from the beginning—during our honeymoon. I told him that I had had an accident when I was younger and I couldn't have any children. He was furious. He felt that I had betrayed him. Of course, I should have told him before we were married, but I couldn't find the courage. I was hoping that he would be sympathetic when I told him why, but he wasn't. Instead, he threatened to leave me—to find a woman who could bear him children. I don't think we slept together after that."

"I'm sorry," Rob said.

Caroline nodded. "He was so callous about it. It took me a long time to recover from it. It finally dawned on me, years later, that your brother was really remarkably immature then. And so, of course, was I."

Caroline stared blankly at her glass of brandy. "I had a baby when I was fourteen," she continued, the words tumbling out in a quiet rush. "Never mind the circumstances. I didn't know anything about sex, obviously. And I didn't know I was pregnant until I was six months along—right in the middle of my freshman year at St. Anne's boarding school, if you can imagine that. I was afraid to tell my family. I ran off and found a home for unwed mothers way out in the middle of Pennsylvania somewhere. They called an aunt I was close to, and she came out. I had the baby. It was premature and stillborn. The doctor completely botched the job. I lost a lot of blood and almost died. At the time, I wished that I had. No one other than my aunt ever knew. And I never told her who was responsible."

Rob touched her hand again.

She sensed what he was thinking and clasped his hand hard. "Don't say anything or I'll start crying again."

"Why?"

"I'm afraid of you."

"Afraid? Why?"

"I don't know."

"Is that the only emotion you feel?"

"You're determined to see me cry again, aren't you."

"No. I just want to . . . understand you."

"Do you really?"

"You don't believe me, do you. Why?"

"I think I'd better go to bed."

Rob followed her down the long hotel corridor toward her room. She turned at the door to say good night. She held the door key in her hand, looking at the big metal weight attached to it.

"What are you afraid of?" Rob asked.

She clicked the keys nervously down the louvres on the door. "The situation. You're Billy's brother. We shouldn't get involved—especially now, when we've come to look for him."

"You never loved him, you told me. You're just worried about impropriety."

A couple of hotel guests walked past on the way to their room, and she waited until they had passed before she spoke: "I'm worried about you, Rob. About what will happen to you. I don't want to fall in love with you."

"Don't want to—"

"You're at war with everybody, even yourself. And I'm afraid of getting caught in the middle of it." Caroline rested her hands on his shoulders and looked up at him, her soft green eyes sad. She leaned her head against his chest, and they stood that way for a long time, not saying anything. Finally she unlocked the door to her room. "I'm a little drunk and I've talked too much."

Rob kissed her good night. It was an uncertain kiss, because he wasn't sure whether to aim for her lips, neck, forehead, or cheek. He ended up catching her awkwardly somewhere between her eye and her nose.

He walked down the hall to his own room, several doors away, not sure whether he felt depressed or elated, or some unlikely mixture of the two. *I'm in love with her,* he thought. *There's no doubt about it. What a terrible time for it.* But some things couldn't be helped.

He unlocked his door and stepped into the darkened room, found the light switch, and turned it on.

A woman was in his bed. Her head was propped against a stack of pillows, and the sheet was pulled up just over her breasts. She was smoking a cigarette and smiling at him.

22

New York City

"You are interfering in my area of responsibility," Otto Brandt said, raising his voice defensively. "And I don't like it." Brandt was Director of Cultural Information for the German Democratic Republic's Mission to the United Nations. In his four years' duty at the mission's headquarters at 58 Park Avenue in Manhattan, he had not once ever dispensed, collected, or otherwise bothered himself with cultural information of any kind. His real job, as the embassy *Resident* for East Germany's Directorate of State Security, was to oversee his government's espionage efforts in the United States. He swung his vinyl-upholstered swivel chair around to face the window, leaving his guest to stare at the back of his head.

"My instructions don't take your opinions into account," Dieter Rheinhart replied.

Brandt stroked his stubbly Vandyke beard angrily, his eyes focused unseeing on the double lane of traffic snaking south along the elevated ramp around Grand Central Station and spilling onto Park Avenue. "And you always follow instructions," he said, his voice heavy with irony.

"You have some objection to that?" Rheinhart challenged.

Brandt swiveled back around and gazed at the bureaucratic clutter of correspondence, reports, files, directives, and memorandums arranged in neat piles on his desk. "Before I help you," he demanded, "I insist that you reveal the details and the objective of this operation to me."

"Those are not my instructions."

Brandt stared at the younger man. His watery blue eyes, magnified behind thick lenses, made him appear even more ponderous and phlegmatic than he was. "You'd have made a good Nazi, Rheinhart," he said.

Rheinhart grinned. "I'm satisfied to make a good Communist."

The cultural attaché frowned and nodded with a barely perceptible tilt of the neck. "I intend to take this up with the ambassador," he said.

Rheinhart shook his head. "There's no need. You outrank him."

"He should be informed, nevertheless," Brandt insisted.

"You'd better think it through. The director expects total secrecy on this."

The cultural attaché swiveled his chair back and forth nervously. Rheinhart waited patiently for him to work out the consequences. He would see that if he told the ambassador, the ambassador—a dim-witted old party hack—would gossip about it to his friends on the SED Politburo and it would get back to Koenig. The director would then retaliate against Brandt's insubordination and ruin him. Rheinhart watched Brandt's hands flutter abstractedly over the piles of paper on his desk as he weighed the advantages of currying the ambassador's favor over risking the director's displeasure.

The director won. Brandt wrung his hands and sighed deeply. "Anyway, I don't know enough about your damned operation to tell him anything worthwhile."

Rheinhart reached into his pocket and withdrew a folded page torn from a notepad. "I will require these," he said, placing the sheet of paper on the corner of Brandt's desk.

Brandt picked up the paper with thumb and forefinger, as though it might be contaminated, shook it open, and held it out at arm's length to read it:

Photographic profile of the Canadair Challenger 600, including front, side, rear, top, and bottom: and interior cabin cockpit, galley, and toilet.

Manufacturer's blueprints and performance specs for the Canadair 600, including schematics for all onboard communications equipment.

Two short-barreled automatic pistols with extra ammo clips.
Four pairs of handcuffs.
A tranquilizing dart gun. Six darts.
Sodium Pentothal.
Two two-way portable HT-1 radios.

"How soon do you need these?"

"Twenty-four hours."

Brandt threw the list toward his desk. It missed and floated to the floor. "Impossible!"

Rheinhart reached down, picked the list up, and placed it on the desk. "Why are you being an obstructionist?"

"I'm not," Brandt snapped. "I have other priorities. And I don't have manpower to burn."

"The director sets the priorities, Herr Brandt."

Fear of the director was the decisive argument in the DDR's espionage service. Brandt cleared his throat. "I'll do what I can. I'm just warning you that it won't be easy. Twenty-four hours is not much time."

Rheinhart brushed off the complaint. "Hire some outsiders. You should spread the purchases around, anyway. Use some of our nationals at the UN." He was referring to the several dozen DDR citizens who worked for the UN Secretariat and General Assembly. Although formally independent from the DDR mission, they were in fact, like all Soviet-bloc citizens employed at the UN, completely under their mission's thumb.

"Is that all?" Brandt demanded.

"No. I need a man."

"What kind of man?"

"Someone with first-rate field experience."

Brandt wheeled his chair a few feet to a low filing cabinet, unlocked a drawer, and fingered rapidly through the tightly packed folders within. After a minute he made an unpleasant grunting noise and pulled out a sheaf of documents and slapped them on the desk near Rheinhart. "This is the individual you want—Wolfgang Hauser."

Rheinhart flipped through the files, then closed them. "I've heard of him. He has a bad reputation."

"So? You are not planning to introduce him to your mother."

"I don't need psychiatric problems."

"He is a dedicated professional. Reliable in a crisis."

"He's a killer."

Brandt shrugged. "He's the best I can do for you. Be reasonable. You won't tell me what the mission is. All I can do is provide you with someone capable of anything you might ask of him."

Rheinhart had no answer for that. Brandt's grudging cooperation was a frustrating nuisance, a perfect example of the drawbacks of Socialist bureaucracy. It was a wonder anything was ever accomplished at all. "You've given him to me because he's expendable," he said.

Brandt sighed and swiveled the chair around to face the window again. "We're all expendable, Herr Rheinhart. Come back tomorrow afternoon. I will have everything here for you. And then I hope never to see you again."

Bangkok, Thailand

Rob Grunwald closed the door of his hotel room and stood in front of it, facing the woman in his bed. She was Caucasian, with short coppery hair and a pointed chin. Her ears were round and stuck out under her hair, her nose long, her face narrow, and there were dark, puffy little bags under her eyes. She was neither particularly attractive nor particularly young.

She threw back the sheet and beckoned him with a crooked index finger. "I always wanted to do this," she said, in a husky, French-accented voice.

"Do what?"

"This. As they do in the James Bond movies." She made a sweeping gesture meant to take in her body and the bed and him all together. Her movements were too quick, suggesting the neurotic more than the sensual.

Rob took a few steps toward the bed, put his hands on his hips, and gazed down at her. Nude save for a wisp of white bra and underpants, her body was smooth and boyish—almost muscular. "Who are you?" he demanded.

She sat up, suddenly embarrassed, and yanked the sheet over her shoulders. "I am Ghislene Ferrer," she announced, as if that would explain everything.

It explained a lot. Rob hid his reaction by scooping up her clothes—an unseductive khaki shirt with perspiration stains under the arms and blue cotton twill trousers—from a nearby chair and tossing them onto the bed.

"I'm flattered by the attention," he said. "But I need a good night's sleep more than sex."

The Frenchwoman slipped on her shirt, took a cigarette from a pack in the pocket, and lit it with a match from the small box on the nightstand. "You American men are so immature," she sneered. "What makes you think I would let you fuck me?" She pronounced the four-letter word with the gusto of one who had only recently learned it and wanted to show it off.

Rob sat down on the edge of the bed. His instincts told him he was overmatched, and it made him feel suddenly exhausted. "Look . . ." he began.

"You are pretending that you don't know who I am," Ferrer accused him. "Why are you doing that? You think I don't know that you are doing that? You are very transparent to me, you know."

"All right," he confessed. "I know who you are."

"Who am I, then?" she demanded, banging the fingers holding the cigarette against her chest. Rob watched a piece of ash fall onto her bra and then roll down the steep pitch of her modest breast and onto the sheet.

"You're a writer—"

"A journalist," she corrected.

"For *Paris-Match*," Rob continued.

She shook her head. "My byline has appeared in over one thousand publications. In many languages. As you well know, I am world famous. So!" Ferrer took a deep puff of her Gitane and blew the smoke at Rob.

"As I well know," Rob repeated.

Ghislene Ferrer seemed intent on extracting all the ego gratification that she could. "Aren't you even a little bit . . . astonished . . . to find me here in your bed?"

"I'll admit it. I'm astonished."

Ferrer smiled. For the first time in their encounter, some trace of sensuality leaked through her aggressive façade. "But you are not pleased," she said.

"I haven't gotten past being astonished."

"Yes, you have," she insisted. She smashed out the cigarette in the ashtray and began buttoning her shirt. "You are very self-centered—like most American men," she concluded, pursing her lips together in a pout. "A healthy man would at least feel some *frisson*."

Rob shook his head in wonderment. "Why didn't you pick a room with a healthier man in it, then? What the hell are you doing here?"

"Enfin, mon ami," Ferrer purred. She threw aside the sheet and stood up on the bed to slip into her trousers. Rob was surprised at how short she was. Her crotch met him at eye level. Behind the cotton he could see a thick patch of dark red hair.

"*Enfin* what?"

"*Enfin* you ask the obvious question," she said. "I want a little favor."

"What kind of favor?"

She buttoned the pants and zipped up the fly with a masculine flourish. "I want a ride."

"I'll call you a cab."

"Tomorrow you are going to northeast Thailand, no? I want a ride."

Rob didn't deny it. "What for?"

"I'm after a story. Just like you."

"We're just a documentary-film crew. We're going to shoot some nature footage, that's all."

"Then you can give me a ride, surely."

"There's no room, I'm afraid."

Ferrer said nothing. She sat back down on the bed, crossed her legs under her, and lit up another Gitane.

"The jeeps will be full," he said. "There are five of us, plus a lot of equipment."

Ferrer laughed. "You are a charming *menteur*."

"I'm sure you can rent your own jeep."

"It would not be safe for a woman like me to go alone."

"Then northeast Thailand will just have to look out for itself."

"You are very droll."

"I guess so. Do you have another room in the hotel you can go to? I'm really pretty tired."

"Not until you consent to take me with you."

"You want me to call the police?"

"You want me to scream rape?"

Rob stood up. "You take this room. I'll go find another one."

Ferrer reached out and snared a belt loop and pulled him back onto the bed. "It is very important that I go with you," she said. "Why do you think that I compromised myself like this? Coming into your bed like this, risking my reputation?"

"I give up. Why?"

"It has to do with my story," she said. "It's a very important story. Its success depends on you, *mon lapin*."

Rob gripped the edge of the mattress with both hands. There was something monstrous about this woman. From the moment he spotted her in the bed, he had guessed what was coming. He felt angry with himself for not having been able to head it off.

Ferrer sucked in a lungful of the dark tobacco smoke. "I intend to be the first one to interview your brother," she said, belching the smoke from her nostrils like a fire-breathing dragon.

Rob tried to look sincerely puzzled: "I honestly don't know what you're talking about."

"It is useless for you to deny it," Ferrer said, flicking her hand at him dismissively. "I have important friends all over the world. They tell me things. I put facts together and come up with new facts. I am not one of the world's most respected journalists for nothing. I have a reputation for getting the stories that no one else can get. I have a genius for enterprise. The many awards that I have won prove it. And when I have made up my mind to get a story, I cannot be stopped. I have interviewed international terrorists, I have—"

"Who told you I was looking for my brother?"

"No one told me. It is a conclusion I arrived at myself—from my own investigation. A magazine editor I know asked my opinion of a story he received about your brother. I told him it was probably a fraud. But then its author, a certain unfortunate Monsieur Duffy, suddenly died. That made me curious. And my curiosity led me to seek out your father. He refused to see me, but your sister was more cooperative. From her I learned that *you* had returned home. When she refused to tell me where I could find you, I became even more curious. From another source—the editor of a magazine for professional soldiers—I discovered that you were busy hiring mercenaries. The rest I figured out for myself. So, *voilà*. Here I am."

"*Voilà* indeed," Rob replied. "You're not going with us. So forget it."

"If I don't go with you, *mon trésor,* you don't go at all. I will publicize your mission. You will be stopped."

"You're treading on dangerous ground."

Ferrer laughed contemptuously. "You think that you can scare me off? I have been shot at in Honduras and El Salvador. I was held a prisoner in Bolivia. My car was shelled in Lebanon. In Northern Ireland a bomb nearly—"

Rob stood up again, grasped Ghislene Ferrer by her copper hair, and pulled her toward the door. He expected her to scream, but she didn't. Instead, she punched and kicked him repeatedly around the stomach and groin. He managed to get the door open while holding her with one hand, and then maneuver her through it, grunting in pain from the blows he was absorbing. When he let her go, she caught her balance against the wall.

"I'll be downstairs waiting," she said, grinning defiantly at him.

"Tomorrow at dawn. And don't worry. I'm the only journalist who knows what you are up to. Your secret is safe with me as long as I go along to record what happens. And I have my own supplies and I don't take up much space. You will hardly know I'm there. And my articles will make you and your brother great heroes. They will appear in dozens of newspapers and magazines all across the world. Millions of people will read of your brave exploits. You will become a celebrity."

Rob crouched in the doorway, resisting the impulse to massage the throbbing in his groin. "And what if I fail?"

The petite French journalist arched her eyebrows in innocent surprise. "Then, of course, they will read about that instead," she replied.

23

The Atlantic Ocean

The chief communications officer of the *Dresden,* a twenty-year-old rust bucket of a submarine of the Foxtrot class, found Captain Helmut Grau in his bed, sipping schnapps and reading a well-thumbed French paperback novel.

"What do you want?" the captain demanded, as the officer hesitated in the doorway. "It's the middle of the night!"

"Sorry to disturb you, Captain," he replied, holding up a folded piece of lined amber paper. "I have a code-yellow radio message from Pankow."

Captain Grau closed his book and dropped it on the blanket. "Pankow?" he asked, incredulous.

"Yes, sir. Priority channel."

The captain pulled his sizable bulk to a sitting position and waved for the officer to come closer. He had never received a coded communication from East Berlin. Although theoretically under East German control, as his country's only submarine in the Warsaw Pact forces, the *Dresden*'s patrol assignments were integrated into those of the Russian Northern Fleet, and his orders always came directly from Supreme Navy Command, in Moscow. "What is it?" he asked, his curiosity aroused.

The officer advanced tentatively into the compartment and handed the captain the cable. "We have to pick up a passenger, sir."

Grau grunted and unfolded the paper. The message instructed him to alter his present course immediately and proceed at top speed to a certain spot in the Atlantic Ocean, precisely spelled out in degrees, minutes, and seconds of longitude and latitude. There he would rendezvous with the *Ivan Kolyshkin,* a Russian submarine depot ship operating out of Cuba, and take aboard "an official of the German Democratic Republic." The official, the message concluded, would be carrying "new orders" for the *Dresden.*

"New orders?" the captain echoed. "Are we a patrol ship or are we a goddamned sight-seeing boat?"

The communications officer shook his head in sympathy.

"Where will these coordinates put us?"

"About three hundred kilometers off the coast of Florida, sir."

"How far is that from here?"

"From our present position," the younger man replied, "it's twelve hours sailing, at eighteen knots."

"Eighteen knots!" the captain thundered. "This old Russian tub can't go that fast—unless we surface."

"It says top speed, sir," the officer mumbled.

Grau dropped the new orders onto his nightstand and settled back against his pillow. "I'm not surfacing under the nose of the U.S. Atlantic Fleet just to pick up some asshole VIP. Even if he *is* a German. Don't exceed fifteen knots. Who's got the watch?"

"The first mate, sir."

"Good. Send a confirmation and then pass the coordinates on to the bridge to feed into the NavCom." The captain picked up the paperback and flipped the pages, searching for his place.

"Is it a good book, sir?" the communications officer inquired.

"Not bad," the captain replied, with a heavy shrug. "It's about this French convict. He escapes from a place called Devil's Island, off the coast of South America. The French used to have a penal colony there."

"Ah, that's *Papillon,*" the officer said brightly. "The Americans made a movie of it. Dustin Hoffman and Steve McQueen. I saw it in Budapest last year."

The captain glared up at his young officer, his mouth tightened in a dangerous frown. "The movie is never as good as the book," he growled. "Tell the watch to wake me when we reach the rendezvous. And fifteen knots. You go a knot faster, I'll tie you onto a torpedo and shoot you at an oil tanker."

Northeast Thailand

Route 5 north was a two-lane blacktop in surprisingly good repair. Once past the suburbs of Bangkok and the new shantytowns around Don Muang Airport, it entered onto a flat, endless sea of shimmering brown and green rice paddies. Mist, baked from the fields by the early-morning sun, shrouded the horizon in a smoky curtain through which an occasional house or line of low trees, or the solitary tableau of buffalo and peasant straining through knee-deep muck at opposite ends of a crude plow, would materialize and then vanish, like a mirage. To the east, the silvery-blue flanks of a mountain ridge lurked behind the haze. The pungent odor of dung and freshly turned earth stung the nostrils.

Rob Grunwald drove the lead jeep, a three-year-old Toyota Land Cruiser, rented in Bangkok. Howard Gilmore sat beside him, and Harris McWhirter crouched in the back, squeezed in among the tightly stacked cases of equipment and supplies.

"Getting hot already," Gilmore murmured, slapping the roof nervously with his big hand and squinting at the sun pouring in the open window on his side.

"We'll make Sara Buri in about an hour," McWhirter replied. "From there to Korat we'll be traveling through those hills over there—the Phetchabuns. It'll be cooler."

Gilmore nodded and drummed his fingers on the roof and began singing softly:

" *'If today was not an endless highway,*
  If tonight was not a crooked trail,
  If tomorrow wasn't such a long time,
  Then lonesome would mean nothing to me at all.' "

Rob swerved too late to miss a pothole. The jeep frame bottomed against its springs, bouncing McWhirter around among the luggage and banging Gilmore's head against the roof. "I feel like a goddamned fool," he muttered.

Gilmore rubbed the top of his bald head gingerly. "That doesn't mean you have to drive like one."

"The woman blackmailed me. What choice did I have?"

"Look. We don't even mind." Gilmore twisted around in his seat. "Do we, Harris?"

"No," McWhirter drawled, sounding bored. "But I hope you let us recruit the next female."

Gilmore chuckled. "You got one good break, though," he said.

Rob eased his foot off the accelerator and moved toward the shoulder to give an approaching truck a wide berth. "What's that?"

"Caroline wasn't armed. Otherwise, I'm positive she'd have blown you away. Never saw a lady that mad in my whole life."

Rob sighed. The showdown in the lobby of the Oriental Hotel in the gray light of dawn two hours earlier had embarrassed him deeply. Ghislene Ferrer was there, just as she had promised to be, standing in a cloud of cigarette smoke in front of three enormous suitcases and two tote bags, checked out and ready to go.

Rob had bowed to the inevitable, but not graciously. After a tortured explanation to the others of how the French journalist had forced her way onto the mission, he had turned to Ferrer and tried to persuade her that the expedition didn't have room for all her luggage. She had responded by ordering a bewildered bellboy to pile her suitcases on the roof rack of one of the jeeps, already laden with supplies. Rob had ordered her to remove them. She had refused. Finally, Rob had climbed onto the roof and thrown the suitcases back onto the pavement, breaking a strap on one of them. Ferrer had cursed him in gutter French.

The standoff was resolved, eventually, but not before Caroline, in a state of jealous outrage, warned Rob that if Ferrer could blackmail him, so could she. Either he took her all the way to Vietnam, or she'd do what Ferrer had threatened to do—expose the mission.

Rob didn't believe her, but Ferrer had already exhausted him, so he placated her, at least temporarily, with a vague promise to consider it. He got his revenge on both women by making them ride together in the second jeep with Wyler.

"I've handicapped the mission," Rob said, "and I know it."

"I wouldn't worry about Ferrer," McWhirter replied. "She looks tougher than stale beef jerky."

"I'm worried about *us*. The woman is a menace. And I'm worried about Caroline. She's going to insist on staying with us all the way now. How can I talk her out of it?"

No one volunteered an answer. Rob looked across at Gilmore. "You think we should let her stay on?"

Gilmore removed his glasses and cleaned them with a shirttail. "No, I don't. If anything happens to her, I'll be as upset as you."

Rob glanced at McWhirter in the rearview mirror. "Harris? What should we do?"

McWhirter grunted. "If she wants to come, let her."

"Don't you think she'll be a burden?"

"You never know."

McWhirter's eyes were hidden behind his aviator sunglasses, so Rob was unable to read his face. "You saying you don't care?"

"I'm saying it's up to you."

Rob looked back at the road, which was rolling beneath the hood in front of him at fifty miles an hour. He was certain that McWhirter was completely disgusted by the unplanned addition of two women to the team. Why was he being so damned polite about it?

The two-jeep caravan, alone on the highway save for an occasional passing motorcycle or bus, reached Sara Buri at eight o'clock, turned onto Route 21, and left behind the rice paddies for the cool hills of the Phetchabun range. At ten o'clock they stopped in Korat, a quiet, graceful little town 150 miles northeast of Bangkok, and bought some fruit from the local vendors in the main square. By one o'clock that afternoon they were in Khon Kaen, 250 miles from Bangkok and deep into northeast Thailand. Instead of a sleepy peasant village, Khon Kaen was an oil boom town, bursting with bars, prostitutes, and Americans in cowboy hats and pickup trucks raising dust on the dry dirt streets.

McWhirter, taking his turn at the wheel, spotted an outdoor restaurant with a gas station in front and pulled the jeep up alongside the single ancient pump. "Have to blink my eyes," he said, "to make sure I'm not in west Texas."

Wyler nosed the second jeep up behind him. After refueling and a quick lunch of noodles and fruit, the caravan continued on, striking east from Khon Kaen on Route 25.

Rob, sitting on the luggage in the back, unfolded the road map of Thailand and steadied it on his lap. "In terms of miles," he said, spanning the distances roughly with the edge of his palm, "we're already halfway there."

"Only in terms of miles," McWhirter warned him. "We're on schedule, that's all. We want to reach the border before dark."

"We'll do that easily," Rob said.

A rickety wooden bus careened around a corner and roared toward them at high speed. Arms and elbows protruded from its windows like legs on a caterpillar, and its roof was stacked with suitcases, boxes, and a few insanely daring passengers clinging to the metal railing like the crew of a storm-tossed sailboat. The bus missed both jeeps by inches.

"For God's sake, don't make any more predictions," Gilmore pleaded.

Half an hour out of Khon Kaen the orchards and rice paddies faded to a dusty, semi-arid terrain, and the villages—forlorn collections of unpainted wood and concrete-block shacks—looked distinctly less prosperous. Oddly, as the quality of the countryside around them deteriorated, the highway improved. Rob wondered aloud about the contradiction.

"We're into guerrilla country now," McWhirter explained. "The government in Bangkok—and Washington—is trying to win the hearts and minds of the locals with better roads. They also want to be able to move the army around fast up here."

As if to prove McWhirter's words, a convoy of six military trucks materialized out of a cloud of dust and bore down on them with the same reckless abandon as had the bus. McWhirter pulled off to the side of the road and let them pass.

Three more times during the next hour they were forced to the side of the road by a similar convoy.

At the tiny hamlet of Ban Si Yaek, they turned off Route 25 north and headed east on a recently paved highway that cut straight toward Route 27 and the border. For fifteen miles they drove through plateau country, the blacktop arrowing across a landscape as featureless and dusty as a stretch of desert. A cluster of tin-roofed shacks appeared, huddled against the road as if seeking protection from the emptiness around them. A ragged child waved from a doorway. A man on a bicycle rode past. Then nothing for five miles.

"According to the map," Rob said, "there should be a town just ahead."

"There's *something* up ahead," Gilmore said, pressing the edge of his palm against the windshield to cut the sun's glare.

McWhirter eased his foot off the accelerator and Rob bent forward from the back to get a better view.

"Another convoy," Gilmore said.

Three hundred yards ahead of them, a pair of olive-green troop transports were parked on opposite sides of the highway. Soldiers sat in the backs of both vehicles, and other uniformed men stood in the roadway. As the trucks and men loomed nearer, Rob saw that some of the soldiers were holding rifles.

McWhirter slowed the jeep to a crawl. "Military roadblock," he muttered.

The jeep came abreast of the trucks' tailgates. The soldiers in the back sat motionless, expectant, waiting for something to happen. One soldier was standing out in the roadway, directly in the jeeps' path. He paused there uncertainly, his rifle butt on his hip, then stepped aside and raised his free arm, as if in salute.

"Wave and smile," McWhirter said.

The jeep idled slowly past the soldier with the raised hand. Rob grinned engagingly and wagged a hand at him. Seconds later a sharp concussion cracked the air.

McWhirter slammed on the brake. The second jeep, with Caroline at the wheel, bumped up against them. Another loud pop of gunfire. Rob glanced to his right and saw three uniformed men crouched on the side of the roadway, their rifles pointed directly at him. The soldier Rob had thought was waving them on through jumped to the side of the jeep and jammed the barrel of his automatic up against McWhirter's neck.

"Stay cool," McWhirter whispered to his companions. "They're spoiling for a little fun. Don't give them any excuses."

Another soldier appeared from behind the truck and joined the one with the rifle pressed against McWhirter. He said something in a low voice in Thai and McWhirter answered him.

"He wants us to get out," McWhirter said. "With our hands on our heads."

24

Dieter Rheinhart waited impatiently just inside a door at the far left end of the private-plane terminal at La Guardia Airport, a green metal toolbox in one hand, a black two-way radio in the other.

He glanced at his watch and then out the small square window in the heavy metal door. The view was of the loading area. A dozen small aircraft were clustered around the tarmac, in various stages of arrival and departure. The plane that monopolized Rheinhart's attention was the large Canadair Challenger, parked off to the left, taking on fuel from a tanker truck. The 68-foot-long twin-jet executive aircraft was the last word in business jets. It could cruise at speeds approaching 600 mph and had a range of 4,600 miles, putting all of the continental United States, Europe, and most of South America within its reach. Gleaming on the white tail fin of the six-million-dollar craft was the Grunwald Industries logo—a thick black capital "I" with a smaller, crimson capital "G" superimposed upon it.

Rheinhart watched one of the ground crew pull the hose from the plane's fueling socket, rewind it into the tanker truck, and drive off. The jet's door, just aft of the cockpit, stood open, its retractable stairway out and waiting for its passengers. Only the pilot and the copilot, whom he had seen enter the craft fifteen minutes earlier, were on board.

Rheinhart flicked his radio's stubby rubber-coated antenna nervously back and forth across his pants leg. He checked his watch again: 9:00 A.M. A workman pushed past him and went out the door. He had been standing at that spot for nearly twenty minutes. *Damn this waiting,* he thought. He wondered whether he should have rubbed a little grease and dirt into his spanking-new white coveralls. They made him feel conspicuous.

The walkie-talkie came to life with a scratchy burst of static. He raised it swiftly to his ear. *"Ja?"*

"Sie kommen," a voice replied.

"Danke."

Rheinhart jammed the radio into a pocket in the coveralls and took a firm grip on the toolbox. Hauser, up on the observation deck, had spotted the limousine. The waiting was over.

He pushed open the door and strode rapidly across the oil-stained tarmac toward the Canadair. They were making it easier for him, he thought, leaving the jet's doorway open and unguarded. He wouldn't have to face the tricky task of talking his way on board.

At the top of the folding steps, he paused, took a breath, and then ducked inside.

The aircraft's interior had been heavily customized. The seats of the original passenger cabin had been removed and the space partitioned into two cabins. In the fore cabin, immediately to his left, was a narrow, benchlike sofa that ran beneath the two window ports on one side, and a desk and swivel chair on the other. The rest of the space was occupied by four heavy armchairs arranged around a polished wood coffee table. A door at the back led to the aft cabin— most likely a small bedroom and toilet, Rheinhart guessed.

To his right was the forward bulkhead, separating the passenger space from the cockpit. Rheinhart stepped quickly through and greeted the crew members seated at the plane's controls.

The pilot, his fingers checking a bank of overhead switches, looked back. "What do you want?"

Rheinhart placed his toolbox on the navigation table behind the copilot's seat and snapped it open. "You reported a malfunctioning oil-pressure light."

The two faces now staring at him were a husband-and-wife team named Don and Marcie Hendry. Hendry, a gangly man in his mid-fifties, had once flown for Pan Am, where he had met Marcie. Grunwald had hired Hendry seven years ago and paid to put Marcie through flight school. Like so many Grunwald employees, they were indebted to their boss, and fiercely loyal. Rheinhart had done his homework, but actually seeing in the flesh the round, pretty female face in the copilot's seat unsettled him.

"That was last week," she said, her eyes narrowing suspiciously. "It was fixed."

Rheinhart drew a snub-nosed .32-caliber Mauser automatic from the toolbox and wagged the short barrel back and forth between the astonished couple. "I'm glad to hear it," he said. "Now, listen to me very carefully and do exactly as I say as soon as I say it. I do not intend to hurt you, but I warn you that I am deadly serious. Do not talk, do not resist. Just obey. Or I will kill you immediately. Do you understand?"

The couple stared at him dumbly.

"Do you understand?"

They nodded. "Listen," Hendry began, "whoever you are, you'll never get away with this. The—"

"Do not talk!" Rheinhart shouted. Hendry shut up. Rheinhart withdrew a pair of handcuffs from his toolbox and tossed them to him. "Lock one end of these onto the bar frame at the front of your seat's left armrest. Don't hesitate. Do it now!"

Hendry clamped one end of the cuff around the steel frame and slid it closed. Rheinhart pointed the pistol at Hendry's wife. "Lock his left wrist in the other end." She glared back at him defiantly. "Quickly!" he barked.

Marcie Hendry complied, fumbling awkwardly to reach the free end of the handcuffs and close the bracelet around her husband's left wrist. When she had locked it closed, manacling the pilot to the armrest, Rheinhart motioned her back into her own seat and tossed her another pair of cuffs. "Lock yourself onto your right-side armrest in the same manner, and do it as fast as you can."

"What are you going to do with us?" she demanded.

"Be quick!" he ordered.

The copilot snapped one end of the cuffs onto the frame, and then fiddled nervously getting the other bracelet around her wrist. Rheinhart held the pistol against her head, grabbed her wrist, and checked that the cuffs were locked. He repeated the procedure with the pilot. Satisfied that both were securely tethered to their seats, he glanced back through the open cockpit door into the forward cabin. What was keeping Hauser?

He turned to the Hendrys. "Let me advise you of the following facts: I am myself an experienced pilot. I am familiar with every aspect of this aircraft, and with all the preflight and takeoff procedures at this airport. I am also familiar with today's airport emergency codewords. If you cooperate with us exactly, I promise that I will not harm you. But any deviation from your normal takeoff routines will be met instantly with a bullet to the brain. Do you understand completely?"

The two said nothing.

"Continue with your preflight checkout. As soon as your passengers come aboard, you will fly the aircraft out of here in the normal manner."

Hauser finally appeared, bounding up the steps and into the plane, breathing heavily. He grinned at Rheinhart as he entered the cockpit. "They're right behind me," he said.

"How many?"

"Just two. Grunwald and his bodyguard."

"Close this door," Rheinhart told him. "Wait until they're both on board." He turned to the husband-and-wife pilots. "Get on with your checkout."

Hendry cleared his throat nervously. "It's kind of hard to do with my left hand tied down."

"You'll manage," Rheinhart replied.

A series of dull squeaks and a slight swaying of the plane's deck warned Rheinhart that the passengers were coming aboard. He heard low voices, clumping footsteps, and a solid thud as the stairs were retracted and the outside door snugged shut into its airtight seal.

Someone banged on the cockpit door. Hauser drew a pistol from a pocket in his coveralls and snapped the safety back. A voice, muffled through the paneling, called out: "Anybody in there? Open the door, for chrissake." After a pause, someone rattled the handle. "What are you two doing in there, playin' with each other? Open the door!"

Rheinhart pulled out the tranquilizer dart gun from the toolbox and slapped it into Hauser's empty hand. "Go ahead," he whispered. Hauser nodded. Rheinhart reached down, twisted the lock, and pulled the door open.

Grunwald's bodyguard, a barrel-chested former New York City cop with a jowly, pocked face, understood the situation instantly. His right hand reached across his chest toward the pistol hidden under his left arm. Hauser fired at him twice at point-blank range, each bullet driving directly into his heart. The big man's hand flopped out from beneath his suit jacket, and he collapsed onto the carpeted cabin floor like an axed steer, shaking the aircraft as he hit.

Grunwald, who had paused by the fore cabin's small desk to make a telephone call, ran toward the rear of the plane. Hauser rushed after him and fired a tranquilizer dart. It whooshed across the cabin and struck him just above the left shoulder blade. Grunwald managed to get through the aft doorway, but Hauser caught up with him before he could wedge it closed. Hauser kicked the door open and fell on Grunwald, pinning his arms to the floor.

"Don't hurt him!" Rheinhart warned.

Grunwald's struggles rapidly grew more feeble as the tranquilizer took effect. Gradually his arms and legs ceased to move altogether. Hauser stood up and straightened his white coveralls fastidiously.

"Drag this one out of the way," Rheinhart ordered, gesturing toward the inert form of the bodyguard, lying face up in a widening stain of blood. "And get the life jackets out. They're under that sofa bench by the side window ports. Get one on Grunwald, then strap him into one of those easy chairs." He turned back to the Hendrys, who had watched the bloody confrontation in stricken silence. "Have you completed the prestart check?"

Hendry nodded.

"Then let's go. But I warn you—the first wrong word over that radio will be your last."

The pilot pulled the mike up to his mouth and keyed it. "Ground control, this is November-9-7-2-Charlie," he said, his voice betraying a slight shakiness. "Requesting start-up clearance."

The scratchy voice of ground control came back instantly: "Roger, November-9-7-2-Charlie."

Hendry fired the engines and maneuvered the jet through the crowd of parked aircraft and out to the edge of the taxiway.

"November-9-7-2-Charlie requesting taxi clearance."

"Roger, 9-7-2-Charlie. Taxi to runway 2-8-left."

As the Canadair began its taxi down the runway, the couple put aside for the moment the fact that they were under a hijacker's gun, and lost themselves in the concentration necessary for getting a plane safely into the air at a busy national airport. Rheinhart strapped himself into the jump seat against the cockpit's rear bulkhead, donned the extra headset by the navigation table, and listened to the chatter of pilot and control tower.

"9-7-2-Charlie, this is ground control. Listen out on 1-6-5-point-7 for takeoff clearance."

"Roger, control."

"7-2-Charlie, hold short of the runway."

An Eastern 727 was ahead of them in the taxi line. Rheinhart watched it swing into position, gun its mighty engines, and roll down the wide tarmac strip, its jet exhaust billowing heat waves as it strained toward takeoff speed.

"7-2-Charlie, you are cleared to lineup."

The Canadair turned onto the runway.

"7-2-Charlie, you are cleared for takeoff. Wind 260 at 12."

"Roger."

Hendry pushed the throttles forward with his free right hand, while his wife steadied the yoke. The craft accelerated rapidly down the runway, until the broken white centerline merged into a continuous strip.

"Eighty knots," Marcie Hendry said, reading out the ground speed from the dial in front of her. "V-1."

Hendry dropped his right hand onto the yoke. "Rotate," he said. The jet hopped effortlessly into the sky in far less space than the 727 that had preceded it.

"V-2," his wife murmured. "Gear up."

Rheinhart heard the faint rumble of the gear carriage retracting up into the nose of the plane.

"7-2-Charlie, climb to six thousand feet. Change to 1-7-9-point-3."

"Roger."

Ten minutes into the flight they had cleared the New York City area and were on their assigned heading south for Washington's National Airport.

"Kill the radio," Rheinhart commanded. "And hand me your headsets."

Marcie quickly complied, but Hendry started to protest. Rheinhart leaned forward and ripped his headset off unceremoniously and tossed it, with the other one, under the nav table. He checked to satisfy himself that all radio switches on the instrument panel were in the OFF position, then returned to his green metal toolbox and drew out a slip of paper.

"Bring the plane around to zero-4-5," he said.

Hendry craned his neck around to look at Rheinhart. "That's out over the ocean."

"That's right."

"We don't have the fuel to get us across the Atlantic," he protested.

"We aren't going across the Atlantic," Rheinhart replied.

"Where are we going, then?" Hendry's wife asked.

Rheinhart ignored her. "Turn on your VOR," he ordered. "And set the dial at 2-8-8."

Marcie Hendry complied. Over his headphones Rheinhart heard the gratifying high-pitched signal, with its superimposed Morse-code identifying letters: "S-S-A."

"What's your readout?" Rheinhart demanded.

Hendry bent forward to read his compass and horizontal-situation indicator. "The beacon is at 110 knots, bearing zero-4-4-point-2."

"Descend to 1,000 feet," Rheinhart said, "and home in on it."

"What's out there?" Mrs. Hendry asked. "What are we homing on?"

Rheinhart took a deep breath and forced his muscles to relax. His quarry was safely in the bag. The most difficult, uncertain parts of the kidnap were behind him. All that remained was the dangerous part. "A black hole," he said, allowing a smug grin to curl his lips. "Into which we shall soon disappear."

Ronkonkoma, Long Island

Al Pickering blinked his eyes at the screen of the large radarscope in front of him. He blinked his eyes again, focusing on one green blip near the top left edge. No, he was not imagining it, he decided. It was inexplicably veering off its southerly heading and moving east. He touched a finger nervously to the microphone on his headset.

"November-9-7-2-Charlie, this is New York Center. Please report your position. . . . November-9-7-2-Charlie, this is New York Center. Please report your position. . . . Do you read me?"

Pickering tapped his microphone in frustration. "This is New York Center calling November-9-7-2-Charlie. Come in, please. You are departing from your flight path. November-9-7-2-Charlie, check your position immediately, please. Do you read me?"

Pickering waited, watching the green blip on the screen. It was now on an east-northeast heading, moving out over the Atlantic Ocean.

"November-9-7-2-Charlie, this is New York Center. Will you come in, please. . . ."

Pickering tried for another minute to raise the aircraft, then stopped to check the plane's flight plan on the computer console beside him. The plane was a private jet, a Canadair Challenger 600, registered to Grunwald Industries, in New York City.

The traffic controller rubbed his chin. *Shit,* he thought. *Maybe it was a hijack.*

The Atlantic Ocean

"How close are we?" Rheinhart demanded.

Hendry checked his instrument panel. "The beacon is at ten knots. We'll be coming up on it in five minutes."

"Slow your airspeed to one hundred knots."

Hendry eased back the throttle and watched the airspeed indicator flicker downward from three hundred to one hundred knots. Rheinhart looked out the side panel of the cockpit windscreen. The ocean was close below them, a thin lace of whitecaps breaking and re-forming across the undulating dark-green surface. The sky was clear, and the midday May sun sparkled on the waves. Rheinhart had hoped for poorer visibility. He scanned the horizon, looking for ships, and saw none.

"What's the wind?" he demanded.

"Steady out of the west at fifteen knots," Marcie Hendry replied.

"Jesus!" It was Hendry, his gaze fixed forward, at a spot just short of the horizon. Rheinhart stood up and looked over Mrs. Hendry's head. He saw it, too.

The long, curving black hull of a submarine was visible, riding motionless in the water, its back exposed above the waves like some enormous whale. A conning tower jutted from the middle of the cylindrical behemoth, and two large yellow inflatable dinghies were moored to its flanks. Rheinhart could just make out the tiny figures of several seamen standing on the narrow deck.

"A submarine?" Hendry asked, his eyes wide in disbelief. "What for?"

"To rescue us. Listen carefully. Fly directly over, waggle your wings, then circle back into the wind and ditch the plane as close to the submarine as you can safely manage. They have rescue crews and boats ready to pick us up."

. "The water's rough," Hendry said, clearly shaken at the idea of ditching in the water.

"You can do it," Rheinhart said. "You're an experienced pilot."

"I've never had to ditch," he replied.

"Don't worry," Rheinhart assured him. "This plane has a very flat underbelly. It'll set down smoothly and it'll float—at least for a few minutes. And that's all we need."

Rheinhart shrugged into his life vest and pulled its cords snug around his chest and waist.

"You're going to let us drown, aren't you," Marcie Hendry said, suppressing her fear with angry grimaces.

"Absolutely not," Rheinhart answered.

"Then why won't you undo our handcuffs? We don't have a chance, otherwise."

Rheinhart called to Hauser to bring him two more life jackets and the dart gun. "As soon as the plane is on the water," he replied, putting all the reassurance into his voice that he could muster, "I am going to give you both a tranquilizer dart. As soon as you're unconscious, we'll unlock your handcuffs, slip the life vests over your heads, and carry you out, just as we intend to do with your boss. You've cooperated. We have what we want. We have no reason to kill you. As long as you make a good landing, you have nothing to fear."

Hauser appeared with the vests and the dart gun.

"As soon as we've stopped moving, get the door open," Rheinhart instructed him. "The door is high, but the waves are rough, so we'll probably ship water. Push Grunwald out immediately, then come up here and help me with these two."

Hauser gave Rheinhart a strange look, then nodded elaborately. There was something so deeply insubordinate about the man that even when following orders to the letter, he seemed to be disobeying them.

The Canadair passed over the submarine, waggled its wings, flew three miles past, and banked around in a wide arc for its return approach. While his wife anxiously read off the distances, Hendry eased the craft down as low as he dared—barely a hundred feet from the waves—and nudged the throttles back until the jet was on the edge of stalling.

"You're doing fine," Rheinhart assured him, watching the conning tower of the submarine looming toward them across the rapidly shortening expanse of sea. "Hit the water as close beside the sub as you can. Flare out and cut the engines. You want the wings to slap down on top of the waves, not slice into them. Once you hit, the plane will skip forward a hundred feet or so, then the water will grab her. The flatter you hit, the longer we'll stay afloat. The closer you hit, the faster our rescue."

The submarine seemed on the same level with them now, growing large as it zoomed toward them.

"You're a little high still," Rheinhart said. "More flaps."

Hendry dropped the flaps briefly, tipping the nose of the jet toward the water, and inched back the throttles.

"Okay, bring it level. . . . Slow it down."

The submarine shot past them to the right.

"We're past it! Flaps up! Flaps up!"

Hendry kicked the flaps up full and killed the engines. The 68-foot-long jet's nose tilted up, as if to climb back into the sky. Then the water caught its tail and it paused, almost motionless, before slapping down on the water, its wings and underbelly smacking against the ocean with a shuddering bang, sending up sheets of water that crashed heavily over the windshields.

Rheinhart gasped, the air knocked out of him. The Canadair Challenger struck the surface a second time, then settled into the sea, silent and still save for the hissing of the water evaporating against the hot metal of its hull.

Rheinhart unsnapped his belt and jumped to the side port window. They had overshot the submarine by nearly a mile.

Ronkonkoma, Long Island

Pickering and his supervisor watched together, following the green blip on the radar screen with a fascinated dread as it drifted farther and farther off course. Another controller had taken over the other traffic on the screen.

"What's his altitude now?" the supervisor asked.

"A thousand feet, and he's reduced speed," Pickering said.

"Can't be a hijack," the supervisor said.

Several other controllers, on their break, sensed the impending drama and were gathering behind Pickering and the supervisor in the dim light of the control room.

"You think he's losing power?"

The supervisor nodded. "He's in trouble, that's for certain. Let's get help."

Pickering grabbed the red telephone and punched the code that would put him through to Air-Sea Rescue.

"We've got a problem," Pickering said, when someone came on the line. "It's a twin-engine private jet, N972C. She's off course and losing altitude. Her present bearings are . . ."

Pickering turned back to check the plane's position, but the green blip had disappeared from the screen. "Shit," he said. "She's down."

The Atlantic Ocean

Rheinhart worked with controlled fury. He shot a tranquilizer dart into the arms of the pilot and his wife, talking to them as he twice loaded, aimed, and fired the small air-charged pistol. "You did it," he said. "Everything is going to be fine. Just fine. You have nothing to worry about now. We'll get you out of here. When you wake up, you'll be safe aboard that submarine, drinking vodka with the crew."

He watched them slump into unconsciousness, then quickly unlocked their handcuffs and dragged them out of their seats and back into the fore cabin. Hauser had already managed to get the aircraft's door open and was struggling with the weight of Grunwald's limp body.

The plane was pitching and rolling with the motion of the sea. A large wave hit the side and green water poured through the doorway and splashed against their legs.

Hauser yelled in fright, dragged Grunwald across the cabin, and pushed him out the door. He bobbed under briefly, then surfaced, his head held above the water by the inflated vest.

Another wave inundated the cabin. Rheinhart grabbed Marcie Hendry under the arms and, splashing backward through knee-deep water, tried to pull her to the door. "Help me!" he yelled. "Hurry!"

Hauser shook his head violently. "We don't have time! Leave them here!"

"Help me, you swine! That's an order!"

Hauser grabbed the handhold over the doorway, the water swirling around his hips. He pulled his pistol from his shoulder holster and shot Don Hendry, who was floating unconscious at the rear of the cabin. Rheinhart dropped Marcie Hendry and lunged toward Hauser, catching his shoulder and pulling him down. He heard another bullet discharge; then Hauser twisted free and dove out the door.

Rheinhart looked around for Mrs. Hendry. The plane was sinking fast. The sea had flooded the cabin almost to the top of the door, and the pressure of the incoming water carried her inert form away from the door and toward the aft bulkhead.

The door disappeared under the water and the cabin turned dark. Rheinhart discovered that Hauser's bullet had punctured his life vest and deflated it. He paddled to keep his head above the surface, now just a foot or so from the ceiling. The craft was now completely under water.

He would never find Mrs. Hendry now. He had to save himself.

He took a deep breath and dove toward the door, but the cabin started to tilt as the nose of the airplane settled into the sea, and he became disoriented. Instead of swimming through the open exit, now below him, he slipped through the door into the aft cabin and surfaced in the bubble of air that had collected near the lavatory at the tail of the plane.

Again and again, as the Canadair Challenger drifted down through the deep and the pressure of the sea built relentlessly against him, Rheinhart tried to find the door. He groped through the pitch-black water that had now flooded the entire craft, and returned after each failed attempt to the diminishing bubble of air in the tail.

A thousand feet down, the ocean crushed his tiny bubble of air with such force that he could no longer exhale his breath. Nitrogen, squeezed into his bloodstream by the tremendous pressure, quickly raced to his brain, causing a narcosis that filled him with a sudden mad euphoria.

He tipped his head into the water, opened his mouth wide, and drank in the sea.

Half an hour later, the East German sailors reached Hauser and the unconscious form of William Grunwald bobbing calmly in the water like a pair of corks. They pulled them aboard the dinghy and rushed them to the deck of the submarine.

Director Koenig was waiting on the conning tower, his eyes scanning the skies nervously for American Coast Guard rescue planes. After Grunwald had been taken below, someone threw a blanket around Hauser's shoulders and handed him a tumbler full of vodka. He drank it down in a single gulp.

"Where is Rheinhart?" Koenig demanded.

"He didn't make it," Hauser replied, shaking his head sadly.

Ronkonkoma, Long Island

"They're going to call the rescue off," the air-traffic-control supervisor told Pickering two days later. "Forty-eight hours and they found nothing. No oil slick, no debris, nothing. They must have gone straight to the bottom."

25

Northeast Thailand

Rob Grunwald opened the passenger-side door of the jeep and stepped cautiously to the ground. Gilmore followed, wrestling his big bulk out from the piles of supplies and squeezing past the front seat-back.

Two soldiers yanked open the jeep's rear door and began pulling their supplies out onto the roadway. Rob started toward them to protest but was stopped by a rifle barrel pressed roughly against his stomach. He raised his hands and looked anxiously across the roof of the jeep to McWhirter, busy exchanging words with a Thai officer. "What do they want?"

"They say guerrillas have been causing trouble here lately. They think we might be supplying them."

Rob glanced back at the second jeep. Wyler was standing in the roadway, hands clasped on his head. Neither Caroline nor the Frenchwoman, Ferrer, had come out yet.

"What are we supposed to do?"

"Stay calm and let them go through our stuff."

The soldier pressing the rifle against Rob's belly was staring at him. Rob stared back. The black almond eyes and smooth brown face looked like those of a boy of fifteen. His olive-green uniform and battle cap were a few sizes too large, making him appear even smaller and younger. The kid grinned at him with a challenging macho leer.

His teeth were bad—small, yellowish-white stumps widely spaced in red, swollen gums.

Rob's eyes fell to the weapon. In the bright sunlight he could discern the manufacturer's stamp on the side of the barrel: a letter "A" enclosed within a "G." He knew what the small print beneath it said without having to read it—"Grunwald Arms, of Westfield, Massachusetts." How beautifully ironic. He was being held up by one of his father's rifles, the GA-16 that McWhirter had disparaged as overpriced. The weapon's safety catch was off, he noticed, and the kid's finger was playing nervously with the trigger.

The young Thai soldier took his finger off the trigger and tapped his wrist instead. Rob breathed easier. The kid repeated his motion, but this time he pointed up at Rob's wristwatch, gleaming in the sun on his raised left arm.

"You want to know what time it is?" Rob asked.

The soldier nodded. Rob brought the arm down and turned it so he could see the dial. He ignored the dial and tapped his wrist again.

"I think he wants the watch, not the time," Gilmore said, standing with his own arms raised a few feet away.

Gilmore was right. The soldier concluded his pantomime by tapping Rob's watch and then his own chest. The watch was the only thing of value Rob had with him. It was a gold Swiss Cartier his mother had given him as a present. Rob shook his head. The soldier nudged his ribs menacingly with the gun barrel.

"For chrissake, Rob, give it to him," Gilmore pleaded.

Reluctantly, Rob slipped the watch from his wrist. The soldier grabbed it and tucked it swiftly into his pants pocket, mumbling something in Thai. He reached into another pocket, produced a cheap disposable cigarette lighter, and pressed it into Rob's hand.

"He's offering you the lighter in trade," Gilmore explained.

Rob turned the worn red plastic object over in his hand. "Just what I always wanted," he muttered.

Loud voices from the second jeep caught their attention. One of the soldiers had pulled a canvas suitcase belonging to Ghislene Ferrer onto the ground, and unable to undo the catches, he had slit it open with a knife, turned it upside down, and emptied its contents onto the road.

Ferrer, who had remained in the jeep with Caroline, burst out and descended on the soldier like a tiger. She kicked his hands away from her scattered possessions, and when he stood up to confront her, she slapped him across the face so hard it knocked his field cap off.

The sound of the slap reverberated through the gang of Thais like enemy gunfire. They jumped toward Ferrer and quickly formed a circle around her, their rifles pointing at her like so many spears.

Ferrer was not in the least intimidated. She pushed through the circle of angry soldiers and stormed over to the two officers now interrogating McWhirter.

"You tell them," she screamed, "that I am a personal friend of the royal family! If they do not apologize and let us go immediately, I will see to it that every one of them is sent to prison!"

Before the astonished McWhirter could translate this threat into Thai, Ferrer repeated it in French, and one of the officers understood her. He started to reply, but Ferrer cut him off.

"I am a world-famous journalist!" she shouted. "We are here in your country at the personal invitation of King Bhumibol and Queen Sirikit!" From the handbag slung over her shoulder, Ferrer produced a beige-colored square of paper and thrust it in front of the officer's face. "When they hear of this outrage, you will be court-martialed!"

The officer, a stocky man in his thirties, took the square of paper and studied it, the arrogance draining from him like air out of a punctured tire. He stopped trying to interrupt her.

"You and your men have acted in a rude and barbaric manner!" she yelled. "We have come to your country on a mission of goodwill, on a mission requested by your own leaders, and we are treated like bandits! Like Communist saboteurs!"

The other officer, who could not understand Ferrer's machine-gun French, looked questioningly at his colleague. The senior officer enlightened him, whispering to him in embarrassed tones.

Ferrer stepped up as close to the senior officer as she could without actually bumping into him. He backed up a step. Ferrer continued to advance on him, her jaw thrust in his face, her arms gesticulating wildly. "Tell your men to put down their weapons and replace our belongings in our vehicles. The sooner you do it, the less devastating will be my report on your behavior." For added emphasis, she kicked dirt on his freshly polished boots. "A report I intend to deliver directly to your defense minister, General Prayoon, by telephone this evening!"

"She must have taken lessons from Billy Martin," Gilmore murmured.

"Billy Martin?" Rob echoed.

"You've been out of the country. It has to do with abusing baseball umpires."

The officer cleared his throat and turned to McWhirter, who had been standing quietly, his face deadpan, throughout Ferrer's performance. The officer growled something in Thai, and McWhirter grinned and nodded.

The officer then strode away from the Americans and began screaming at his soldiers in a high-pitched, hysterical voice.

"A good example of displacement," Gilmore said. "He loses face with Ferrer, so he takes it out on his troops."

The soldier who had been pressing the rifle into Rob's stomach suddenly pulled it away and scurried to the edge of the road, where the rest of the troops were falling into formation. The officer berated them for several minutes, then ordered them to replace the supplies in the backs of the jeeps. They hopped to the task in double time, cramming the cases and crates inside in a disordered jumble that barely left room for the passengers.

"We'll sort it out later," McWhirter said. "Let's just get the hell out of here before they recover and decide to shoot us."

Ferrer retrieved her square of beige paper and stalked back to the jeep. Wyler, holding the door open for her, laughed his hyena laugh and threw her a kiss. She patted him affectionately on the cheek as she got in. Rob could see Caroline still sitting at the wheel. She was the only one who had not come out to face the soldiers. He felt a certain perverse satisfaction for the scare the incident must have caused her. But, fortunately, they had left her alone. If they hadn't, he wasn't sure what he would have done. Thank God he hadn't had to find out.

"I'm still shaking," Gilmore said, when they had put the roadblock several miles behind them. "What the hell was on that card she flung at him?"

McWhirter laughed. "An engraved invitation to Citralada Palace from the king and queen of Thailand."

"I thought she was just bullshitting him."

"Of course not," Rob said acidly. "She's a world-famous journalist."

Gilmore adjusted his glasses on his nose. "Whatever she is, she was fucking magnificent."

"She might have got us killed," McWhirter said.

"I should have asked her to get my watch back," Rob muttered.

They arrived at Mukdahan, the last town before the Laotian border, at five o'clock. Crowds of soldiers wandered the main street, a dusty stretch of dismal bars, cheap restaurants, and noisy sidewalk vendors. Military convoys and heavily armed border police in jeeps were in evidence everywhere.

Following McWhirter's directions, Rob drove north out of town for several miles on Route 27, the highway that parallels the border, then turned off onto a barely passable dirt track that wound through a heavy thicket of low-growing shrubs and dead-ended near the top of a steep hill.

"This is it," McWhirter said.

Rob pulled up the emergency brake and turned off the engine. The other jeep, with Caroline still driving, pulled up beside them.

McWhirter got out and beckoned for the others to follow him. He took them up to the crest of the hill, some hundred feet beyond the parked jeeps, and paused near the edge of a long drop-off.

"There's the border," he said, pointing down the hill to the bottom of a narrow wooded valley. The floor of the valley was bisected by a wide, muddy-brown stretch of the Mekong River. "The far bank is Laos. And this is where we cross to get to it—tomorrow morning, before dawn."

"How do we get across the river?" Ghislene Ferrer demanded.

"You'll find out tomorrow."

"What do we do tonight?" she asked.

"We're invited to be the special guests of His Royal Lowness, Mr. Sammy Rep," McWhirter replied, mocking the words on Ferrer's invitation to the royal palace. "Exalted and serene dope smuggler, whoremaster, and proprietor of the world's sleaziest hotel."

The North Atlantic

Grunwald thought at first that he had awakened from a dream within a dream. It sometimes happened to him. He was back in Chemnitz, before the war, standing in a large field with his mother. She was a pale-blond woman in her mid-twenties. He was middle-aged. She was holding his hand and crying softly. He told her not to cry, that he was rich and powerful now. An ambassador. But it seemed that everything he said only made her sobbing more intense. Finally she dropped his hand and walked away from him across the field. He ran after her, stumbling on the uneven ground like a small boy, unable to see over the high grass that slashed against his face and bare arms. He ran and ran, but he couldn't catch up. He stopped, finally, out of breath, and looked across the field. It had turned into an enormous lake, and his mother was gone.

Now he was lying on a cot in a dimly lit chamber. He lay still and focused his eyes overhead. The ceiling was low and obscured with rows of pipes, like a dingy tenement basement. A throbbing hum that seemed to originate from deep within the walls vibrated his entire body and made him feel slightly sick. He closed his eyes to wake from this second dream, but when he opened them again he was still in this same place.

Alarmed, he pulled himself upright and swung his feet off the cot. It was no dream. The space around him, illuminated from overhead by a single low-wattage bulb enclosed in a mesh cage, seemed more like a metal box than a room. The air was clammy and stale and smelled faintly of salt and oil. There were no windows, and the walls and ceiling were made of welded-steel panels. The only opening was a low door, also steel, with a very high threshold and rounded corners. He tried the door's leverlike handle, yanking up and down on it with anxious ferocity. It refused to move.

He must be inside a ship, he thought. But how could it have happened? He looked down at his clothes. His gray suit was gone, replaced by a cotton shirt and trousers little more substantial than a pair of pajamas. A number was stenciled across the front of the shirt. In place of his dress shoes were cheap slippers of woven hemp. He felt for pockets, but the trousers contained none. His wallet was gone, and his key case, his penknife, and his belt. He pushed back the sleeve on his left wrist. His watch was gone as well.

He rubbed his hands over his head in confusion, and got another shock. His head was shaved.

He had just stepped aboard his jet, he remembered, on his way to Washington. Two men were there. They shot John, his bodyguard, and he had run to barricade himself in the aft cabin. Beyond that he remembered nothing. They must have knocked him out. When? How much time had passed? A night? A whole day? He wished he had his watch.

Grunwald explored the room. It was roughly twelve feet long and eight feet wide. It was impossible to guess what it had been used for. Aside from the narrow cot against the wall, the space contained a small metal chair, a chemical toilet, and a basin half full of water resting on a special stand that prevented the basin from sliding off. On a shelf built into the stand he found a towel, a washcloth, a piece of soap, and a roll of toilet paper. He dipped his hands in the water in the basin and splashed some against his face. It was the same temperature as the room. He pulled out the towel, a thin, scratchy rag that smelled of disinfectant, and patted his face dry.

He paced the cramped cell, stumbling frequently in the ill-fitting hemp slippers, trying to determine what had happened to him. The steady deep hum that vibrated the walls disturbed him. This ship didn't sound or act a bit like any ship he had ever been on. There was no pitching or rolling, no voices, no echoing of footsteps overhead, no clanging of machinery. Just that ceaseless vibrating hum. Grunwald wondered if it was actually moving at all.

He sat down on the edge of the cot. If he was on a ship, whose ship was it? He thought of Demopoulis, his Greek rival, who had once vowed revenge against him for outmaneuvering him on a big Indonesian oil contract. But that was years ago. And Demopoulis, violent a man as he was, didn't bear grudges. Who, then? Arab terrorists? That was a frightening possibility. He was the new ambassador to Israel, after all. They might be holding him hostage in return for U.S. concessions.

Grunwald had just about convinced himself that he was in the hands of the Arabs, when he began to feel a new and peculiar sensation, as if the whole chamber was tipping slightly on its side. He went over to the basin and studied the water. The ship's vibration caused it to ripple slightly, but otherwise it was still. No, not quite. It was beginning to climb up one side of the basin.

For half an hour, Grunwald stood mesmerized, watching the surface of the water in the basin tilt at a sharper and sharper angle. It climbed to within an inch of the basin's lip, stayed that way for about fifteen minutes, and then gradually returned level with the sides of the basin.

It didn't take a degree in engineering to explain the mystery of the water's movement in the basin. It meant that the vessel he was on had just changed altitude. Ships could not do that. But airplanes could.

Was he on an airplane? He ran his fingers along the steel plates and gazed up at the maze of piping over his head. No airplane in the world would be constructed of such heavy material. And the noise of its engines would be unmistakable.

But what else could change altitude?

When the answer dawned on him, it stunned him. He collapsed on the cot, suddenly dizzy and sick.

He was on a submarine.

The vibrations he felt were the diesel engines turning the huge worm-screw shaft that powered the sub's propeller.

Then he had been kidnapped by a government, not a band of terrorists. And only a handful of nations possessed submarines. It was crazy! Why would any country do such a thing? He pounded the wall with the bottom of his fist in frustration. The contact of his flesh against the steel made a hollow, drumlike *bong*. He tried the door handle again, knowing it was locked, then lay back down on the cot and tried to compose himself.

He gazed up at the dim, flickering bulb in its cage overhead. There was one good thing, he thought. His disappearance must be creating a hell of a fuss. It would be the lead item on the network evening news, and it would be splashed across every newspaper in the United States and Europe. Half the world would be wondering where he was. Far from being forgotten, this kidnapping was going to make him the center of the world's attention. So it was unlikely that any real harm would come to him. Governments, unlike terrorists, were relatively responsible organizations. They might play rough, but they seldom played crazy.

Marginally comforted by these thoughts, he concentrated his attention on determining which country had kidnapped him. Which hostile nations possessed submarines that could be active in the Atlantic? There weren't many. He tried to remember the figures that he had once heard from one of his admiral friends in Washington. Russia allowed only three nations in the Warsaw Pact—Bulgaria, Hungary, and East Germany—to have any at all, and these were only a handful of obsolescent hand-me-downs.

So it must be the Russians.

What invidious gambit had they conceived that would make him such a valuable hostage? He could not think of one. Still, it had to be the Russians.

He wondered how Cornelia was taking all this. Would she be worried? Yes and no, he decided. She would put on a great show of being distraught, and she would get everyone's sympathy, but deep down inside would she really care that much? Despite her enthusiasm about Israel and the ambassadorship, they led separate lives. His disappearance would have almost no effect on her daily existence. It was sad, but it was true. His daughter Sarah would care, of course. And maybe his secretary, Flory. Yes, Flory would be very upset. Flory needed his protection. Who else would care? Jim Safier? Yes, he would certainly be shaken. Who else?

He couldn't think of anyone else.

His nausea gradually eased, and in its place he began to feel pangs of hunger. They were old sensations, left behind with his childhood, and they disturbed long-buried memories. He saw himself, a skinny urchin roaming the streets of Chemnitz in search of something to fill his belly. He saw the bakery on Charlottenstrasse, where he had once been caught stealing bread. He saw his mother—frail, broken-spirited, her face red from crying. She had so many things to cry about—the lack of food, the lack of work, the burden of caring for him and his younger sister. She even cried for the Weimar Republic, God bless her poor Lutheran soul. And for the chaos and despair that had settled upon it like a biblical plague. Everybody was so unhappy in Germany in those days.

He saw his father, his lungs burned by gas at Verdun, sitting all day in the house in his dirty long-sleeved underwear, drinking cheap beer and coughing. He could hear that hateful cough now, the gagging heaviness of it, as if there was something inside him that wanted to escape.

The submarine chamber was damp and cold, and he shivered violently in his flimsy cotton pajamas. He paced the floor again, slapping his arms against his sides to stimulate his circulation. By now a whole day must have passed, he guessed. He needed some food to help warm him up.

These Russian bastards, he thought. They were not going out of their way to make him comfortable. And they would regret it. They underestimated his influence, his resources, his power. They underestimated his resolve. Someday, he vowed, the individuals responsible for this outrage would feel his revenge.

When were the bastards going to feed him? he wondered.

26

Northeast Thailand

Sammy Rep's hotel sat, or rather was heaped together, at the top of a dusty rise on the outskirts of Mukdahan—one swaybacked, tin-roofed, two-story concrete-block structure hemmed in by a crowd of ramshackle one-story wood-and-thatch wings that jutted out from the main building's walls at odd angles and uneven intervals. More than a dwelling, it resembled some kind of sluggish female monster with a brood of nursing infants huddled against her belly.

As they parked the jeeps in the front yard, putting a score of chickens and bare-bottomed children to flight, the master of the house, a middle-aged Thai, ran out to greet them. He recognized McWhirter instantly, and grabbed his hand and pumped it so energetically it looked as if he was trying to shake it loose.

"Sammy's the local Godfather," McWhirter said, turning to introduce him to the others. "Nobody can pronounce his full name, so we call him 'Sammy Rep.' "

Sammy Rep raised his hands in the air, as if bestowing his blessing, and shouted out a greeting in Thai. He was a short man, skinny and tough as a hickory stick, and he affected a style of dress that made his wrinkled body the battleground of a major East-West culture clash—greasy felt cowboy hat, saffron neckerchief, olive-drab military camouflage jacket over a white T-shirt, native red pantaloons, and high-topped canvas jungle boots with no socks. This electric outfit was further highlighted by a pile of accessories—several large gold rings, gold bracelets, an enormous hunk of polished jade suspended around his neck by a strip of rawhide, and a .45 revolver strapped to his narrow waist by a thick black belt bristling with metal studs.

He was enormously good-humored and enthusiastic. The party's arrival seemed to set him in perpetual motion, running along before them, showing them around the establishment, shouting orders at the amazing number of women and children who seemed to be lurking behind every doorway. His movements were as abrupt as a marionette on strings, and they caused the big jade stone to bounce constantly against his ribs. He didn't so much speak as bark. To each of McWhirter's inquiries, he would open his mouth wide, displaying a set of large, loosely fitting false teeth, and clack back an answer.

A shouted command brought a stream of girls from one of the doorways. They surrounded Caroline and Ghislene Ferrer and escorted them inside one of the house's many wings, giggling self-consciously. After another bark, three teenage boys appeared and began unloading the luggage from the jeeps and hauling it into another wing.

"Who are all these people?" Rob asked. "It looks like the whole village is up here."

"Sammy's extended family," McWhirter explained. "Wives, mistresses, friends of wives and mistresses, in-laws, sons and daughters, grandchildren."

"Incredible," Gilmore said. "How does he support them all?"

"He doesn't. They support him. He puts them to work running his enterprises. He's involved in everything. He keeps this inn, plants a big garden, does a little loan-sharking, a little pimping, and, when he can get away with it, a little drug-smuggling and gunrunning. The Bangkok authorities leave him alone. In exchange for turning a blind eye, he keeps them up to speed on guerrilla and bandit activity in the area, and anything funny going on across the river in Laos. He's chief of the village, so he also collects the taxes, dispenses patronage, and generally keeps the lid on things."

Sammy Rep led the four men around a corner, down a sharp incline, and onto a path through a thick stand of prickly bushes. At the end of the path stood a concrete-block shed with garage doors on it. Sammy Rep yanked open one of the doors to reveal the interior—a packed dirt floor empty save for a dozen bales of hay stacked against the back wall.

"This is where he's going to hide the jeeps for us."

"Can we trust him?" Rob asked. "If he's such a big shot, won't word get around about what he's doing?"

"Probably," McWhirter admitted. "But he's the law around here. No one would dream of crossing him. He's the *only* one around here we can trust." McWhirter mimed a counting out of dollar bills. "And we're making it worth his while, don't forget."

They parked the jeeps in Sammy Rep's shed, along with the camera equipment they had rented for their cover as a documentary-film crew. Sammy, meanwhile, dragged out two long wooden crates from underneath the hay bales and pried them open with the edge of an ax blade.

Rob knelt down with McWhirter and brushed aside the sawdust packing. One crate contained five Kalashnikovs and an RPG antitank weapon. The other crate contained ammunition and an assortment of grenades, Claymore mines, and rockets for the RPG. Every item appeared to be new. Rob nodded at Sammy, hovering before him.

"A-okay?" Sammy asked, holding out a gnarled fist with the thumb sticking up.

Rob grinned and held up his own thumb in response, feeling distinctly foolish doing it.

But it pleased Sammy. "A-okay!" he cried, in his reedy voice.

McWhirter fished out an automatic pistol from one of the crates and tested its action. He bent down, found a cardboard box of pistol shells, and opened it. "I'll see you tomorrow," he said, pushing bullets into the pistol's clip.

"Where're you going?"

"Across the river," McWhirter answered. He slid the clip into place inside the grip and stuck the pistol in his belt. "I have to meet with Tan, the tribal chief. Check out his men and transportation and tell him we're ready to move. If everything's straight, I'll stay there tonight and meet up with you in the morning. Unpack these weapons and get all five of you down to that spot by the river I showed you. Be there by dawn, armed and ready for business. Sammy'll take you across."

Before Rob could answer, McWhirter had disappeared out the door of the shed.

That evening Sammy Rep's kitchen produced a lavish and tasty dinner of *pla taw,* a fish from the Mekong River, beef curry, chicken and bamboo shoots, and an endless supply of Chinese beer.

The dining room was a pleasant verandalike shed decorated with plants and open on three sides with a long view to the east, the direction of their future travels. While Sammy Rep's relatives and offspring rushed dishes back and forth from the kitchen, the five sat at a big table, recalling their encounter with the Thai soldiers and speculating on tomorrow.

Rob sat at the end of the table, with Gilmore and Caroline on one side, Ghislene Ferrer and Wyler on the other. Ferrer did much of the talking, retailing anecdotes from her travels among the famous with a characteristic combination of skillful narration and shameless self-promotion. She stopped in the course of a long monologue to let Wyler light a cigarette for her. She had made a deep impression on Wyler, Rob noticed. She pretended to be dependent on him, and was constantly making small demands of him. And Wyler was loving every minute of it.

Rob looked down the table at Caroline. She had washed, combed her hair, and applied a discreet touch of makeup around her eyes. Her khaki safari shirt had stubbornly held its freshly pressed look against the day's wilting heat. She looked glamorous and out of place, like an actress in the wrong role. He noticed that their hosts were in awe of her. The women stared and the children tried to sneak up on her, their eyes wide with shy reverence, to touch her clothes and hair. Rob had several times caught old Sammy Rep himself shoot a gleaming eye in her direction.

She had not spoken to him since their confrontation early in the day, and he had not been able to catch even a glance from her all evening. She was obviously still angry about the sudden appearance of Ferrer, and he hadn't yet been able to convince her that it wasn't his fault.

Gilmore was in a positively jovial mood. He drank great quantities of the tart Chinese beer and toasted everything and everybody in sight. He pressed numerous bottles of the brew on Sammy Rep, and the old man, already overstimulated by the whole occasion, became hilariously drunk. He laughed and barked, clapped his hands, staggered around pinching the bottoms of the females in his household, and capped his performance by carting out from some back room an old salute cannon. With Wyler's help, he packed it with gunpowder and fired it from the edge of the veranda. The tiny cannon produced an earsplitting boom, and Rob half expected the hills across the river in Laos to erupt with a return barrage.

Later, Sammy grabbed Rob's arm and tugged him off to a small storage shed at the back of the rambling inn. There, in the flickering gloom of a kerosene lantern, he fished a quart-sized plastic bag out from under a pile of rice and grain sacks, removed a rubber band from it, withdrew a smaller bag, and pressed this firmly into Rob's hand. "For good luck on trip!" he shouted.

Rob held the plastic bag up closer to the kerosene lamp. It weighed about a pound and appeared to be filled with small, irregularly shaped transparent brown stones.

"What is it?" he asked.

"Rock!" Sammy replied, grinning strenuously.

Rob gazed at the bag, still mystified.

Sammy opened the bag, took out one of the pebbles, held it up to his nose, and sniffed hard. "Pure rock," he repeated, holding the piece under Rob's nose.

Rob took the piece and touched it to his tongue. The taste of it was unmistakable. A fearful thrill swept through him. He quickly handed the bag back.

Sammy's black eyes narrowed in offended anger. "You keep! You keep!" he cried, pushing Rob's hand away forcefully. "No charge. You keep!"

Rob gave up and slipped the bag into his pants pocket. He could dispose of it tomorrow, he decided. Just throw it into the jungle somewhere. The thought amused him. He had never encountered it in its pure rock form before. How much was a pound of raw cocaine worth? he wondered.

Back in the dining room, Rob drank another Chinese beer and watched Wyler and Sammy Rep drunkenly trying to pack another charge of gunpowder into the salute cannon. After they had fired it, three of Sammy's girls put on an impromptu dance exhibition—an artful and highly suggestive melange of movements that owed more to the strip joints of Petchburi Road than to any local folk tradition. Later, someone produced a beat-up guitar and Gilmore launched enthusiastically into a version of "The House of the Rising Sun."

Rob found a bathroom on the second floor, and then wandered into a small bedroom and flopped down on a mattress spread out on the rough floorboards. He rested his head against the wall and sat listening to Gilmore's songs drifting up through the wide cracks in the floor. He pulled the bag of cocaine from his pocket, took out a few pebbles, and turned them over thoughtfully in his hand. He rubbed the edge of one piece with his thumb, causing it to flake off into a powder. The stuff he had built his habit on was cut three to one with aspirin. A little bit of this would blow his anxieties away like a heady March wind.

Downstairs, Gilmore began a ballad, his big voice hugging the sad words with earnest emotion:

" 'No use crying, talking to a stranger,
Naming the sorrows you've seen. . . .' "

Rob dropped the pieces back in the bag and then took them out again. For a long time he sat crouched forward over them in the dim light. Why had Sammy given the coke to him? Reckless generosity? Or had someone told him about his past habit? Was he being tested? Or was he being tempted?

" 'Too many sad times, too many bad times,
Nobody knows what you mean. . . .' "

Tomorrow they would be in Laos. The real dangers of the mission had not yet even begun. If he yielded to the coke now, how much more irresistible would it be tomorrow? He crumbled three of the pebbles into a powder in the palm of his hand and stared at it. Why did he need it? He had been doing so well without it. Why test his willpower now?

It wasn't that he needed it, he decided; it was that he wanted it. A little reassurance, that was all. Once would not kill him. Hell, it would shore him up. Give him the confidence to go on. Once wouldn't hurt him at all. Nor twice, for that matter. Nor three times. Nor ten.

Still, he well knew its evil charm. Like all beautiful things, it possessed the power to corrupt and enslave.

He sniffed gingerly at the small mound of powder in his hand. He deserved the reward of it, he told himself. A momentary lapse of discipline wouldn't matter. He was a different person now from the one in Belize. Stronger. More sure of himself. He could handle a little coke. And he needed the solace of it.

He wanted it.

He needed it.

A shadow by the doorway broke his trancelike concentration. Wordlessly it moved into the dim interior of the bedroom and knelt quickly beside him on the mattress. A hand grasped his wrist and swung it away from him, spilling the mound of coke to the floor, like a handful of dust.

"You damned fool!" Caroline hissed.

He fell back against the mattress and closed his eyes. "Go away."

She picked up the bag of cocaine crystals and heaved it toward the open window. It caught the edge of the frame and spilled back into the room, scattering small pebbles across the floor and the mattress. "You idiot, you don't care about anything!"

Rob pressed his hands over his face. "What do you care?"

Caroline balled her fist and pounded it against his chest. "What do I care? You're not the only one with something at stake, you bastard. There are other people depending on you now. Don't you understand that?"

"Don't get hysterical. If I took a snort of coke, it wouldn't be the end of the world."

Caroline stood up and paced the room. "How could you risk it, Rob? After all you've accomplished these last weeks? How could you dare? Are you really that self-destructive?"

"What have I accomplished? I've already fucked up the mission— by letting you and Ferrer come along."

"How can you say that?" Caroline demanded, her voice rising in anger. "After what she did for us this afternoon?"

"Now you're championing her cause?"

"You're an ungrateful son of a bitch."

Rob rested his hands over the spot that Caroline had hit on his chest, savoring the dull hurt of it, and stared at the ceiling. Caroline leaned against the wall and crossed her arms. He couldn't see her face in the dark, but he felt her eyes on him. From below, Gilmore's voice filtered through the background of laughter and talk:

" 'But if you could pack up your sorrows,
   And give them all to me.
   You would lose them, I know how to use them. Give them all
     to me. . . .' "

"Are you crying?"

"I'm too mad to cry."

"What have I accomplished?"

"This whole mission is your doing. You put it together and you got it here. Against great odds. Nobody thought you could do it. Nobody. I didn't. Your sister didn't. Your father didn't. Nobody did. But if you sabotage it by your own self-indulgence you'll throw away everything."

"I'm not sabotaging it."

"You can't take coke—that's all there is to it. You should know better, but apparently you don't."

"Don't lecture me."

For a long time neither of them spoke. Then Caroline broke the silence. "I'm going all the way to Vietnam," she declared.

"I don't want you to."

"I'm not asking you. I'm going."

"Who do you think you are? We don't need you."

Caroline pushed away from the wall and stepped to the mattress. Rob saw her tower over him briefly, then kneel down beside him.

"You *do* need me," she said.

Rob hunched forward, his arms folded self-protectively over his chest. "No. I don't need you. I don't need anyone."

A full ten minutes passed. Both of them remained motionless and silent, each caught in the quicksand of their private emotions. Finally, Caroline braced herself on her hands, leaned over, and slowly lowered herself down on top of him. Her knee fell between his thighs. He felt her fingers at the back of his neck and her mouth against his ear.

"*I* need *you*," she whispered. "I wish I didn't, but I do."

Rob reached up and pulled her to him.

"Tell me that you need me," she whispered.

"I need you," he said, overwhelmed with the simple truth of the words.

Before his spinning head had sorted out the miracle of what was happening, Caroline had removed her shorts and shirt—all she was wearing—unzipped him, straddled him, and engulfed him with a suddenness that made him cry out.

They made love for a long time—eagerly, then languorously, lost to time and place, consuming their passions in an unself-conscious greed for each other.

Later, adrift in an ecstatic haze halfway between waking and sleeping, Rob opened his eyes. Caroline lay half on top of him, her head by his shoulder. He pressed his hand gently against her back, luxuriating in the sensation of her soft weight.

She stirred and rested a cheek on his chest. "I've fallen in love with a trapeze artist," she murmured sleepily.

"What do you mean?"

"Howard told me about your life—in Europe and Belize."

"Damn Howard."

"I pried it out of him."

Rob laughed. "He told you I was a trapeze artist?"

"No, silly. I mean you've been careless with your life."

"You intend to be my net?"

"If you want me to be."

"You've caught me once already."

Caroline raised her head. Strands of her hair shadowed her face. "To tell you the truth, I wish we could end the mission right here. It will be so much harder now, to face Billy."

"Who's being selfish now?"

"I feel we're betraying him."

"By falling in love? It's been twelve years. And after all you've told me, I don't think you need to worry."

"I know. But I'm scared. That's why I got so upset when I saw you with the cocaine. I'm afraid of what might happen to you. . . . To all of us."

"I'm just finding my purpose in life," Rob said. "You don't want to take it away, do you?"

Caroline rested her head on his chest again. Below them, Gilmore was still singing. His voice staggered drunkenly over the notes, punctuated by the giggles of one of Sammy's girls:

" 'No use gambling, running in the darkness,
   Looking for a spirit that's free.
   Too many wrong times, too many long times,
   Nobody knows what you see. . . .' "

Rob felt Caroline's warm tears on his skin.

27

The North Atlantic

By lying on his side near the edge of the cot, Grunwald was able to wrap the thin mattress around him and hold it across his chest with one hand. But as soon as he began to fall asleep, his grip would relax and the part of the mattress wrapped around him would slide off and the cold would wake him up again.

He huddled this way for hours, balanced between waking and sleeping, between hunger and nightmares. His emotions were beginning to cartwheel out of control, spinning through cycles of fear and anxiety, self-pity and rage.

The bastards were tormenting him, he decided, softening him up for something. He was determined to resist, to show them that he was a lot tougher than they thought. He struggled to keep his mental equilibrium, to think things through.

He was more than just a hostage. The way he was being treated told him that somebody wanted to punish him. But who? And for what reason? What could be the point of such bizarre cruelty? Was he in the hands of madmen?

He wished again for his watch. He missed the inability to measure time almost as much as he missed food. He needed to know what day it was, and whether it was daylight or dark. The disorientation was as frightening to him as the growing uncertainty of his fate.

There were people nearby—just beyond the steel bulkheads that imprisoned him—who knew what time it was, who knew where they were and what they were doing, who had warm clothes and food in their stomachs. Surely someone would soon open that door and explain to him what this was all about. Surely they must want something from him. Why didn't they come to get it?

Why didn't someone come?

Laos

In a chilly dawn mist, Rob and his party gathered outside Sammy Rep's inn and helped one another strap on rucksacks and weapons for the half-mile walk down to the crossing point on the banks of the Mekong River. The mood, after the revelry of the night just past, was subdued and tense.

Sammy Rep led the way to the river, his dirty Stetson pulled low over his forehead, his holstered revolver slapping against his bony hip. Three of Sammy's sons, mobilized to carry the expedition's extra baggage—boxes of canned food, tents, hammocks, and ammunition— followed behind him, trailed by Caroline, Rob, Gilmore, Wyler, and Ferrer. Wyler carried Ferrer's two cases for her so she could take photographs. The track, worn smooth by the passage of many feet, led over a short rise and then meandered downhill through a broad stand of bamboo trees. "It looks like a smuggler's trail," Gilmore whispered. "They're all over Southeast Asia. The guerrillas use them, too."

At the river, Sammy instructed everyone to lie down out of sight in the bushes near the bank. For a long time the old Thai trained his binoculars on the opposite bank, inching them back and forth across the landscape with the patience of a bird-watcher. Finally persuaded that there were no Laotian border patrols in the vicinity, he stuck two fingers in his mouth and produced a low, birdlike whistle. Almost immediately it was answered and the compact form of Harris McWhirter emerged from the foliage on the opposite shore and waved a hand.

One of Sammy's sons crept to the edge of the bank and tugged hard on a thick vine. At the other end of it, hidden under the muddy water by a scrap-metal anchor and a couple of large rocks, was lashed a crude homemade boat, square-shaped and flat-bottomed, like a bricklayer's mortar box. While his sons hauled the boat onto the bank and emptied out the water, Sammy went to another hiding place and retrieved a long wooden pole.

Minutes later Sammy took on his first passengers, Wyler and Ferrer, and poled them swiftly across the river. Two trips later, the whole mission, with all its supplies, was safely across in Laos.

McWhirter paid Sammy Rep off with a large roll of American bills, and Sammy, his false teeth grinning in his wizened face, shook hands with each of them vigorously, wished them well, and quickly retreated with his sons back across the river.

"Everything's set," McWhirter assured them, picking up his back-pack from the pile of supplies and throwing it over his shoulder. "Let's get all this shit out of sight."

Rob helped Caroline tighten the straps on her pack, and then stepped over to Gilmore to help him with his. "How are you feeling?" he asked.

"Just as fucking ruined as you look," Gilmore replied, in a scratchy voice. "From now on, let's enforce a curfew."

McWhirter led them onto a trail that wound up from the river through tall grass and bushes and then along the edge of a steep embankment. His appearance surprised Rob. Everybody looked a little bedraggled, but the normally trim and soldierly Oklahoman looked as if he hadn't slept at all. His clothes were wrinkled and sweat-stained and his face unshaven. Behind his aviator sunglasses, his customary laconic demeanor seemed even more pronounced than usual. At the top of a rise, McWhirter paused to get his bearings and then took them off the path and into a heavily wooded hollow. There, shaded under a dense umbrella of palms, a dozen men were squatting in a ragged circle.

McWhirter called out a brief greeting, and one of the men rose from the group and walked out to meet them. He was dressed in a black loincloth and was incredibly squat, like a nine-foot-tall bronze statue that had been hammered down to five. His broad face and thick neck were supported on apelike shoulders and arms, a beer-barrel trunk, thick legs, and huge feet. His bare chest was crossed with ammunition belts, and the butt of a big revolver protruded from the holster hanging from his waist. Knives were strapped to both thighs, their sheaths running almost from hip to knee. Bands of tooled metal hugged his wrists and upper arms, and a heavy necklace of bones dangled from his neck. To further enhance his general ferocity, he had painted black and red streaks around his eyes and mouth. He looked both ridiculous and terrifying.

He exchanged a few words with McWhirter, then signaled for the other men to join him. They scrambled quickly from the ground and fell into a disorderly double rank behind him. There were ten of them, plus a small, one-armed boy who hung shyly behind the back row. They all carried automatic rifles and, with minor variations, were clothed in the same primitive fashion as their leader. Most wore crude rubber sandals, but several were barefoot. Many were scarred and two walked with limps. None managed to appear quite as formidable as the leader, but they were a rough-looking bunch by anyone's standard.

"This is Tan," McWhirter said, turning to the others behind him. "Chief of the Souei tribe."

Tan nodded his big head a fraction of an inch and cracked his lips in a leaden smile. He was long overdue for the dentist. All that remained of his teeth were eroded stumps stained reddish brown by years of chewing betel nut. His men stared at the party of Westerners with the stony boldness of a street gang looking over intruders in the neighborhood.

"They're tough," McWhirter admitted, catching the look of shock on Rob's and Gilmore's faces. "I hear they even practice ritual cannibalism. They eat a killed enemy's brains and testicles. They say it gives them the victim's strength and courage."

"Aren't we lucky to have them on our side," Gilmore said, scratching his beard.

McWhirter laughed. "The cannibalism stuff is probably just bullshit, but it makes good propaganda. It keeps the Pathet Lao off their case."

At his signal, Tan's men filed out of the woods and followed McWhirter back down the path to the riverbank to retrieve the rest of the party's supplies. When they returned, Tan led everyone on a long, difficult hike through dense groves of bamboo and thick patches of briers that ripped at clothes and drew blood from exposed flesh.

" 'Wait-a-minute bushes,' we called them," Gilmore said, pushing a branch of bristling thorns aside with his shirt sleeve. "Used to drive us crazy on patrols."

The morning mist had burned off and even under the protective shade of the trees, Rob felt the building pressure of the late-morning sun. Behind him, he could hear Ferrer complaining about it to Wyler, her words punctuated by periodic yipes of pain as another thorn snagged her. Caroline, directly ahead of him, was bearing the march in silence. He noticed wide stains of perspiration spreading out from under her arms, and her face, from the occasional side glimpses he caught of it, seemed dangerously red.

"You okay?" he asked her.

She looked back and smiled. "Tired," she said.

"Want me to take your pack for a while?"

She shook her head. "No. I'll manage. Really."

At midday they stopped for a short rest on a shaded patch of grass by a small stream. Rob and the Western contingent filled their depleted canteens from the stream and dropped in iodine pills to purify the water. Tan and his men simply fell flat on their bellies and slurped it up noisily.

When everyone had taken their fill of water, one of the Laotians removed a grenade from his bandolier, pulled the pin with his teeth, and heaved the explosive into the stream. There was a deep, earth-shaking thump, and the water erupted in a huge, angry bubble that spilled onto the banks. A minute later, dead fish began popping to the surface by the dozens. With a joyful whoop, the Laotians waded in and began collecting the harvest.

McWhirter stepped over to Rob. "Tan's trucks are just off Highway 9, about a mile away. We can rest here and wait until dark or we can go now."

"What do you think?"

"Go now. It might be safer to travel by night, but we'll lose half a day if we wait here. It's about a hundred and seventy-five miles to the Vietnamese border. The roads are bad and Tan's trucks are worse. A dozen things can delay us. But if we leave now, there's a better than even chance that we can make Vietnam before first light tomorrow. That would be ideal."

"What are the risks if we leave now?"

"Pathet Lao patrols. But if we wait until tonight, we risk getting our asses caught in the daylight over on the other side of Laos, and that's probably more dangerous. The terrain is terrible over there, and these guys won't be operating on their home turf."

They reached the trucks half an hour later. Two of Tan's ragtag army had stayed behind to guard them. One was passing the time preparing a chew of betel nut by smearing betel-palm seeds and lime paste onto a betel-pepper leaf and rolling it into a small wad. The other, apparently the company cook, was busily plucking the feathers from a live chicken. When he saw his chief returning, he tied the chicken to his waist and walked over to join his comrades.

The trucks were a depressing sight. One was a vintage World War II French military lorry, the other an American Dodge rackbody, circa 1948. All the fenders were badly dented, and large sections of their frames were rusted completely through. The hood and the door on the driver's side of the French vehicle was pocked with bullet holes. The Dodge was missing most of its windows.

"Where the hell do you suppose they found those?" Gilmore said, staring at the two vehicles with the disbelieving expression of a man discovering UFOs in his backyard.

Rob frowned. "I imagine they just stopped them on the road somewhere, shot the drivers and passengers, ate them, and kept the trucks."

Gilmore pushed his glasses up on his nose. "Yeah. Dumb of me not to think of that."

It was decided that Tan and ten of his men would occupy the French truck and take the lead position. Rob's party, along with two of Tan's men—one driving, the other riding shotgun—would follow in the Dodge. This suited everybody but Ghislene Ferrer, who insisted on riding with Tan in the lead vehicle. She was clearly fascinated by the hulking warrior and eager to interview him. After some debate, and over the jealous objections of Wyler, Ferrer switched places with the one-armed Laotian boy and the expedition moved out.

The trucks crept along at ten miles an hour. The stake body of the Dodge pounded against the frame with jarring repetition. The canvas top that had once covered the body had long since rotted away, and for the first three hours on Highway 9, the sun beat down on them with the intensity of a torch. The rutted, unpaved road twisted snakelike up and down through an exotic and spectacular landscape of valleys and cloud-shrouded karst mountains—knifelike peaks and jagged saw-edges that punctured the thick skin of jungle in breathtaking thrusts.

The country seemed deserted, ghostlike. The villages they passed were strangely still, as if their occupants had suddenly fled. On the highway itself, all afternoon, Rob counted only six trucks, four old women on foot, one man in a cart, and another man on a bicycle. He mentioned it to Gilmore, and got more of an explanation than he expected.

"Tan's reputation is preceding him," Gilmore said. "Everybody in the neighborhood is giving him a wide berth. The same thing used to happen to us on patrol. It was eerie as hell. You had the feeling there were people there, just ahead of you, around the corner, or just behind you, but you never saw them. It spooked you because you were thinking all the time that it was the VC, luring you into an ambush. But it was just the locals—terrified old men, women, and children just trying to keep the hell out of our way. We'd arrive at a village—half a dozen hooches, maybe—and it would be empty. Fires going, food and tools lying around, but no people. You knew they had just run off into the woods and were watching you."

Gilmore shook his head sadly. "Something about it crushed your spirit," he added, after a pause. "Especially when you began to realize that what they were doing made such good sense. Along with our candy bars and Cokes and aspirin, we also were known to hand out rape, torture, and sudden death. We were just as terrified of them, of course—of their deceit and hatred and booby traps. We thought we were doing what we had to do. But the bottom line was that we should never have been there in the first place. Of course they ran and hid. We were a goddamned doomsday caravan, spreading panic and destruction wherever we went."

At four in the afternoon, a towering wall of cumulus clouds rolled in from the west and lashed the earth below in rain. Water descended in a violent cascade, crashing into the foliage with such force that the jungle seemed to writhe under the impact, leaves and branches jumping and twisting in a struggle to remain upright against the assault from above.

Those caught in the back of the truck rigged a nylon tarpaulin over the body's side panels, tying it to the corners to make a temporary roof. Still the rain battered it like a sail in a hurricane, and a big pocket of water rapidly collected in the center of the canvas and bulged it downward. With all hands pushing from underneath, they were able to force the water over the sides, but the wet trickled and beat in on them from every direction, and the battle to keep dry was hopelessly lost.

The driver of the lead truck, meanwhile, skidded off the shoulder and mired the wheels in half a foot of viscous clay mud. The second truck braked to a halt alongside.

Tan's men produced a coil of braided hemp and tied it around the rear bumper of the first truck and the front bumper of the second. The homemade rope snapped twice, but finally, after much revving of engines and shouting and running around, the old Dodge managed to pull the French lorry back onto the highway.

McWhirter climbed out to have a conference with Tan and the drivers. Rob folded back a corner of the tarpaulin and surveyed the world around them. The clouds, now drained of their moisture, were pulling apart like ripped wads of cotton, and low in the west the sun was burning through again, igniting their undersides in a bright-orange glow. The jungle glistened, and a thick veil of steam collected in the air, turning the countryside into an immense, shimmering-green Turkish bath.

Rob stood aside to let Wyler jump out, and watched him as he swaggered over to the cab of the lead truck to check up on Ferrer. Tan's motley crew was lounging aimlessly around the truck, their weapons slung over their shoulders, chewing betel nut or smoking marijuana. Two were dozing in the mud. The one with the live, half-plucked chicken had untied it from his belt and busied himself ripping off its remaining feathers. Ferrer photographed him.

"Attila the Hun would have been proud of these men," Rob cracked, looking back at Howard Gilmore. Gilmore didn't answer. He was sprawled out on the boxes of supplies, sound asleep.

McWhirter returned briefly to apprise Rob of the situation. "Tan thinks we're only ten miles from the border. He wants to make camp here for the evening and send out a recon patrol on foot to check the border area. If it's clean, we can set out again at midnight and be well inside Vietnam by dawn."

Up in a front corner, Caroline was sitting beside the Laotian boy. Rob had been watching the two of them during the long ride with growing fascination. The boy had clearly decided that Caroline was something special. Gradually, surreptitiously, he had worked his way across the space in the back of the truck until he was next to her. His concentration on her was total. Caroline had ignored him at first, then began meeting his stares with polite smiles.

Finally the boy had reached out tentatively and touched Caroline's arm. Caroline had stiffened, and the boy took his hand away. Rob could understand her diffidence. One-armed, clad in ragged shorts and plastered liberally with dirt, cuts, and bruises from his head of disheveled black hair to the thick, blackened soles of his bare feet, he was an off-putting sight.

But now Caroline was holding the boy's hand and talking to him in low whispers. He sat scrunched up beside her, his big eyes fixed on her with the rapt adoration of a puppy.

"The kid seems to have a thing for blondes," Rob said.

"His mother died when he was born," Caroline replied.

"How did you find that out?"

"He speaks a little French."

"What's his name?"

"Lin Pao. One of Tan's soldiers is his father."

Rob knelt and extended his hand.

The boy stared at it suspiciously. Rob straightened up. "I think he's afraid that if he lets go of your hand, he'll never get it back again. Are you holding up all right?"

"I could use a bath, a vodka and tonic, and a nap. Otherwise, I'm fine."

"I've been thinking about you all day," Rob said. "You and the ten thousand dollars' worth of coke you threw out the window last night."

Caroline pulled a strand of hair back from her eyes and smiled seductively. "Would you rather have had the coke?"

"I'll have to admit," Rob said, pretending to ponder the question seriously, "that you're a better high."

"Gee, thanks."

"And probably even more habit-forming."

"I hope so."

A loud explosion shook the air. Instinctively Rob fell forward, grabbed Caroline and Lin Pao, and pulled them down with him to the floor of the truck.

There was a long silence, then a chorus of shouts and exultant laughter. Rob jumped down from the tailgate and rushed up to the lead vehicle. Tan's soldiers were running up the road in front of the French truck, howling gleefully and brandishing their rifles in the air. Tan, McWhirter, Wyler, and Ferrer were standing together by the side of the truck, watching them. One man remained standing in the back of the truck, balancing a bazooka-like device on his shoulder. He was pounding the roof of the cab with his free hand and grinning proudly.

McWhirter pointed down the highway. Tan's men were converging on the smoldering wreckage of a military jeep. "They just wiped out a government patrol with the RPG."

Rob watched, horror-stricken, as the men swarmed over the remains of the vehicle. Like a pack of hungry jackals, they pulled the dead and dying bodies of the Laotian soldiers out onto the roadway, stripped them naked, and began hacking them to pieces with knives.

McWhirter exposed his teeth in a broad grimace and adjusted his sunglasses carefully on the bridge of his nose. "Let's move on," he said.

28

The North Atlantic

The cold steel handle that he had stared at for so long finally turned, and the door to Grunwald's underwater prison opened at last. Two uniformed men stepped inside. One cradled a submachine gun, the other a rectangular tin tray covered with a paper napkin.

Grunwald stumbled off the cot but stopped when the sailor pointed the machine gun at him. "Where am I?" he demanded. "What time is it?"

Neither man answered him. The one carrying the tray deposited it on the floor, and before Grunwald could think of anything else to say, they were gone. He dropped to his knees by the tray and pulled the napkin off, his heart pounding.

He found a bowl of soup, a square hunk of black bread, and a spoon. That was all. He picked the tray up carefully, brought it over to the cot, and rested it on his lap. Nervously he dipped the spoon into the soup and tasted it. Potato. When had he last eaten such crude peasant fare? Years ago, during the war. Tears flooded his eyes and he had to set the spoon down and wipe them with the sleeve of his pajama shirt.

He forced himself to eat the soup and bread slowly. As the creamy liquid warmed his stomach, he reflected how simple hunger had made him start to feel sorry for himself. He had to push such dangerous emotions back, he realized. He must not feel pathetically grateful for the food. The bastards were just trying to weaken his resistance. He must not allow them to strip him of his self-respect.

Far from sating him, the meager quantity of food only inflamed his appetite. After he had licked the last drop of soup from the bowl and consumed the last crumb of bread, he placed the tray out of sight under the cot, to take his mind off the gnawing in his belly.

Again, he wished desperately that he had some way of telling the time. He had lived for so many years by the clock, letting his assistants and secretaries slice it into precious minutes and half hours and dole it out to subordinates, supplicants, and petitioners in carefully rationed quantities. There were few people in the world who were allowed to take up more of William Grunwald's time than he cared to permit. Now some faceless kidnappers were squandering hours of it, days of it, discarding it as carelessly as if it had no value at all.

But they had kidnapped him, after all, because he *was* so valuable. He remembered the published accounts of other kidnapped executives, and how easily they had become prey to their own inner anxieties, making their captors' jobs that much easier. He must not allow that to happen to him.

The food made Grunwald drowsy. He had begun to fall asleep when he heard someone at the door again. He pushed himself upright on the cot and listened. The steel handle turned and the heavy door swung inward on its hinges to reveal the slender figure of an old man.

"Guten Abend, Herr Grunwald," the old man said, stepping over the high threshold and closing the steel door behind him. *"Was gibt's sonst?"*

The German words shocked Grunwald. "Don't you speak English?"

The old man's lips parted in a mocking grin. "I'm afraid not," he replied in German. "And, in any case, as fellow countrymen, I think it appropriate that we converse in the tongue of the fatherland. Don't you agree?"

"I am a citizen of the United States," Grunwald announced, finding the words in German and delivering them in as severe a tone as he could muster. "As you very well must know."

The old man opened his mouth and emitted a harsh cackle. "Well, your German remains excellent, Herr Grunwald. I congratulate you on that."

Grunwald stared at the decrepit figure in bewilderment. Up close, he saw that he was not such an old man after all, but he looked unhealthy. His face was weather-beaten to the point of appearing ravaged, and his eyes, with their watery red rims and dark crescents, gave him a haunted demeanor. "Who are you?" Grunwald demanded.

"My name is Karl Koenig," the German replied. "For the time being, I am your custodian."

"How did I get here?"

"We removed you from your aircraft a hundred miles off the coast of the United States."

"Where are the others? The Hendrys? And John?"

Koenig sighed. "Regrettably, they did not survive."

"You killed them?"

"They did not survive," Koenig repeated, looking straight into Grunwald's surprised eyes.

Grunwald swallowed. "Who the hell are you . . . really?"

"I hold an important post in the government of the German Democratic Republic."

"What do you want from me?"

Koenig chuckled, causing a fan of deep wrinkles to radiate out from his temples. "I am tempted to say your soul. But you'll get a full explanation of everything in due course."

"Why have you kidnapped me? How the hell do you expect to get away with it?"

Koenig dragged the metal chair a few feet until it was more or less in the center of the room, facing Grunwald's cot. "We have already gotten away with it," he answered, sitting in the chair.

"Are you people crazy?" Grunwald thundered, finding some authority in his voice at last. "Is the East German government now stooping to terrorism? How do you expect to explain this to the world?"

Koenig laughed again. "No explanation is necessary, my friend. The world already knows what has happened to William Grunwald."

Grunwald ignored Koenig's cryptic reply. After all the hours of anxiety, he at last had a target on which to unleash his indignation and fury. "If you bastards harm me," he warned, jabbing a finger at Koenig, "you'll have the U.S. government to answer to. We can put the screws to that puppet regime of yours in Pankow in dozens of ways—economically and politically—and you know it. Kidnapping an ambassador amounts to an act of war. Are your masters in Moscow prepared to back up such barbaric behavior? I demand you release me at once!"

Grunwald's protest did not intimidate Koenig in the slightest. In fact, it seemed to touch some ferocious nerve in the man, for his face turned a mottled red, as if set afire from within. Instead of replying, he turned to the door and clapped his hands together loudly. The door opened immediately, and a young seaman stepped through, carrying a small cassette recorder. He handed it to Koenig and then withdrew.

"We taped this some hours ago," Koenig said, cradling the recorder on his lap. "From the BBC. I think you'll find it of interest."

Grunwald heard the hiss of tape and then the voice of an English newscaster:

". . . And finally we have this item from Kevin Ruark, in our New York bureau." The anchorman's cultivated tones were replaced by the voice of the journalist: "Both the financial and diplomatic communities in the United States were upset today by the sudden death of William Grunwald, the multimillionaire industrialist who had just this week been appointed by the President as his new ambassador to Israel. Grunwald's private jet, on a flight from New York to Washington, mysteriously veered off course and crashed into the Atlantic Ocean. By the time rescue craft reached the area, no trace remained of Grunwald's plane or of its passengers—Grunwald; the pilots, Mr. Donald Hendry and his wife, Marcia Hendry; and Grunwald's personal bodyguard, John Fitzpatrick. Rescue efforts were abandoned just this evening, after a forty-eight-hour search of the area failed to turn up any evidence of survivors. 'We have lost a great American,' the President was quoted as saying this afternoon, responding to a question put to him by a newsman as he rushed for his helicopter on the White House's south lawn. . . .'"

Koenig turned the recorder off and stood up. "So you see, no one is looking for you at all. Your disappearance does not threaten international peace or cooperation in even the smallest degree. William Grunwald is of no consequence to anyone anymore. William Grunwald is dead, and the world has gone on to other business. So your future welfare is completely in my hands, and the sooner you accept this new status of yours, the better it will be for you. I want you to reflect on this before our next conversation."

"I demand you tell me why you have kidnapped me!" Grunwald cried, straining for that tone of command that only a few days ago was so comfortably his.

Koenig stepped toward the door. "You had better remove that word 'demand' from your vocabulary," he warned. "I find it annoying. You'll receive answers to all your questions eventually."

"I want more food—and clothes," Grunwald said, less belligerently.

The German rapped on the door and waited for it to open. "Those are peculiar demands for a dead man to make," he retorted, revealing his bad teeth in a mocking grin.

"I'm not dead, you son of a bitch!" Grunwald exploded, restraining himself from leaping at the frail figure and throttling him with his bare hands. "I'm alive and I intend to stay that way!"

Koenig glowered at his captive. "William Grunwald is dead," he repeated, articulating the words with a somber finality. "Dead and gone to hell."

The door opened and Koenig lifted his legs carefully over the threshold. "That's your situation," he said, not looking back. "Dead and gone to hell. Where you belong."

Rhinebeck, New York

"How is she?" Safier asked.

Sarah Grunwald closed the door to her mother's bedroom and walked with her fiancé down the second-floor hallway. "She'd be fine if it wasn't for that damned doctor of hers," she said. "He can't resist shooting her up with tranquilizers. She can barely stand at the moment."

"It must be hard for her," Safier said. "Thank God she has you. You're the strong one in this family."

Sarah shook her head. "I'm just the least high-strung."

They walked silently down the stairs. The ground-floor hall was crowded with wreaths of flowers, filling the stairwell with their sweet funereal odor.

"I tell everybody not to send the damned things," she said, waving at the masses of blossoms. "People pay no attention."

"I've got to get back to the city," Safier said.

Sarah leaned her head against his shoulder. "I'd better stay here for a few more days."

Safier kissed her on the forehead. "Your father was a great man," he said, his voice suddenly cracking with emotion. "He had his share of enemies, but he was a great man. I feel like he was my father, too."

"He thought the world of you, Jim."

"He treated me like a son. I owe him everything."

Sarah smiled, embarrassed. "Stop it. You'll make me think we're practicing incest."

They embraced briefly. "I'd better go," Safier said. "Things are pretty wild at the office. The vultures are closing in from everywhere, hoping for a piece of Grunwald Industries."

"You can handle them, if anyone can."

Sarah followed him out the front door and waved good-bye as he climbed into his Porsche and sped down the drive. She wished he

252 / TOM HYMAN

would get rid of that damned sports car. He always defended it by saying that it was safer than other cars because it handled so well. She was convinced it just made him a more reckless driver.

Perhaps she was too hard on him. The sports car was about the only thing frivolous about James Safier. At least the only thing frivolous that he revealed about himself. There was a lot to discover in him, she thought, and that probably accounted for her interest in him. He was a mystery. He seemed to have almost no life outside his work, yet he was obviously a passionate, caring man.

Sarah was touched by his devotion to her father. And she was grateful that he was there to fill the void. Without Safier to steady things, she dreaded to think of the difficulties the company could be facing. Certainly no one in the family was capable of stepping in and taking charge.

She would have to think about that, she realized. At the moment, the disposition of her father's will depended on the outcome of Rob's mission to rescue Billy.

As she stood there, looking across the big lawn toward the gate house and the apple orchard, a chilling thought overtook her.

It was Jim Safier who stood to lose the most. He felt like a son, but he was not a son. There would be no inheritance for him, beyond a possible trust fund. He would get no ownership in Grunwald Industries. He had only his job, and with his boss gone, even that was now in jeopardy. If Billy came back, he would want to take over, and Safier would be left with nothing.

Only by marrying her could he hope to hold, even indirectly, any real power or influence in the company to which he had devoted his life. Sarah didn't want to take that away from him, but neither did she want it to be the reason he was marrying her.

29

Laos

After the destruction of the military patrol, the expedition drove several miles farther east, hid the trucks well off the highway, and camped for the night. Tan sent two men out to reconnoiter the border area. They returned at three in the morning, with bad news.

"They ran into a checkpoint near Tchepone, two miles up the road," McWhirter said, shaking Rob awake, "and two more between there and the border. We'll have to leave the trucks here and hoof it the rest of the way."

Rob sat up and rubbed the sleep from his face. "How far?"

"Four miles. Our best route is along the stream that parallels the highway. It branches out of the Bang Hieng River about a mile from here, crosses the highway, and then stays just south of it all the way to Khe Sanh."

"I remember it from the map," Rob replied. "Is it the best place to cross the border?"

In the moonlight, Rob could see McWhirter offer one of his characteristic shrugs. "Tan thinks so."

"You think he's right?"

McWhirter hesitated. "Sure," he said. "This is his turf."

"I thought this part of Laos *wasn't* his turf."

"Well, shit, it's more his than ours."

McWhirter's mood disturbed Rob. He seemed hourly to grow more short-tempered and preoccupied. "What's our timetable?" he asked him.

"Off the road we'll have to move by day. Let's get a few more hours' sleep, then pack up and leave at first light."

Rob passed the word to the others while McWhirter went back to confer with Tan.

Getting back to sleep was difficult for Rob. By the time he had managed to force from his mind all his concerns for the mission, now approaching its critical hours, the hammock, wonderfully restful when he had first climbed into it early that evening, had become a torture device. Lying on his back, folded into a shallow V like a diver coming out of a back flip, put constant pressure on the nape of his neck and under his heels. After an hour or so the discomfort would become unendurable and he would start thrashing around in search of a more bearable position.

In addition to the discomfort, he felt vulnerable, outside at night in the Laotian rain forest. It brought back an irrational fear of the dark he hadn't experienced since childhood.

During the daylight hours, the jungle had seemed oppressively still. Save for the occasional squawk of a parrot overhead, the dense curtains of foliage that rose up on each side of the highway hid its secrets in a claustrophobic green silence. But at sunset the lethargic daytime paralysis shifted into a madhouse of disquiet. A cacophony of noise—from the pulsing peeps of thousands of tree frogs to the lugubrious trills and whistles of unfamiliar birds and mammals—reverberated through the wild night. Twice Rob was awakened by the nearby scuffle of nocturnal feet along the forest floor. And once, a distant, blood-freezing animal shriek brought him bolt upright in the hammock.

A ghostly illumination from a three-quarter moon trickled down through the jungle canopy, and occasionally, through the intricate web of light and shadow, Rob caught a glimpse of movement over-head—the darting silhouette of a bat, or the movement of a branch, signaling the presence of some prowling creature.

Rob shifted wearily onto his side. He had watched the moon travel all the way from the jagged edges of the mountains in the east to the flat western horizons, where it was about to disappear. Already its light had retreated out of the forest understory, leaving the world below the canopy in a thick predawn darkness.

Angry, shouting voices rang out suddenly over the clearing, destroying his last hopes of sleep. He threw his legs over the side of the hammock and sat up, nervously alert. The jungle's nocturnal racket had ceased and a gray, mist-laden light had just begun to dilute the blackness.

He pulled on shirt and pants, kicked his feet into his canvas shoes, and walked, sleep-starved and groggy, in the direction of the noise. Out in the clearing he saw Frank Wyler waving a fist under the chin of the Souei chief, Tan, and cursing him loudly. Tan stood with his arms crossed over his massive chest, his bull-like physique pulled up to its full height. His posture was defiant, but the expression on his face was puzzlement. A pace behind Wyler, Ghislene Ferrer was hurling her own invective at the Laotian.

"What's going on?" Rob demanded.

Wyler turned, his face muscles working. "I'm going to kill the little shit," he snarled. "Tell this son of a bitch to go find him. Because I'm going to kill him!"

McWhirter and Gilmore appeared. McWhirter stepped over to the former Marine and pulled his fist down out of the vicinity of Tan's face. "What the hell's the matter, Frank?"

"One of his little yellow bastards attacked her!" Wyler spluttered. "Ask her!"

"He tried to rape me," Ferrer declared, gesturing toward the two trucks, where the soldiers were sleeping. "Didn't anybody hear me yell for help?"

"What did he do to you?" Rob asked.

"He attacked me," she insisted. "With a gun!"

"Did he actually rape you?"

"I fought him off!"

Wyler stalked over to Rob. "You taking their side? The little bastard jumped her—with a gun!"

"Take it easy, Frank," Rob said, trying to placate him.

Wyler exploded: "Take it easy! I'm going to shoot the little gook bastard full of holes!"

McWhirter translated Ferrer's complaint to the Souei chief. When he understood, he acted decisively. He bellowed some words in Laotian that silenced everyone. Seconds later his men, who had remained out of sight, stepped out warily from behind the trucks and the bushes surrounding the clearing. Tan bellowed another command, and the men, in bad humor, formed a line in front of him.

Tan addressed a question to McWhirter. McWhirter turned to Ferrer. "He wants you to point out the one who attacked you."

Ferrer stepped up, hands on her hips, and began inspecting the ragged row of warriors. She stalked down the line, stopping directly in front of each one and looking him over. She seemed to be enjoying it. Wyler walked along behind her, fists clenched.

"Don't drag it out," McWhirter warned her. "If you don't know who it is, say so."

"I don't need your advice," Ferrer snapped back.

"Frank, get the hell away from her," McWhirter said. "Let these people settle it among themselves."

Wyler ignored him. Ferrer finally pointed an accusing finger at one of the younger, more presentable members of the gang. "This one," she said, her tone emphatic.

Tan shouted a question at him. The tribesman did not seem intimidated by his chief's bullying tone. He answered in a loud, confident voice, obviously denying Ferrer's charge. Wyler advanced toward him, his fist raised. McWhirter and Gilmore grabbed Wyler and pulled him back.

Tan and the accused man exchanged shouted remarks for several minutes.

Rob turned to McWhirter: "What are they saying?"

"The guy claims he didn't try to rape her at all. He admits he threatened her with a gun—because she kept snapping his photograph after he had warned her not to."

Ferrer overheard McWhirter and reacted contemptuously. "That's absurd! That's the most absurd thing I have ever heard in my life! I have photographed the world's leaders! How dare he say he objected? He didn't object! He held a gun on me and he grabbed me and pushed me to the ground!"

Caroline appeared near the edge of the clearing, with Lin Pao beside her. When the boy saw the line of men, he rushed over and stationed himself behind the one Ferrer had accused, grabbing his shirt for security.

McWhirter translated Ferrer's rejoinder to Tan. Tan spoke to the accused man again, this time in a low and ominous voice. The soldier's wide brown face looked worried for the first time, but he rejected Ferrer's accusation vigorously.

"He's claiming that you came on to him," McWhirter told Ferrer. "And you're just trying to get even with him because he wouldn't have anything to do with you."

Ferrer was outraged. "That's a damned lie!" she cried. "This man tried to rape me! Are you going to take his word against mine?"

McWhirter shrugged. "I'm just translating, sweetheart."

"Then tell his chief what I just said!" Ferrer demanded. McWhirter did.

"Would being photographed bother him that much?" Rob asked.

"It might," McWhirter said. "These people are animists. They believe the spirit lives inside things. Taking somebody's photograph can steal his soul from him."

Rob was beginning to think the incident was a bad joke. He suspected that Ferrer probably *had* tried to turn the soldier on, just as she had Wyler and the Souei chief, to get her way. In this particular case, just to get a few photographs. Now she was looking for revenge because he hadn't cooperated. And she obviously had both Wyler and Tan on her side. "This is idiotic," he said. "Tell Tan to tell the man to apologize to Ferrer, and let's get on with what we came here for."

McWhirter shook his head. "We'll have to let Tan settle it."

Tan did settle it. After a final heated exchange of words, he drew out his big .45 revolver from its handmade holster, cocked the hammer back, pressed the muzzle against the man's forehead, and shot him.

The crack of the explosion was quickly swallowed by the encircling wall of foliage. The soldier crumpled slowly backward. His son, Lin Pao, was still standing behind him, his one hand clutching his shirt. His father fell on top of him, momentarily smothering him in the leaves. The boy screamed and struggled to get out from beneath him. The rest of Tan's men moved quickly aside, as if proximity to the dead man might in itself be fatal.

The boy pushed himself to his feet. His face, neck, and chest were cloaked with blood, and his eyes were wide with terror. He staggered around the clearing as if he, too, had been mortally wounded, and then he disappeared into the woods, his throat racked with sobs that were unbearable to hear.

Ghislene Ferrer clutched the sides of her head with both hands, her face distorted in abject disbelief. *"Oh, mon Dieu,"* she gasped. *"Oh, mon Dieu. . . ."*

30

The North Atlantic

Koenig returned, carrying a small blanket, and sat in the metal chair. Grunwald remained on the cot, lying on his side, his legs drawn up for warmth. He wondered if the blanket was for him.

"Sit up, please," Koenig ordered, his voice crisp.

Grudgingly Grunwald swung his feet over the side of the cot. He had thought a lot about the German since his first visit. He had taken on many tough men in the years of building his industrial empire— rival businessmen, bankers, venture capitalists, regulatory bosses, powerful governors, union leaders, Mafia chiefs. The list was long. Sizing a man up, ferreting out his weaknesses, had become second nature to him. His success—sometimes even his survival—had depended on it, and he believed that he was good at it.

He had come to some tentative conclusions about Koenig, and none of them was reassuring. He represented a kind of toughness that Grunwald had never experienced—at least not since his youth in Germany. Koenig was a true believer, a man who saw himself as part of an ideology bigger and more important than himself—or any individual. And, like most fanatics, he probably had little interest in his own material well-being. This made him virtually impervious to either temptation or threat.

And to have risen to a position of power in East Germany, he was no doubt a decisive and ruthless man who knew how to exert his will effectively. He had already proven that with frightening persuasiveness. He had commandeered a submarine, taken Grunwald prisoner, isolated him, starved him, stripped him of his possessions, and deprived him even of the basics by which a human being measured his activities and his life—daylight and dark, the calendar and the clock. He had even forced his choice of language on Grunwald. He had done all this, and Grunwald had yet to discover why.

"How long have I been here?"

"I have been listening to your obituaries on the shortwave," Koenig said, ignoring his question. "You were a very rich man."

Was it a simple ransom the Germans were after? "I need more to eat," he said.

Koenig folded his arms across his chest and studied the ceiling. "You Jews have a knack for making money. Why is that?"

The German's question astonished Grunwald.

"You must have some theories," Koenig persisted.

"Because we're smarter than everybody else," Grunwald retorted.

Koenig laughed. "Smarter! About making money, yes. But you know what money represents?"

"It represents power."

"Does it?" his captor challenged. "I am not a rich man. But I have considerable power. Look at the power I have over you now. Life and death. What do you say to that?"

"There are other forms of power besides money."

"You expect me to say that money is theft," Koenig continued, bringing his eyes down level with Grunwald's. "Give you the party line, so to speak."

"I suppose you might believe that," Grunwald muttered.

Koenig revealed his yellowed teeth. "Money is excrement!" he said harshly. "And you Jews love to wallow in it. That's why you're so good at making money. Admit it! You love to wallow in shit!"

Grunwald sighed and looked down at his feet. They were jammed into the hemp slippers, the heels of which stuck out an inch behind his own.

"That's why there are so few Jews in the German Democratic Republic. Jews don't fare so well in a Socialist climate. They prefer the capitalist countries, where there's more shit for them to wallow in."

"I would think that the reason you have so few Jews in East Germany," Grunwald replied in an even tone, "is that you murdered them all in the forties."

Koenig seemed perversely pleased by Grunwald's answer. He nodded his head like a schoolmaster acknowledging a good point made by a student. "We didn't kill *you,* though, did we?" he said.

"No."

"Why not, I wonder?"

"I was lucky."

"You were in Dachau."

"Yes."

"How long were you there?"

Grunwald folded his arms across his chest and tipped his chin down to keep warm. "A short time."

"How short?"

"About a year. The camp was liberated soon after I arrived."

"And so you made your way to America—the land of opportunity."

"That's right."

"Where you married a woman with money."

Grunwald said nothing.

"So you could wallow in shit all of your life, along with all those other money-grubbing Jews in America."

"Your prejudice does you no credit," Grunwald said.

Koenig showed his teeth again. "What's the matter? Do you object to being called a money-grubbing Jew?"

"Of course I object."

"But that's what you are," Koenig persisted. "Isn't it?"

Grunwald wondered why the man was baiting him. "Whatever you say."

"*Not* whatever I say," Koenig replied. "Don't you have the will to deny it?"

"Are you expecting me to argue with you?"

"Not at all. I'm expecting you to correct me, if I should mis-state the truth. If you are not a money-grubbing Jew, you should correct me."

Grunwald felt baffled. What was the man getting at? "Your state-ment is a slur. I can't respond to it."

Koenig seemed to change the subject. "When we undressed you," he said, "to change your clothes, we noticed that you didn't have a number tattooed on your forearm."

"I told you I was in Dachau a short time. Things were confused. The war was nearly over."

"But all concentration-camp inmates received their tattoo as soon as they were admitted. How did they miss you?"

Grunwald shivered. "I don't know," he muttered. "Do you doubt that I was there?"

Koenig's eyelids lifted and his rheumy eyes blazed with mock surprise. "Doubt that you were there?" he echoed. "Why, of course not! I'll bet you could draw me a map!"

"What do you want from me?"

Koenig pulled back the sleeve of his jacket and then unbuttoned his shirt cuff and rolled it up. The German's arm was thin, the skin laced with blue veins. "I was at Dachau, too," he said. "And I have my number to prove it!" He pointed to his wrist. "Do you see my number?"

Grunwald saw the black row of numerals burned into the skin just back of the wrist. After forty years, they had barely faded.

Koenig folded his cuff back down and buttoned it. "Don't you recognize me, Herr Grunwald?"

Grunwald shook his head. His heart had begun to pound and he pressed his arm over it, as if to hold it in.

"What do you say? No?"

"No," he croaked.

Koenig laughed. Grunwald felt something swelling inside, tightening against his rib cage.

"Well, I'm not surprised," Koenig went on, folding the thin blanket in his arms until it was barely a foot square. "We met only briefly, after all. And it was so many years ago. How could I expect you to remember?"

Grunwald swallowed. His spine trembled with cold. He could feel the hairs raising up along it. Koenig stood up, ramrod straight, and advanced a step toward him. "It was a very memorable occasion for me, however," he said, his voice suddenly soft, caressing. "One I knew I would never forget. Indeed, I remember everything about that day. I was dying of dysentery in the Revier. You remember the Revier?"

Grunwald nodded.

Koenig stepped closer and draped the folded blanket over his arm. "And on the day I was to die, an incredible thing happened. The Americans came. Of course you remember that?"

"Yes," Grunwald whispered.

"Yes," Koenig purred. "The Americans came. Do you remember what they did?"

Grunwald stared at him.

"Do you remember?" Koenig repeated.

"They liberated the camp."

"What else did they do?"

"I don't know."

262 / TOM HYMAN

"They executed the guards!"

Grunwald said nothing.

"You must remember that! It was a moment of great joy! They lined up the SS guards against the wall of the prison block and cut them down with machine guns. You all stood in the Appellplatz and cheered them on! Remember?"

Grunwald looked at his striped pajamalike trousers. Some part of him had known that this was coming. Still, consciously he had resisted it. "Yes," he whispered. "I remember."

Koenig stepped directly in front of him, his chest inches from Grunwald's face, forcing Grunwald to lean back. "What did you do after the Americans shot the SS guards?"

"I don't know. It was a long time ago."

"Didn't you go to the Revier?"

"It's possible."

"It's more than possible," Koenig whispered. "Because that's where we met—in the Revier."

"If you say so."

Koenig reached out and pressed his bony fingers gently against Grunwald's chest. "These numbers on your tunic," he said. "They should help you remember better."

Grunwald bent his face down to watch Koenig's hand slowly trace the stencil on his chest.

"I thought you more intelligent," Koenig said, his voice still teasing him. "I thought the numbers would have some meaning for you."

"No," Grunwald replied. "No meaning."

"You have repressed it," Koenig decided. "Look at the numbers and read them aloud to me."

Grunwald docilely obeyed Koenig's directions. Like a subject in a hypnotic trance, he gazed at the numbers, upside down from his view, and began saying them out loud: *"Vier . . . drei . . . fünf . . . zwei . . . sechs."*

"Very good," Koenig murmured. With two fingers of his right hand, he traced a double lightning stroke against Grunwald's chest. "Now, if you put an 'SS' in front of them, you would see that they are your Waffen-SS I.D. number. Am I correct?"

Grunwald looked up into Koenig's eyes. At such close range he felt the man's hatred full force.

"Am I correct?" Koenig demanded.

Grunwald stared, unable to move.

"You took a blanket, like the one in my hands, and used it to suffocate the old man in the bunk beside me. Then you took his clothes—a pathetic pair of prison pajamas like the ones you now wear—and you escaped. Now do you remember?"

Grunwald shivered violently.

"*Now* do you remember?" Koenig shouted.

Grunwald nodded.

Koenig held the blanket up and laughed. "I have waited all my life for this moment, Willi Gruen. I have followed you and your career every step of the way, waiting for my chance. Now it has come."

Koenig leaned forward, clapped the blanket over Grunwald's face, and held it there, pressing his captive's head against the steel bulkhead. Grunwald screamed and clawed at Koenig's wrists.

In the blur of terror that followed, Grunwald ripped the blanket free and rolled onto the floor, striking out at his tormentor with the desperation of a cornered animal.

Other hands were on him, suddenly, pulling him away from Koenig and slamming him hard against the wall. Fists pounded into his face and chest and groin and knocked him to the floor again. Boots kicked him repeatedly. He twisted and squirmed, trying to dodge them. Finally, defenseless and exhausted, he rolled himself into a ball and let the blows crash into him at will.

His brain came to his rescue, pulling him into unconsciousness. His screams began to sound far away, and then he couldn't hear anything at all.

31

Laos

A grave was dug in a patch of sandy ground not far from the trucks, and the Souei tribesman—Rob never did learn his name—was hastily thrown in, wrapped in his homemade hammock, and buried without ceremony. One of Tan's men built a small kairn of stones on top of the grave, placed a few objects inside to propitiate the local spirits, and the expedition prepared to move on.

Numbed by the event, Rob and the others lost themselves in preparations—unloading the trucks and repacking the supplies they would have to carry the rest of the way on their backs. No one spoke, except to confer on some essential detail related to the job of packing. Ghislene Ferrer was especially subdued. After the shooting, she had stayed well away from Tan and his men, occupying herself writing furiously in her notebook. Of all who had witnessed the brutal execution, only Wyler remained cheerful.

The death weighed heavily on Rob. "It should never have happened," he told McWhirter.

"Put it behind you," McWhirter advised. "These people don't play by the same rules we do."

"Tan's judgment was compromised by Ferrer."

McWhirter offered his shrug. "Maybe. But he has to be tough to keep men like this in line."

"Ferrer lied," Rob persisted. "The rape charge was her revenge against the man because he wouldn't let her take his fucking picture."

"She miscalculated and she knows it," McWhirter replied. "At least she'll probably keep her mouth shut from now on."

Rob unpacked a box of freeze-dried food and arranged its contents in six separate piles on the ground. "What about the rifles and ammo?" he asked McWhirter. "Shouldn't we divide them up now? Let everybody carry his own?"

McWhirter shook his head. "They're too damned heavy. Let the Laotians tote them for us. That's what we're paying them for."

"What if we run into trouble? Are we going to have time to hand out weapons?"

"We won't run into any trouble today that Tan and his men can't handle."

Rob looked down at the mounds of sealed aluminum packets. It was uncharacteristic of McWhirter to treat the matter so casually. "I don't agree," he said. "We ought to have our weapons."

McWhirter stared at him. It was the same intimidating look he had used when Rob first recruited him, back at that bar in Oklahoma in April. It seemed as if years had passed since that night. "I guess you're the boss," he said, finally, managing a faint grin.

Rob asked Wyler to sort out the rifles and ammunition and pass them out. He finished dividing up the food packets and took Caroline's share over to her hammock. Her rucksack and belongings were there, but she was not.

He searched the campsite and the woods around it, and began to feel a tinge of panic. One disaster a day was surely enough. He remembered how easy it was to get lost in the jungle. He had once strayed just a short distance off a path in the rain forest south of Belize and ended up spending the night there, miserable and terrified, shivering against the trunk of a large mahogany tree. He was about to enlist some help for a serious search, when he heard a faint splashing noise in the woods directly ahead of him.

The sound led him to a stream, and a short distance to the right the small creek widened into a pool of clear water.

Caroline was there, sitting on a flat rock that hung over the pool's edge. Submerged to his knees in the water in front of her was Lin Pao, the one-armed boy, his naked little body shivering in the humid midday heat. Caroline was washing him with a hand cloth and bar of soap, murmuring to him reassuringly as she scrubbed away the blood and dirt.

Rob had forgotten about the boy. He watched the two of them for a moment, reluctant to disturb them, then stepped out to the rock and announced his presence. "I was afraid you were lost," he said.

The boy's lips were drawn back from his chattering teeth like a wounded animal's. His face, stressed by more pain and fear than the wretched child knew how to handle, caused Rob to avert his eyes.

"He doesn't have anybody now," Caroline said, her voice matter-of-fact.

"No relatives back in his village?"

"No."

"What will he do?"

Caroline squeezed the hand cloth out in the water and rubbed more soap into it. "He doesn't know. He's on his own, he told me."

Rob nodded and watched her apply the cloth to the boy's ears and neck. She began talking to him again, in a soothing, healing voice that would eventually, he was sure, rescue the boy from his grief. How incredibly beautiful she looked at this moment, he thought—in her wrinkled shorts and shirt, her hair pinned roughly back. And how thankful he felt, suddenly, that she had come with them after all.

"We'll be along in a minute," she replied, pushing a strand of hair from her face with a wet hand.

He wanted to sit down beside her on the rock and embrace her, and tell her how much he loved her. "I'll help you pack," he said, and started back to the campsite.

The expedition set out on foot at one o'clock in the afternoon, stepping cautiously along a narrow path that wound through heavy foliage down to the banks of a muddy brook. They followed the stream until it crossed Highway 9 and emptied into a larger river flowing east.

Rob saw Lin Pao marching up near the front of the line, stumbling along with his dead father's rucksack and rifle slung over his back. Upset and angry, he asked McWhirter about it.

"He has to take his father's place if he wants to stay with Tan's men."

"That's monstrous. The boy's only eleven years old!"

McWhirter shrugged. "Next thing you'll be saying the kid should be in school."

At five o'clock they stopped to make camp for the night. Rob pulled out the terrain map and compass from his pack and estimated their location. "It looks like we're about two miles from Vietnam," he said, pointing out the spot on the map to Gilmore and McWhirter.

"We're only four or five from our target, then," Gilmore said, sounding surprised. "We'll be there tomorrow."

Rob glanced sideways at McWhirter. "Are we going to have problems getting across the border?"

McWhirter removed his sunglasses and squinted down the river. It was narrow at this point, and its brown waters—the accumulated runoff from the steep slopes of the Annam Cordillera—tumbled furiously through the twisting corridor of green foliage. "Tan will send out another recon patrol before daylight. We'll have to wait on them."

Rob was about to ask another question, but McWhirter suddenly got up and walked away.

"What's eating him?" Gilmore asked.

Rob scratched a tick bite. "I think the mission's beginning to bore him."

The North Atlantic

"Wake up, Herr Gruen."

Grunwald rolled over onto his back and tried to open his eyes. The swelling of his face had closed them nearly shut. He started to hoist himself up to a sitting position but quickly changed his mind. The slightest exertion made him dizzy and exacerbated the pain that seemed to inhabit every corner of his body.

The physical beating, combined with Koenig's tearing out of him the terrible secret he had lived with for thirty-seven years, was having a complicated effect on Grunwald. On the one hand, he was devastated, intellectually and emotionally, and, for the first time since his capture, afraid that Koenig might kill him after all.

On the other hand, he had experienced an extraordinary psychological catharsis that he didn't completely understand. The violent events had triggered within him an immense release, lanced some crippling psychic infection and drained away the poisons of fear and guilt. Whatever might happen to him now, he knew that at least he would never suffer another anxiety attack.

Koenig looked his captive over. "A few bruises, Herr Gruen, that's all. You must get used to such things. You must learn humility."

Grunwald felt light-headed. He closed his eyes and the cot seemed to roll beneath him, like a porch swing. "I need something to eat," he said.

"We are going to talk first," Koenig commanded.

Grunwald looked up at the German. The dim light from the overhead bulb fell down across Koenig's features at an oblique angle, lengthening the shadows under his brow, nose, and cheeks, imparting to his already menacing visage a chiaroscuro of waxen surfaces and black hollows that resembled a death's-head.

"What about?" Grunwald asked, struggling to articulate the words through his swollen mouth.

"About you," Koenig replied. "And your family. I know a great deal about you, you see. More, in some respects, than you know yourself."

Grunwald shook his head in confusion.

"You see, Herr Gruen, ever since that night in the Revier, when you killed Simon Grunwald, I have maintained a very special interest in your activities. For thirty-seven years I have shadowed you from afar, followed you through your life every step of the way, from the day you first escaped justice at the hands of the American soldiers until this very moment. I watched you immigrate to the United States and ingratiate yourself, as the Jew Grunwald, among the very people who only a short while before you were shoveling into the crematorium at Dachau. I watched you marry into a prominent Jewish family. I watched you take that family's money and parlay it, with a criminal ruthlessness unusual even for America, into a great capitalist fortune. I watched your children—rich, arrogant, complacent—grow and make their way in the world, innocent of the truth about their father, about their own true heritage. I watched it all. A classic case study of capitalistic greed and degeneracy that fascinated me even as it repulsed me. I watched and I waited."

Grunwald raised his hands and pressed them gently over the bruised flesh around his eyes. "I believe you are insane," he muttered.

Koenig stared at the gray pipes over Grunwald's head. "Sometimes I have thought so myself," he admitted. "Most men were eager to forget those horrible times. Something in me made it impossible to forget. I am by nature unforgiving. I believe too deeply in justice. In retribution. But also I was too deeply scarred. My family was destroyed by the Nazis. Destroyed hideously. We were Socialists and we spoke out against the Nazi party from the beginning. They threatened my family repeatedly, attacked my father in the streets, fire-bombed our house. And when they seized power, they were quick to exact a fuller revenge.

"They came one night—I was not there—and dragged my father, mother, brother, and little sister away. I never saw any of them again. Indeed, it took me years to learn of their fates. My brother, after weeks of torture at the hands of the Gestapo, managed to hang himself in his cell. My parents and sister were not as lucky. What they did to them is too monstrous for me to speak of, even after all these years.

Suffice it to say they all died horribly. I lived in hiding for three years before they caught me and took me to the camps."

Koenig removed a cigarette from the pack in his pocket but didn't light it. "So I was a witness to many atrocities before Dachau," he said.

"In you, I saw the distillation of everything evil in capitalism and National Socialism. You were the end product, the young Teutonic pig fresh from the Hitler Youth, the narcissistic, brainwashed bully who was willing to commit any crime for his masters as long as you got your rewards and privileges. You were truly the scum, the swinish, greedy cowards of the human race. You had failed every test of humanity. Rather than resist the subhuman temptations of Nazism, or stand up against it, as some of us did—rather even than fight and die for your country on the front lines in Africa, Europe, or the East— you chose to skulk in protected comfort behind the lines, strutting around in your preposterous uniforms with your skull and crossbones, bringing daily humiliation, torture, and death to the thousands of brave humans who could not defend themselves against your clubs and your dogs and your bullets. . . ."

Out of breath, Koenig interrupted his tirade and tipped his head back to catch a sudden flood of angry tears. "How many days, years, I burned with these thoughts I can't say, but my experience convinced me in a way nothing else could, of the bankruptcy of European civilization. Only a corrupt and rotting social and economic system could have allowed such a malignancy to thrive. No other explanation is possible. And your act, the night Dachau was liberated, was the final outrage for me. You murdered a noble human being, a gentle, saintly man who had already suffered more pain in his life than a thousand Willi Gruens. You killed him for the last thing he owned, a dirty pair of concentration-camp pajamas. You killed him when he was only hours, perhaps minutes, from being saved. You killed him, and then desecrated his memory by appropriating his identity to save your own foul guts. And you not only got away with your monstrous act, you improved upon it shamelessly, exploiting your sham Jewishness into a triumph of truly despicable proportions. And each victory of yours only strengthened my determination to see justice done. I knew that if I could one day bring you to account, Simon Grunwald's death would have some meaning, some value."

"What do you want from me, for God's sake?" Grunwald whispered.

"I want your most treasured possession—that which you love most in your life," Koenig answered. "I want your son Billy."

"But, my God, why? He's not responsible for anything that I've done."

"I want him, nevertheless."

Through the depths of his anguish, Grunwald laughed at the cruel irony of Koenig's demand. "He's been missing in Vietnam for twelve years. You must know that."

Koenig didn't answer immediately. When he did, his tone was calm, almost regretful. "Yes, he is in Vietnam. But he is not a prisoner. If he were, then I would not require your assistance."

Not a prisoner? Grunwald thought. *Then he has escaped!* "I won't betray Billy," he declared, hurling out his words in a defiant shout. He heard his voice reverberate against the steel walls of his prison. To his horror, it sounded thin and pathetic—the hollow whining of a defeated man.

Koenig stood up to leave. "I think you will, Herr Gruen, when you learn the truth about him."

32

Laos

Rob opened his eyes to see Gilmore looming over his hammock in the misty predawn light. "The Laotians are gone," he whispered.

Rob sat up and pulled back the mosquito netting. "What? Gone where?"

"Gone. Bugged out."

Rob threw on his clothes and joined the others, now gathering in a group around the cold cook-fire, extinguished by the night's rain. He looked around for signs of Tan and his men, but Gilmore was right: they were gone.

He found McWhirter. The Oklahoman was kneeling on the ground, quietly rolling up his hammock. "What the hell happened?"

"They cut and ran," McWhirter answered, folding the hammock ropes neatly inside the cloth.

Rob felt as if someone had just plunged a knife into his chest. He was too stunned to feel the pain yet, but he knew it was on its way. "Why, for chrissake?"

McWhirter finished folding his hammock and tucked it into his rucksack. "I don't know. Maybe his scouts picked up something near the border that scared them off."

"Why didn't they tell us?"

McWhirter shrugged and started rolling up his mosquito net. Frank

Wyler appeared, muscles twitching in anger. "You hired those fuckers," he said, pointing a finger at McWhirter. "This is your fault."

"We got a bad break."

"Bad break!" Wyler bellowed. "The whole fucking mission is ruined! How are we going to liberate a prison camp with four men and two girls?"

"We aren't going to liberate anything," McWhirter said. "We're getting out of here as fast as we can."

"How?" Gilmore demanded. "Walk across Laos?"

"I can get you across," McWhirter said. "We've got the supplies and weapons and I know the way."

Rob walked off, leaving Gilmore and Wyler arguing with McWhirter. He stopped out in the center of the small clearing that had been their camp for the night, and tried to clear his head. His thoughts whirled. He had gone through so much to get this far. Billy was only a few miles away. *So close. So close.*

Ghislene Ferrer appeared at his side, her camera hanging from her shoulder. She looked as if she had been up and dressed for hours. "I know how you must feel," she said. "It is all McWhirter's fault, no?"

"I don't know," Rob replied, barely hearing her words. "It's my fault for thinking the whole thing was possible in the first place."

Ferrer gave him an odd, patronizing look. "*Mon cher,* you have made a mistake in trusting McWhirter too much. That is my instinct."

"I'm not impressed with your instincts," Rob replied.

Ferrer sighed. "I am sorry. I was as horrified by the killing of the boy's father as you. I regret it very deeply. But I still believe McWhirter is hiding something from you."

Rob glared at her. Ferrer threw out her hands in a gesture of surrender and walked off. "If no one else is going to make breakfast," he heard her saying as she approached the cold remains of the cookfire, "then I suppose that I must do it myself."

Rob paced around the clearing, his brain churning, oblivious of the activity around him. He walked back to McWhirter. "Can we hire some other men?" he asked. "Put together another team?"

McWhirter paused in his packing and looked up. Without his sunglasses, he seemed naked and vulnerable. "Let's get back to Sammy Rep's first, then we'll see what's what."

"We already know what's what," Rob snapped. "The mission's collapsed."

"Sammy will help us," McWhirter insisted.

"You're taking this thing pretty calmly."

"I take everything pretty calmly," McWhirter said, an edge in his voice. "You oughta know that by now. Just like I'm taking pretty calmly the idea of marching you amateurs out of this fucking jungle."

"For chrissake, Harris," Rob pleaded, "don't you even feel disappointed? After all our effort? This is a tragedy."

McWhirter laughed. "Tragedy? Shit, no," he replied, his tone hostile. "Tragedy is when your kid dies of leukemia, or you get your legs shot off. Or the town you live in is wiped out by an earthquake. Or you get captured by some barbarians who torture you to death. Those I'd call tragedies. This I'd call just one of life's little frustrations." He hefted his half-packed rucksack and, with a show of irritation, tossed it to one side. "Don't take it so hard. It's not the end of the world. It's not even the end of the day."

Rob shook his head. "I don't believe you're that callous. What's wrong with you? You've been acting as if you *wanted* the mission to fail."

McWhirter sat back on the ground, resting his arms on his knees. "Look, I *am* sorry about what's happened. That's the honest truth. I'm sorry as hell. I'm as disappointed as you are, for reasons you wouldn't even understand. But I learned a long time ago not to waste time feeling sorry—for myself or for anybody else. It takes too much out of you and there isn't any money in it. We got fucked on this one, that's all. The odds were always against us, anyway. I told you a hundred times not to get your hopes up on a mission like this. No reason for you to feel bad. You did your best. We all did our best. We just didn't get lucky. Accept it."

"That's not the truth, Harris."

It was Caroline. Rob turned to see her standing behind him, her face tight with anger. To his amazement, the Laotian boy, Lin Pao, was still with her, his father's rifle slung jauntily over his armless shoulder. "Tan didn't desert us," Caroline said, her voice shaking. "Harris sent him home."

Rob stared at McWhirter in open-mouthed disbelief.

"Lin Pao overheard them yesterday evening," she added. "Harris paid Tan off and told him to slip out during the night."

"Is that true, Harris?"

McWhirter went back to packing his rucksack. "Of course it isn't true."

Rob pulled Caroline and Lin Pao off to the side and questioned the boy closely. With Caroline translating his halting French, Lin Pao stuck to his story. Rob felt physically ill. He walked over to his own hammock, barely ten feet from McWhirter, and picked up his rifle. He remembered that McWhirter had wanted Tan's men to carry all their weapons and ammunition. Thank God he had insisted otherwise. He leveled the barrel at McWhirter. "Tell me the truth, you son of a bitch."

McWhirter stopped packing and looked up. "You're not going to shoot me. Put that thing down."

Instead, Rob pulled the bolt handle back and released it, cocking the hammer and bringing a round up from the magazine into the chamber. Caroline started toward him, to intervene, but he waved her back. His hands were drenched with perspiration. He knew he could kill McWhirter right there, and that sudden self-knowledge shocked him as much as the imminent failure of the mission. "Tell me the truth, Harris," he warned.

The other members of the party had all stopped what they were doing and were standing nearby, watching the confrontation in stricken silence.

McWhirter rubbed his hands over his face and groaned to himself. "I had to do it," he admitted.

"Why?"

"Some people don't want your brother found. You're not supposed to know about it. They told me to derail the mission—and do it so you'd never know it wasn't just bad luck."

"What people?"

"People with power in the government."

"You let them buy you off?"

McWhirter shook his head. "They blackmailed me."

"How could they do that?"

"It's a long story."

Rob lowered the rifle, easing his trembling finger off the trigger. "You break my heart, Harris," he said. "I mean it."

McWhirter stared at the ground. "They'd have stopped you anyway, no matter what I did. And they might not have been real nice about it. I figured that at least I could control how it was done, since it was going to be done anyway."

"Why did you bring us this far, for chrissake?" Rob demanded. "Why didn't you just warn me? That's all you had to do."

"No. I had to stop you. You're stubborn. You'd try to go through with this if you had half a chance. I had to make certain you couldn't."

Disgusted, Rob turned and walked away.

"There was another reason, too," McWhirter said, to Rob's back. "I didn't want you to think I'd do something like this to you. I'll give you your money back."

Rob whirled around. "I don't want the fucking money back, Harris!" he shouted, his voice breaking. "I want us to rescue Billy!"

"We can't stand up against these people," McWhirter insisted. "Take my word for it. I can't. You can't. But I got you here and I'll get you out again. That's the best I can do."

Wyler, who had been listening to the conversation, suddenly lumbered forward and began berating McWhirter in a loud voice. The anguish in his face was startling. He seemed even angrier than Rob. Ghislene Ferrer, acting in the unusual role of peacemaker, interposed her small frame between the two men and gradually, like a lion tamer with an enraged beast, cajoled Wyler into backing away.

While the others broke camp—moving about in a depressed silence, dividing up supplies and packing rucksacks—Ferrer lit a fire and produced some hot instant coffee, scrambled powdered eggs, and canned grapefruit juice.

Rob walked to the edge of the clearing and stood for a long time staring into the shadowy recesses of the jungle, trying to regain control of his emotions. Even as he agonized over what he was going to do, he marveled at the clarity of his dilemma, at how absolutely his life had been placed on a crossroads.

Arms encircled his waist from behind and a head leaned against his back. "The mission is already a success," Caroline said. "Even if we don't find Billy."

Rob pressed his hands over hers and said nothing.

"You don't have to prove anything more," she whispered. "You've done all anyone could possibly expect."

He pushed out of her embrace and turned to face her. "Why did he betray us like this? I don't understand it."

"Don't dismiss his reasons."

"What reasons? That they'd have stopped us anyway?"

"Yes."

"I don't believe in his mysterious 'they.' He took a bribe, that's all."

"He said he was blackmailed. I believe him."

"Why?"

"Everything I've seen. And everything you've told me about him. How hard he worked training you. How much effort he put into the whole project. It wasn't just for the money you paid him. He's a proud man. He wanted this mission to succeed as much as you did. I believe that."

Rob pulled her close to him and held her tightly. "It doesn't matter now, anyway. He's sabotaged us."

"I'm sorry it's happened," Caroline said. "But I'm glad we're going back. All I want now is to get you and Lin Pao out of here, alive and well."

"Lin Pao?"

"I'm taking him back with us. I want to adopt him."

Rob looked at Caroline.

"He needs me," she said. "And I need him."

Her reasons were unassailable.

"He needs a father, too," she added.

Rob glanced across the clearing. Lin Pao was busy cleaning his father's rifle—*his* rifle now. Rob marveled at how dextrously he managed the task with only one hand, using his body and legs to hold the piece in place while he disassembled it. The boy had spirit. He was a survivor.

"I'm going to go on," Rob said.

He felt her fingers dig into his arm. "No. Don't even think it."

"I can't give up now, at this first setback. Not when we're so close."

"Please don't do it."

"I want the rest of you to come. The hell with McWhirter."

Caroline twisted away from him. "No," she said.

"We're so close. Who knows what's possible? We have to look, at least."

"What chance will we have? It's a foolish risk."

"I'll go alone, if I have to."

"What about us?"

"You told me once I couldn't love anybody until I learned to respect myself," he said. "Well, that's why I'm going on. For my self-respect. If I turn back now, I'll lose it." He reached for her hands and clasped them tightly. "I've staked everything on this. I need this success. Without it, what's happened between us won't be worth a damn. This mission is to rescue me as much as Billy. If I don't go through with it, I'd rather not come back at all."

Caroline pulled her hands away. "I won't go with you," she replied, her voice trembling. "It's crazy. If I can't stop you, I can at least stop Lin Pao. We're going back with Harris."

"Will you at least wait for me at Sammy Rep's?"

"How long do you want me to wait?" Caroline retorted, her eyes furious. "Another twelve years?"

Rob reached out for her, but she stalked away from him.

He took his decision to the others. Wyler agreed instantly to continue on with him, and so did Ferrer: "Of course, *cheri*," she said. "I don't have my story yet."

Gilmore tried hard to talk Rob out of it, but finally, realizing that he was adamant, he also agreed to stay on.

Rob approached McWhirter again. He was standing by the dying embers of the cook-fire, a paper cup of Ferrer's coffee in his hand, looking defeated. "We're going on without you, Harris."

McWhirter tossed the dregs of the coffee onto the fire. "That's plain asinine," he muttered. "You'll never make it."

"That's no longer your concern."

"You're damned right it is. I'm supposed to see you don't get there."

"You just said we'll never make it. What are you worried about?"

"Don't be an asshole, Grunwald. I'll get you out safely. You can come back later with another team, if you're so goddamned determined."

Caroline and Lin Pao appeared alongside McWhirter, packs on their backs, ready to leave. Her eyes were red-rimmed from crying.

"Caroline, please come with us," Rob begged. She shook her head firmly.

"If you take on that prison camp with just the four of you," McWhirter warned, "you'll be committing suicide."

"Then you'll have survived *two* failed rescue missions."

McWhirter's mouth tightened into a scowl. "Just listen to me: If you make it to the camp, do all the surveillance you want, but don't do anything more. Just get the hell out. Don't try to snatch Billy. If by some miracle you did get him out, I promise you they'd never let you get him to Thailand in one piece."

"I don't need your advice anymore, Harris."

McWhirter pulled on his rucksack, tied a pouchful of ammunition to his belt, and hoisted his rifle strap onto his shoulder. He faced Rob for the last time. "I could force you to come back at gunpoint."

Rob shook his head. "Not really practical. You'd have to disarm us first. And then you'd have to stay awake all the way across Laos."

McWhirter nodded and headed toward the edge of the jungle clearing.

"You'll never be able to live with yourself, Harris!" Rob shouted.

If he hadn't been laden with a pack and a rifle, McWhirter undoubtedly would have shrugged. Instead, he just waved his hand behind him. "I haven't been living with myself for years," he said.

Rob called to Caroline: "I'll meet you at Sammy Rep's. In ten days. I promise it. Wait for us there. . . ."

Caroline followed Lin Pao and McWhirter out of the clearing.

"Please wait for me, Caroline."

She didn't answer him or even look back.

Rob watched her disappear into the jungle. He balled his fists at his sides, and turned, finally, to join the others. His stomach felt clenched even tighter than his hands. The anger, bitterness, and remorse that had been washing over him for the past hour had been so strong it wasn't until he saw the others, the loyal remnants of his rescue party, that he remembered that he was also more frightened than he had ever been in his life.

33

The North Atlantic

Koenig sat on the metal chair, knees comfortably crossed, and watched Grunwald eat his first meal in twenty-four hours—a bowl of watery potato soup and a two-inch-square chunk of black bread. "Not quite in a class with the Wall Street executive lunch, is it, Herr Gruen?"

Grunwald concentrated on the arduous task of chewing the hard bread. The swelling around his eyes and mouth had gone down, but every movement of his jaw sent electric jolts of pain down his neck. He feared it might be broken. "You enjoy watching me?" he asked.

"Yes. Thoroughly," Koenig admitted.

The taste of the food had whetted Grunwald's atrophied appetite. He felt ravenous suddenly. "I need more to eat," he said.

"You'll adjust to your new rations, Herr Gruen. You can credit your Nazi doctors for that. They discovered that a man could subsist on fewer calories than previously thought. The body, by some marvelous mechanism, responds to starvation by extracting more value from its reduced supply of fuel. You'll be weak and fatigued, but you'll survive. Just like I did."

Koenig's words implied a long imprisonment. "When do you intend to let me go?"

"You will have the answers to all your questions soon enough," the

German replied. "Today we will deal with the matter of your son Billy."

Grunwald lay back on the cot and hid his eyes under the palms of his hands and steeled himself for whatever he was about to hear.

"First, let me remove any doubts from your mind that I know what I am talking about," Koenig began, uncrossing his legs and leaning forward. "I have kept open an active intelligence file on you for many years. When your son was captured by the North Vietnamese Army, it came quickly to my attention. I was curious about him. He had established an enviable reputation during his school years. Since our department had trained many of the top people in North Vietnam's intelligence service, it was a simple matter for me to arrange to travel to Hanoi to talk to your son in person. This I did. In fact, I conducted Billy's interrogation myself. It lasted many months."

"You tortured him?"

Koenig laughed. "No. But he was very resistant to our questioning. I had expected that, of course, because he had an image of himself as a leader. He imagined that in everything he did he was setting an example for his men. We separated him from the others and kept at him. We didn't torture him; we simply demoralized him, undermined the delusions about Western capitalism and communism that he clung to so tenaciously. We wore him down eventually, but it was a difficult task. He was unusually stubborn, unusually rigid. I can't pretend that we made any kind of convert of him. And that was not our intention, in any case. Indeed, his hatred of us is no doubt stronger today than it was ten years ago—not because we treated him brutally, but because we forced him to confront some unpleasant truths."

Grunwald removed his hands from his eyes and looked at Koenig. "What truths?"

"Your son Billy was the officer in charge of a company of Marines sent in to search the village of Long Ba, in the Central Highlands, on February 24, 1970. They told the villagers they were looking for stores of Vietcong weapons. They herded everyone together in a large open square and searched each house. Some they set fire to, some they pulled down, some they looted. The villagers were kept out in the square, under the guard of Marines with automatic rifles, from early in the morning until late in the afternoon. No weapons or ammunition were found. The villagers thought the Marines would then leave, but they did not. They remained, keeping the villagers at gunpoint out in the square."

Koenig pulled out his cigarette pack and selected one from it. When he had lighted it and taken his first puff, he continued: "At about four o'clock in the afternoon, your son Billy ordered his men to open fire on the villagers. In a matter of a few minutes they had murdered one hundred and forty-three defenseless human beings, shooting them like sheep in a slaughterhouse pen. Almost all of them were women, children, and old men. Only four villagers survived. As the Marines were about to leave, they were discovered by part of a regiment of North Vietnamese regulars that happened to be moving through the area. After a battle that lasted well into dark, the Vietnamese soldiers liberated the village and discovered the massacre. They took twenty Marines captive, your son among them. The Americans were marched to Hanoi, imprisoned and interrogated. It was clear, from their confessions, and from the testimony of the four surviving villagers, that many of the Marines had participated, to some degree, in the massacre, but it was also clear that your son bore the primary responsibility. He was in command of the company and he had ordered his men to open fire."

Koenig tapped the ash from his cigarette onto the floor with a bony forefinger. "Your son was brought to trial in a military court. An unusual proceeding, but you must remember that the Vietnamese did not consider the Geneva Conventions to apply to Americans taken prisoner in Vietnam. He was tried, in effect, for crimes against the people of Vietnam. He was found guilty and sentenced to life at hard labor. Six of his own men testified against him. That is why he was not returned with the rest of the American POWs during the prisoner exchange of 1973. Your own military learned of the massacre when it debriefed the POWs, but to protect its own reputation it chose to suppress the truth. It granted all those involved general discharges and closed its files on the matter. I had many times personally urged Hanoi to make the facts of the massacre and your son's involvement public, but for reasons of its own, the government chose not to do so. I suspect it thought it might use your son as a pawn in some future negotiations with the United States. It might well have done so, too. But three years ago, after many years in a work camp north of Hanoi, Billy Grunwald escaped."

Koenig dropped the butt of his cigarette onto the floor and crushed it vigorously under his heel. "The Vietnamese government believes that he is still in hiding somewhere inside the country. But it has not been able to recapture him. Why are they so sure he is still in the country? The answer to that is complicated, but I will tell you this much: Your son realizes that returning home would mean a court-martial. The massacre and his role in it would become public, bringing shame upon him and the Grunwald family. Someone of your son's personality makeup could never stand to confront such a situation. So he hides somewhere in the jungles of Vietnam, a disgraced and broken human being, a fugitive in every sense of the word."

Koenig paused in his monologue and stood up to pace the small chamber. "We have now arrived at the reason for your kidnapping, Herr Gruen. You have information from a source in France—a Brian Duffy, now dead—on your son's location. We have tried to obtain it, but powerful circles within your own military establishment have prevented it. We know that you still have this information, however. We know that your younger son, Rob, has undertaken a rescue attempt based on it." Koenig stopped pacing and faced Grunwald, his hands clasped behind his back. "I want you to tell me where this information is located, and assist me in obtaining it. I, in turn, intend to assist the Vietnamese in recapturing Billy before either your son Rob or the United States government can prevent it. This is important to the Vietnamese government. And to me."

Koenig watched Grunwald in silence for a moment, gauging the effect of his words on him. When he spoke again, his voice was soft and reasonable. "I want you to give me this information now. When you have done so, I will see to it that your diet is improved. And I promise you that we will not harm you further."

"No."

Koenig's tone turned cold. "Do you want me to make public a complete account of the massacre at Long Ba and your son's criminal responsibility for it? And make public the truth about your own past as an SS guard at Dachau? It doesn't take a man of exceptional imagination to understand the effect this will have on you and your family."

"I don't believe this massacre story of yours," Grunwald replied, his voice shaking with emotion. "And I will never cooperate with you to endanger my son. Never."

Koenig sighed. "I am prepared to resort to force, Herr Gruen."

Grunwald said nothing.

"As a last resort, I will use it to extract the information we need. If that fails—which is unlikely—then you will be bound with weights and thrown overboard as a meal for the sharks of the North Atlantic. So you see, a show of bravery is really useless. You are less than nothing now, Herr Gruen. You must understand that. You no longer have money or powerful friends to help you. You have no legal protection. No rights. You are just an object to be manipulated. Your very existence depends on your cooperation."

Koenig walked to the door and knocked for it to be opened. "Think about it, Herr Gruen. I will give you a few hours."

Vietnam

With Rob in the lead, taking compass bearings, the remaining four members of the mission set out to cross the Vietnamese border.

They walked from the clearing straight into the jungle. The heavy canopy shaded them from the burning sun, but the exertion of traveling along the uneven ground, struggling through heavy vines and over large root systems with heavy backpacks in the high humidity had soon soaked everyone in sweat.

Keeping a steady eastward bearing proved impossible. Steep hills blocked the terrain in front of them, forcing them on long detours. Their progress became an exhaustingly slow zigzag, punctuated by monsoon-flooded streams, patches of muddy quicksand, and impenetrable walls of thornbushes and thickets that had to be hacked through with a machete.

After three hours of steady effort, Rob felt certain that they were across the border and inside Vietnam. He adjusted their route slightly to the south, in the direction of their target, which he calculated to be four miles away. The plan was to get within a mile, establish a well-hidden camp, and scout the area around the prison the following day.

Late afternoon brought them through a narrow pass between two steep hills. Beyond the pass the land dropped gradually and leveled out onto a wide rift valley that stretched southeastward between the shoulders of a chain of hills on either side.

Down on the plain, they entered a dramatically altered landscape. The lush green foliage that had formed a virtual ceiling over their heads for miles disappeared altogether, and they found themselves traveling through a devastated world of bare, rotting tree trunks and sparse, stunted bushes poking out of bare soil. The jungle profusion of flowers and birds was absent totally. Dead lianas hung from the skeletons of the trees like strands of giant cobwebs. It was a vast dead zone, stretching out around them for thousands of acres.

"Forest fire?" Rob asked Gilmore.

"Agent Orange," Gilmore replied.

"Jesus. After all these years?"

"Imagine what it did to the people who used to live here."

They walked through the blasted wilderness in gloomy silence, their footsteps crunching on a decaying carpet of leaves and branches. Rob wondered how much of Vietnam still looked like this. It was as if the machinery of war, frustrated with its inability to win a military victory, had decided to kill the very land itself.

When they regained the cover of live jungle again, Rob ordered a rest stop. He unscrewed the top of his canteen, held it to his mouth, and discovered that it was empty. Everyone else's was low, as well. A lot of water was required to replace the moisture lost in perspiration, and it was burdensome to carry more than a canteen-full at a time.

He pulled out the terrain map again, unfolded it on the flat surface of a rock, and studied it with great care. The pressure of his new responsibilities still weighed on him heavily. He dreaded making a mistake that might plunge them all into deeper difficulties. "There's a stream about a mile ahead," he concluded finally. "Let's make camp there."

On the move again, Rob felt a surge of optimism. They had crossed into Vietnam without incident, and were only two or three miles from their destination. And they had done it without either McWhirter or the Laotians. Tomorrow, he prayed, they would find the prison camp.

A sudden scream interrupted his train of thought. He whirled around and ducked down into a crouch. Gilmore and Wyler hit the ground simultaneously, their rifles out in front of them.

It was Ferrer. She was standing, feet apart, arms raised dramatically over her head. Her eyes were fastened on something on the ground in front of her. "It just landed here," she gasped. "It just landed here—right in my path!"

Rob walked back and looked. Wyler and Gilmore jumped up and joined him.

A human skull lay on its side in the dirt near the exposed root of a large tree, one hollow eye-socket staring up from the bleached round cranium. The bottom front edge of the skull was fringed with a row of teeth. Gold fillings on the back molars were plainly visible. The jawbone was missing.

"Someone threw it at me!" Ferrer insisted.

Rob craned his neck upward. High overhead, half hidden in leaves and shadows near the roof of the jungle canopy, he saw the explanation. Like the discarded toy of some Brobdingnagian child, a military helicopter hung suspended in the thick net of branches that formed the forest overstory. It pointed nose down, its rotor blades entwined in the branches of one tree, its undercarriage caught in another. Much of the green-and-brown camouflage paint had flaked off, baring shiny patches of aluminum, and the front windscreen was shattered. The big sliding door on one side was ripped from its track and hung, like shedding skin, from the ship's flank. The rusted barrel of an M-60 machine gun, still moored to its firing post inside the door, jutted out like an exposed bone from a wound. Vines had woven their way through the openings of the derelict craft and branched out in veinlike networks over much of its exposed surface.

"Mother of Christ," Wyler whispered. "It's a Huey."

A movement from inside the helicopter caused everyone to freeze. After a tense pause, a face appeared in the doorway. It belonged to a large brown-and-black macaque. It stared down at the party below, eyes wide, teeth bared, and held up a bone nearly as long as the monkey itself. The animal made a series of gruff, threatening barks, then threw the bone down. It missed Wyler's head by inches, bounced in the leaves, and came to rest several feet from the skull.

The macaque disappeared from the doorway and returned seconds later with another bone. It barked again, like an impudent vandal determined to flaunt his gruesome pranks, and started to bang the bone on the side of the helicopter door frame, sending a hollow clang reverberating through the forest.

Before anyone had time to stop him, Wyler raised his rifle and fired off a burst of bullets that ripped through the monkey and knocked it back out of sight into the interior of the ship.

"You stupid ass!" Gilmore yelled. "They'll hear that for miles!"

Before Rob could do or say anything, Gilmore had plunged off through the jungle. The others followed, struggling to keep up with him.

After a fifteen-minute chase, they crossed a trail, and Gilmore turned onto it to make better time. "Howard!" Rob gasped. "Slow down. You're going the wrong way!"

Gilmore stopped.

Rob caught up with him. "You'll get us lost, for God's sake."

Gilmore stood motionless, staring down the narrow trail ahead of him.

"What is it?"

Ferrer and Wyler caught up and crowded behind Rob. "What the fuck's he doing?" Wyler demanded.

"What's the matter, Howard?"

Gilmore continued to stand rigid as a statue. Rob put his hand on his back and felt his friend's muscles tense. He removed his hand, utterly baffled.

"Get out," Gilmore rasped, his voice barely audible.

"What?"

"Get out!"

Rob looked down at Gilmore's legs, frozen in mid-stride. A thin wire glinted in the light. It ran horizontally across the trail about a foot above the ground. Gilmore's shin was pressing against it.

34

The North Atlantic

Koenig woke Grunwald from a fitful sleep. The two German sailors who had beaten him earlier carried a tall metal clothes locker into his cell and stood it in a corner, while Koenig looked on. "We are forced to improvise," he said, cryptically.

The two seamen picked Grunwald up roughly from the cot, jammed him upright into the locker, and slammed its door. He heard a padlock slip into place and snap shut. The locker was tall enough to accommodate his height, but there was room for his shoulders only if he stood diagonally, facing one of the locker's corners. He expected that they intended to carry him out in the locker, but, to his bafflement, they left him where he was.

"I'll be back in a while, Herr Gruen," he heard Koenig say. "I'm sure you'll be in a far more cooperative frame of mind by then."

Grunwald heard the men leave and the door to his cell close. The locker smelled faintly of sweat and seawater. He felt around its interior with his hands, reassured to find a row of ventilation slats on the door to let in air. A stupid punishment, he thought—like locking someone in a closet.

Several hours would pass before Grunwald would fully appreciate what Koenig had inflicted on him.

Laos

McWhirter's technique for getting Caroline, Lin Pao, and himself safely back across Laos was simple, swift, and effective. Once they reached Highway 9, he hijacked the first civilian truck headed westward. It was an old Citroën, its canvas-covered rear body loaded with sacks of rice and grain for the market in Savannakhet.

McWhirter hid Caroline and Lin Pao in the rear among the sacks and sat up in front holding his rifle on the driver, a young Lao named Kwan Lee. Once under way, McWhirter produced three thousand dollars' worth of Laotian currency and offered it to the young man in return for putting his foot to the floor all the way to the Thai border.

With that to encourage him, the driver made the 175-mile run across Highway 9 to Savannakhet in under six hours. They were stopped once by a military patrol. McWhirter hurriedly joined Caroline and the boy among the sacks in the back, while Kwan Lee used his money to bribe the soldiers not to search it.

By late afternoon they reached the Mekong, only to find it heavily patrolled. They waited until dark and swam the river, McWhirter carrying the one-armed Lin Pao across on his back. By nine o'clock that evening they were back at Sammy Rep's.

Sammy galvanized the kitchen to produce a meal for them. McWhirter wolfed it down with several beers and decided to leave immediately for Bangkok.

"I'll borrow one of the jeeps," he said, rising from Sammy's big communal table, where only a few nights earlier the others had toasted the success of the mission. "If he makes it back and you need an extra vehicle, Sammy can arrange it."

"I hope you mean *when*, not *if*," Caroline replied.

McWhirter shrugged. "How long do you plan to wait for him?"

"I don't know."

"Well, you'll be all right here with Sammy."

Caroline looked up from her plate. "Thank you for getting us out, Mr. McWhirter," she said, her tone distant and formal. She had barely spoken to him all the way across Laos.

McWhirter grunted. "You can always spot good breeding," he said. "You hate my guts, but you're too polite not to thank me."

"I don't hate you at all," she said. "I feel sorry for you."

"I'd feel better if you just hated my guts."

Caroline watched Lin Pao, sitting beside her, his chin close to the table's edge, hungrily shoveling food into his mouth with a pair of chopsticks. "I'm not being condescending. I feel sorry for all of you.

You, Frank, Howard, Billy—even Rob. You're all casualties of war."

McWhirter thought about it. "Well, you better include yourself and the boy here in that list, too." He saw Sammy lurking behind the kitchen doorway, a hand cupped comically to his ear, trying to overhear their conversation. "At least we're walking wounded. And if you have to be wounded, walking sure as hell beats maimed or dead."

Caroline smiled bleakly at him. "That's a survivor's philosophy, I suppose."

"I suppose it is." McWhirter grabbed his rucksack from the corner by the door and threw it over his shoulder. "Listen," he said, "I'm sorry about what I had to do. But I think Rob's still got a chance of pulling it off. Everybody's underestimated that guy all his life. I don't."

He paused briefly by the veranda's bamboo screen door, his smooth, deadpan manner creased with embarrassment. "Anyway, good luck," he said.

The North Atlantic

Koenig returned sometime later and pounded on the metal door of the locker. "Are you ready to give me the information about your son, Herr Gruen?"

Grunwald didn't answer him. He was concentrating all his energy on standing up. The innocent locker, he had discovered, was a diabolical instrument of torture. Its narrow confines gave him no room to change his position. He could not bend, turn, sit, or squat. He could only stand. When his legs eventually reached the degree of fatigue beyond which they could no longer support him, his knees would buckle and press themselves into the corner, a distance of a mere four inches. When the pain in his knees became unbearable, he would be forced to stand again—or suffer the pain. He had tried with the weight of his upper body to topple the locker onto its side, but they had wedged it firmly into the corner.

"You must know by now that you will succumb eventually," Koenig said.

"Go to hell," Grunwald whispered.

"If you think about it," Koenig continued, "you'll realize that you really don't want Billy to be rescued. Imagine what his homecoming would be like. There would be questions, suspicions, accusations. The Marine Corps, whether it wished to or not, would have to court-martial him for the Long Ba massacre. The same POWs who testified against him in Hanoi would be called on to testify again. Public attention would be intense, merciless. You know how your press works. Journalists would be competing eagerly to exploit the story. Your son's criminal acts would be trumpeted daily on television. Long and lurid articles about him would appear in newspapers and magazines. Wouldn't it be better if he never came home? Think of the advantages. His reputation is saved—and, by implication, yours and your family's. Isn't that worth more to you than seeing Billy publicly humiliated? And sent to prison, probably for life?''

Grunwald smelled the sharp smoke from one of Koenig's cigarettes filtering through the vents of the locker. He tried to block the meaning of Koenig's words from his mind, to prevent himself from succumbing to their remorseless logic.

"I suppose you just can't bring yourself to believe that Billy was capable of any such atrocity, can you? Well, I can't prove it to you, of course, but ask yourself this: Why hasn't he tried to come home? After all, he escaped from us a long time ago. Why is he still in Vietnam? He could have gotten out by now, surely—crossed the border into China or Laos or escaped by sea. There are a thousand possible ways for someone of your son's ingenuity and daring. Why hasn't he tried them? The reason is clear, isn't it? He can't face the ordeal he knows awaits him. He can't face his family, knowing the disgrace he will bring to it. Even if Rob finds him, it won't matter. He will never come home. So you see, Herr Gruen, you are putting yourself through needless torment.''

35

Vietnam

Rob knelt down and followed the wire from Gilmore's shin to each side of the trail. Five feet to the right, it was wound around a small sapling. To the left, it terminated on the cotter pin of a fragmentation grenade, lashed to another sapling. The pin was still firmly in place.

"It's okay," Rob said, standing up. "You didn't budge it."

Gilmore seemed unable to move. His face was white and his arms gooseflesh in the ninety-degree heat. Rob squeezed his shoulder gently. "It's okay, Howard. We'll just walk around it."

Wyler came up and examined the booby trap himself. "It's been here awhile," he said, rubbing a finger around the pin. "Already some rust."

"Leave the damned thing alone," Rob told him. "Come on, Howard. Nothing's going to happen."

Slowly Rob was able to coax Gilmore from his trance. He removed the weight of his pack from his back and took him by the elbow and led him back down the trail. Suddenly Gilmore's legs buckled. He sat down and started to shake violently, like someone seized by a fit.

Rob watched his friend with alarm. "Howard, are you all right? What can I do?"

Gilmore shook his head and spread out on the ground. He rolled over, his hands clutched to his chest, and began to gasp for breath.

Ferrer bent down and felt the cold surface of his skin. "He needs a tranquilizer," she said.

Gilmore heard her and nodded. Rob searched hurriedly through his pack for his medicine. He found the tranquilizers, removed a capsule, and pushed it into Gilmore's mouth. Gilmore swallowed it, then lay back on his side, his rib cage heaving convulsively.

Gradually his breathing returned to normal and he sat up. His face was pallid and slick with sweat. "Jesus, I'm sorry," he said.

"Don't apologize."

"It was the damned wire. It put me right back there. Brought it all back. All the bad shit. I thought I was rid of it. But it's still there."

"You just need a rest," Rob decided. "Let's camp right here and get our bearings. We'll find the prison camp tomorrow."

The mission spent a restless, uncomfortable night, huddled on the ground in their sleeping bags under a hastily rigged roof of plastic tarpaulins. Just before dawn a heavy rain hit, accompanied by strong winds. Rivulets of water inundated the ground sheets under their sleeping bags, and the wind finally ripped the tarpaulins loose, ending any further hope of sleep.

Soaked and miserable, the four packed up their soggy belongings as soon as the light permitted, and, without breakfast, moved off to find a better campsite.

The rain stopped at around eight o'clock and they halted in a small grassy clearing at the edge of a bamboo forest. "Let's put up a bamboo shelter so we can hang the hammocks," Rob said. "I could live without having to lie all night in half a foot of water again."

"I could live with fewer of these sons of bitches," Wyler said. He pulled up a pants leg to reveal clusters of four-inch-long leeches clinging to his ankles.

"Maybe they'll eat my ticks," Rob joked, pulling up his own pants legs. "I counted fifty on me earlier."

"You must burn them off with a cigarette, *cheri*," Ferrer advised. "Watch, I will show you." She lit a cigarette, puffed up a good red ash, and then held it against a tick feeding on her ankle. The little triangular-shaped insect immediately released its pincerlike hold on her skin and fell to the ground.

Rob looked over at Gilmore. He was sitting quietly on a rock, arms resting on his legs, his head down. "You okay, Howard?"

Gilmore looked up and managed a weak smile.

"Why is anybody mining trails around here in the first place?" Rob said. "The Vietnam War is over, isn't it?"

"Guerrillas," Wyler replied.

"Guerrillas? We're in Vietnam, not Thailand."

Rob and Wyler began cutting down bamboo for the shelter, while Gilmore, still unsteady from his scare with the grenade, hunted up some dry wood to build a cook-fire. Ghislene Ferrer made the breakfast. The work was warming and the party's mood lifted somewhat. After coffee and some freeze-dried scrambled eggs, they trussed together a bamboo frame, draped a plastic tarpaulin over it, ran rope through the grommet holes, and secured it tightly. By the time they finished the shelter, the sun had come out, and they quickly took advantage of it by spreading the contents of their packs out to dry in the grass.

By midafternoon they got the hammocks hung, and fell into them, exhausted.

Rob extracted a map from its case, unfolded it, and set to work with a compass to determine where they were. He found their last known location, near the helicopter, and traced his finger outward from it in each possible direction. To the north was a highway; to the west, a nearly continuous range of steep mountains; to the east, several large streams, none of which they had encountered. By default, that left the south. He tried to match the terrain he remembered from yesterday's panicky retreat with the features on the map. The map kept confirming the same answer: south. He folded it up and hurried over to Gilmore, at the other end of the shelter. The big man was lying with his arms and legs dangling over the sides of his hammock.

"If what you want requires physical motion of any kind," Gilmore warned him, "I'm not going to volunteer."

"If my estimates are right," Rob said, unfolding the map on Gilmore's chest, "we're about two miles south of the helicopter." He explained how he had worked it out. "That would put us about here, on the east side of this hill. You see where that is? Right on top of our target. The camp is barely a quarter of a mile from here."

He looked up and pointed in the direction he believed would take them to their target. Beyond the end of his finger, he saw a cluster of leaves in the wall of foliage tremble slightly, as if caught by a breeze. But the air was still. A bird or animal, he supposed, startled by his gesture.

Gilmore forced himself to a sitting position and studied the map. Rob squatted on the ground beside him. "We're close, Howard," he said, the excitement rising in his voice. "I know it. We're close."

Gilmore fell back against the hammock. "I'd rather die right here than go looking for it now, if that's what you're thinking."

Rob looked across Gilmore's lap down the row of hammocks. Ferrer, next door, was writing in her notebook; Wyler was sleeping. Twenty feet beyond Rob's empty hammock at the other end, the bamboo grove began. A line of perfectly straight yellow-brown trunks against a pea-green backdrop of foliage, it reminded him of a wallpaper pattern from the Grunwalds' summer house in Maine, years ago.

Again he noticed a subtle movement of leaves. A trick of the light, or was there something there? He kept his eyes on the spot.

"What're you looking at?" Gilmore demanded.

"Don't turn," Rob whispered. "Someone's watching us."

As the words left his lips, a figure stepped out into the clearing, brandishing a rifle. He shouted something and a dozen others materialized out of the foliage and closed in on the shelter from all directions.

"My God," Gilmore groaned.

They swarmed around the hammocks, cocked their rifles, and leveled them at four astonished faces. Rob waited to hear the crack of gunfire and feel his flesh ripped by bullets—an ignoble, squalid end to a foolhardy adventure.

It didn't happen. Two of the raiders pressed the bores of their rifles against Rob's side and gestured for him to rise. It seemed like a replay of the Thai incident, but with an ominous difference: These soldiers had a savage, underfed look about them. Their battle fatigues were dirty and patched and their boots in poor condition. In ironic contrast to their ragged attire, each of them wore a black beret, tipped at a rakish angle toward one ear.

Rob stood up, heart pounding, and raised his hands over his head. Their leader, a solid stump of a man with officer's bars on his shoulders, advanced toward him and yelled a question at him in Vietnamese.

Rob shook his head to indicate that he didn't understand. "What do we tell them?" he whispered.

"I don't know," Gilmore replied.

The officer overheard them. "American?" he screamed, pointing at Rob. Rob nodded.

"You American?" he repeated, either failing to understand Rob's nod or not believing it.

"Yes. We're all Americans," he replied.

The officer turned to his men. "American!" he bellowed, and then laughed loudly, as if he had just heard the funniest joke of his life. The others laughed with him.

Ferrer pushed aside a rifle pointed at her and approached the officer, her face loaded with the same sham outrage she had used to such good effect in Thailand. Rob held his breath.

"Je ne suis pas américaine," she began, gesticulating forcefully with both hands. *"Je suis française. Et je vous demande—"*

"Ferme ta geule!" the officer cried. His voice was baritone, and had the volume and density of a carnival barker's.

Ferrer switched to English: "You cannot address me that way!"

"Shut up!" the officer cried, even louder than before.

"Take his advice, Ghislene," Rob muttered, "and shut up."

Instead, Ferrer slapped the officer in the face.

No one dared move. The Vietnamese touched his face, his eyes widened in disbelief, as if a bee had appeared from nowhere and stung him on the cheek. He looked at Ferrer, then pulled his arm back and smacked her with his open palm so hard that she was knocked sideways to the ground. She shrieked, and then tucked her head under her arms anticipating more blows. The officer kicked her lightly in the side, mocking her fright, and started laughing again.

Rob saw Wyler's eyes kindle with a berserk fury. He lunged at the officer, threw him to the ground, and dropped his hands swiftly around his throat. He outweighed the Vietnamese by at least a hundred pounds, and with his enormous wrestler's strength, Rob knew that he could easily strangle him.

The soldiers jumped to their leader's defense. One swung his rifle butt full force against the back of Wyler's skull and knocked him to the side, where he was met with another rifle butt to his temple. For nearly ten minutes he struggled against the odds, a madman out of control, absorbing kicks and blows that would have destroyed a horse.

Finally, he collapsed to the ground and stayed there. Blood ran from his mouth and nose. The black eye patch was gone, revealing the pucker of scar tissue that had grown over the empty socket. One of the soldiers kicked him viciously between his legs, but Wyler was unconscious and didn't react. They bound his wrists and ankles, kicked him a few more times for good measure, and left him on the ground.

During Wyler's beating, the officer had brushed off his uniform and recovered his dignity. He ordered Rob, Ferrer, and Gilmore marched to the edge of the clearing, where soldiers prodded them into a tight cluster and bound their wrists. Rob glanced at the others. Gilmore looked utterly defeated, his face drawn in pain. Ferrer appeared distraught. She was shaking and whimpering uncontrollably. Her bluff had been called—brutally—and it seemed to have shattered her.

While they watched, the band of black berets pulled out all their knapsacks and supplies and sifted through them, dumping items of little interest onto the ground. The officer, restless to get moving, ordered them to tear down the shelter and pack everything up. Then he walked over to Rob.

"American, eh?" he said, pushing his chin out pugnaciously.

Rob nodded, trying not to appear either friendly or hostile.

"Land off the free, home to the grave," the officer said, demonstrating his mastery of English. Rob thought of correcting him but restrained the impulse. The Vietnamese turned and stalked proudly away.

When they had finished dismantling the shelter and packed up everything they considered worth taking, they tied their prisoners together in a line—Ferrer first, then Gilmore and Rob. Two of the soldiers brought up a thick bamboo pole that had been part of the shelter, ran it under Wyler's bound wrists and ankles, and lifted the pole onto their shoulders, with Wyler suspended beneath it like a trussed boar.

The officer bellowed a command, and the procession moved off into the jungle. After a few minutes beating through heavy undergrowth, they turned onto a well-trodden path and stepped up the pace to a fast trot, prodding their prisoners along with occasional slaps from a rifle butt on the back of the neck.

Bleak thoughts chased one another through Rob's mind. He should have accepted defeat with McWhirter's betrayal and let everyone go home. Now he had compounded the mission's failure. His eyes rested on Gilmore's back, two feet in front of him. His friend's hands had been tied very tightly at the wrists and were beginning to swell, and his shirt was so soaked with perspiration that it clung to him as if he had just been dunked in a river. Rob could hear Gilmore's panting breath over his own. He prayed they didn't have far to go.

Rob caught his foot on a hidden root beneath him and pitched forward, pulling the others down with him. Amid a barrage of pokes and angry reprimands, the soldiers quickly yanked them back on their feet.

Twice more, someone in the line lost his balance and pulled everyone to the ground in a tangled heap. Still the Vietnamese refused to slacken the pace. After what Rob judged to be about three quarters of an hour, they came to a sudden halt in the middle of nowhere.

He looked toward the front of the column to see why they had stopped. One of the soldiers was stepping cautiously forward, his gaze fixed low on the path in front of him. He suddenly dropped to his hands and knees and crawled a few feet forward, feeling ahead of him with one hand. Finally he stood and waved back at the officer, and the column started up again. When Rob drew abreast of him, he saw the device. It was another grenade, lashed to a tree alongside the trail. When everyone was safely past, the soldier fixed the trip wire in place again and rejoined the column.

Fifty feet farther along, they stopped again and the soldier disconnected another trip wire from another grenade. Fifty feet beyond that, the column was marched off the path and into the thickest and tallest wall of thornbushes Rob had ever seen.

Through the seemingly impenetrable mass of shrubbery, a zigzagging passage had been cleverly tunneled. They followed it until it terminated against a high wall of bamboo. The officer opened a small door cut into the wall, and the column filed quickly through. On the other side they were assembled in a small open area of packed earth not much bigger than someone's backyard.

They were inside a stockade of some sort. High bamboo walls surrounded it on four sides. Directly in front of them, two old women were tending a fire, and behind them, sitting at a crude table of planks, four other women were busy working at some task that Rob could not discern. He counted four low thatch-roofed huts and several other smaller huts in the enclosure, including a kitchen and a storage shed. Beyond the far wall, he could see a crude wooden watchtower. Someone was in it, peering at them through a pair of binoculars.

The wall, the watchtower, and the arrangement of the huts—there was something eerily familiar about them. He had seen them before, somewhere. Abruptly it struck him. "Harris' model," he said, astonished. "This is it. This is Billy's prison camp."

Gilmore, standing beside him, flicked his eyes nervously around the enclosure. "But no prisoners."

"No talk!" a soldier yelled. To emphasize his point, he jabbed his rifle barrel into the small of Rob's back.

The officer reappeared from one of the huts holding what looked like white handkerchiefs. He passed them out, one each, to three of the soldiers. They in turn walked over to their captives and began blindfolding them.

Rob felt the chill grip of terror around the bottom of his spine. Ferrer started to plead with the soldiers in French, her voice quavering and reedy with fear. He saw the officer slap her again. Then one of the blindfolds was jerked tight across his eyes and knotted against the back of his head.

Hands grabbed his upper arms from behind and pushed him forward, steering him in the direction they wanted him to go. He was marched for a short distance across the yard, then guided through a doorway.

After a short wait someone wrapped a heavy strap of some kind around his chest and under his arms and secured it in back. He heard Ferrer cry out in fright.

"Shut up!" the officer yelled.

Ferrer continued to whimper, but her voice seemed to be disappearing into the ground. After an agonizing interval, Rob was prodded forward several steps and down into a sitting position. As soon as his seat touched the packed dirt floor, someone shoved his legs into a hole of some kind. He heard voices below him; then hands pushed him off the edge, so that he was dangling in midair by the harness around his chest.

He bit his lip to hold in the fear. Quickly, in a series of rough bounces, he was lowered downward. The blindfold and his panicky state of mind prevented him from even guessing how far down he went, but when he felt something solid under his feet, he fell forward onto his knees, sick with relief.

He thought they were being dropped into an underground dungeon, but what happened next confused him further. The harness was removed and hands once again grabbed him by the upper arms and steered him forward.

They were led along a narrow tunnel. The air was cool and damp, and the soft plod of their footsteps was muffled by the closeness of the earth around them. Rob's shoulders frequently brushed the sides of the passage as the invisible hands pushed him onward. They proceeded in a straight line for a distance, then were turned at a right angle into another branch of the tunnel, which Rob sensed was larger. After several more turns, they were stopped and made to wait.

Rob heard a low conversation in Vietnamese, and then the sound of what he guessed was someone pulling open a door. The smell of fresh air rushed into the tunnel, and bright daylight whitened the surface of his blindfold. Hands were guiding him again. They shoved him foward urgently, then pressed on his shoulders to make him sit down.

Minutes ticked by. Pungent cooking smells tickled his nostrils, and the sounds of voices swirled around him, as if he were standing on a busy city sidewalk.

He heard Ferrer exclaim something in French. A few seconds later, fingers were tugging at the knot of his blindfold. When it fell away, he blinked in the bright afternoon light and looked around.

Ferrer and Gilmore were sitting near him on a patch of bare earth in the middle of a large grove. The undergrowth and many of the trees had been removed, leaving only enough of the larger ones to maintain the jungle canopy, high overhead. The grove appeared to be situated on an immense mountain ledge—one side butting against a nearly vertical mountain wall, which towered up over the canopy and out of sight; the other side, some four or five hundred feet away, terminating at the edge of a precipice, where blue sky penetrated between the trees.

The grove was teeming with soldiers, most wearing the distinctive black berets. They seemed in a relaxed, festive mood, laughing and joking freely. Dotted across the expanse of cleared ground were half a dozen small fires where women were busy preparing food. No houses, huts, or structures of any kind were anywhere in sight.

The soldiers posted to guard Rob, Ferrer, and Gilmore relaxed their vigilance in the presence of their comrades, and amid the noise and distractions, Rob chanced a whispered conversation:

"Where's Wyler?"

"They kept him in the tunnel," Ferrer replied.

"How do you know?"

"I rubbed my blindfold halfway off against the wall of the tunnel," she replied, recovering her old arrogant self-confidence. "I saw them take him another way. These tunnels were part of the Ho Chi Minh Trail. When I was a guest of Hanoi, they showed me some very much like these but farther north. Very elaborate."

"This can't be their regular army," Rob said. "Look at that guy over there by the big table. He must be fifty or more."

Ferrer shifted her position to take the pressure off her bound wrists. "They're ignoring us completely," she complained.

"Don't be discouraged," Gilmore retorted. "Those old crones by the fires may be preparing cannibal soup."

"I think we're here to meet the local big shot," Rob said.

"You are right, *mon cher,*" Ferrer answered, tilting her head in the direction of the mountain wall.

Rob turned to look. A door opened in the rock face and several officers filed out. One of them shouted an order. From where Rob sat, the sound of his voice was almost inaudible, but it appeared that every soldier—as many as two hundred of them scattered around the grove—heard the command. A silence fell almost immediately, and the disordered crowd of uniforms quickly converged on a central spot in the grove and formed into ranks.

The officer who had given the order walked in front of them, inspecting their ranks, and then turned to face the opening in the rock. A profound silence engulfed the entire grove.

A minute of suspense passed, then another. The soldiers, standing at parade rest, remained as still as statuary. Two guards with submachine guns came out the entrance and took up positions on either side of it. Rob fixed his eyes on the black opening cut into the side of the mountain, and marveled at the shrewd sense of timing displayed by whoever it was they were all waiting for.

When it seemed that the grove would explode from the waiting, more figures emerged from the entrance in the rock. Two were young women, both wearing the same camouflage costume and black berets as the males. Behind them, flanked by a crowd of officers, came, at last, the object of all the anticipation.

The officer gave a quick signal, and the soldiers came to attention with a crisp and audible snap.

The two women turned to face their leader, then raised their hands and applauded. This was the signal for an incredible roar of approbation from the ranks of the soldiers. They saluted, and then shouted out a chant that to Rob sounded something like "Hip, hip, hooray!"

The leader returned their salute with a modest touch of the finger to his forehead and then, with the two young women a step behind him, he walked out in front of the formation, one hand on his hip, the other grasping a swagger stick, which he switched against the side of his pants at regular intervals. His dress was identical to that of his men—black beret and camouflage gear—but his pants and short-sleeved shirt looked newer and cleaner, and his shoes were leather instead of canvas.

"Look at that son of a bitch," Gilmore whispered. "He's the biggest Vietnamese I've ever seen. Must be six-three or -four."

"He's Caucasian," Ferrer insisted, her eyes widening in awe as the tall man strolled along in front of his men, grinning and shaking hands.

Rob followed the leader's movements himself with growing disbelief. Everything that he had been doing for the past several months—every assumption made, every contingency planned for—was being kicked over, turned on its head.

"It's Billy," he said.

36

The Norwegian Sea

Grunwald remained on his feet for eighteen hours. He shifted his weight a thousand times, wedged his shoulders against the sides of the locker until his arms were numb, but the effort was useless. Increasingly, his knees began slipping forward against the corner. Finally his thigh and calf muscles, cramped and burning beyond endurance, could no longer hold his legs upright. They collapsed against the corner and stayed there, putting the full weight of his upper body on his knees. Soon his head began to drop against the side of the locker, seeking to escape into unconsciousness, but the agony in his legs kept him awake.

The pain spread through him like a fire—from his knees down his calf muscles and into his ankles and upward to his thighs and groin. As it spread, it took control of his senses and his conscious thought, blotting out everything but the terrible experience of the pain.

He heard Koenig's voice through the fog of his agony: "Have you had enough, Herr Gruen?"

He answered yes, and wept with shame when they opened the locker and pulled him out. His pants were stained with urine, and he was unable to stand. They dragged him to the cot and sat him on the edge.

"You are inhuman," he whispered.

"Merely determined," Koenig replied. "Where is the material?"

"I will never betray my son."

Koenig sighed. "You disappoint me," he said. "You have a misguided notion of your own bravery. There is no one around to impress except me, and my opinion of you cannot be altered."

"I won't betray him."

Koenig paced the room, deep in thought. Finally he stopped, lit a cigarette, and walked over to the cot. "Since the possibility of Billy's shame and imprisonment doesn't seem to mean much to you, perhaps it will interest you to know that Billy is aware of your past. He knows your true name and identity. He knows because I told him. As you can imagine, he was considerably shaken by it. He now knows that everything you stood for was a lie. You no longer have his love or his respect. He despises you; he blames you for all his problems. And of course that's another reason he doesn't want to come home. If he did, you would have to face his contempt. Are you prepared to do it? I don't think you are. Now, why don't you tell me where the tape and transcript are located? The Vietnamese do not intend to kill Billy, after all. Merely to return him to prison."

Grunwald shook his head.

Koenig smoked in silence for a moment, then got up to go. "Put him back in the locker," he said.

Vietnam

The leader, the two young Vietnamese women and the officer trailing behind him, reached the end of the front rank of his soldiers and turned to look around him. His officer said something to him, and he glanced over in Rob's direction and nodded.

It seemed to take an eternity, but eventually he crossed the short distance to Rob's party and paused directly in front of them, his hands clasped loosely behind his back, switching the swagger stick like a cat twitching its tail. His black beret was tilted over one ear, and his sandy hair spilled out from under it in rich clumps. His face seeemed older than his thirty-five years. It was lean and weather-beaten, like the face of a man who had worked all his life out in the elements. His eyes were ringed by dark circles. They had lost their youthful luster and taken on the squinted, insomniac look of someone accustomed to getting by on little sleep.

The officer muttered something in his ear, and he replied in fluent Vietnamese. His voice reinforced the same fatigued quality. Raspy and poorly modulated, it seemed to crack and falter under the simple stress of conversation.

He let his gaze rest briefly on each of the three captives, then settled it on Ghislene Ferrer. "You're Americans?" he asked her, slapping the switch against his leg.

"I am French," Ferrer replied, in an uncharacteristically fawning voice. "*They* are American."

Billy stared at Rob, his chin jutting out at him challengingly. "You're an American?"

Rob was not prepared for such a moment. He had imagined something so different—a daring rescue, a swirl of action in which his brother, weak and broken from long imprisonment, would collapse on Rob's shoulders and whisper his pathetic gratitude. This situation was beyond him utterly. An enormous lump choked his throat. He swallowed twice to clear it, then managed two words: "Hello, Billy."

Billy slapped the swagger stick against his thigh, then held it out, suspended in midair a foot from his leg, his eyes squinting at Rob in utter puzzlement. The silence across the crowded grove was absolute. Every pair of eyes was fixed on William Grunwald, Jr., and the three captives.

Rob watched the mystification collect on his brother's face, then harden into disbelief. He stepped up closer and peered at Rob from barely a foot away.

"Robbie?"

Rob nodded.

"Really you?"

"Yes."

Billy reached out and cupped Rob's face between his palms and studied him intently. Then he pulled Rob against him and embraced him fiercely. His hands still tied, Rob stumbled and fell against him.

The Vietnamese officer, standing just behind Billy, reacted to the unexpected reunion with comic incredulity. His mouth flapped open in wonderment, like some innocent primitive witnessing feats of stage magic. He stepped back several paces, as if afraid he might be asked to participate.

And he was. Seeing the ropes binding their wrists, Billy directed him to cut them free. With servile alacrity, the officer pulled out a knife, stepped around in back of them, and sawed hurriedly through the cords.

Billy swung around to face the grove, pulling Rob around with him. He clasped his shoulders and walked forward with him, toward the ranks of soldiers, still standing at attention. He shouted an explanation to them in Vietnamese. The effect of his words was astonishing. Their solemn faces came alive with smiles, as if the occasion represented a personal cause for celebration, and the entire grove broke into a prolonged applause.

The officer, now understanding the situation, ran out in front of them and joined in the celebration. Everyone in the grove—the women, the soldiers, everyone—began clapping in unison. Billy, his face beaming, grabbed Rob's hand and held it aloft with his own, acknowledging the applause.

It went on for a long time. Billy paraded before them, still clutching Rob, soaking up the approbation like a political campaigner. He led him to the platform back near the entrance into the mountain and pushed him up the four steps ahead of him. Again he caught his hand and held it in the air. Wild cheers augmented the applause. Rob could scarcely believe what was happening. The noise thundered off the mountain wall behind them and echoed through the grove until the trees themselves seemed to vibrate from the ovation.

Billy raised his arms aloft, palms downward, and the crowd, like an orchestra taking its cue from a conductor, began to hush. By the time his hands had reached his sides, the grove was silent.

Billy addressed the crowd for about ten minutes, his hoarse voice climbing and falling among the exotic tonal pitches of the Vietnamese tongue with an easy mastery that astounded Rob, so alien and un-expected did the language seem in Billy's mouth. It was a powerful reminder of the enormous stretch of time that had passed since they last saw each other—a stretch wide enough to encompass the creation of an entirely new existence.

Amid the applause that followed his speech, Billy escorted Rob down the platform steps and back toward the opening cut into the side of the hill. Billy's personal entourage—the two women and the officer—followed them at a discreet distance. Before they stepped through the entrance, Rob managed to stop Billy long enough to remind him that his two colleagues were still under guard.

Billy called over a soldier and gestured toward Ferrer and Gilmore, at the back of the grove. He turned back to Rob. "Your friends are now official VIPs. Food and drink are on their way. Come on, I want to show you something."

Billy ushered Rob through the doorway in the face of the cliff and down a long concrete-walled tunnel. Bare light bulbs strung along the ceiling at widely spaced intervals provided a dim twilight illumination. It was much cooler in the passageway, and Rob felt a faint breeze against his face, carrying damp odors of earth and mildew. They passed several tunnels that branched off on both sides, then turned right onto a corridor that led to a doorway guarded by a black-bereted soldier. Beyond the doorway was a cramped and humid flight of steps that spiraled upward through the rock like the stairs in the tower of a medieval cathedral.

After a long climb, they reached a landing where another soldier was standing guard. He saluted Billy smartly and hurried to pull open a heavy plank door directly behind him.

"Welcome to my house," Billy said, gesturing for Rob to step inside. He lit a small kerosene lamp with a lighter and adjusted the wick. "When we get another generator we'll be able to run electric power up here. Meanwhile, things are a little old fashioned." He led Rob through a series of small, windowless chambers that formed a subterranean apartment. Rob saw a primitive kitchen and pantry, a bathroom with a metal sink and a toilet, and a small bedroom with several mattresses on the floor.

The lack of windows made the atmosphere claustrophobic and dismal. It wasn't a house; it was an underground lair, a bunker.

At the end of the row of chambers was a large space that served as Billy's study, living room, and bedroom. It was modestly comfortable, furnished with a sofa and a few chairs, a high antique chest, a couple of crates converted to coffee tables, a small bookcase, an old record player, and, most astonishing of all, a beat-up American television set. A tiger skin lay on the rough concrete floor in front of it, the tiger's glass eyes staring at the blank screen. In the corner farthest from the door, another kind of screen, a large folding one, covered with intricately painted silk cloth, was stretched out to hide the narrow metal army cot that served as Billy's bed.

His brother beckoned Rob over to a section of drapery hanging across part of one wall. He pulled it aside and daylight streamed in. A window five feet high and five feet wide looked out over a broad jungle valley to a row of hazy mountain peaks that rose up from the carpet of green foliage in a series of blue-gray sawtooth silhouettes, like ancient mammoths rising in rebirth through the crust of the earth. Giant thunderheads were banked above them, and along the horizon, bolts of lightning crackled back and forth inside the clouds, charging them momentarily with an orange glow, and then flashed down through a dark curtain of rain to strike the earth.

"What do you think?" Billy demanded.

"Nice view," Rob admitted, too astonished to think of anything else to say.

Billy laughed. "It's cut into solid rock a hundred feet above that grove we left a few minutes ago. From here I have a clear line of sight in three directions—one hundred and eighty degrees, half the compass."

Billy opened the antique chest and removed a bottle and a couple of glasses. He seemed bemused and nervous. "We're having a little celebration tonight—that's the reason for all the activity down in the grove." He filled the glasses and handed one to Rob. "Well, now, damn it, we really have something to celebrate!" He held his glass up. "I don't know what the hell you're doing here, or how you found me, but I'll bet it's one son of a bitch of a story." Billy shook his head in amazement. "It's been a long time, hasn't it. Jesus, Robbie, it's been a lifetime."

Rob touched his glass to his brother's. They clinked together harder than he had intended, and liquid spilled down both their hands. Billy laughed at their discomfort. "You had some guts coming out here. I would never have imagined you had it in you."

"I didn't think I did, either," Rob admitted, trying to keep his emotional turmoil in check.

They drank. It was a coarse-tasting vodka and it made Rob choke.

"How's your life been?" Billy asked.

"Difficult."

His brother nodded. "Mine, too," he said.

"I thought you were in a prison camp."

Billy poured more vodka into the glasses. His hands trembled. "I was always sorry I couldn't get some word to the family. To let you know what was happening."

Rob rested his glass on the thick stone window ledge, his curiosity burning in him like a fuse. "What *is* happening?" he demanded. "What are you doing here?"

Billy tipped the glass to his lips and emptied it in a single gulp. "In good time. Tell me about the family, for chrissake. How is Sarah? And Mother? My God, it's been so long. A dozen years. Do you ever see Caroline? I had a dream about her the other night."

The two Vietnamese women who had been so conspicuous at Billy's side earlier entered the room. They smiled and dipped their heads and waited for introductions. Billy seemed both embarrassed and annoyed by their appearance. "This is Mai Ling," he said, holding his hand out toward the taller of the two. "And this is Hoa." He muttered something in Vietnamese to the women, and they nodded solemnly.

Both women were unusually attractive. The taller one, Mai Ling, was robust and sensual, her movements unrestrained. She had a full figure, and her breasts and hips pressed provocatively against her uniform. Hoa was more delicate and feminine, in the classic tradition of Asian women, with large dark eyes and high cheekbones.

"These girls are my family," Billy said.

"Family?"

"Wives," Billy clarified, with a sheepish grin. He clapped an arm around Rob's shoulder and guided him out of the room. "Come on, kid brother, I've got a lot to show you."

At the bottom of the long spiral of steps, Rob found his voice again. "Who are these 'wives' of yours?" he demanded. "And all these soldiers? What the hell is going on?"

The heartiness drained from Billy's manner. "Don't push me, Robbie," he warned, his eyes flashing. "You've stumbled into something you're not supposed to know about. You shouldn't have come. But you're here, so we'll just have to make the best of it."

37

New York City

In the days immediately following William Grunwald's plane crash, James Safier was too busy to grieve.

Grunwald Industries was taking a pounding. The small amount of public stock available lost a third of its value in three days, and contracts with its subsidiaries were being canceled at an alarming rate. Key employees were being hired away by competing firms. The problem, pointed out with brutal accuracy in an article in the *Wall Street Journal*, was that Grunwald Industries had a long-standing reputation as a one-man company. And with that man missing, the corporation was assumed by the business and investment communities to be floundering and directionless. And the business community was acting accordingly, cutting its financial ties with the Grunwald empire as fast as it could. The loss of confidence was having the same effect on the company as a run on a bank: It was turning the perception into a reality. Grunwald Industries had become, overnight, a wounded giant, and panic had hit the corporation's executive suites.

It fell to James Safier, the only individual with sufficient knowledge and experience in the overall operation of the company, and sufficient support from a majority of the top executives and shareholders, to prevent a crisis from deteriorating into a collapse.

After the initial jolts of grief and disbelief at the disappearance of

William Grunwald had subsided, Safier moved rapidly to consolidate his position. Although Grunwald's will could not be made public until the legal obstacles surrounding his uncertain status had been removed, Safier had long known its main provisions.

He waited until past midnight, when the nightly crew of cleaning ladies had finished their work and left the building, before he let himself into Grunwald's office and opened the safe. He riffled quickly through the stack of documents, found the folder with the photocopy of the will, and sat down on the sofa to study it.

It contained no surprises. It only confirmed the precarious position he was in.

Grunwald had left his wife, Cornelia, a large trust fund. Safier was also the recipient of a substantial trust, as were Grunwald's secretary, Florence Weld, and Billy Grunwald's wife, Caroline. But the important inheritance—Grunwald's corporate holdings, which amounted to ninety-four percent of the total stock in Grunwald Industries—had been split sixty-forty between his son Billy and his daughter Sarah, with the larger share going to Billy. The will went on to declare that in Billy's absence the sixty percent would be managed by a special trust, to be headed by James Safier, until Billy either returned to claim his share or was proven dead. In the event of the latter, the sixty percent would be divided equally between Caroline and Sarah.

Rob was to get nothing.

Safier decided that he must do two things immediately.

First, he must persuade Sarah to advance their wedding date. The sooner they were married, the stronger his position would be, both in and outside the company. As soon as Grunwald was declared legally dead, Safier would have an executor's control of Billy's sixty percent and indirectly, through Sarah, control of the other forty percent. Even though he would personally own no stock, he would have a virtual monopoly position in the management of the corporation.

If Billy was eventually proven dead, he would lose control of his sixty percent, but Sarah's share would then jump to seventy percent, a still comfortable—indeed, an unassailable—majority position.

But, if Billy returned home alive, then he would get his sixty percent and, with it, control of Grunwald Industries.

The possibility that Billy Grunwald might one day take over the business had always been there, hanging over Safier's head like a Damoclean sword, threatening to deprive him of everything he had struggled for for so long. In the past it had been only an implication. Now, with William Grunwald almost certainly dead, Billy's stake was spelled out. Explicitly.

With control of the corporation almost within Safier's grasp, Billy suddenly loomed as more of a threat than ever. The possibility of losing everything to him haunted Safier. He had an almost preternatural sense that if he left it to chance, it would surely come to pass.

So there was the second thing he must do: prevent that possibility from becoming a reality.

He mixed himself a scotch and water from Grunwald's bar and moved to the windows behind the desk. The drapes were pulled back, offering an extravagant nighttime panorama of New York Harbor. Safier stood there for a long time, staring out at the silent carnival of lights, concentrating on the search for a solution to his problem.

Several hours and several scotches later, he found his answer. It wasn't the perfect answer, he realized, but it was pretty damned good.

He opened the safe again, rummaged once more through the documents, pulled out the extra photocopy of Duffy's transcript that he had withheld from Captain Short, and carried it to the desk.

Perhaps Short had told him the truth: Perhaps the transcript was phony, worthless. He hoped so. But, just in case it wasn't, he planned to deliver it personally to the Vietnamese ambassador to the UN first thing in the morning. The ambassador would know whether there was any truth in it.

And when the ambassador was told of the rescue party on its way to find and free Billy Grunwald, Safier knew he could depend on the Vietnamese to do something to prevent it. If it wasn't already too late.

Northeast Thailand

Lin Pao pressed a finger against Caroline's nose.

" 'Nose,' " Caroline said.

" 'Nose,' " Lin Pao repeated. He moved his finger to her mouth.

" 'Mouth,' " she said.

" 'Mouse,' " he replied.

"No, '*mouth*,' " she corrected.

" 'Mouse,' " he repeated.

Caroline drilled him until he got it right. They went on through "teeth," "lips," "ear," "hair," "neck," "eyebrow," and "chin." "Teeth" and "mouth" gave him the most trouble, since the *th* sound was not common to his native tongue.

Lin Pao pressed his finger against her breast.

"Stop it," Caroline warned.

He poked her in the breast again and giggled.

"Stop it!" she ordered, slapping his hand away.

"Stop it!" Lin Pao repeated, giggling louder. "Stop it!"

Caroline stood up. "That's enough lesson for now, you little sex maniac. Let's go for a walk."

She took his hand and they walked around back of Sammy Rep's hotel, down past the shed that hid the mission's remaining jeep, and along the path that led east toward the Mekong. At a high promontory overlooking the river, they stopped and sat down. From this vantage point, they could see a wide stretch of the muddy river that divided the countries of Thailand and Laos, and directly below them, the place on the bank where the rescue party had departed on its quest to find Billy.

This was the third day they had come here. Too soon to expect anyone, Caroline told herself. But it helped fill the hours of waiting.

It seemed to her that she had spent her whole life waiting. And just when she thought she had finally taken control of it, she found herself back in the same passive situation—waiting for somebody else so she could start living her life. Waiting and enduring the low-grade pain of uncertainty, of not knowing. She wished now that they had stayed with Rob. For probably the first time in his life he had found the courage to admit that he needed someone. And she had deserted him.

She hugged her arms to her chest and rocked slowly back and forth, her eyes fixed on the eastern horizon. She fended off her guilt by telling herself that she had done the right thing. Staying would have been simply too dangerous. But any danger was beginning to seem better than this damned waiting.

They remained there by the river until the early evening, then returned to Sammy's for dinner and more English lessons.

The Norwegian Sea

Grunwald was unconscious when they opened the locker, slumped down inside the narrow space like a corpse in a coffin that had been stood on end.

He revived and began to weep as they pulled him out and carried him to the cot.

Koenig sat in the metal chair, smoking a cigarette and watching him as he collapsed on his back and tried, unsuccessfully, to straighten his knees. The flesh around them was hot, swollen, and seared with pain. Below his knees, he could feel nothing at all.

"Your ordeal is over," Koenig said.

"I told you nothing."

Koenig smiled. "Yes, you can award yourself a prize for holding out on me. But your brave little effort was wasted. We have the transcript now."

Grunwald imagined that Koenig must be trying to trick him. "Not possible," he mumbled.

Koenig flicked the ash from his cigarette onto the floor. "You should consider yourself lucky. Another few hours in there and you might never have walked again." He opened a small notebook and read aloud some details from the transcript. "Aren't you curious to know how we got it, Herr Gruen?"

Grunwald didn't reply.

"Your minion, Mr. Safier, delivered it to the Vietnamese embassy in New York this morning. Pure ironic luck, isn't it? He obviously had no idea how desperately we have been looking for it."

"My God."

"Herr Safier is only putting to good use those invaluable principles of American business that you taught him so well. He's moving to consolidate his position. Isn't that how you'd phrase it? Having Billy Grunwald around would be a major nuisance for him, after all. So he very wisely decided to give him to us."

"He's betrayed me," Grunwald whispered.

Koenig sucked on his cigarette and exhaled the smoke in a long, thick plume. "He assumes you're dead," he said. "And with you and Billy out of the way, and with his marriage to your daughter, he knows that Grunwald Industries will soon be all his. Lock, stock, and barrel, as they say in America."

Koenig put away his notebook. "We'll get some ice for your knees," he said.

38

Vietnam

"This whole complex of tunnels used to be part of the old Ho Chi Minh Trail," Billy said, taking Rob through a guarded door into a wide, low chamber lit by a string of naked bulbs. "It was a major base—a storage and transshipment point for soldiers and supplies coming down from Laos and North Vietnam. Its location was so well guarded that the U.S. never even knew it existed. They bombed the shit out of every inch of the trail itself, many times over, but never touched any of this. From the air, it's impossible to see anything. Just jungle and mountains. It's a secret fortress. We restored and expanded it."

A dirty makeshift plywood table supported on wooden sawhorses took up much of the room, with a collection of broken stools and chairs scattered around it. The far wall was obscured behind a large bank of radio and communications gear, manned by a bored-looking middle-aged Vietnamese wearing earphones and smoking. The air was stale and hot, and a blue haze of cigarette smoke hung over the room. Immediately behind the table several large terrain maps, similar to the ones Rob had used to find his way to Billy, hung from a large blackboard.

"Headquarters," Billy announced, taking in the room and its disordered contents with a wave of his arm.

"Headquarters for what?" Rob asked.

"The ANV," Billy responded. "Army of the New Vietnam."

Rob thought his brother was joking. "Give me that again?"

Billy's red-rimmed eyes flickered with a self-satisfied gleam. "I'm leading a revolution, Robbie. Against Hanoi."

Rob leaned against the table for support. "I don't believe it."

Billy flopped casually into one of the chairs, hoisted his feet up on the table, and pulled out a small cigar from the pocket of his shirt. "It takes a little explaining," he began. "I escaped from a prison north of Hanoi three years ago. I did more than that, actually. I led a mass escape of over two hundred men. Most of them were former officers from the South Vietnamese military. They had nothing to lose. After the north took over in 1975, the Communists let most of the ARVN enlisted men off with a little time in a reeducation camp. But they were really brutal with the officers. They beat them, tortured them. Many were shot."

Billy found a match and struck it. It crackled loudly in the concrete-lined bunker. When his cigar was lit, he shook the match out and tossed it on the floor. "I made it into the jungle, along with about a hundred others. We'd planned things pretty carefully. We knew there was a fledgling guerrilla movement already operating in the Southern Highlands. They were tribesmen—mostly Jarai, Rhade, and Bahnar—carrying on low-level harassment against the government with captured American weapons. Once we fell in with them, we were pretty safe. We had weapons, the jungle, and the local people to protect us."

As he talked, each sentence seemed to fuel his enthusiasm. He was like a lonely missionary who had at last found a sympathetic ear. " 'FULRO'—that was the old acronym: 'Front Unifié pour la Lutte des Races Opprimées,' if memory serves. FULRO had the right idea, but it just wasn't very effective. I saw that it would be only a matter of time before Hanoi whittled them down to nothing. They had a sort of shadow government—Y Ghok Nie Krieng was president and Y Drun Nie foreign minister. I offered to join forces with them. With my hundred men—all well-trained people, representing every major military and political discipline—I knew I had the cadre of an absolutely first-rate fighting force.

"For a while the alliance worked. I really started organizing things for them. Because it's so remote, Hanoi used this part of the country for exiling dissidents—POWs from Saigon, political opponents, and so on. We took advantage of that immediately, and started recruiting them into the movement. We scrounged weapons everywhere we could.

We made contact with Hanoi's enemies—the Khmer Rouge in Cambodia, and the Chinese—and persuaded them to help supply us. We even got the Ho Chi Minh Trail operating again. And we found this underground fortress and started enlarging it.

"But FULRO was a problem. We were doing all the work and they wanted to call all the shots. The politics and the infighting got to be ridiculous. Without us, they would never have survived, and after a time we realized that unless some changes were made, we might not survive, either. So we just took over. Sort of a bloodless coup. Many of the FULRO people supported us. They saw what was needed and they went along. Most of them are still here, in fact, working with us."

Staggered by what his brother was telling him, Rob stared blankly around the room. "And you're in charge of all this?"

Billy puffed on his cigar and grinned at him.

"I don't understand. Why should they pick you? You're not even Vietnamese."

"I took over a moribund insurgent movement and gave it life and hope," Billy replied. He pushed himself up out of his chair and poked his finger at one of the terrain maps on the blackboard. "Here's our fortress, right here. We control the area around it for about ten miles." He ran his finger in a large circle over the center of the map. "We govern it completely—make the laws and collect taxes. Hanoi doesn't even dare venture into the area anymore. And our control is spreading. Another five or six miles out is contested terrain. The government's there in the daytime; we're there at night. And our strength is growing every day. We don't control much population yet, but the word is getting out. We're recruiting at the rate of ten a day now, and they come from every part of Vietnamese society—from former South Vietnamese soldiers, from the local tribes, the peasant farmers, the professional and intellectual classes . . . All the disenfranchised, all those oppressed by the present government—a number that grows bigger every day." Billy jabbed the cigarillo menacingly in the air. "The people of Vietnam hate the Communists, Robbie, no matter what you read in the Western press. The tragedy of the boat people speaks eloquently of that hatred. The population is so desperate that it'll take any risk to get out from under Hanoi's rule. It's a harsh, totalitarian regime. It maintains its rule by force, against the will of its citizens. My movement proves that. And my movement offers hope."

Rob shook his head. "Jesus, Billy! You're fighting the Vietnam War all over again. We lost it once, using half a million men and dropping more bombs than they used in all of World War Two. And now you're going to win it all by yourself? With this ragtag collection of men?"

"It's not numbers that count," Billy replied calmly. "It's the moral force of the cause, the ideals we stand for."

"Moral force? America is ashamed it ever got involved. You haven't been home in a long time. Maybe you don't know that."

Billy narrowed his eyes. "Are you ashamed?" he demanded.

"You're damned right."

"Did you fight?"

Rob caught his breath. He realized that Billy didn't know anything about his draft protests or his flight to Canada. "Yeah, I fought. I fought against the war."

"What's that mean?"

"I protested. I refused to be drafted."

Billy dropped back into his chair. "How did you get out of it?"

"I went to Canada."

Billy studied his brother for a long time.

Rob steeled himself for an argument, but none came. "A lot of people went to Canada," he added. "I wasn't the only one. There was a huge movement—"

"I know all about it," Billy interrupted. He pointed to the bank of communications equipment. "We do get the news here, you know."

Rob looked over at the rows of switches and dials. A panel of tiny red lights on one console flickered dimly, and a faint hum radiated from a speaker somewhere. "It looks like state-of-the-art gear," he said, anxious to change the subject. "Where'd it come from?"

"From China," Billy replied. "Down the Ho Chi Minh Trail." He jumped up from the chair and patted Rob on the shoulder. "Come on. Let me show you the rest of the place."

Billy led his younger brother through a network of tunnels that seemed to extend endlessly in every direction, like a multitiered maze, connecting together an underground encampment as big as an entire town. Rob saw kitchens, communal dining rooms, baths, and barracks-like dormitories with long rows of cots.

"Maybe you did the right thing," Billy said, eager to continue the dialogue. "Even if for the wrong reasons. It was a stupid war, the way we fought it. We backed the wrong people, for openers. Saigon was worse than a puppet government. After Diem, it degenerated into a gang of thieves, getting rich off us while we fought the war for them." A very young Vietnamese soldier squeezed past them in the tunnel, and Billy slapped his thin shoulder affectionately. "The U.S.

never knew what it wanted out of Vietnam," he said. "So naturally it couldn't figure out how to get it."

"And when big countries make mistakes, small countries pay," Rob answered.

Billy nodded. "Well, that's all over now. We've got something real going here. The Army of the New Vietnam is for real. It's grass roots. It speaks to the desires of the people to be free, and the people are rallying to our cause. You'll see."

They arrived at a junction of two tunnels, and Billy stopped. "I know it sounds like an exaggeration, Robbie, but this is a genuine revolution. I've been in this country for twelve years, and I've experienced it as no other Westerner possibly could. I've seen its best and its worst, and I've come to understand and to love these people. They are a great race, still struggling for the government they deserve. They've made me the leader of that struggle. My future is here, with them. My life is dedicated to their liberation."

"Is that why you didn't come home?"

"What do you mean?"

"You escaped from prison, you said, three years ago. You could have gotten out of the country if you wanted to, couldn't you?"

Billy furrowed his brow, as if hurt by Rob's words. "Of course. But that would have meant letting down the others—the men I'd led on the escape."

"Is that the only reason?"

"There are some others," Billy admitted. "But, in retrospect, they really aren't very important. The important thing is what's happening here. This is my destiny, Robbie. This is why fate put me here. When the Hanoi government refused to repatriate me, I saw that my misfortune had a reason. I always believed that I would play an important role in the affairs of my time, but I never realized the form that it would take. I used to daydream about being a senator from New York. About running for president. I suppose that was because Father wanted that for me. Christ, imagine—the old man buying me a Senate seat. Buying me the presidency. Such nonsense. Me a fucking senator? Making windbag speeches on transportation bond issues and the need to balance the federal budget? Such bullshit. America doesn't need leaders anymore, Robbie, because it isn't going anywhere. It's already arrived. Its glory is behind it. It's too rich to have any goals anymore. It wants salesmen, not leaders, PR types to tempt it with tax cuts and higher wages. It's at a dead end. It's countries like this that need leaders. And history has chosen me to lead these people. I believe that."

Along another dimly lit passageway, Billy showed Rob a row of storerooms stacked floor to ceiling with crates and boxes of canned and dried food, clothing and boots, mechanical equipment and tools, tents, bicycles, beds, furniture, and a thousand other items. Several large rats scurried out from behind a crate and disappeared into the shadows.

"Agent Orange," Billy explained. "It killed off most of the bird and animal population in the area. The rats gorged themselves and they've multiplied like hell. They're everywhere."

"You can't get rid of them?"

Billy shook his head. "Don't want to," he said.

"Why not?"

"Emergency food supply."

Rob's eyes widened. "You'd eat rats?"

Billy smiled grimly. "There were times, in the camps, when I'd have given anything for one. Hard to believe, I guess, if you've never been through it, but the need for protein overcomes a lot of squeamishness. I developed some pretty tricky strategies for trapping them. Boiled, they taste something like rabbit. Or even veal." Billy laughed. "Not the kind of dish Mother would serve at Greenwood, but they're a hell of a lot better than insects. I've eaten a lot of those, too."

They stopped by an infirmary—a narrow space with a long row of cots visible under a couple of light bulbs. All the cots were occupied and the fetid stink of sweat, excrement, and urine was overwhelming. Rob saw one Vietnamese—an old man—moving slowly among the cots, doing the work of an orderly.

"We've been hit pretty bad with hepatitis," Billy said, walking into the ward and bending over the first cot. A frail young boy with a jaundiced face looked up at him solemnly. Billy pressed a hand against his forehead and said something to him in Vietnamese. The boy smiled manfully and nodded. "It's a sanitation problem," Billy continued, moving on to the next bed. "Living underground like this. We're working on it, but it's a problem."

Rob suddenly remembered Wyler. In the excitement of the reunion with Billy, the wrestler had totally escaped his mind. "Your men beat up one of our party and carried him off down here somewhere. He might need some medical attention."

"He's all right," Billy assured him. "We put him in the punishment cell. One of our women went down to clean him up and feed him. I'll send word down to release him."

"He knows you," Rob said.

Billy's eyes flashed in surprise. "He does?"

"It's Frank Wyler. He was in your company. Captured with you at Long Ba. You remember him?"

Billy bent his face toward Rob. "Frank Wyler?"

"Yes. A big guy. He's a professional wrestler now."

Billy scratched his chin thoughtfully. An expression of pain, or anger—or both—tightened the muscles of his jaw dramatically.

"He said you saved his life."

Rob's brother stared at him. "Did I?"

"That's what he said."

"I don't remember," he replied, dismissing the subject. "I saved a lot of lives." He turned away and bent down to talk to another sickbed patient. When he had completed his rounds of the infirmary, they descended a ladder to a lower level, which housed a big diesel power plant for generating electricity and operating the air-circulation system, and two enormous subterranean depots, one crowded with large drums of kerosene, oil, and gasoline, the other a bulging arsenal of armaments of every description—crates upon crates of rifles, ammunition, pistols, knives, mortars, grenades, bazookas, Claymore mines, small artillery pieces, hand-held antitank guns, and one-man surface-to-air rocket-propelled missile launchers. The stencils on most of the crates were in English.

Rob gawked at the enormous stockpile of arms. "American weapons?"

Billy nodded.

"From who? The CIA?"

"No."

"You can't tell me?"

"It's a special-operations group in the Pentagon."

"Is that what we're not supposed to know about?"

"Naturally they want to keep it quiet."

Rob felt sick with disgust. "They're back at it again. Don't those bastards ever learn anything?"

"A revolution takes its help where it can get it," Billy snapped.

"Without the Pentagon footing the bill, I can't believe there would be any revolution," Rob answered. "Or anything else going on here. You can't possibly expect you're going to overthrow the Vietnamese government with a bunch of retreads from the Saigon regime? And the Pentagon can't expect it, either. They're using you as a pawn!"

Billy shook his head condescendingly. "You don't understand what's going on."

"Yes, I think I do. You're a cheap, deniable way for them to keep the heat on the Vietnamese government. They're using you for their own ends. And when your movement is crushed, they won't give a damn."

"They use me, I use them. What's the difference? But this movement will never be crushed. Not as long as I'm alive."

Rob threw open his hands in a gesture of futility.

Billy laughed good-naturedly and slapped him on the back. "You always were a pain in the ass, Robbie," he said. "I guess a lot of it had to do with being a kid brother. You've been bitching about everything I ever did as long as I can remember."

"You bullied me," Rob retorted. "And you always had the old man on your side."

"Sibling rivalry, Robbie, that's all it was. Sibling rivalry. Sure, we fought. And I won because I was older and bigger. You were always crying to Mother—Billy did this, Billy did that. You were just jealous. You wanted everything I had. You wanted to do everything I did. And if you couldn't have it or couldn't do it, you complained. Just like you're complaining now. You're jealous of what I've got here. I can read it in your attitude."

"Jealous?" Rob echoed. "You think I'm jealous?"

"Why the hell did you come here, then?" Billy demanded. "You want to horn in on this, don't you?"

"Jesus, Billy, no," Rob whispered, alarmed at his older brother's paranoid reasoning.

"Why did you come here, then?"

"I came to bring you home."

Billy thought about it for a minute, scratching his grizzled chin slowly with an index finger; then he laughed savagely. "I can't go home, you damned fool."

Washington, D.C.

Walker's wheezy voice vibrated softly from the intercom speaker in back of Short's head. "Is McWhirter lying?" he asked.

"I can't judge that," Short replied, staring out the limousine's windshield at the looming hulk of the old red brick Smithsonian building, dark and empty under a bright half-moon. He could just discern the silhouette of Walker's chauffeur-bodyguard, leaning against a tree trunk about a hundred feet down Jefferson Drive. At two in the morning the vast common was deserted, a panoramic still life of silvery lawns bordered by pools of dim yellow streetlight and the squat giant shadows of government buildings. The dome of the Capitol, nearly a mile away, glittered pale gold under the moon, like some gigantic alien spaceship hovering over the city.

"Give me your best guess," Walker insisted.

"McWhirter said he left them in Laos, near the border. He tried to persuade them to turn back, but they refused."

"Why would they refuse?" Walker persisted. "It doesn't make sense."

"McWhirter couldn't tell me why."

"They must have guessed that he was responsible for the tribesmen abandoning them."

"I don't know. McWhirter claims they have no chance of getting anywhere."

"He's wrong," Walker said.

"You want me to send some people in? Find them?"

"No," Walker said. "It no longer matters. I've decided to terminate the operation."

Short felt a secret surge of joy at the words. Nothing would give him greater pleasure than to be done with this business. "Why?" he probed, his voice deadpan.

"The Vietnamese are moving into the area in force."

Short was about to ask Walker how he knew that, but he caught himself. Walker was privy to all the intercepted radio signal traffic from NSA, the photo reconnaissance from the CIA's spy satellites, and probably half a dozen other sources of intelligence Short had never even heard of. "They've tried to smoke out Monarch Eagle before," Short said. "What makes you so sure they can find him this time?"

Walker's voice sounded distinctly depressed when he answered. "Someone has apparently leaked the location to them. That man Safier, no doubt. They wouldn't put this level of resources in unless they knew their target. The roads along the Khe Sanh–Quang Tri axis are choked with military vehicles. All headed in his direction. They've got him pinpointed. They wouldn't haul in artillery otherwise."

"What do you want to do? Try to pull him out?"

Walker didn't answer. Short waited patiently, listening to the faint wheeze of the man's breath keeping a lethargic syncopation with the metallic tock of the analog clock on the dash. Short repeated his question.

"There's nothing to salvage," Walker said, as if talking to himself. "Monarch Eagle is over. All we can do now is hide the evidence of our involvement."

"How do we do that?"

"By sacrificing Grunwald."

"What if the Viets capture him? They could build a show around him."

"No, they can't do that," Walker answered. "It would be too humiliating for them to admit the existence of his movement publicly. They would simply put him away somewhere. For good."

"What if he survives their attack and escapes?"

"Yes," Walker admitted. "That is what we must prepare for. I want you to get men and helicopters to the Thailand–Laos border area. As many as you can as soon as you can. I'll give you priority clearance on everything you need."

Short heard a sharp, gasping intake of breath. "He must not be allowed to come out," Walker wheezed. "Not under any circumstances."

39

The Norwegian Sea

It was two days after his ordeal in the locker before William Grunwald was able to walk again. But his food was increased, and with its regular arrival, he was able to begin a rough calculation of the passage of time. His stomach told him that Koenig was now feeding him twice a day—a cup of weak tea and a piece of bread for what he decided to call breakfast, and a bowl of soup and a larger piece of bread for what he decided was dinner. The only variety in the fare was in the soup. Sometimes it contained only potato, other times bits of vegetables—beets or cauliflower, usually—and twice there had been some pieces of meat.

So far, since Koenig had freed him from the locker, he had counted eight meals and four days. The days before the locker remained an indistinct blur, but, judging from the growth of his beard, he estimated that he had been held captive for a total of eleven days.

Eleven days in which his life had been turned inside out.

He had contemplated suicide. He determined that he could hang himself from one of the pipes that ran across the ceiling. All he needed to accomplish the act was at hand—a sheet that could be converted to a noose, and a chair from which to step. But he had rejected the idea. He had survived adversity in his life before. He would survive this, too.

He organized his time into a simple routine. After "breakfast," he washed himself in the basin, used the chemical toilet, and then put himself through an hour of calisthenics. "Physical therapy" was a better description. As soon as he was able to stand and bend his knees again, he tried push-ups and was shocked to discover that he could not do any. Two weeks ago he could easily have run through fifty.

The remainder of the time before "dinner" he lay quietly on his cot, staring at the gray steel ceiling, reviewing his life. After "dinner," he waited for Koenig.

He had come to anticipate these sessions with his captor eagerly. It was sad, he reflected, that Koenig had become the most important event in his day, but he was his only contact with the world. And although he feared and despised him, he was also completely dependent on him for everything. Koenig controlled his existence utterly and in every detail. Koenig *was* his existence.

The ordeal in the locker had marked a watershed. Before, he could think of nothing but escape and revenge. Now he accepted the impossibility of escape, the pointlessness of resistance. Now he sought only to engage Koenig with words, to win a different, more profound struggle—that of justifying his life to his enemy. And Koenig was a formidable opponent. He thought and argued like a Jesuit—his view of the world whole and unbroken, admitting of no paradox, contradiction, or shadings of gray. He was dogmatic but agile, quick to seize on another's inconsistencies and weaknesses, sure-footed in the advancement of his own views, and well armed with fact and anecdote to support every generality.

Grunwald, by contrast, was a weak debater. He was a man of action, not reflection, and his case was a subtle one, demanding an appreciation of fine distinctions, of extenuating circumstances, of the commonly accepted weaknesses of human nature. Koenig beat him down on these matters with ease, using harsh polemics and rhetorical devices that were difficult to counteract. But, after each argument, Grunwald became more determined than ever to make Koenig understand, even to win his sympathy. And the fact that Koenig chose to sit each day and engage him in these verbal wrestling matches was in itself an encouragement. Each successive session helped Grunwald to strip away the false and the presumptuous from his own arguments, helped him to find and understand the truth. He had surrendered tremendous ground—confessed to so many things—that at last he began to feel that he was standing at the bedrock of his personality. Koenig could drive him down no further.

Fate had decided to appoint his most bitter enemy his judge and his confessor. So be it. He would struggle, he told himself; he would temper himself in the crucible of self-examination and become strong again. He would survive.

Vietnam

Hundreds of torches, constructed of large tin cans fitted with home-made wicks and filled with oil, had been set out on dozens of tables throughout the grove, bringing the humid night forest alive with danc-ing yellow flames. A growing crowd of soldiers, their projected shad-ows jumping against the canopy of leaves overhead like giant figures in a light show, milled around the big roasting pit, where the carcasses of six pigs turned slowly on their spits over a huge bed of red coals. The tables were decorated for the occasion with an incongruous mix-ture of jungle orchids and buckets of palm wine and warm beer. Laughter echoed across the grove in quick, rippling waves. Hordes of insects, enticed from the dark by the dazzling islands of light, flung themselves to their deaths by the thousands, and piled up in the oil of the tin lamps until the bottoms were thick with their cremated bodies.

"What do we do now?" Rob asked Howard Gilmore, who was sitting with him at one end of the table reserved for Billy and his guests of honor.

"We send out for some cold beer," Gilmore retorted, twisting the top off a bottle of the warm Chinese brew and sniffing it suspiciously. "Then we go home."

"We have to persuade Billy to come with us."

"He doesn't look ready to leave any time soon," Gilmore said. "I think we'd better skip it and just hightail it the hell out of here."

"What have we gone through all this for? Just to stop in and say hello?"

Gilmore settled his glasses on his nose nervously. "This isn't quite the situation we expected," he replied. "To tell you the truth, ol' buddy, I don't see a whole lot wrong with leaving things just as they stand. Your brother's not in prison, after all. And he obviously thinks he's got a good thing going here. And maybe he has."

Rob shook his head emphatically. "The situation here is doomed. It's only a matter of time. We've got to talk him into giving it up. Billy's sick. He's living some crazy delusion of glory, and what he's doing is sick, as well. He's trying to fight the Vietnam War all over again—with the help of some maniacs in the U.S. government who never know when to leave well enough alone. We ought to try and stop it."

"Stop it?" Gilmore echoed, incredulous. "Who's suffering from delusions? We have less of a chance of breaking this act up than your brother has of marching into Hanoi."

"We *do* have a chance," Rob insisted. "And if we don't do something, Billy'll end up dead, along with everyone else here. I think he knows that, deep down, but he's afraid to leave. We've got to get him to change his mind."

"What's he afraid of?"

"He's afraid of not coming home a hero."

Gilmore pulled at his beard. "He might also be afraid of what the people who put him up to this will do if he decides to back out on them."

At a table nearby, Ferrer was chatting animatedly in French with several soldiers. Her tape recorder was out, Rob noticed, and from the boisterous nature of the voices, it was clear she had them competing to spill their innermost thoughts about themselves, Billy, and their experiences as part of the Army of the New Vietnam.

"We'll have to put pressure on him," Rob said. "If I threaten to make public what's going on here, he won't have any choice but to come home."

Gilmore narrowed his eyes in shock. "If you tell him that, he won't let us leave."

Billy emerged, suddenly, from the tunnel entrance, and their conversation was interrupted by a loud cheer from the crowd. Billy waved, swagger stick in hand, and was soon swallowed up in a throng of well-wishers who flocked around him in a growing circle of shouts and extended arms. Watching his brother, Rob felt an irrational anger swelling in his chest. He had risked so much to find him, only to be accused of jealousy. Billy was still bullying him.

"He can't keep us here."

"Why can't he?" Gilmore argued. "Have you already forgotten this morning? We were captured, remember? They took our weapons, kicked Wyler unconscious, tied us up, and marched us off into the jungle. If we had turned out to be strangers, who knows what would have happened to us by now? You may be right about your brother's delusions, but he's still the law around here."

Frank Wyler woke up in the dark and groped around him with his hands. He felt the edges of a thin mattress and the cool clay of a dirt floor. His sleeping bag had been thrown over him, but he still felt a chill. How could it be so cold? The last thing he remembered, he was walking through steaming jungle.

He moved to sit up, and felt waves of pain splash over him. His head spun, forcing him to lie back down again. He remembered now. The attack and the beating. *God have mercy on me*, he groaned. *I'm a prisoner again.*

He examined himself carefully, palpating his flesh with his fingers, locating and identifying the bruises and sore spots that crowded his body. He felt the bandage wrapped around his head. It was stiff and crusted with blood. He tested his limbs, and satisfied himself that he had broken no bones. Painfully he raised himself onto his hands and knees and began to explore his surroundings.

The cell was small and square. There were two other mattresses on the dirt floor, but they were empty. Where were the others? he wondered. Dead?

Sounds of footsteps. He held his breath, listening. A key rattled in a lock and suddenly the beam of a flashlight pierced the dark. He blinked his good eye and held a hand up over his face.

Someone walked in, stopped in front of Wyler's mattress, and shined the flashlight on him. Wyler saw the barrel end of an automatic pistol pointed down at him. Behind it, he could make out the dim figure of a Vietnamese dressed in camouflage fatigues and beret.

"Vous venez avec moi," the soldier said.

Wyler shook his head, indicating that he didn't understand. The man rattled off some more French, and Wyler just stared back at him. *Dumb gook,* he thought. "I'm an American," he answered, finally, to make him shut up.

The Vietnamese nodded vigorously. "American," he echoed, and then laughed in that nervous way Wyler noticed that Orientals sometimes laughed when nothing was funny. The sound froze Wyler's blood. He had been tortured close to death by a Vietnamese with a similar laugh.

The soldier gestured for him to get up. Wyler did so, very carefully, his eye mesmerized by the pistol leveled at him. He could smell beer on the soldier's breath.

The Vietnamese prodded him in the small of the back with the barrel of the automatic, and directed the beam of the flashlight toward the open doorway. Wyler walked through, ducking his head under the lintel, and found himself in a long, narrow tunnel.

"Allons-y," the soldier ordered, pointing the flashlight down the passageway. With the pistol pressing against Wyler's back, the soldier

hustled him down the tunnel, pushing him at a pace that caused him to stumble repeatedly.

They came to a bend in the passageway. The light bulb nearest the corner had burned out, leaving the area immediately near it quite dark.

Wyler saw his opportunity. He pretended to stumble, and as he recovered, he reached an arm back swiftly, closed it around the Vietnamese's neck in a hammerlock, and lunged forward, driving the soldier headfirst into the rock wall of the tunnel.

The pistol clattered to the ground. Wyler pulled back, the Vietnamese still tucked firmly under his arm, and rammed his head into the wall again and again, with all the force he could muster. The Vietnamese had ceased to struggle with the second blow, but Wyler, his powerful muscles inflated with adrenaline, couldn't stop.

Only when he was gasping for breath and felt his arms cramping did he finally release his hold. The soldier fell to the ground limp as a sack of rice, his skull a matted mess of blood, hair, and flesh. Wyler snatched up the flashlight and the pistol and ran off down the tunnel.

40

Vietnam

Rob left the drunken revelry in the grove and retreated back into the tunnels, looking for Ferrer. He glanced at his bare wrist, still expecting to see the luminous dial of his missing wristwatch. Around midnight, he guessed. The heavy night air and the beer in his stomach made him drowsy. He planted his hands against the walls for support as he trudged the steep, twisting stairwell to Billy's quarters. The wall surfaces felt slick and gelatinous, like the hull of a sunken ship, and his perspiring hands slipped against them.

The guard's station at the top landing was deserted. He opened the door to Billy's rooms and groped his way in the darkness, directing the white beam of his flashlight around the black spaces, looking for a lantern to light. The gloom was palpable, oppressive. Shadows darted and weaved around him, thrown into silent commotion by the movement of his light.

"Ghislene?" he called. No response. He found his way into the main room. Light and noise from the grove drifted up through the window cut into the hillside rock. He walked over to it and leaned forward against the curtain of mosquito netting. The revelry below seemed to be reaching a frenzy.

A burst of gunfire racketed against the mountainside, and as the explosions echoed through the hills and died, the grove fell silent. He saw a drunken soldier staggering around in circles, an automatic rifle braced on his hip and pointed skyward. He loosed another burst, scattering the celebrants near him. A woman screamed. Two other soldiers jumped him from behind, wrestled him to the ground, and took the rifle away. The woman who had screamed came up and pulled the drunk to his feet. Amid a raucous chorus of hoots and jeers, he took three steps and fell down again. Someone poured the contents of a bottle on his head and the crowd around him broke into helpless laughter.

A rustle of movement in the dark caused Rob to turn around. It was Ferrer, barefoot in a short cotton nightgown. She leaned beside him at the window ledge.

"What is happening?"

"The party's getting out of hand."

"*Les pauvres petits,*" she whispered, looking down at the grove. "It is not a good life they have."

"You're shameless," Rob chided. "You don't give a damn what kind of life they have."

Ferrer slapped him playfully on the cheek. "You are a cynic, *mon cher*. I have spent much of the day talking to them, and my head is full of their problems. At this moment it makes me feel good to feel sorry for them. To sympathize. Tomorrow I will feel other things. Is that wrong?"

"I don't know."

"I sympathize with you, also."

"Feel sorry for me, you mean?"

Ferrer favored him with a husky laugh. "Yes, a little bit, I do."

"Why?"

Ferrer wrapped her arms tightly around Rob's waist. It surprised him, but he didn't resist it. He felt the heat of her slim figure through her thin nightshirt.

"Make love to me," she whispered, "and maybe I will tell you."

Rob put his hands on her shoulders, trying to frame some reply, but she didn't wait. She reached her arms around his neck and pulled herself against him, pressing a knee between his legs and her lips against an ear. "Make love to me now, *mon amour*. I am a little drunk—and I am so hot!" She flicked her tongue inside his ear, wetting it thoroughly, and then blew her breath in short puffs against it. An electric chill zipped through him, creating goose bumps and the start of an erection, which she teased with the edge of her knee. Still, he resisted.

Ferrer giggled. "You are thinking of Caroline?"

He nodded.

"She will not mind. You will have each other for a long time. I will have you only tonight."

She coaxed him back into the small room with the mattress on the floor, and they lay down on it.

"Let me undress you, *mon cher,*" Ferrer whispered. She pressed him back against the mattress and fumbled in the dark with his belt. He felt her hands around him, then her mouth sucking on him, skillfully orchestrating an intense erection.

Her mouth came away. "I can't wait," she said. "I want to fuck you." She straddled him, pulling her cotton gown up around her waist. He strained to see her, but the dark was complete. She raised herself up, quickly worked him partway into her, and slid down on him, engulfing him tightly. She stopped, her pelvis pressed against his, and caught her breath. Then, with a series of shuddering spasms, she pulled away, pressed down, and pulled away again. He grasped her thighs to follow her movement.She felt slight as a child on top of him.

"I heard you make love to Caroline," she gasped. "At Sammy's. I was in the room next to you. My God, it excited me so much! I wanted to come in and make love to both of you. I went crazy listening to you and playing with myself."

Aroused by her own words, Ferrer quickened her pace. She trembled. "I am going to come, *cheri.* Now!"

Ferrer collapsed against him, holding him tightly imprisoned inside her. When he began to soften, she flexed her vaginal muscles, pumping him up again. "I am not letting you go yet," she said, with a low giggle. "Just giving you a little rest."

"Why don't you rest," he replied, "and I'll get on top."

"No. I prefer it like this, *mon amour.* I can come much better this way."

Rob smiled. "You like to set the pace, don't you."

"Yes. That is the secret I have learned from you men. Control. In many ways I am more like a man than a woman. I accept it. I have made love to both. I honestly don't know which I prefer. I think I am lucky to be able to enjoy both. Women are soft, sensual, reassuring. The lovemaking is tender. And a little bit forbidden. With men there is more thrill, excitement. And I most enjoy sex when times are dangerous. Like now. Danger is a powerful aphrodisiac for me."

"Are we in danger now?"

"Yes. Great danger."

He felt her squeezing him again. "Think of Caroline," Ferrer whispered, slowly flexing her belly against his. "We will both think of

Caroline. That will be very exciting! We will have a tremendous or-gasm together."

Rob tried briefly to resist Ferrer's erotic manipulations but quickly succumbed. She was right, damn her! It *was* exciting. Someday he would tell Caroline, he thought, as Ferrer rode him skillfully toward a second climax, and they would laugh about it. And maybe she would find it exciting, too.

A match flared in the darkness and Rob blinked in surprise. He had drifted off to sleep, and Ferrer was sitting beside him on the mattress, lighting a cigarette. The match light illuminated her face and hands briefly, then died. He watched the red glow of the Gitane as it traveled from her mouth to her lap and back again.

"I came up here to ask a favor from you," he said.

"I have already favored you, *mon lapin.*"

"Something else, I mean."

"What is it?"

"You came here for a story. . . ."

"Yes?"

"And you have it now, don't you?"

Ferrer was silent for a moment. "Yes, most of it," she replied.

"What's missing?"

"The conclusion."

"Don't wait for that."

"Why not?"

"I want to get my brother out of here."

"I don't think that is possible."

"It is, if you'll agree to what I ask."

"Perhaps. Tell me."

"I want you to leave tomorrow. With Gilmore. Get back to Thailand and file your story. When I tell Billy what you plan to do, he'll have to accept that his days here are numbered. When your story appears, the Vietnamese government will swarm all over this place. With that facing him, I might be able to persuade him to come home with me."

Ferrer took a deep puff on her cigarette and said nothing.

"It'll be risky," he continued. "But it's even riskier for you to stay here. He might decide not to let any of us leave."

"It's too late," Ferrer replied.

"Why?"

"Hanoi has already found him. The soldiers told me tonight that their patrols are spotting government convoys and artillery moving in. We are surrounded. A big attack is coming."

Rob sat up, suddenly furious. "Christ, why didn't you tell me?"

Ferrer's voice was contrite: "I intended to. I wanted to enjoy the danger, first."

"Does Billy know about this?"

"Of course. He is down in the command center now, planning the defense."

Bangkok, Thailand

The nightclub on Petchburi Road was jammed with a jostling, noisy herd of male Japanese tourists in wash-and-wear suits, and dozens of bar girls and prostitutes in shorts and bare breasts. Harris McWhirter crouched at the bar at the back of the club, nearly hidden in the dim light and the mist of cigarette smoke. He was concentrating on drinking himself insensible.

A go-go dancer clopped along the top of the bar in her high heels and squatted down in front of McWhirter's face, giving him a close-up view of the inside of her thighs and the black thatch of pubic hair that divided them. He gazed blankly at the sight.

"You want to play?" the girl asked.

"No."

"Come on, you sourpuss," the girl urged. "You here every night, you no play."

McWhirter sipped his drink. The girl reached down between her thighs with both hands and spread the carmine lips of her vagina. "Put some dollars in my pussy, sourpuss," she demanded.

"Beat it."

"Come on," she coaxed, wetting a finger and probing her vulva with it. "Show me you're a man."

"Maybe it needs a drink," he muttered.

The girl giggled. "You buy my pussy a drink?"

"Sure," McWhirter replied. He picked up his glass and tossed the whiskey and ice cubes into the go-go girl's crotch. She shrieked and jumped up. McWhirter grinned.

"You son-of-a-bitch bastard!" she yelled, grabbing the bartender's towel and drying herself. "I get you kicked out of here!"

"Don't bother," McWhirter said. He grabbed the stack of American bills he had piled in front of him, snapped a ten off the top, threw it at her, and stood up to leave.

A pair of big hands settled heavily on his shoulders and pushed him back down onto the barstool. He tried to turn around to see who it was, but the hands prevented him.

"You owe the lady an apology, McWhirter."

The words came from a freckle-faced man with sandy hair, sitting on the stool next to him: Captain Short, the man Walker had sent to debrief him about the Grunwald mission. McWhirter, in his stuporous state, hadn't even noticed him. The man with his hands clamped onto his shoulders he was still unable to see.

McWhirter grimaced from the pain shooting through his shoulder blades. "What the fuck do you want now?"

"We're organizing a rescue party. We're gonna go rescue those people you carelessly abandoned in Laos."

McWhirter picked up his empty glass and tilted it to his lips. "What do you need me for?"

"To show us the way."

"Show you the way," McWhirter repeated.

"That's right."

Moving his arms with difficulty against the pressure on his shoulders, McWhirter peeled another ten off the pile of bills still clutched in his palm and waved it in front of Short. "She can stick them up her cunt," he mumbled, pointing unsteadily in the direction of the go-go dancer, now squatting in front of another customer farther on down the bar. "Let's see you stick this one up your ass."

The next thing McWhirter knew, the surface of the bar was rushing up at him with tremendous velocity. It smashed him in the face and knocked him out cold.

41

Vietnam

Rob Grunwald fumbled around in the dark, searching for his clothes. The small underground room was oppressively hot, the air stale and heavy with odors. He felt both nervous and drained at the same time. *Where the hell is Ferrer?* he wondered. She had set out to find the bathroom and never come back. Impatient with waiting, Rob located his pants, shirt, and canvas boots, struggled into them, and groped his way to the big window in the main room and leaned out for a breath of air. The lights from the party below had been extinguished, and the grove was barely visible under the glow of a quarter moon.

A match flared suddenly from a corner of the room, illuminating a pair of cupped hands and the undersides of a face.

"Ghislene?"

"She's gone."

It was Billy.

"You scared me," Rob breathed.

Billy's hand moved the flaring match to a lantern in front of him and applied it to its wick. A wisp of orange smoke curled up; then the flame caught the kerosene and evened out along the wick into a steady yellow glow. Billy adjusted it, replaced the glass chimney, and carried the light to the table in the center of the room. "You always scared easily," he said.

"Did I?"

"Yeah. Remember the night light in your room? Gerta told me it was there because you were afraid of the dark."

"It's more than the dark I'm scared of now."

Billy laughed. "Welcome to Vietnam. I've been scared for twelve years. I don't think I'd know what it felt like not to be."

"Ferrer tells me we're about to be attacked."

Billy dropped heavily into a chair. Rob could see his strained eyes glittering in the lamplight.

"Tell me some news from home, Robbie."

"What do you want to know?"

"Tell me about Caroline. What's she doing? Is she happy?"

"She's in Thailand. Waiting for us."

His older brother laughed again. "What are you trying to arrange, Robbie? A family reunion?"

"I want to get you out of here."

"You fucking her?"

Rob held his breath. Billy's words hung there, unanswered, in the thick gloom.

"I don't care if you are," he said. "Somebody must be fucking her, after all this time. Might as well keep it in the family."

"I'll tell her you said that," Rob replied. "She'll be thrilled to hear how much you've missed her."

"I went nine years without sleeping with a woman," Billy said, ignoring Rob's sarcasm. "That's a long time, nine years." He expelled his breath in a long hiss. "We never really got along. Did she tell you that?"

"Not in so many words."

"I think she just wanted the family money."

"You don't understand a damned thing about her."

Billy pulled himself upright. His face, in the dim light of the lantern, seemed to hang suspended by itself staring at him with haunted eyes. "You're in love with her."

"Yes."

Billy's taunting mood dissolved abruptly into a weary sadness. "I'm sorry, Robbie. There's a lot of bitterness left in me." He slouched back and sighed deeply. "The old man's dead. Did I tell you that?"

Was his brother losing touch with reality? "How did you get that idea?"

"It's not an idea I got," Billy snapped. "Stop treating me like I'm feebleminded. We picked it up on the shortwave, two days ago. Voice of America. His plane went down in the Atlantic."

Rob bowed his head, his confusion complete.

"You never liked the old man very much, did you?"

Rob shook his head. He thought how many times in past years he had wished his father dead. How many times he had imagined the pleasure he would feel, being free of him at last. Now that it had happened, he felt neither remorse nor satisfaction. He felt cheated. The chance to prove something to him was gone forever. There would be no scores settled, no understandings reached. The focus of a lifetime of defiance had been snatched away from him.

"You don't seem very sad about it," Billy said.

"Neither do you," Rob replied. "And you're the only one he really loved."

His brother started to laugh. The quality of it was so eerie that it made Rob shiver. Billy produced a cigarillo from the breast pocket of his shirt and leaned forward to hold the tip over the chimney of the lamp. He puffed on it until it ignited.

"You're going to see some fireworks around here in a few hours," he said, abruptly shifting the topic of conversation again. "Hanoi is going to throw the works at us. In the past, we've always hit and run, in classic guerrilla style. This time we'll have to hold our ground and slug it out with them. It'll be a bitch."

"Why not hit and run again?"

Billy leaned back and blew smoke at the lantern. "Because I believe we can beat them back."

"Because they have you trapped," Rob contradicted him.

"I've been trapped before, but I've survived. And the Army of the New Vietnam will survive, too. We're tough and committed. Every day I'm called on to make decisions that may mean life or death to my people." Billy jammed the cigarillo in his mouth and bit down on it. "They're going to remember me," he said, his voice low, as if talking to himself. "I'm going to be a part of this country's history. Someday the world may even look back on me as a turning point. The first non-Marxist revolutionary of this century. The first man to turn the tide against communism."

"How are you going to break the trap? If you stand and fight, they can just starve you out, can't they?"

"Our friends in Washington may have to help us."

"They'll just cut you adrift."

"No. They have too big a stake in my success."

"Do they?"

"What I'm wondering," Billy said, his voice chill, "is how they found our location in the first place." He dropped the cigarillo on the floor beside his chair and crushed it under his heel, then reached for something on the antique chest behind him. His hand returned, clutching a large automatic pistol. He brought it close under the light, snapped its clip out, and counted the bullets in it. Rob watched, mesmerized. The pistol's polished blue-black surface gleamed dully in the amber lamplight, like the carapace of an enormous insect.

"You came here to destroy me," Billy whispered. He shoved the automatic's cartridge back into the grip with a loud click.

"That's crazy talk."

"You think so?" he asked, flicking the safety off with his thumb.

"You're under a lot of stress."

Billy pointed the pistol at his brother. "Is it just a funny coincidence that Hanoi arrives right behind you?"

Rob stared across the table at the barrel of the automatic, its .45-caliber bore hole leveled at his head. During their childhood Billy had pointed so many cap pistols and BB guns at him that the experience had a depressing familiarity to it. He found it difficult to accept that this time the pistol was real.

"Tell me about the French reporter," Billy demanded. "Why'd you bring her?"

"She blackmailed her way in."

"How?"

"By threatening to expose our rescue mission."

"What did she want in return?"

"The story of your escape."

Billy laughed. "My escape? From what?"

"We thought you were in a prison camp!"

Rob's explanation didn't seem to interest his brother at all. The laugh faded and he abruptly shifted to another subject: "Why did you bring Frank Wyler?"

"He was in your outfit. He worshiped you. He begged me to take him."

"Begged you?"

"Yes."

Billy shook his head sadly. "Robbie, Robbie," he chided. "Don't lie to your older brother."

"I'm not lying, for chrissake!"

"You came here to *destroy* me," Billy repeated.

Rob saw the pistol's bore flash bright orange. A bullet exploded past his head and caromed off the wall behind him, kicking up a shower of rock dust. His ears rang as if a siren had been tripped inside his head, and the sudden bath of adrenaline through his veins made him hot and dizzy. The acrid odor of cordite stung his nostrils. "You crazy fool," he gasped.

"The only reason Wyler would come here is to kill me," Billy said, wagging the pistol at Rob. "I intended to bring him up here and confront him, but he killed the soldier I sent to get him. He's loose down on the bottom level—with the soldier's gun."

"Please believe me," Rob pleaded. "He doesn't even know you're here!"

"You brought him here to kill me," Billy repeated. "You want my movement crushed. Don't deny it. I hear it in everything you've done and said since you got here."

"I just wanted to get you out!"

"You think my movement is a fantasy," Billy accused him. "But it's not. It's profoundly real. I've overcome incredible odds to create it. Put my life on the line to maintain it. This movement is my reason for being. This is my reality. And you're in it. And in my reality, kid brother, I call the shots."

Rob didn't try to answer him.

Billy pushed back the chair and stood up. "I'm going to give you a chance to prove you're not lying," he said. He jammed the pistol into his belt and picked up a large flashlight from the top of the chest. "We'll go find Wyler and ask him."

The Norwegian Sea

"I was a victim of the times," Grunwald said, staring up at the ceiling, the rows of pipes now as familiar to him as his bedroom at Greenwood.

Koenig sat in the chair, legs crossed, shrouded in a nimbus of blue cigarette smoke that curled from his hand and hung suspended in the stale air. "Every man has his excuses," he replied.

"You became a Communist because your family was Communist. My family believed in National Socialism."

"My family was Socialist. There's a difference. But I became a Communist because I hated capitalism. Capitalism was responsible for the rise of Hitler."

"It was Germany's humiliation after the First World War. Hitler took advantage of that."

"Yes. A humiliation concocted by the greedy bankers of Europe and the United States. The Treaty of Versailles squeezed every last pfennig out of the German nation, stripped it clean of everything, until the puppet Weimar Republic, collaborating in the rape of its own country, could no longer take the strain and collapsed. So much for democracy."

"At least you understand the discontent that existed. My father was a laborer. He was wounded at Verdun. Mustard gas destroyed his lungs. After the war he could no longer work. His military pension became worthless when the currency collapsed in the twenties. He turned to alcohol. We survived on charity from my mother's parents. When Hitler came along, my father embraced his cause like a new religion. National Socialism saved us. It put father back to work, gave him a sense of pride and dignity again. He even stopped drinking."

"Back to work? In the S.A.?"

"Yes."

"Beating up Jews in the streets? Smashing the windows of Jewish shops? You call that going back to work?"

"He did organizing in the party offices."

"That's what he told you, of course."

"He was never part of the street gangs. He needed crutches just to get around."

"He approved of their depredations, obviously."

"He hated the Jews, that's true. He blamed them for all our problems. I grew up in that atmosphere. Everything I heard—around the house, from neighbors, from friends—all reinforced those same beliefs. How could I have thought otherwise? How was I to judge? I was a child."

"You can be excused your prejudice, Herr Gruen," Koenig replied, knocking the long ash from his cigarette. "It was common enough, I admit. Even my family indulged in it. It was only through the KPD that I learned about the class struggle and saw that the Jews were victims, too. But you did not stop at mere prejudice, Herr Gruen. You were a member of Waffen SS, the Death's Head. You were part of the machinery of terror and mass extermination. A little prejudice is one thing; the wanton butchery of human life is another. And it wasn't just the Jews that your maniacal organization sought to destroy. There were Poles, Russians, Slavs, homosexuals, political dissidents, Gypsies, the mentally retarded. . . . The list is depressingly long. Don't insult me with excuses for your behavior."

"You killed my pilots, Herr Koenig. The Hendrys. They were innocent people, yet you killed them. What excuses do you make for that?"

Koenig shook his head. "Their death was an accident."

"That's a callous dismissal of their lives. How can you call it an accident? You created the conditions that killed them."

Koenig decided not to reply. He smoked his cigarette in silence, his rheumy eyes focused on the blank wall in back of Grunwald's bunk.

"Have you enough to eat, Herr Gruen?" he asked, finally.

Grunwald nodded.

"Is there anything else I can do for you?"

"Let me out for some fresh air."

"We are in a submarine."

"Just let me out of this damned prison for a few minutes."

"I'll think about it," Koenig promised. "Anything else?"

"Give me a watch, so that I can keep the time."

"You have no need of the time."

"Then give me the answers to my questions. Where are we? Where am I being taken? When will I be released?"

Koenig stood up. "Soon, Herr Gruen. I promise you I will answer those questions very soon." The German tapped on the bulkhead door for the guard to open it. "But," he added, his pocked face drawn in a tight grin, "I can't promise that you will like any of the answers."

42

Vietnam

Rob preceded Billy down the narrow steps that led into the main tunnel complex. His brother's mood had shifted again. Minutes before he had been abusive; now he seemed melancholy.

"What makes you think Wyler wants to kill you?"

"Long Ba," Billy replied, his voice flat. "You ever hear of Long Ba?"

"Wyler told me you were trapped there by a NVA regiment."

"Is that all he told you?"

"He said they wiped you out. And massacred the villagers."

"He lied to you," Billy murmured. As they twisted down the spiral well of steps, Billy's voice alternately faded and swelled. "The NVA didn't kill the villagers."

At the bottom of the well, Billy stopped and played his light down the tunnel. The long passage swallowed the flashlight beam in darkness. "We turned the electric generator off," he explained. "The enemy has sensors that can pick up vibrations."

"Where are your men?"

"Deployed outside the tunnels. We're going to ambush some of their convoys. Put them on the defensive."

"You said the NVA didn't kill the villagers."

Billy nodded. "We had been taking steady casualties from the place for months. At least two snipers were operating out of there, and they were setting up mines and booby traps everywhere, picking us off one by one. And under our rules of engagement, there wasn't a damned thing we could do about it. Every time we searched the place we found nothing. This time we were determined to end the harassment. We moved in at dawn and stayed there all day. We rounded everyone up in the main square and tore every inch of the ville apart. We found a few pistols and an old entrance to a tunnel complex. That was it. We interrogated a few people, but, as usual, they denied everything.''

Billy led Rob down a side tunnel. Several of the wooden supports overhead had rotted away, leaving a mound of spilled earth and rock in the middle of the tunnel floor. They stepped over the debris.

"Who killed the villagers, then?" Rob asked. He feared he knew the answer already. That obscure newspaper article Gilmore had searched out with his computer weeks ago had hinted at it.

"You have to understand a few things, Robbie," his brother said. "Fear and hate, and how they can act on you. The villagers and us— we feared and hated them; they feared and hated us. We were both victims of circumstance—the poor inhabitants of that godforsaken little collection of thatched huts, and the bunch of ignorant and confused American kids in my company. We were caught in the middle, between the ruthlessness of the Vietcong and the stupidity and insensitivity of the U.S. military. But if we were going to have to stay in the area, I had to make it safe for my men to operate there. We had to pacify that village. That was what was on my mind that day. We couldn't walk away from it again and lose another man to sniper fire or a booby trap the next day. We had to clean that place out, somehow. . . . I had lost radio contact with headquarters, so I sent two men back for a new radio and to request instructions. We waited, but they never returned. We kept the villagers out in the square all day. . . .''

Billy broke off his narrative and directed the flashlight beam into a low, cryptlike chamber off the passageway. "We put Wyler in here," Billy said. Rob shone his own light around the airless dungeon and shuddered. The body of Wyler's victim had been dragged inside and left there. He lay on his back in the middle of the earth floor, arms and legs flung out, his head turned to the side. Blood from his nose and mouth caked his neck and the side of his head. Insects were crawling on his face, and the smell was overpoweringly fetid.

Billy let his beam play briefly over the body. "His name was Nguyen Din Vien," he said. "He was from the south—Mekong Delta area. He came to me a year ago. His father was a local official for the Thieu government. The Communists killed him." Billy led Rob back out into the passageway and closed the door to the cell. "We'll bury him at first light," he said. "Before the rats get him."

He flashed the light quickly down the tunnel in opposite directions to satisfy himself that no one was lurking nearby, and picked up the thread of his narrative again: "My men were going crazy with the suspense, waiting for me to give some order. The villagers must have sensed the danger they were in. The tension in the square was something you could feel."

Billy paused for a long time, as if reviewing the incident in his mind. "I should have ordered a withdrawal. But I was blinded by my own fear of losing the respect of my men. They were spoiling for revenge, and if I called a retreat, after all those hours, I was afraid they might even refuse my order. I might lose my authority over them."

Rob waited silently for his brother to go on. Billy seemed lost in thought. He stared at the wall of the tunnel near him, as if for a moment he wasn't sure where he was. "I put Wyler in charge of guarding the villagers in the square," he said, finally. "Wyler and three other men. That was a mistake. I knew Wyler was unstable. He had lost a buddy the week before to a Claymore and he was aching to kill somebody. . . . He claimed later that a kid threw a rock at him. He opened fire and killed the kid. The villagers went berserk, and the other Marines started shooting. Once it started, I couldn't stop it. I lost control of my men. In a couple of minutes the square was a carpet of dead bodies."

Billy shined the flashlight down the passageway again. "I learned a lot about leadership that day," he said.

They walked in silence, their flashlight beams illuminating the deserted subterranean warren in cones of ghostly white.

Billy continued: "I made a lot of mistakes that day. I took so long trying to decide what to do, I gave some villager time to slip away and alert a nearby NVA regiment. They surrounded the village and I had no way to call in help. They decimated us."

He paused, then began again, speaking rapidly, as if eager to be rid of the words and the thoughts attached to them. "Those of us who lived were marched to North Vietnam. It took two months. We were paraded through dozens of villages, and at each stop the locals were encouraged to torment us. Somehow they learned that Wyler had started things, and he was singled out for the worst punishment. That's how he lost his eye. Twice I managed to intervene and save him. Six of us died on that march."

Billy raised the pistol and tapped the barrel against Rob's chest, using it like his forefinger to emphasize a point. "In Hanoi they brought me to trial for the killings in the village." His eyes flashed, and his voice became hoarse with emotion. "Wyler testified against me. He said I had ordered the massacre. He said I had threatened the men with court-martials if they refused to obey. He was very convincing. His head was bandaged from the eye injury, and he groveled and whined and played for sympathy before those North Vietnamese military judges. He told them he had felt horror at being forced to carry out my orders. Imagine. He felt horror! He was a member of the exploited working class, he said. He cited examples from his childhood. And I was the idle son of a rich family whose father had bought me an officer's commission. The massacre was just another example of capitalist oppression!"

Billy waved the pistol menacingly in Rob's face. "That was Wyler's repayment for my saving his life. After the trial they took me away and I never saw him again." Billy let the pistol fall heavily to his side. He dropped his chin against his chest in dejection. "I was found guilty," he said, his voice suddenly weak. "I was sent to a special place north of Hanoi. I lived there for five years in solitary. I never spoke to a soul. Even the guards were forbidden to speak to me. So I talked to myself. In whispers. I learned to think out loud in Vietnamese. I still do it. It's a habit now. I didn't even know about the peace treaty and the repatriation of the American POWs until two years after it happened. That was in 1975, when the north took over the south. When that happened, I realized that they would probably never let me go home."

Billy stopped at a trapdoor and pulled it open. "Wyler must be down here," he said, "on the bottom level. It's the best place to hide."

Rob nodded. The flood of adrenaline following Billy's near miss with a bullet had worn off, and weariness was overtaking him. His leg muscles fluttered from fatigue. The flashlight and the pistol began to feel like barbells in his hands.

Billy showed no hint of slowing down. He looked so desiccated, so sickly, yet his metabolism raced. Rob wondered if he ever slept or ate. He seemed to be consuming himself, burning energy from some internal fire and fueling it with his own flesh.

"Let's rest for a minute, first," Rob said. Without waiting for a reply, he flopped down beside the trapdoor and draped his arms over his knees. "I don't have your energy."

Billy remained standing. "It's not energy," he said. "It's willpower. That's one thing all those years in Vietnamese prisons teach you. You need a lot of it to survive."

Rob let his head sag forward against his knees. "Were you treated badly?"

"They brought in this East German, Koenig, to interrogate me. He took me apart and tried to build someone else out of the pieces."

"Did he?"

"He hammered at me until I didn't know what to believe about anything. He was diabolical. He burrowed his way into my head, into my dreams, until he seemed to live inside me, a parasite eating away at my brain. He was clever and pitiless. It's painful to talk about him. Part of him is still with me. He still terrifies me. It's because of him that I don't sleep very well anymore."

Billy slumped against the wall of the tunnel. "After Koenig I felt that I had died. I knew then that I could never return home, even if they ever decided to free me. Home was a place that wasn't there anymore. It was dead and gone. A previous life."

"Because of Long Ba?"

"Yeah. I knew the Marines would court-martial me. Hang it all around my neck. I'd have been a disgrace. But that wasn't the only reason. Koenig told me about our old man. He knew all about him, what he had done. Everything."

A low-pitched boom vibrated the floor of the tunnel. Several more explosions followed, rumbling in the distance like summer thunder.

"Artillery," Billy said. "The softening up before the attack."

Another shell exploded somewhere far overhead, and Billy tilted his face upward, listening. "They can shell us all night long. They won't make a dent." Billy waved his arm. "Let's find Wyler."

Rob pushed himself to his feet. "What did Koenig know about our father?"

"It doesn't matter anymore."

"Don't pull big brother on me now. It had to do with Dachau, didn't it. He did something dishonorable when he was there."

Billy laughed.

"Tell me, for chrissake!"

"Our father was one of the camp guards. He was in the SS."

"That can't be true."

"It's true, all right. His real name was Willi Gruen. He escaped capture by disguising himself as a prisoner. Then he spent his whole life pretending to be a Jew."

Rob felt as if there was no air left to breathe. He pressed his palms against his eyes and leaned his head on his knees and tried to get his breath back. His mind began tripping over a mad jumble of images and recollections of his father. It would take him a long time to sort it all out, but he had the overwhelming intuition that it was all going to make sense now. His brother had just handed him the key to everything.

"Koenig, the East German," Billy muttered. "He knew all that because he'd been a prisoner at Dachau. He saw our father kill one of his friends the night the camp was liberated. A middle-aged Jew named Simon Grunwald. He killed him and stole his prison clothes. Koenig showed me proof. He had painstakingly documented our father's entire life. He was obsessed by him—by what he had done. He said that one day he planned to destroy him. He didn't know how yet, but he said one day he'd do it."

Billy held the pistol up and pointed it at an imaginary target beyond the tunnel wall. "I worshiped our father," he said. "Then I learn his whole life was a fucking lie. And our world was built on it. Built on it! Imagine, Robbie. Imagine our disgrace if that story ever gets out! Koenig still holds this over us. He promised me that we would all be punished for what our father had done. And he's a man of his word. How could I come home and face that? I'd rather take my punishment here."

Billy reached down and pulled Rob to his feet. "Let's go find Wyler," he said. "I want to tell the dumb bastard that he never had anything to worry about. If he'd just stayed home, his dirty little secret would never have left Vietnam. But he outsmarted himself."

Rob staggered on his feet. He felt sick from the emotional shock. He waved the flashlight around as if the light might drive away the claustrophobic blackness that pressed in on them. His eyes caught something in the beam of light, and he moved it back and steadied it on the long section of tunnels directly ahead of him.

Wyler was not on the bottom level after all. He was standing right there in front of them, not thirty feet away.

He looked enormous in the narrow confines of the tunnel, his broad shoulders seeming to brush the walls. His hair was matted with sweat, and his face looked wild—lips drawn back against his teeth, his one eye popped open like a clown miming surprise. He was pointing a pistol at them.

"Put down the gun, Frank," Billy said. His tone was stern, an officer giving an order to a recruit.

Wyler stared at Billy with undisguised terror. "You can't come home, you bastard!" he shouted. "Never!"

"I'm not *going* home, Frank. Give me the gun."

"I have to kill you," Wyler replied, his voice trembling. "I have to."

Billy laughed. "You came all this way for nothing, Frank. It's not necessary to kill me at all."

"I have to," Wyler repeated. He steadied the pistol with both hands and opened fire. The explosions ricocheted in the tunnel with a deafening clamor. Rob fell flat and hugged the packed-earth floor.

"Turn out your light!" Billy yelled.

Rob grappled for the switch on his flashlight and turned it off. Total blackness. Wyler's last shot echoed down the tunnel and died, and in the awful silence, Rob heard his blood booming in his neck. Then the vibration of a deeper sound—Wyler's feet thudding heavily toward them.

Rob pulled up into a crouch and scrambled away on all fours, leaving his flashlight behind. A loud groan and the sudden smack of flesh against flesh made him stop. Wyler had found Billy in the dark.

Still on all fours, Rob groped around desperately for the flashlight. He found it, finally, turned it on, and aimed it at the noise.

Wyler was kneeling in the dirt, with Billy's neck gripped in an arm lock. He balled up his free hand and smashed it into Billy's face. Billy was kicking, his fists beating ineffectually on Wyler's back.

Wyler rose to his feet, bringing Billy up with him, and rammed Billy's head against the tunnel wall. He pulled back to repeat the blow, but Billy tripped him. They fell back into the dirt. Wyler transferred his hands to Billy's throat and closed them around it in a choke hold. He pulled his head up toward him, then slammed it against the ground with tremendous force.

"Stop it, Wyler!" Rob screamed. "Jesus Christ, stop it!"

Billy was no match for Wyler's maniacal strength. He flailed his fists against the wrestler's arms, but Wyler, his weight crushed down against Billy's neck, barely noticed.

Still yelling, Rob dropped the light and threw himself against Wyler's back, wrapping one arm around his throat and seizing his hair with the other. Wyler released his grip on Billy, pushed himself to his feet, and lunged backward, pinning Rob against the wall. He twisted around, breaking Rob's hold, snatched an arm, jerked it over his neck, and sent him flying.

Rob landed on top of Billy's pistol. It struck him directly in the chest, knocking the wind out of him. He lay there gasping.

The beam of the fallen flashlight shone along the tunnel floor, catching Billy's inert form in its path. He lay on his back, his arms at his sides, his head turned away. Wyler landed his knees hard on his stomach, then pulled his unresisting victim up by a wrist, spun him around, and smashed him into the wall. Billy slumped to the ground and Wyler jumped on him, his hands closing around his throat again.

Still wheezing from lack of air, Rob picked up the pistol and willed himself to his feet. Fighting to remain conscious, he stumbled toward Wyler. He lost his balance, fell onto the big man's arching back, and clutched his arms around his neck for support, like a child climbing on for a piggyback ride. Before Wyler could throw him off again, Rob jammed the pistol against the base of his skull and squeezed the trigger.

The bullet exploded through Wyler's brain and collapsed him like a flat tire onto Billy. Rob rolled him off and shot him twice more— once in the chest and once in the head—and then threw the pistol into the darkness. The stink of gunpowder and blasted flesh sickened him. The tunnel floor beneath him began to tilt and spin.

He dropped to his knees beside his brother and pressed a hand to his neck. Billy was still breathing. He leaned against him for support, and waited for the waves of dizziness to subside. "Don't die on me now, Billy," he whispered. "Please don't die on me now."

Thailand

Caroline had promised herself that she wouldn't even think of expecting Rob for a week, but she could think of nothing else. Sammy Rep, without intending it, made the hours pass more slowly by treating her like visiting royalty, ordering his vast horde of relatives and hangers-on to wait on her every whim. She pleaded with him to let her help in the kitchen or run errands for the hotel, but Sammy, his sense of propriety offended at the idea, adamantly refused.

Each morning after breakfast she and Lin Pao, the big revolver that Sammy had given him strapped to his skinny waist, took long trips on foot, roaming over the wild landscapes along the border of eastern Thailand. Caroline varied his daylong language lesson with as much ingenuity as she could, interspersing the drills with long stories about herself, her family, and what life was like back in the United States. This last subject particularly fascinated Lin Pao, and he would listen attentively for hours and still be eager for more.

Their walks always ended in the same place—the spot overlooking the Mekong River. Each day they spent more time there, watching the far bank, hoping to see the mission return.

Six days passed, each one doubling the anxiety of the day before.

At dusk on the seventh day something happened.

As they returned to Sammy's along the path from the river, Lin Pao suddenly stopped and held up his hand. Caroline cast her eyes rapidly along the trail in front of them, expecting to see another snake. Several days ago they had run into a cobra, and Lin Pao had killed it.

The boy pointed toward the shed that stored the expedition's one remaining jeep. Part of it was visible at a bend in the path, some distance ahead of them. "Men," he whispered.

They crouched down and watched. One man appeared around the corner of the structure, then another. Both were Caucasian. They examined the shed and the ground around it carefully but did not try to break in.

The same men returned the next day. But this time they stayed away from the shed, settling instead behind a thick screen of bushes some distance away where they could keep a watch on it.

"They wait to catch your Rob," Lin Pao said.

43

Vietnam

Dr. Huong conducted his examination with painstaking thoroughness, probing and squeezing and kneading the patient on the mattress before him with his delicate hands, nodding his head every minute or so, as if in confirmation of some as yet unspoken diagnosis. Rob stood by the window, alternately gazing out at the blasted remnants of the tropical jungle that had stretched so magnificently across the valleys to the east only the day before, and turning impatiently to see if the doctor was through. Billy lay limp under the man's probing, his eyes staring at the ceiling in a dreamy languor beyond pain.

Gilmore knelt beside Rob at the window, steadying a pair of binoculars on the ledge. "Four or five batteries off to the east, about three miles from here," he said. "They're walking them across, finding the range."

Gilmore's words were confirmed by a flash of white light, followed a split second later by a thunderous blast. Four more explosions followed, each one increasing in intensity. Five columns of smoke billowed up through the jungle canopy, forming a straight line, the farthest about a mile away on the near slope of the valley, the closest barely a half mile.

The next cluster fell to the left, about five hundred yards away. Another battery opened up from behind a second ridge line. A few minutes later a third battery joined the rising chorus of destruction, then a fourth. Shells exploded continuously across the entire valley, shredding the jewel-green jungle vegetation. The tunnel complex vibrated incessantly from the pounding.

"We're going to catch hell," Gilmore said, letting the binoculars fall on their strap against his chest.

Finally the doctor climbed up off his knees. He seemed so cool-mannered and self-contained, Rob was surprised to see the sweat streaming down his brow. Huong wiped his forehead with the sleeve of his uniform and dried his hands on the sides of his trousers.

"He has much damage," he said, his Parisian-polyclinic accent giving his English words a soft comic effect, as if he were Charles Aznavour instead of a physician who had been tending dying men all night long without sleep. "There are broken ribs, and he has damaged a lung. He has internal bleeding in the chest cavity and, most serious, a brain concussion, with signs of cerebral hemorrhage."

"What can we do?"

Huong sighed and wiped his hands against his trousers again. Rob noticed for the first time that they were smeared with blood. "I will come back later and bandage his chest. That is all I can do. He must get to a hospital."

"You know that's not possible," Rob replied, angrily.

Huong sighed again. "I will give him morphine." He reached into a canvas bag he had brought with him and searched it for a hypodermic syringe.

"He's already on drugs, isn't he?" Rob said.

"Yes," Huong replied. "I prescribed some sleeping medication."

"Is that all?"

"A stimulant."

"What kind?"

Huong found the syringe and busied himself preparing a shot. "Amphetamine," he murmured.

"You've got him hooked on the stuff."

Huong shrugged. "I tried to moderate his use. But he demanded them."

Rob dropped the subject. It was a pointless matter to debate at this stage. He watched Huong tip a bottle of alcohol onto a patch of cotton, swab Billy's upper arm, then deftly inject the needle. He packed up quickly and made a curt bow. "I will come back this evening," he promised.

"How long will he live?" Rob demanded, watching Billy's eyes flutter slightly at the question.

Huong thought about it for a minute. "Maybe not long," he said.

The doctor's answer startled him. He realized that Huong meant it in a hopeful sense: Maybe not long before he's out of his misery.

Huong hefted his canvas bag, bowed again, and left, headed back to the infirmary down on the second level from which Rob had summoned him. Filled with the screaming, untreated bodies of the burned, shot, and dismembered, it had become a cave of horrors, a vestibule of suffering. Rob had discovered that Billy's American sponsors had supplied him with tons of weapons and ammunition but almost no medical supplies. It was killing Vietnamese, not saving them, that interested the bureaucrats who had nurtured this particular folly.

Rob knelt down beside his brother and clasped his hand. In the dripping heat it felt cold and dry. "Billy?"

Billy opened his eyes and squeezed Rob's fingers. "What's the situation?" he mumbled.

"The doctor says you've got serious injuries—"

Billy shook his head. "No, no . . . What's the situation . . . down below?"

"Bad. We're going to get you out of here."

"No, no," Billy said. He tried to sit up but quickly abandoned the effort. He closed his eyes and rocked his head back and forth on the pillow, talking to himself. "Must get up," he repeated in a barely audible voice. "Must get up . . . Defend the revolution."

A whistling noise overhead made Rob duck instinctively. A round exploded in the grove. The room flashed bright white for an instant, and the mosquito netting that had been hooked to the side of the window opening flapped inward like a flag in a stiff wind. Behind the clap of the first concussion there followed a deep, shuddering roar, like that of a long wave crashing onto a beach. A choking stink of smoke and sulphur drifted into the room.

"We better get out," Gilmore said, crouching beneath the window ledge.

"Where's Ferrer? And Billy's wives?"

"Down with the wounded."

"Will you get one of them up here to take care of Billy? Then meet me in the command post. I'm going to talk to Colonel Tieu."

Rob found Colonel Tieu sitting with three members of his staff at the big table that dominated the cavelike interior of the command post. Billy had introduced him to the colonel earlier. A broad-faced, handsome man in his early forties, he defied the stereotype of the career military officer in almost every respect. He was soft-spoken and gentle, a man of culture and education, who had taught economics at the University of Saigon before enlisting in the South Vietnamese army. Rob had liked him instantly.

A small portable generator was chugging quietly in a far corner, powering the radios and two overhead lights. The Vietnamese officers looked pale and disheveled from lack of sleep.

Their eyes followed Rob anxiously as he moved to Billy's empty chair at the end of the table and stood behind it. "My brother's dying," he said bluntly. "You'll have to carry on without him."

Colonel Tieu translated his words to the other officers. They greeted the news with resignation. They had already assumed as much.

"What's your situation?" Rob asked Tieu.

Tieu stood up and stepped to the pair of large maps pinned to the blackboard. One was hand-drawn in heavy ink markers and showed the tunnel system. The other was a large topographical map of the Khe Sanh–Lang Vei area.

"There are three main forces moving in on us down these roads," Tieu explained, in his cool, professorial manner. "One from the northeast, one from the east, one from the south. There are no main routes in from the west; it's too near the border. The one reconnaissance we've made there shows only the usual patrols along the river. The main forces are still three or four miles away, waiting for the shelling to stop. We think they'll fan out through the jungle during the night and attack tomorrow at dawn."

"How many troops do they have?"

Tieu conferred in Vietnamese with the other officers. "We estimate fifty thousand."

Rob shook his head. "You're hopelessly outnumbered. What do you plan to do?"

Tieu looked at the other officers, then back at Rob. "We're safe in the tunnels. The enemy can't see us, can't hit us. If they try to overrun us, their casualties will be unacceptably high. We have less than two hundred men left, but we're better trained than the government troops." Tieu paused, and then added, with heavy emphasis: "And we have far more reason to fight."

"What's to prevent them from simply surrounding you and starving you out?" Rob asked.

"We can't be surrounded in the classic sense," Tieu replied, stiffly. "The tunnel system is vast. There are several exits, some of them a mile from here. The enemy cannot find them all."

"How many casualties did you take last night?"

Tieu refused to answer.

Gilmore walked in and Rob confronted him immediately. "How many wounded in the infirmary, Howard?"

Gilmore adjusted his glasses. "Forty or fifty," he replied.

Rob turned to Tieu. "So you must have left at least half that many dead behind. What went wrong?"

Tieu cleared his throat and stared at the blackboard. "We planned to ambush two convoys, but we were spotted and cut off. We were fortunate to get anyone back."

Rob nodded. "Who's in charge now? Are you?"

Tieu averted his eyes. One of the officers muttered something in Vietnamese and shook his head. Tieu answered him sharply. Rob waited but got no response. He repeated the question, and to his amazement, Tieu just sat down.

"Someone has to command the defense of the tunnels," he said to Tieu. "Aren't you the senior officer?"

Tieu nodded. "Yes, I am," he began, "But . . ."

Rob waited for him to complete his thought, but he left it hanging in the air. "Your brother has led us well. None of us can replace him," he said.

"*Someone* had better replace him," Rob replied, alarmed at his attitude. "Your situation is desperate."

Tieu and the other officers just stared at him politely, as if they were privy to some secret knowledge they could not share with him. The truth dawned on him, suddenly. Billy had no second-in-command. No one wielded any real authority but him. And none of his officers, faced with such a grim situation, was anxious to assume responsibility.

From behind him, Rob felt Gilmore's hand fall on his shoulder. "Can I have a private word with you?"

Mystified, Rob followed his friend out into the passageway.

"Don't you see what's going on in there?" Gilmore said.

"Yes. A leadership crisis. Nobody knows what to do."

Gilmore nodded solemnly. "That's part of it."

"What's the rest?"

"They want you to take Billy's place."

Rob looked at Gilmore as if he had just grown a second head. "What have you been smoking, Howard?"

"It's true. They've already talked to me about it. They are too polite to ask you outright. They know that that would be too big an imposition. But if you volunteered, then they could accept without feeling guilty about it. And if you volunteered, it would further persuade them that you're the right choice to take over."

356 / TOM HYMAN

"Jesus Christ, this is ridiculous. Not only am I the least qualified, I don't even embrace their cause. I just want to get Billy out of here."

"That may be the only way to do it."

Rob planted his hands on his hips. "It's crazy, Howard."

"I'll admit it sounds it, but these people sometimes know things that we don't. They see you as Billy's brother. That's what's important to them. They believe you must possess the same qualities. The same karma. And maybe they're right."

"You agree with them?" Rob asked, incredulous.

Gilmore nodded. "They're paralyzed in there. Afraid to act. They want your leadership. Give it to them. Don't worry about your lack of experience. They understand that as well as you. That's not what they're looking for. They know they're in deep trouble, and they think you'll have the same instinct to do the best thing that Billy had. They want your luck, not your experience."

"My luck? What luck?"

"Look," Gilmore said. "You saw how they acted when you demanded to know who was in charge. Everything you said was only confirming what they already believe. That you're the one to take over. They just don't know how to approach you about it. You have to show them you're willing to take charge. And what do you have to lose? We'll all be helping you. Do it, for chrissake. We're in a desperate situation."

"Jesus, Howard, you're scaring the hell out of me."

"Nonsense. I've watched your transformation since that night you first showed up on my doorstep in Wilmington. You're the man. You can do it, if anyone can. They believe it. I believe it."

"They just want a scapegoat," Rob protested. "Someone to pin the blame on. They're not getting out of here and they know it. They just want to take me down with them."

Gilmore squeezed Rob's shoulder with his big palm. "You've been drafted, ol' buddy. And this is one draft you aren't going to evade."

Rob looked at his friend, astonished. Gilmore just nodded.

They walked back into the command post. No one spoke. Rob saw four frightened faces around the table, watching him. The thunder of the enemy guns above them penetrated the silence. Rob turned to Colonel Tieu. The gentle professor's mouth was drawn in a tense frown. "I, ah, I'll take command," Rob murmured. "If you like."

Tieu translated Rob's offer to the other three. A brief discussion followed, and Rob saw each man nod his head. Tieu cleared his throat. "You are Billy's blood," he replied. "We accept your offer."

"I don't promise anything."

Tieu tilted his head solemnly. "We understand."

Rob looked at Gilmore. Gilmore grinned back at him. Well, why not? he thought. What was there to lose? He walked over to Billy's empty chair and sat in it. The tension that had hovered in the chamber from the moment he first entered evaporated almost visibly. A gulf had been crossed. A decision made.

"Thank you for your confidence in me," he said, hardly believing what was happening even as he spoke. "It's probably misplaced, but I'll try to live up to it. I'll need the help of all of you."

Tieu translated, and the officers smiled reassuringly.

Rob's instinct told him that he must act at once to inspire some confidence. They wanted a leader, so he had better start playing that role.

"We're about to be overrun," he declared. "It doesn't take a military genius to see that. What are our choices? First, we can stay here and fight. We're surrounded and outnumbered, so sooner or later we'll all be killed or captured. Does anyone disagree with that analysis?"

Tieu translated. No one disagreed.

"Second, we can surrender right now. Save lives. Get it over with. Admit defeat. We'll be taken prisoner, but we'll survive. And the wounded will get medical attention."

Tieu flinched in dismay. "Most of us are wanted men," he said. "If we surrender, they'll kill us, and Billy for certain. It's him they want most."

"That leaves escape."

Tieu looked puzzled. "Escape?"

"Why not?"

"But, as you say, we are surrounded."

"That doesn't mean we can't get out. You escaped with Billy from a government prison three years ago, didn't you?"

Tieu nodded. "Tell us how we can do it, then."

Rob glanced up at the maps on the blackboard. How indeed. He stood up and invited Tieu to join him in front of the maps. "How many exits are there from the tunnels, Colonel?"

"Five," Tieu replied, pointing them out on the map.

"What's their status?"

"The north one, here, is useless. We retreated through it this morning. The enemy found it and dynamited it. The east one is near an artillery emplacement. This one, to the southeast, is near an occupied village road. We'd be spotted quickly. This one, to the southwest, opens into harsh terrain. Mountains and heavy jungle. Travel would be very slow."

"What about the last one?" Rob asked.

Tieu shrugged. "That's far to the west."

"That's the one we were brought in through, isn't it?"

"Yes."

"It's well hidden inside a stockade. What's the matter with it?"

"It's a long tunnel, very narrow. Hard to move men and supplies. The far end is in the middle of heavy jungle. Hard to move from there."

"It sounds perfect," Rob said. "We'll use it. And it's only about two miles from the Laotian border. How many men are fit enough to travel?"

Tieu conferred with the other officers. "We estimate about one hundred men," he replied.

"Get them together right away. Load everyone with all the ammo belts and grenades he can carry, a canteen of water, and two days' supply of food. Take all the RPGs we can manage, as well. We'll start moving out as soon as it gets dark. We can assemble tonight in the stockade at the other end of the exit and plan our next move from there. The main thing is to get as far away from here as we can before the main attack comes."

Tieu rubbed his chin nervously. "That means abandoning the wounded."

"We have no choice. They'll be better off as prisoners. And the quicker it happens, the faster they'll get proper medical treatment."

"What about Billy?" Gilmore asked.

"We're taking Billy with us," Rob replied. "That's the whole point, isn't it?"

Tieu translated Rob's words to the other officers. One of them replied at some length. Tieu nodded, and the other two officers seemed to agree.

Tieu related his remarks to Rob. "Escape is no good," he said, with a trembling sigh. "We must stay and fight."

"Why?"

Tieu hesitated, searching for the right words: "We'll all die if we leave here. Even if we escape, we have no place to go. They will hunt us down."

Rob wondered if his tenure as commander hadn't just come to an end. He glared angrily at the officers. "You want to hole up here and die like rats? We *have* to escape!"

"Where can we go?" Tieu persisted. "We cannot return home. We will all be fugitives."

"Look," Rob replied, "I can't promise you'll all make it. All I can promise is that you'll at least have a chance if you get out of this death-trap. A hundred men is a powerful guerrilla force. And you're well trained for it. You can run, you can hide, you can hit back. You'll have a chance."

Tieu translated this, but the others shook their heads. "We still don't know where we will go," Tieu repeated.

Rob sat back and took a deep breath. He understood. These men were homeless in their own land. Exiles. He looked at the map, his eyes moving up and down the long, thin stocking of Vietnam, sensing the desolation they must feel. To them, there was nowhere that wasn't behind enemy lines. Their resistance movement, however futile and misguided, gave them a place. A home, a cause. Now it had collapsed, and with it, their hope.

Suddenly he knew where they could go. It was the obvious answer. The only solution. Both to his problem and theirs. "Thailand," he declared.

"Where?"

"Thailand."

Tieu's eyes widened. "Thailand?"

"The Thai government will grant you asylum."

Tieu translated. The officers shook their heads. "It is not possible to get there," Tieu said.

"Of course it is," Rob replied. He reached up and put his finger on the map at Khe Sanh and drew it six inches across to the left. "We go right through Laos."

Tieu was visibly stunned. "Through Laos? How?"

Rob rested his hands on his hips and grinned. "Simple," he said. "We fight our way across."

Eastern Thailand

Sammy Rep objected, but he didn't try to stop them. He and one of his sons took them down to the river before dawn on the eighth day, pulled the rowboat from its hiding place in the water, and rowed them across to the other side. Each carried a full backpack, weighted with one of Sammy's revolvers and a box of .38 shells. Lin Pao had wanted to take his father's automatic rifle, but Sammy persuaded him that pistols were much safer.

Going had been Lin Pao's idea. At first Caroline had dismissed it as too dangerous. But finally she accepted the necessity of it. They must get to Rob and warn him before he walked into the trap waiting for him by the shed.

And she doubted that she could have stood another day of waiting, anyway.

44

Vietnam

Rob looked at the faces crowded around him, their expressions grim in the weak yellow light of the kerosene lamps. A heavy blanket had been nailed across the big window as a blackout curtain, shutting off the fresh air from outside. The crush of bodies was raising the temperature of the room to the oppressive levels of a steam bath, draining energy from every movement, making even the act of drawing breath unpleasant.

Colonel Tieu had gathered seven of his best men to coordinate the evacuation. They were all in their thirties and forties—too old and too proud to start life over again under the Communists. They had all been with Billy in the great prison breakout north of Hanoi three years earlier and were marked by the present regime as criminals.

"Are we ready?" he asked Tieu.

Tieu nodded solemnly.

"Weapons? Ammunition? Food? Water?"

"All we can carry," Tieu replied.

"What's the condition of the west tunnel?"

"The air is bad," Tieu said. "But the tunnel is clear."

"Including the stockade at the other end?"

"Clear."

"What if it's not clear by the time we get there? Are there any alternatives? The last thing we want is to get trapped underground."

"There is an additional emergency escape exit off the tunnel," Tieu informed him. "The main one comes up inside the stockade village. The other is a distance away, in the jungle. It's well hidden."

"Okay. Now, somebody responsible has to stay here and formally surrender the place. Who do we have who's willing to stay behind to do that?"

Before Tieu could answer, Ghislene Ferrer called out from her place near the window. "I'll do it."

"Aren't you coming with us?"

"I can be of more help this way. I will stay and help get the wounded moved out onto the grove. They can't be left down below much longer. The air is becoming impossible. They will suffocate."

"You'll be taken prisoner," Rob warned her.

Ferrer treated him to her superior smile. "*Mon cher*, you forget who I am."

"How can I," Rob joked, "when you constantly remind me?"

"I am a personal friend of Premier Pham Van Dong," she declared. "Far from being taken prisoner, I will be treated very well."

"They'll be in an ugly mood when they don't find Billy."

"I will persuade them not to be. And I will use my influence to get the best possible treatment for the wounded."

"That's very generous of you."

"Not entirely," she admitted. "If I go with you, I think I will be exposed to greater danger than if I stay behind. And I am anxious to file my story."

"From here?"

"From the nearest town with a telephone," she replied.

"Will the government let you?"

"I don't intend to ask their permission. Our wire service, Agence France Presse, has a bureau in Hanoi. I will call there."

"And the bureau chief is a close friend of yours," Rob said.

"You mock me."

Rob smiled. "Good luck," he said.

Ferrer threw her arms around him and kissed him fiercely on the mouth. "It is you who need the good luck," she whispered. "Whatever happens, you can be sure that I will tell the world your story."

Rob laughed uncomfortably, embarrassed in front of the others. "Don't write any epitaphs, Ghislene. Believe it or not, I expect to live through this."

Ferrer's eyes filmed with tears. "I am sorry," she blurted out. "My Gallic emotion is showing." With that confession, she snatched a kerosene lamp from the table and disappeared down the corridor toward the tunnels below.

Rob looked at Tieu and the officers, then turned to Gilmore, who had been patiently standing against the back wall. "Let's get Billy," he said, "and get the hell out of here."

In the adjoining room, Billy was lying with his head propped up on a rolled blanket. His two Vietnamese mistresses had changed his clothes, washed him, and combed his hair. They had decided to stay behind and take their chances with the government. They sat on each side of him, sniffling back the tears while Dr. Huong injected a shot of morphine into his arm.

The doctor rummaged in his canvas sack and produced a packet of disposable hypodermic needles and a bottle of liquid. "This is enough painkiller to last for a few days," he said, handing the bottle and the needles to Rob. "Inject him every four hours."

"I wish you were coming with us, Doctor," Rob said, holding the equipment awkwardly in his hand, not sure where to store it.

"I am needed here."

"Of course. How is Billy?"

"About the same. No better, no worse."

"Any advice?"

Huong scratched the plunger end of the hypo he had just used against his smooth chin. "Time is the crucial thing," he said.

Rob and Gilmore strapped Billy into the special stretcher they had constructed. Its poles would rest in harnesses on their shoulders, to stabilize it on uneven ground and to allow them free use of their hands in an emergency. Two of Billy's younger officers, men who had served him as informal aides and bodyguards, agreed to bracket Rob and Gilmore, one in front and one in back, and to alternate with them in carrying the stretcher.

Billy opened his eyes. "Leave me here, Robbie," he whispered.

"You need a hospital," Rob replied.

"I belong here . . . with these people."

"They're coming with you, so be quiet. Save your energy."

His brother managed a feeble grin. "Getting your way at last."

"You're going home."

"Can't face it."

Rob lay the palm of his hand lightly on Billy's forehead. "You have to face it."

With Gilmore he hoisted the stretcher from the floor and stood, holding the poles at his sides, like the handles of a wheelbarrow. Its heaviness surprised him.

"We'll have to maneuver it like this down those stairs," Gilmore said, "and probably through the tunnels. When we're outside, we can hoist him on our shoulders. He'll feel a lot lighter then."

"Let's go," Rob replied.

The winding stairs were impossible to negotiate, and finally Gilmore unstrapped Billy and carried him down piggyback. Rob followed with the rolled-up stretcher.

The one hundred remaining members of the Army of the New Vietnam were already in place, standing in line with their equipment and weapons along the main passageway to the west tunnel, waiting to begin the breakout. Tieu led the way to the front of the line, followed by the other officers, then the two bodyguards, now carrying Billy's stretcher. Rob and Gilmore brought up the rear. Everyone they passed saluted Billy in the stretcher and then saluted Rob.

Rob was surprised and moved. He looked each soldier in the face and touched him on the shoulder as he walked by. Several in the ranks were young women. One hundred strangers, he thought, putting their lives in his hands. And for no other reason than that he was Billy's brother. It sent chills through him.

When they reached the entrance into the west tunnel, no order was necessary. Rob simply gave Tieu a little nod and they started down the narrow passageway. The soldiers at the front of the line fell in behind them, and the entire column followed.

To the damp and rotting odors that normally permeated these underground passages were now added smoke fumes and an acrid, slaughterhouse stench that increased in strength the farther they progressed. The beams from their flashlights materialized into dancing shafts of light, like a car's headlights in a night fog.

Rob gagged. "What the hell is it?" he complained.

"Smells of battle," Gilmore said. "Probably sucked down from the surface shelling."

A hundred yards along, the procession suddenly stopped. Rob stepped up beside one of the bodyguards carrying Billy's stretcher. His face was filmed with sweat. "Are we at the exit?"

The bodyguard shook his head. "No, no," he whispered, his expression tense. "Much farther."

The delay continued. Rob walked up to Tieu, at the front of the column. Incredibly, he saw the colonel talking to an old Vietnamese woman with a child in her arms. She had just come down the west tunnel from the other direction.

Tieu saw Rob and shook his head with agitation. "They've captured the stockade," he said.

"How many of them?"

Tieu asked her. She didn't know.

"Do they know about this tunnel?"

Tieu repeated Rob's question. Rob saw, from the expression on her leathery face, what the answer was before Tieu translated it.

"Yes," he said. "They've set up an ambush at the top of the ladder at the other end. This woman was in the tunnel when they discovered it, on her way back to the stockade. She and her grandchild hid when she heard them. She said there are probably a dozen soldiers in the hut that sits over the trapdoor."

"Are any of them in the tunnel?"

"She says not so far."

Rob thanked the woman. Tieu assigned a soldier to escort her and the child back up the tunnel to the command post, where she'd be safe until the surrender.

"How far back from the main exit is the branch off to the emergency exit?"

"Twenty meters," he said. "Maybe less."

"Not very far. Can we sneak by?"

"If no one is in the tunnel, they can't see us."

"One of us will have to go out there first and see."

"There is a better way," Tieu advised him. "All the exits are mined with explosives. We can blow the tunnel shaft closed." Tieu reached up and patted the wooden beam over his head. "The charge is placed here, in the support timbers, just before the ladder. Enough dynamite to collapse the roof of the tunnel."

"And then we duck out the emergency hatch," Rob said.

"Yes. It will take us far away from the stockade."

"How far is that?"

Tieu thought again. "A hundred meters."

"Little better than a football field."

"Very heavy jungle," Tieu reminded him.

"If it's still there," Rob said, thinking of the relentless shelling that had been going on all day long.

The soldier who had escorted the old woman returned at a run, talking rapidly. As Tieu listened to him, his expression turned bleak.

"What's he saying?'" Rob asked.

"The enemy has taken the whole place. He said they are everywhere overhead. They must have infiltrated one of the other tunnels. He left the woman and child on their own and came back as fast as he could."

"Did anyone see him?"

"No. He says he closed the bulkhead door off the main passageway and jammed it shut from this side."

Only Tieu's flashlight was turned on, and the faces of the men around Rob were hidden in shadow. He didn't have to see them to know what they were thinking.

Gilmore moved up beside Rob. "They'll find this tunnel before long," he said. "What'll they do then?"

Tieu spread his hands out. "Blast it shut."

"What if someone tells them we're in here?" Rob asked. "Like that old woman we just let go?"

Tieu chewed on his lip, thinking about it, then just shook his head in despair.

"Never mind," Rob said, holding his voice as steady as his nerves would allow. "Our choice is simple. We go out the emergency exit. And we better get out fast."

"What about the dynamite?" Tieu asked.

"We leave it alone. So far no one knows we're here. Let's keep it that way."

Tieu nodded and brushed the sleeve of his uniform across his brow. "They might see us from the stockade exit," he whispered.

"With a little luck, they won't," Rob replied. "We'll sneak through in the dark. Bring someone up here who knows this tunnel."

Tieu pointed to one of the other officers standing beside them. "He supervised work on it last spring."

Tieu translated what he had said, and the officer, a young man from Hue named Captain Deng, nodded eagerly.

Rob shook his hand. "Tell him to run up and check the emergency exit all the way to the end and get back here as fast as possible."

Captain Deng set out immediately. Rob watched him disappear into the darkness beyond the glow of their flashlights, his hand on the tunnel wall to guide him.

The minutes passed with glacial slowness. Rob marveled at the discipline of the soldiers standing in the long column behind him. They were facing the terrifying prospect of being trapped alive underground, and the delay must be working on their nerves as much as on his. He suspected that part of their self-control stemmed from their faith in him. *God help me not to disappoint them*, he prayed.

The young officer returned ten minutes later, his mud-covered face stricken. He spilled out a jumble of words to Tieu while Rob waited impatiently for the translation. When he got it, he couldn't believe it.

Government troops had set up a field camp right at the emergency exit. In fact, the exit hatchway, Captain Deng explained, carefully concealed under a movable flat rock, was now inside the enemy's mess tent.

Laos

Caroline sat under the shade of a large tree and looked out across the village's unkempt collection of bamboo huts, raised on platforms to keep out the snakes and the rain, and contemplated their situation.

A cloud of flies buzzed around her in the heat. She felt more exhausted and depressed than she could ever remember. The day thus far had been both an ordeal and a failure. She and Lin Pao had walked for four hours over rugged, dangerous trails to Lin Pao's village to ask for help, and the village had refused.

The problem was starkly simple: None of the men in the village could even consider going without their chief's permission, and the formidable Tan wouldn't give it. Caroline pleaded with him personally, but the squat giant had stood his ground, his thick arms crossed over his chest, his normally menacing demeanor polite but unmoved. His reasons, as best she could make out from Lin Pao's halting efforts at translation, had to do with spirits. Rob's expedition had too many bad ghosts. It was unlucky. If he let any of his men go, they would be unlucky, too. And so would she. And Lin Pao.

His complacent stubbornness had infuriated her. She had lectured him, telling him that he at least owed Lin Pao a favor, having killed his father. But Tan had not been persuaded. As a last resort, she had offered him a substantial sum of money. He had turned the offer down without hesitation.

Bad spirits, she realized, were an argument that just could not be overcome.

She watched Lin Pao emerge from one of the huts carrying a couple of wooden bowls squeezed between his one arm and his chest. It always moved her to see how bravely and well he coped with the thousand small daily activities of life made more difficult by having only that one arm.

The bowls contained a fermented fish of some kind on a bed of rice. The smell of rotting fish made her gag. She picked listlessly at the rice around the edges and gave the rest to Lin Pao, who gobbled it down voraciously. She wondered how he would take to a Big Mac or a Whopper.

"We can stay tonight," he said, pointing to an unused hut near the edge of the forest. "Over there."

"Then what?" she asked him.

He smiled up at her mischievously. "Go find Rob," he replied.

"By ourselves?"

He nodded. He rummaged in the pocket of his shorts and pulled out an ignition key and dangled it in front of her. "We take the big truck," he said.

45

Vietnam

"We'll have to surrender," Gilmore said.

Rob looked at his friend's face in the reflected glow of the flashlights. He was stroking his beard nervously. Rob turned to Colonel Tieu. "Do you agree?"

"Yes," Tieu said.

"What'll they do to us?"

"For you," Tieu replied, "I cannot say. For most of the soldiers, it will mean a long time in the work camps. For us," he added, taking in his fellow officers with a short motion of his arm, "it will mean death."

"Then there's no point in it," Rob snapped. "No point at all."

Rob switched off his flashlight to save the batteries, and the others followed his example. In the pitch-blackness the stale air seemed to settle on them like a suffocating blanket. He sat and listened to the hard breathing of the men around him. Not one of them had yet complained or even raised his voice in circumstances that would have panicked many. But the pressure was building on them. Waiting there, contemplating their situation, was simply too terrifying to be borne for very long. The demons of the imagination would assure their destruction before enemy fire even got a chance.

"Can we fight our way out the main exit under the stockade?" he asked Tieu.

Tieu thought about it for a moment, then said no. "The ladder and the trapdoor present an impossible bottleneck."

"Suppose we retreat back to the main tunnel complex," Rob said. "Could we fight our way to one of the other exits?"

Tieu said no.

Either way, forward or backward, meant certain capture. The only possibility that remained was the emergency exit. It was still open, still undiscovered.

Rob turned to Colonel Tieu again. "Ask Captain Deng if there was anybody in the mess tent."

"He says no one," Tieu replied.

"Ask him how big the tent is."

Tieu discussed this with Deng. "He thinks about ten meters by twenty meters. But it was hard to be sure in the dark."

"What could he see in the tent?"

"Field stoves, counters, sinks, stacks of supplies," Tieu replied. "And two log tables."

Rob performed some rapid mathematical calculations in his head. "That's big enough to feed about two hundred men, am I right?"

Tieu had no idea.

"I'm right," Rob said. "What time is it?"

Gilmore held his luminous dial up to his eyes. "Half-past two in the morning."

"What time do you think they eat breakfast?"

Tieu said that five-thirty was standard in the Vietnamese army.

"You thinking of joining them?" Gilmore asked.

"Why not?"

Rob rapidly sketched out a plan. They would exit through the emergency tunnel and gather in the mess tent, which he estimated was big enough to hold all of them. The camp would be asleep and the sentries would be posted only around the perimeter. No one would conceivably anticipate any threat from inside.

"With stealth and a little luck," he said, "we should be able to walk right out through the camp. The main problem will be the sentries at the perimeter. We'll try to deal with them quietly. If the alarm goes up, we ought to be able to hold our own. They don't outnumber us by more than two or three to one, and we have surprise on our side. We ought to be able to shoot our way out before they find their socks."

Gilmore stroked his bald head and whistled softly through his teeth. "This is one we never learned in Officers' Training."

Tieu, even more startled by the plan than Gilmore, began raising objections. "Captain Deng says the branch tunnel to the emergency exit is very small, very narrow. You have to crawl through for thirty, maybe forty meters."

"Is anybody too big to fit?"

"No, but—"

"We'll crawl through, then."

Rob met a few more objections, then silenced the colonel. "We don't have time for a debate," he said. "There may be a better plan, but no one's come up with it. So let's go with this. Pass the word down the line. We'll have to move in total darkness and silence. Each soldier should hold on to the belt of the man ahead of him so he won't get lost. You and I will take the lead with Captain Deng here, who knows the tunnel. Then Billy and his stretcher bearers. The next dozen men behind us should load their rifles. When we get into the mess tent, they should fan out around the sides and be ready to hold off anybody until we all get through. If things go bad, we'll just have to make the mess tent a beachhead. Send the officers back down the line now. Make sure everybody understands exactly what we're doing. We'll leave as soon as they send word back that everyone's ready. Any questions?"

No one spoke. "Good," he said. "Pass the word back."

Tieu gave the orders to the officers and they started back down the line, explaining the plan.

While they waited, Rob heard Billy start to groan. He turned on his flashlight and crouched down beside him. His brother's eyes fluttered open and he gritted his teeth in pain. Rob dug out one of the disposable syringes and injected the drug in his arm. "Hang on," he whispered. "We're on our way."

Billy closed his eyes and began to drift off again.

"Let me take up the rear," Gilmore said.

"You sure?"

"Positive. Small tunnels make me claustrophobic. And if anybody's big enough to get stuck, it's me. I don't want anybody behind me if I have to back up."

"If you get stuck," Rob warned him, "I'm coming back and blasting you out with dynamite."

Nearly half an hour passed before one of the officers returned with the word that the line was ready. Rob took a deep breath, motioned for the bodyguards to pick up Billy's stretcher, then stepped behind Captain Deng and grabbed his belt. He waited until he felt Tieu grip his belt from behind; then he switched off his flashlight and prodded Deng gently to start the advance.

The sensation of movement in the utter blackness of the tunnel was eerie, and as they crept forward along one wall, Rob felt as if he was floating, not certain which way was right or left, up or down. The tug on his belt became sometimes heavy as the long train of soldiers behind him struggled to keep in step.

Suddenly Deng stopped and knelt down on all fours. Rob felt him crawling to his right. He ducked down and followed him, inching along on his knees. It was no longer possible to hold on to Deng's belt, and with great reluctance he let go.

He felt the walls of the branch tunnel closing around him. It was barely three feet high and two feet wide, a crude, damp burrow dug through the earth. He swallowed hard and pushed ahead. Tieu scrambled in behind him.

They moved on hands and knees through muck several inches deep. The hot, fetid stench of vegetable decay added to the discomfort. He worried about Billy behind him, being dragged through the slime. There wasn't anything to be done about it.

Captain Deng stopped and made a low hissing noise to signal that he was near the exit. Rob listened in the darkness, his senses strained. He heard a soft whooshing noise, and a rush of sweet night air hit his face. He gulped it in gratefully.

A tense minute passed while Deng stuck his head up out of the hole and looked around the tent.

Deng's flashlight flicked on and off directly in front of his eyes. The way was clear. Rob flicked his own light back down the tunnel behind him and crawled forward to the exit hole and pushed himself up through it, feeling a sick tremble of relief to be above ground again. Faint moonlight penetrated the gauze mosquito netting draped to form the tent's walls. The objects inside the tent loomed around him, their unfamiliar silhouettes casting vaguely menacing shadows.

Tieu and the next dozen men came up fast and fanned out quickly among the tables and boxes and crouched down along the tent sides, their rifles ready. Getting Billy through was slow and difficult. Rob prayed that he had given him enough morphine to keep him quiet.

Rob stood by the exit and watched each man come up. It seemed a geologic age, although it was only about ten minutes, before he saw the welcome bulk of Howard Gilmore, gasping with exertion as he pushed his big frame up through the narrow hole.

Rob clasped his hand wordlessly and led Gilmore over to the slit in the gauze screen that served as the tent's front entrance. Tieu was already there. Rob pulled the netting aside and peered out.

He noticed the sky first—the bright half-moon and low, fast-moving clouds. One moment the campsite was hidden in darkness; the next it stood revealed in the moonlight—rows of plastic tarpaulins stretched over bamboo poles, several more large tents, and a couple of crude thatch-roofed open shelters.

Tieu pointed to the space between two large tents directly across the clearing. The contours of a rough roadway were visible, bulldozed through the jungle. Rob nodded. That was their destination. They had agreed beforehand that the safest way to escape the camp would be right out the front door. It would arouse the least suspicion if anyone was watching, and it was the only way to avoid the mines and booby traps almost certainly sown around the camp's perimeter.

Rob squeezed Tieu's arm. "Let's go," he whispered. "Good luck."

They walked out of the mess tent in double columns of twenty—Rob, Gilmore, Tieu, and Billy with his stretcher bearers leading the first wave.

Tieu followed a beaten footpath that wound past one of the thatch-roofed huts. As they neared it, Rob could see a long row of hammocks inside, shrouded in mosquito netting.

Suddenly the hammock at the end wriggled and its occupant pulled the netting aside. Tieu stopped, bringing the column to a halt. Rob clenched his teeth and laid his fingers on the trigger guard of his Kalashnikov. The shadowy figure in the hut muttered something in Vietnamese. Rob watched as Tieu glanced at his watch and calmly replied. The occupant of the hammock groaned and pulled the nettting back into place. He had asked Tieu for the correct time.

Rob let himself breathe again.

In less than a minute they had crossed the campsite and were approaching the roadway leading out into the jungle. On the right, Rob could make out a line of six stake-bodied military trucks parked in an improvised depot and surrounded by portable gasoline tanks, extra tires, and a stack of jerricans. On the left, he saw a soldier on sentry duty. He was squatting against a tree trunk, his rifle resting across his lap, his head bent forward. Rob approached him, his AK-47 directed at his lap.

"Asleep," Tieu whispered.

Rob nodded. He looked at Captain Deng. Deng pulled out a knife and made a throat-slitting gesture with it. Rob shook his head. He stepped next to Deng and chopped gently on the back of his neck with the edge of his palm. Deng understood. He tiptoed over to the sentry and dealt his exposed neck a karate chop that toppled him forward onto the ground without a murmur.

Everyone made it across the campsite, past the trucks, and out onto the rutted roadway without incident. As the secure black folds of the jungle closed around him Rob felt a welling exultation. Their escape from the tunnels seemed miraculous, even though he knew it wasn't. The government troops, after all, had little motivation to be on their guard. They had probably been told that the tunnel complex had already fallen, and believed that their battle was over.

He turned and waited with Tieu and Gilmore in the dark for the last elements of their party to catch up with them. The next challenge was to find the border as fast as possible.

"What time is it?" he asked Gilmore.

"Three forty-five."

"It'll start to get light in an hour."

Gilmore agreed. "We can't possibly hike to the border in that time. We'll have to hide somewhere."

"No good. We've got to keep moving."

"They'll be looking for us with everything they can get in the air and on the road," Gilmore argued.

"Of course!" Rob said, slapping his friend across the chest with the back of his hand. "The road. Let's go back and grab those trucks."

"Are you crazy?"

"What can they do? Chase us in their bare feet? With those trucks, we can punch our way right across the border and keep on going."

Rob consulted Tieu and the other officers. Predictably, they rejected the idea. Rob overruled them.

"How many trucks you want to take?" Tieu asked.

"All six of them. Pick five teams of drivers, as fast as you can. Gilmore and I will drive the lead vehicle. We'll go back and steal them as soon as you pick the men. When we come back through here, have everybody ready to jump on. Let's load twenty to a truck. Leave the last truck empty, as a spare."

Rob led Gilmore and the five pairs of drivers back toward the camp. As soon as it was in sight, one of the Vietnamese volunteered to check for the location of the ignition keys. If they weren't somewhere in the trucks' cabs, they would be out of luck. He came back minutes later with good news. The keys for each vehicle were in the glove compartment.

They crept up closer. The lone sentry was still sprawled unconscious by the roadway. As quietly as they could, they loaded several extra jerricans of gasoline into the back of each vehicle, and then each team climbed into the cabs. Rob had given them careful instructions. "Don't close the doors until you're moving, and wait for me to start the first truck."

"It's completely unfamiliar," Rob muttered, feeling around the cab for the ignition switch and the gearshift. "Turn the flashlight on for a second."

While Gilmore held the light close to the dash, shielding the beam with his hand, Rob slid the key into the ignition and turned it half a turn to the right. A red light glowed on the dashboard, but the key wouldn't turn further to fire the engine. He twisted it back and forth, in mounting frustration. "The son of a bitch doesn't work!" he rasped.

"It's Russian," Gilmore replied, spotting some Cyrillic lettering on the dash.

Rob craned his head down near the key slot to see what was preventing it from turning.

"Oh, shit," Gilmore croaked. "Here they come."

Rob looked up. Through the windshield he saw the light of a lantern bouncing in the dark. He cursed, yanked at the key desperately, then was hit with an inspiration. The truck must have a separate starter, like his brother's old MG. He started grabbing knobs, working his way along the dash. He could see more lights moving toward them.

His fumbling turned on the windshield wiper, then the headlights. Gilmore whimpered audibly and slid down in the cab until his head was below the windshield.

Rob found the right knob and yanked it hard. The starter motor made a high-pitched whining racket; then a deep-throated roar filled the cab. Rob jabbed a foot down on the clutch and wrestled the shift lever into what he hoped was low gear. A chorus of revving motors alongside him told him the other trucks were ready. As their headlights flashed on, they illuminated a chaotic scene. The camp, fully alerted now, was swarming with movement like an ant's nest someone had stepped on. An automatic rifle opened fire somewhere, its angry chatter barely audible over the roaring truck engines.

Rob popped the clutch and tromped hard on the accelerator. The big rack-bodied vehicle heaved forward, smashing into a stack of jerricans. Not certain of reverse gear, Rob rode over the cans, cramping the stiff, unyielding steering wheel hard to the right to swing around to the roadway. The truck ground over more obstacles, then bounced onto the rutted road surface.

The other trucks fell in behind him. In the rearview mirror he counted their headlights, dancing in the blackness. All five pairs were moving. His own headlights picked up Colonel Tieu and the others almost immediately. He drove abreast of them, braked hard, and jumped out. The soldiers began piling into the back.

The machine-gun fire from the camp was deafening. Rob ducked down and ran back to the last truck, stalled some hundred feet behind the others. All four of the dual-wheel rear tires had been shot flat. He waved at the men in the cab to abandon it. They scrambled out and ran for the tailgate of the next truck up.

Rob stopped one of them long enough to pull two grenades from the bandolier around his chest. He yanked the pin on the first one and lobbed it toward the crippled truck. It bounced over the back and exploded behind the vehicle. The enemy gunfire slackened somewhat. He pulled the pin on the second one, took careful aim, tossed it, and ran.

The grenade bounced on the top of the cab, rolled down between the cab and the stake body, and wedged itself there, directly against the gas tank.

The big Russian truck exploded like a string of Chinese firecrackers—first the grenade, then the gas tank, then the jerricans in the back—lighting up the surrounding jungle like a magnesium flare. Rob dashed for the lead truck. The men stood in the backs of the trucks and cheered wildly as he ran past. Behind him the gunfire had ceased altogether, replaced by the loud crackle of the burning vehicle.

Rob pulled himself into the cab, slammed the door, threw the engine into gear, and roared forward.

"We're on our way, Howard, god damn it!" he cried. "Let's have a song!"

Gilmore cleared his throat but couldn't get his vocal cords unstuck. Rob punched him hard on the shoulder and then began singing himself, in a loud, out-of-tune voice, drunk with euphoria:

" *'On the road to Mandala-ay!*
Where the flyin'-fishes play-ay!
An' the dawn comes up like thunder
Outer China 'crost the bay!' "

The Barents Sea

"My father was killed during the Night of the Long Knives," Grunwald said, scratching his fingers thoughtfully in the stubble of his new beard. "Of course, I didn't understand the politics of it then, the struggle for power that was going on inside the party. I was told the Jews were to blame, and naturally I believed it. I guess I was brainwashed from childhood. By the time I was in the Hitler Youth, I was a rabid Jew hater. I blamed them for the death of my father. And for everything— the destitution and humiliation our family had suffered for so long." Grunwald paused and gazed up at the maze of pipes overhead. "I was an unhappy child," he said. "I had a lot of hostility in me—from my father, I guess. His life had been so frustrating. He failed at everything. Even as a husband. My mother cheated on him, and after he died, there was a steady stream of men. I was in my teens, and jealous. She brought men home, drunk usually, and they would have sex in the bedroom. The bed was right against the wall where I slept in the little sitting room. I could hear everything, even feel the bed shaking through the wall."

Grunwald looked at Koenig. He was smoking one of his foul-smelling cigarettes, his legs crossed in the chair, his harsh features composed in placid indifference. But Grunwald knew that he was paying attention. When he didn't fidget with his hands, he was paying attention. It was astonishing, Grunwald thought, how attuned he had become to Koenig's various frames of mind. Like a dog whose life revolves around its master, he had learned to interpret Koenig's every expression and mannerism.

"One night I tried to kill one of them," he went on, settling back against the cot. "He was an officer in the Kripo, a gross and stupid man. A bully. He sometimes slapped my mother around, and once he had threatened me. I had my knife from the Hitler Youth. The Fahrtenmesser. It was my prized possession. I cleaned and polished it every day, even took it to bed with me. It was my Excalibur, my friend and protector.

"In the morning, when he was sleeping off a drunk, I stalked right into the bedroom and plunged the knife into his stomach. Right through the sheet. I remember how swiftly it turned red around the knife. My mother woke and started screaming. She stopped me from stabbing him again. He lost a lot of blood, but the bastard lived. No charges were pressed against me, and he never showed up at the apartment again. So you see, the only man I ever tried to kill was a Nazi."

Koenig nodded slowly. "You don't count your killing of Simon Grunwald, then? Because he was just a Jew?"

Grunwald didn't reply.

"It seems to me," Koenig added, "that you had precisely the violent streak the SS was looking for in a camp guard."

"I was only nineteen. Dachau was a nightmare for me. We had heard rumors of what was going on—medical experiments, mass exterminations—but nothing, not even my hatred of the Jews, could have prepared me for such a place. You suffered, as a prisoner, and I know well what you were put through, but you at least had the dignity of knowing you were the victim of terrible injustice. For me, my whole world began to crumble. No amount of brainwashing could justify the organized brutality of the place. Being a Jew hater was not enough. For one thing, most of the prisoners at Dachau weren't even Jews. We guards spent a lot of time trying to convince each other that the inmates were all criminals, subhuman types worse than animals, to help harden us against what we had to endure. But I still could not witness their treatment without revulsion. And guilt. I felt sorry for them. I wished they would all die, so they would not suffer anymore and so we would not have to continue doing what we were doing. My dreams of heroism, of doing great deeds at the front for the fatherland, were shattered at Dachau. I began to see how monstrous and perverted an ideal National Socialism had become."

Koenig lit another cigarette. "A pretty little speech, Herr Gruen. You had the weak stomach of a coward, that's all. Don't try to pass it off as a wakening of moral scruples."

"I don't profess to anything noble. Far from it. I confess only that I was one of many. I was common. Unexceptional. I was not evil. The times were evil."

"The times have always been evil, Herr Gruen. And it has always been men who have made them so. The Holocaust is only one of thousands of such organized slaughters that man has perpetrated on his own kind."

"But I was not guilty of anything! I was only guilty of not resisting! What could I have done? Sacrifice my own life just to protest the evil around me? What good would it have done? Who did that, in Germany? Who dared resist? Who dared object? Who?"

"Not very many," Koenig admitted.

"I was swept along, like the rest of Germany, into something that we couldn't stop."

"And so you found your own way to save your neck. To violate your victim even further by posing under his skin. You personally conspired against the Jews in a uniquely evil fashion. As a capitalist, as an exploiter of the labor of others, you have managed the extraordinary feat of having your own greed and ruthlessness counted against the Jewish stereotype. You have smeared them with your excrement, Herr Gruen. And that has nothing to do with the evil of the times. It was your own private doing. And it is that act which of all your crimes I find most reprehensible."

Grunwald rubbed his hands over his eyes. "My God, Herr Koenig! How wrong that is. Even if you don't approve of my life, you must give me credit for an act of atonement. I was brought up to despise the Jews. It was deeply ingrained. By my family, by the Hitler Youth, by the SS. We were daily indoctrinated in this hate. No one could have resisted it. At first I acted only to save myself, that is true. It was purely a question of survival. The Americans would have killed me, otherwise."

"So you became a Jew," Koenig said. "And availed yourself of all the help, all the outpouring of sympathy for those who just a few days earlier you had been brutalizing."

"I intended to drop my disguise as soon as it was possible. It pained me greatly to be taken as a Jew. It was an awful feeling. It tore me apart. But it saved me in more ways than I then knew. By becoming my victim, I came to understand him. I came to lose that hatred, to see what the world looked like from his point of view, to understand the nature of the evil that had been done against him. I took the place of my victim, subjected myself to the same prejudices, the same ill will, the same ostracisms that he had lived with all along. I atoned. I made myself whole. It was a rebirth for me. I was glad to be a Jew. It gave me strength to go on. It made it possible for me to build the great industrial empire that I did—an achievement I take great pride in, despite your views about capitalism."

Koenig mocked him. "What it made possible, of course, was for you to escape justice. The ease with which you surrendered your supposedly deeply ingrained principles for an entirely new and far more convenient set does not impress me, Herr Gruen. You built your empire by marrying into a Jewish family with money, and by using the network of Jewish wealth to advance yourself. I would be more impressed by your argument if you confessed to me that you still hate the Jews. It would indicate more character to me than you show by your shameless expedience. You are without scruples, Herr Gruen."

"You would give a man no credit for growth, for change?"

"Men change very little after the age of six."

"If you believe that, then your Marxist revolution is in deep trouble."

"Not at all. Future generations, having no experience with the chaos and inequities of capitalist society, will not miss it at all."

"Because they won't know any better, you mean."

Koenig's hands began to fidget. He abruptly changed the subject. "We will arrive in port late tomorrow."

Grunwald pushed himself up on the cot. "In port? Where?" he asked, his pulse racing at the prospect of his impending release.

Koenig struck a wooden match against his heel and held it up to another cigarette. When it was lit, he shook the match out and returned it to the matchbox, an act that Grunwald wondered, every time he saw it, why it never set off the other matches in the box. "Severomorsk," he said.

"Severomorsk?" Grunwald echoed, the surprise on his face transparent. "Russia?"

"We have sailed a long way together, Herr Gruen," Koenig said. "All the way across the North Atlantic, over the Faeroe–Iceland Ridge, and across the Norwegian Sea. We stand now about a hundred miles off the northern tip of Norway, in the Barents Sea."

"A long way from home," Grunwald complained.

"Yes," Koenig admitted. He blew a perfect smoke ring and watched it ascend toward the ceiling, his expression composed and benign. "Farther away from home than you realize, Herr Gruen."

46

Bangkok, Thailand

McWhirter awoke with another hangover. He was getting to like them. The pain not only took his mind off his problems; it had a nostalgic quality to it. Getting drunk and being hung over were as familiar and comfortable as baseball in the summertime. If he looked back on the happiest hours of his life, not counting those spent in the cockpit of an airplane, they had all happened under the influence of alcohol. That was the whole point of drinking in the first place. To make the good times roll.

He reached across the king-sized bed to feel for bodies. His hand came up with empty sheet. He slid over a few feet and tried again. Still nothing. Funny. He was sure there'd been somebody there last night. Maybe it was the night before.

He sat up carefully, fearful his head might roll off onto the floor, and squinted at the clock by the bed. Eight-thirty. That would be morning, he decided, noticing the slivers of light seeping around the edges of the tightly pulled drapes.

After a hot shower, a cold shower, some aspirin and Alka-Seltzer, he felt marginally restored. Even his pair of black eyes from the pounding he had taken in the bar on Petchburi Road were fading to a tolerable yellowish-purple. By the time he emerged from the bath, room service had delivered his breakfast—two eggs over hard, a small grilled steak medium rare, a pot of coffee, a pitcher of orange juice, a stack of toast with a jar of grape jelly on the side, and two ice-cold bottles of Budweiser.

McWhirter twisted the top off one of the beers and unfolded the copy of the English-language *Asian Times* that the hotel threw in free with his twenty-dollar breakfast.

A headline under the fold immediately caught his eye: "American Brothers Escape from Guerrilla Base Inside Vietnam." He sat down hard on the side of the bed, the beer in one hand, the paper in the other. The article was syndicated by a French agency, and the byline read "Ghislene Ferrer." He scanned the story, his amazement mounting. It was a long account, detailing the whole incredible story of Billy Grunwald and his Army of the New Vietnam. When McWhirter had finished it, he drank the bottle of Budweiser, opened the other one, and reread the article a second and a third time.

The breakfast remained uneaten. Finally McWhirter tossed the paper aside and went to the window. He yanked back the drapes and pushed open the window, letting the steamy morning heat and noise of the city pour into the air-conditioned suite. "Son of a bitch," he muttered out loud. "He's pulling it off."

And if he was to succeed, McWhirter thought, Walker would be even more unhappy with Harris McWhirter than he already was. If that was possible.

But how *could* Rob Grunwald succeed? Even if he got his brother out of those tunnels, how the hell could they get out of Vietnam, with the Vietnamese army all over them? And if they did get out of Vietnam, how the hell could a hundred of them ever get across Laos? He swore in disbelief. *A hundred men. Jesus Christ!*

The more McWhirter thought about it, the more agitated he became. He felt pain beyond the hangover. He had let Grunwald down, but Grunwald had gone ahead and pulled it off, anyway. He knew the guy was gutsy, but Ferrer's story, even allowing for some obvious exaggeration, made him out to be Superman.

Son of a bitch!

McWhirter sat down and ate the cold steak, his mind churning. He read the article a fourth time, then dressed, threw all his money into a briefcase, and left the hotel.

By 9:30 A.M. he was driving north on Route 5 out of the city in a rented Toyota jeep, his foot punishing the accelerator.

Passing Don Muang Airport, he was seized with an inspiration. Why drive when he could fly? He swung the jeep into the airport-approach road and turned off toward the small cluster of private planes he had noticed from the highway. He scanned the lines of light aircraft—mostly Cessnas, Pipers, Beechcraft, and a few Learjets. But, parked by the side of a small hangar, her fat wings and oversized prop almost hidden from view, was something that made his heart skip.

Inside the hangar he found a young-looking Chinese standing behind a counter. A big sign suspended by wire over his head said: "Chinaman Chin's Flying Dragons—Anything, Anywhere, Anytime."

"You Chinaman Chin?"

The man smiled condescendingly. "No. He's my father," he said, in impeccable English. "I'm Harold Chin."

"Your English is damned good," McWhirter replied, genuinely impressed.

"It ought to be. I majored in it at the University of Michigan."

"English majors are probably in big demand out here," McWhirter observed, annoyed at Chin's arch manner.

"What can I do for you?" Chin asked.

"I'd like to rent a plane from you."

Chin turned on his smile again. "I'm sorry, but we're a freight service. We don't rent out our aircraft. There's a flying school not far from Don Muang. You might have better luck there."

"Then how about flying me somewhere? I'll pay a premium rate."

Chin narrowed his eyes. "Freight," he repeated frostily. "Not passengers. Freight."

McWhirter sighed. "You're a hard man to warm to, Harold. Let me put it this way. I need an airplane, right now." He plopped his briefcase on the counter, opened it, pulled out a dog-eared packet of documents, and pressed it into Chin's hand. "I'm an expert pilot. These papers will prove it." He left the case open so that Chin could see the stacks of American bills. "And I'm prepared to let you rip me off for the privilege of borrowing one of your rickety crates out there."

Chin browsed through McWhirter's documents. He pretended not to notice the money in the case.

"Where do you want to go?" he asked.

"I need to pick up some friends in Khon Kaen."

Chin nodded. "Excuse me a minute, please." The Chinese took McWhirter's documents and disappeared into a small office behind the counter and shut the door behind him.

He emerged ten minutes later wearing an unctuous grin. McWhirter guessed that his father had told him to make a deal. Chin cast a swift glance in the direction of the briefcase. "I might be able to sell you a plane," he murmured.

"For how much?"

Chin cleared his throat. "A hundred thousand dollars," he said.

McWhirter came back with a counteroffer. "You thieving chink," he said. "I didn't see a plane out there worth ten."

"I'm trying to accommodate you, Mr. McWhirter. Perhaps you could tell me what kind of a plane you'd like?"

"Yes. I want that old tail dragger behind the hangar."

Chin raised his eyebrows all the way to his hairline. "The Helio?"

"That's the one. Is she airworthy?"

"Yes, but it's an extremely difficult plane to fly. I'd suggest the Cessna 182—"

"Harold, I've spent more hours at the stick of that tail dragger than you have jerking off, which you can appreciate is a hell of a lot of time."

Chin cleared his throat again. "The Helio Courier is a very special plane. But if you are familiar with it, as you claim, then I'll let you have it for fifty thousand."

"I'll give you twenty."

"Forty thousand is absolutely the lowest."

"I'll report your opium smuggling to the authorities."

McWhirter had made a good guess. Chin blanched and quickly said, "Thirty."

"That Helio is at least twenty years old," McWhirter retorted. "It's probably been to the sun and back. I'm going to count out twenty-five thousand American cash dollars from this briefcase and give it to you right now for the papers on that beat-up old piece of crap."

"I'll have to think about it."

"After thirty seconds my offer drops to twenty."

"You are a very obnoxious individual," Chin complained.

"Ten seconds left."

"Give me the twenty-five," Chin demanded.

McWhirter dealt out twenty-five thousand dollars in hundred-dollar bills, stacked it like a deck of cards, and slapped it down in front of Chin. Chin scraped the stack deftly into a drawer under the counter.

McWhirter held up another hundred-dollar bill. "Gas it up and change the oil, Harold, and I'll be on my way."

Chin grabbed the hundred and slipped it into his trouser pocket. "It's your funeral, as they say back in the States."

Vietnam

The remnants of the Army of the New Vietnam bumped onto Highway 9 at Lang Vei just before dawn in five Russian military trucks, turned west, and headed for the border.

"How far?" Rob asked, his eyes glued to the road surface as he maneuvered the ponderous vehicle down the highway.

Gilmore trained his flashlight on the map, trying to hold it steady against the bouncing motion of the truck. "Three miles," he replied.

"Five minutes from now," Rob estimated. "Let's stop."

Rob pulled the caravan over to the side of the road and hopped out. Gilmore followed him to the tailgate of the truck. Colonel Tieu jumped down from the back.

"How's Billy?" Rob asked.

"A lot of fever," Tieu replied, shaking his head.

Rob hoisted himself into the back of the truck, squeezed through the crowd of soldiers, and knelt by his brother, lying on a makeshift bed of rucksacks piled on the floor. His skin was dry and his forehead burning. With the bodyguards' help, Rob peeled off his clothes down to his underpants to give him more ventilation, and administered another shot of morphine.

He unscrewed the cap from his canteen, soaked Billy's shirt with water, and wrapped it around his head. "Keep the shirt wet," he told the bodyguards in French, handing over the canteen. "The evaporation will help cool him."

Tieu, the other officers, and the four teams of drivers had gathered by the tailgate. Rob joined them. "The border's just ahead," he told the colonel. "What can we expect?"

Tieu tugged thoughtfully at an earlobe. "Maybe six guards at this hour."

"Any physical obstacles?"

"A guardhouse, a customs shed, and a gate. That's all."

"How about the Laotian side?"

"Not so much. A small customs shed. They close the border at night. Maybe one or two guards there now. No more."

He looked at Gilmore. "You think they've been alerted?"

"We can count on it."

"We need a plan," Rob said. "Fast."

The three of them devised one, and ten minutes later the convoy hit the border.

The sudden harsh glare of lights over a cluster of tin shacks interrupted the dark of the predawn jungle with a jarring sharpness.

Rob switched off the headlights, shifted down into second gear, and pressed the gas pedal to the floor. The truck lumbered forward, its elephantine bulk gathering momentum like an avalanche.

As it closed on the border, Rob saw the heads of soldiers jammed in the two guardhouses that straddled the crossing. Far more than six. More like fifty.

The men in the back of the truck were in position. Two grenade throwers stood directly behind the cab, sandwiched between a machine gunner and another soldier manning an RPG. Along the slatted side rails the barrels of a dozen automatic rifles protruded.

The machine gun opened up first, spraying a concentrated fire at the left guardhouse. The RPG fired two rockets in rapid succession, scoring a direct hit on the right guardhouse.

Rob and Gilmore crouched down as low as possible in the cab. Gilmore trained his rifle out the window and fired at stray soldiers running from the sheds.

The truck hit the long steel pole barricading the border crossing at fifty miles an hour. The pole whipped back on its hinge and knifed sideways into the customs shed, collapsing the flimsy structure on the heads of its occupants.

Amid the colossal din of the rifle fire, Rob heard the sharp ping of bullets hitting the cab.

The convoy smashed over the border and roared on into Laos. Behind them, the border post was in flames, the handful of survivors busy pulling the dead and wounded from the burning sheds.

Laos

With Lin Pao bouncing happily in the seat beside her, Caroline gingerly maneuvered the old Dodge onto Highway 9 several miles east of Savannakhet and coaxed it slowly up a long gradient that wound up the side of a mountain. The roadway was narrow and laced with ruts, and the Dodge's ancient frame, its leaf springs rusted and brittle with age, bottomed out with a spine-jolting clunk every time she hit one.

She was still shaking from Lin Pao's bold theft of the truck an hour earlier. It was hidden in the trees at the edge of the village, parked on a steep incline so it could be started if its weak battery failed to turn over. Lin Pao had jumped in, released the hand brake, and rolled it silently right out of the village without anyone noticing.

The late-morning sun beat down on the hood of the cab. As the truck labored up the long incline, Caroline watched the water-temperature gauge anxiously. Its needle was all the way over in the red. Either it was broken or the radiator was about to boil over.

The Dodge crested the long rise without exploding. Caroline sighed with relief, jerked the balky shift into neutral, and let the vehicle coast downhill. The water-temperature needle dropped back out of the red, but then she discovered another problem.

The first time she applied the brakes to slow the truck around a sharp corner, the pedal gave way with a sickeningly spongy sensation, carrying her foot all the way to the floorboard. She pumped the pedal madly and slowed the Dodge just enough to prevent it from careening off the steep drop that bordered the outside edge of the hairpin curve.

Before the next big hill, she mastered the technique of shifting down. It was an arcane skill she had learned one summer on an uncle's farm in Maine. The farm truck was an old Dodge rack body with the same recalcitrant gearbox. The technique for overcoming the problem consisted of disengaging the clutch briefly at neutral after slipping it out of one gear and before slipping it into a lower one. Double-clutching, her uncle called it. It worked best, she discovered, if she also applied her foot to the gas pedal when the shift was resting in neutral.

That helped solve the braking problem. The overheating she could do little about but pray. She was grateful that at least the truck was moving. And each kilometer was bringing them closer to Rob.

There was little traffic, and most of it was bicycle and oxcart. In the village of Seno, where Highway 9 was intersected by a north-south road, Route 13, they stopped and Lin Pao bartered at a produce stand and returned with some shriveled oranges and a container of cooked rice.

Caroline noticed a soldier in uniform watching her from the front of a store across the road. A Caucasian woman driving a truck was not an everyday sight in downtown Seno. She wondered if her blond hair was showing beneath her cap. He started to walk over.

She glanced at Lin Pao. "What is he?" she asked.

Lin Pao didn't know the word in English. "Bad soldier," he said, in French. "He tells people to go to jail."

"A policeman. I don't think we want to talk with him, then." She cranked the ignition, wrestled the gearshift up into first, and drove off. In the rearview mirror, she saw him standing in the middle of the street, his arms on his hips.

Beyond Seno the land flattened out and they drove through miles of rice paddies. At the town of Muong Phine they met a second north-south road, Route 23. From here on, Caroline remembered, looking at the hazy blue wall of mountains ahead of them, Highway 9 began its long, circuitous climb up through the peaks of the Annam Cordillera. The truck's odometer had long since failed, but she estimated that in four hours they had traveled nearly a hundred miles. More than halfway across Laos. She had not let herself hope that they might meet Rob so soon, but now, with each vehicle that approached them, she felt her pulse begin to race. And each time, as she saw only strange Asian faces staring back at her as they passed, her anxiety increased. On the other side of the mountains was Vietnam. If they didn't find him soon, they would have to turn back.

The truck labored up a long incline, then followed the road on a twisting path through the mountains. Highway 9 became little more than a one-lane blacktop, a thin, dirty scar nicked into the flanks of the giant green hills. On one side of them a wall of rock; on the other, a vista of distant valleys and gorges.

"Look, look!" Lin Pao cried. He leaned out the window on his side, pointing a finger at something out over the precipice on their left.

Caroline slowed down but was afraid to take her eyes off the treacherous roadway for even a second. "What is it?"

Lin Pao shouted something in Laotian. Over the noise of the truck's straining engine, she heard a deep, whining rumble and then a heavy thumping, like a fast heartbeat.

She glanced quickly to the left and saw it. A helicopter. It was flying alongside them, out over the gorge. A male Caucasian face was grinning at her from behind the plastic-bubble windshield and making a thumbs-up gesture.

Who were they?

The chopper edged over the roadway in front of them, its tail twitching back and forth dangerously close to the truck. Caroline pumped the brakes, shifted down to first, and brought the vehicle to a shuddering stop. The helicopter hovered briefly in the air, danced around sideways to the Dodge, and settled on the road, effectively blocking their path.

A short, sandy-haired man carrying a pistol hopped out and came trotting over. He slapped his palm down on the top of the open door frame. "Mrs. Grunwald? My name is Captain Henry Short. I'm with the U.S. government. We're sure glad we found you!"

Caroline could hardly hide her astonishment. "What is it?" she asked timidly, like a driver caught going through a red light.

"Can I ask what you're doing out here?"

Caroline didn't know what to say. Whose side was he on?

"We're here to help you," he prompted, his freckled face spread in a wide grin. "You're in danger out here."

Caroline recovered her poise. "Danger of what?"

Short laughed. "Hey, you're in a Communist country illegally."

"Am I really?"

"We're here to help," he repeated.

"Who sent you? I didn't ask anyone for help."

"Hey, listen, I don't want to argue with you, but we've risked our asses to come out here."

It must be McWhirter's doing, she thought. His guilt had finally gotten the better of him.

"Then help me find Rob Grunwald."

"That's what we're here for," Short replied, pointing with his pistol at his colleague waiting in the helicopter. "Let's get in the chopper and we'll go find him."

Caroline hesitated. Short's answer sounded almost flip. She felt Lin Pao pressing his knuckles against the side of her leg. She looked at him. His brown eyes were solemn. He shook his head.

"Who's the kid?" Short asked, leaning against the door frame and peering in. His tone was condescending.

"He's a friend," Caroline replied.

"He from around here?"

"He's with me."

"Laotian?"

"Yes, but—"

Short cut her off decisively. "We can't take him with us, sorry."

"I'm not going anywhere without him."

The captain sighed disagreeably. "I'm trying to be nice, lady. The point is, I was sent out here to pick you up—before you create an incident that might embarrass the United States."

"Then you lied. You're not looking for Rob Grunwald at all."

"We're looking for him, all right."

"I'm not going without Lin Pao. If you don't like it, then you can damned well leave us alone."

"I don't have all day to argue, Mrs. Grunwald."

Caroline put her hand on the ignition key. "Get out of our way," she snarled.

Short's ferretlike eyes appraised her coolly. He reached his decision. He yanked open the door and grabbed her arm. Caroline clutched the steering wheel with both hands. Short banged her fingers with the grip end of the pistol and forced them loose. He grabbed a wrist and dragged her roughly out of the truck. She slid onto the ground in front of him, kicking at him.

Two explosions rent the air directly over her head. She felt Short's grip on her wrist relax and then saw him crumple over backward.

Lin Pao was crouching in the cab, his pistol still aimed at Short, writhing on the road. One bullet had severed an artery in his neck, and a bright gusher of blood was pumping out into a puddle on the ground. Lin Pao shot him twice more, and he lay still.

Caroline climbed back into the cab. Through the windshield she saw the other man in the helicopter steadying a rifle at her. She ducked down across the seat just as the windshield shattered. Shards of glass cascaded over both of them. Lin Pao popped his head up and squeezed off two shots through the broken glass. Caroline yanked him down next to her. Bullets pinged off the metal surfaces of the cab.

Still lying on the seat, Caroline twisted onto her side, reached up and knocked the shift lever into neutral, and then twisted the ignition key. The engine coughed and died. She twisted it again, this time reaching down and pressing a hand on the accelerator pedal. The engine rumbled into life.

She slid forward so that she could reach both arms down to the pedals. She depressed the clutch with her left hand, pushed the shift into first gear with her right, then quickly brought her right hand down to the gas pedal.

She released the clutch and pressed hard on the gas. "God help us," she murmured.

The old Dodge bucked violently, then rumbled forward. She held her right hand on the accelerator and grabbed the steering wheel with her left, to keep the truck on course.

It roared ahead in low gear. The gunfire intensified. Lin Pao crouched beside her, his hands braced firmly against the dash.

The truck plowed into the helicopter broadside with a rending shriek of metal and shuddered to a stop. Caroline, knocked under the steering wheel, grasped the accelerator hard and jammed it to the floorboard. The truck whined and chattered and began inching forward again. Over the racing engine, she heard the landing gear of the helicopter scraping loudly over the road.

Suddenly the scraping stopped and the truck lurched forward. She released the gas pedal and pressed both hands on the brake pedal. Over her head, Lin Pao turned off the ignition and slapped the gearshift into reverse. Amid a crunching of gear teeth, the truck wobbled to a halt.

She crawled out from under the steering wheel and looked around. Thirty feet behind the truck, Short's body lay on its back. The truck itself had scored deep tire burns into the road surface and had ended its short journey stalled six feet from the edge of the precipice. The helicopter was nowhere in sight.

Caroline stepped, weak-kneed, out of the cab to examine the damage to the truck. One front tire was flat, and the radiator had been shot full of holes. The precious water was trickling out of it in a dozen different places. Lin Pao, still clutching his pistol, scrambled out and walked over to the edge of the cliff and looked down. The helicopter was a thousand feet below him, resting on a flat rock ledge, a twisted pile of expensive metal with a small curl of blue smoke spiraling up from it.

Caroline went over to him. His face wore a big smile, but he was shaking violently. She pulled him against her and held him tightly.

47

Laos

"You want me to take the wheel?" Gilmore asked.

Rob shook his head. "Not yet. I feel okay."

Gilmore removed his glasses and cleaned them with forefinger and thumb. "I'm glad to hear it," he said. "Because I'm hungry, thirsty, and tired. And scared. Not necessarily in that order."

"I'm sorry I got you into all this."

Gilmore laughed. "Well, I figure if we ever get away with this, I'll be able to dine out on it for the rest of my life."

"We'll get away with it," Rob said.

"Or at least die trying," Gilmore added.

"How about a chorus of 'Waist Deep in the Big Muddy'?"

"You're really enjoying yourself, aren't you."

Rob glanced over at his friend and then grinned.

Gilmore suppressed a nervous yawn. "You've come a long way for a former draft dodger," he said. "And I say that with love."

Someone started banging on the roof of the cab. Rob looked out the side-view mirror. The truck behind them was stalled in the middle of the highway, its front end listing to the side at a steep angle. He stopped and backed up to it.

The truck's right front wheel had fallen off. Gilmore bent down to inspect the damage. "The wheel lugs snapped right off," he said, pointing out the broken studs of metal protruding from the inside rim. "Nothing we can do about it—except sue the Russians."

Rob turned to Colonel Tieu. "Let's get the men out and into the other trucks."

The third, fourth, and fifth trucks pulled around in front of the crippled vehicle, and the twenty men in the back quickly picked up their equipment and moved.

"Let's block the road with it," Rob said. "Back one of the other trucks into its nose and shove it around sideways across the highway."

When they had pushed the damaged Russian vehicle around, Rob borrowed another grenade from the bandolier of one of the soldiers and tossed it into the cab. It blew the doors out and set the vehicle on fire. "If anyone's chasing us," Rob said, "this'll at least slow them down."

"If anyone's chasing us," Gilmore replied, "it's likely to be from the air."

"You think so? Does Laos have an air force?"

"No, but Vietnam does."

"They'd violate Laotian airspace?"

"Of course they'd violate it," Gilmore retorted. Colonel Tieu agreed.

"We need a spotter, then," Rob decided. He handed Tieu his binoculars. "Keep a watch for aircraft," he said. "And bang like hell on the cab roof if you see any."

The convoy moved out again, its four remaining trucks heavily laden, and began a long, slow climb up the steep flanks of the Annam Cordillera.

Northeast Thailand

The Helio was as beautiful as any he'd ever piloted. A loose-jointed, rackety old ship whose every strut and wire, every piston and control surface, he knew as completely as if they were extensions of himself. He had flown with her sisters on many incredible voyages. They had shared glorious adventures, desperate moments, narrow escapes. Every Helio had her own peculiar weaknesses and strengths, but they were all from the same family, blood relations whose character he admired and whose personality he understood. Many times he had asked for all they could give him, and they had never let him down. If it was possible for a man to love a machine, then it would be said that Harris McWhirter loved this airplane.

Once out of the traffic pattern of Don Muang, he leveled out at four thousand feet, set a north-northeast heading toward Sammy Rep's hotel in Mukdahan, on the Thai–Laotian border, and pushed the throttle to the stops, watching the old Lycoming engine wind the airspeed indicator up to a modest 160 knots. The Helio was not a fast ship. On the other hand, he reflected, there wasn't an aircraft in the world, not counting helicopters, that could stay airborne at only twenty-six knots. And that was a talent sometimes worth a lot more than speed.

Two hours later McWhirter landed the Helio across the wind in front of Sammy's hotel, using up less than two hundred feet of bumpy dirt roadway. He taxied up to Sammy's front door and saw the old man running out to confront him, brandishing his revolver over his head.

McWhirter killed the engine and opened the door. When Sammy saw who it was, he put away the pistol and welcomed McWhirter in a loud voice, tugging at his sleeve in his haste to get him out of the plane.

"Any sign of Rob Grunwald?"

Sammy shook his head.

"Are Caroline and the boy still here?"

Sammy shook his head again.

"Where did they go?"

Sammy told him.

McWhirter couldn't believe it. "Why the hell would they do anything so crazy? Why did you let them go?"

Sammy told McWhirter about the men staked out by the shed.

"They still there?"

"Yeah. They still there," Sammy repeated.

"How long ago did Caroline leave?"

"Two day now."

McWhirter pulled the old man's hand free of his shirt sleeve. "See you later, Sammy."

He took off against the crosswind, roaring along the roadway on one wheel, rudder and flaps at full extension. The plane banked so steeply to hold a straight takeoff course that the Helio's fat wing was scything off the tops of weeds along the roadside.

As soon as he had gained maneuverable altitude, he pointed the craft eastward, toward Laos, and gave it full throttle. At the Mekong River he banked southeast, to pick up Highway 9 about five miles north of Savannakhet. At ten in the morning it was already blazing hot, the air so expanded with moisture that even the nearly empty Helio, with its tremendous lift, felt sluggish, as if he was flying at ten thousand feet. Behind him, a wall of thunderheads was building. Poor flying weather, and promising to get worse.

He kept to a course about a hundred feet above Highway 9 and far enough off to the right so he could keep the road in view without banking the craft. With a map in his lap, he counted the villages as he flew past, praying that he'd find them out on the road somewhere. And find them soon. He passed Ban Pho, Seno, Ban Na, Dong Hene, and Muong Phalane. Then Ban Phone Mouang and Ban Kepo at the foot of the mountains. Still no sign of them.

He trimmed the tabs and eased the Helio into a climb. Against the slope of the hill ahead of him he could see Highway 9 snaking upward in a long series of hairpin turns. He scanned the roadway with growing pessimism. He doubted that they could have made it this far.

The road leveled off onto a saddle between two peaks and then girdled the side of a nearly vertical face of mountain.

He spotted a truck by the side of the road, its cab poised right at the edge of the precipice. He dropped down for a closer look. Immediately he recognized it. It was the beat-up old Dodge they had taken on the mission. Near it, a figure lay sprawled on the ground.

He flew on ahead, checked the highway for approaching traffic, then circled back into the wind. Edging in alongside the mountain wall carefully, he settled the Helio onto the surface and taxied down the road to the truck. With no nose gear for steering, the old tail dragger's direction had to be controlled entirely by rudder and flaps, but McWhirter was so skilled at it that he drove the plane along the bumpy, narrow ledge of highway as easily as if it were an automobile, leaning out the side door to keep the road surface in view.

He cut the engine and walked over to the body. A thick pool of blood around the neck had attracted a lively mass of flies and insects. He bent down for a closer look. The freckled face of Captain Short stared back at him, mouth fixed open in a permanent expression of astonishment.

McWhirter examined the truck and saw the bullet holes in the radiator grille and the evaporating puddle of water under it. The key was not in the ignition, or anywhere else in the cab.

How Short had managed to get himself killed, he couldn't imagine, but Caroline and the Laotian boy must have been in the truck. Had they abandoned it? Been kidnapped? Murdered? What?

He called out Caroline's name at the top of his voice, and listened to his echo bounce back across the gorge. He called several more times, then gave up. He walked back to the Helio, held a wetted finger up to check wind direction, took a quick look around for traffic, and climbed in.

He saw them as soon as he had settled into his seat, descending a steep chimney cut into the face of the cliff overlooking the road.

They ran around to the passenger-side door and scrambled in. McWhirter fired the ignition, gave it full throttle, and peeled the Helio off the high ledge of road just seconds in front of a large diesel tanker truck chugging east.

"There's a bottle of water under the seat," he yelled, over the noise of the climbing engine.

Caroline found it and shared it with Lin Pao. They both looked exhausted and dirty. She explained briefly what had happened. "We decided to hide," she said. "We didn't know what else to do."

"Why didn't you answer me when I yelled?"

"We didn't know whose side you were on."

McWhirter glanced sidelong at her. Her hair was as matted as a bird's nest, and her face sunburned and peeling. He'd never seen her looking so good.

She smiled knowingly at him. "I decided to take the chance that you're a better man than you pretend to be," she said.

McWhirter felt a sharp sting of embarrassment. "Rob found Billy," he said, quickly changing the subject. He pulled the folded-up clipping with Ferrer's story from his breast pocket and handed it to her. "He's coming out with a whole goddamn army."

New York City

James Safier came out the front entrance of his Sutton Place apartment building at eight o'clock, as he did every workday morning, and strode across the sidewalk to his waiting limousine. He exchanged brief pleasantries with his chauffeur, climbed into the air-conditioned back recesses, and relaxed against the cool leather upholstery.

As soon as the limousine reached the relatively smooth road surface of the FDR Drive, Safier reached beside him and scooped up the copies of the *Wall Street Journal* and the *New York Times* that were always placed on the left side of the seat for him.

He thumbed leisurely through the *Journal,* pausing to read a report on a small mining company in Minnesota that Grunwald Industries was secretly preparing to buy out. Rumors that the company was in financial trouble had been judiciously sown some months ago, and Safier was gratified to see that the *Journal* had finally picked up on them. The story was certain to drop the company's OTC stock substantially, making the takeover much easier and cheaper.

As they passed the Fourteenth Street exit, Safier picked up the *Times* and glanced quickly at the headlines.

Below the fold he saw a long two-column story with an accompanying photograph that looked remarkably familiar. It was a posed studio head-shot of a young man in a Marine dress uniform. It was so familiar, in fact, that seeing it on the front page of the *Times* startled him. It was the same photograph that had stood on the corner of William Grunwald's desk for over twelve years.

Safier caught his breath. His eyes stayed riveted on the young face, not daring to move to the column of text beside it.

He steeled himself for the worst, and began reading the story. It took him a long time to get through it, because he had trouble keeping his eyes focused on the words. He stopped frequently to look away.

Rob bringing Billy out. Against all odds. It was unbelievable, but there it was, an eyewitness account by a reputable French journalist.

Safier squeezed the bottom half of the front page in his hand, tearing it away from the rest of the paper and crunching it into a tight ball. When he released it, his hand was covered with newspaper ink. He retrieved a scented moistened towel from a side compartment, ripped open its sealed pouch, and wiped the ink carefully from his trembling fingers.

There were always a thousand things to do in a crisis, he had learned, and in his years with Grunwald, he had handled many of them. Crisis management. He had thrived in that environment. He prided himself on being good at it.

What terrified him now was the realization that with everything in his life at stake, he couldn't think of anything to do.

He had already done everything. And it hadn't been enough.

Laos

Rob braced a hand against the dash and studied the unfolded map on his lap. "A few klicks ahead we drop down into Muong Phine. After that we'll be out of the mountains."

"But not out of the woods," Gilmore replied, his big hands clutching the steering wheel of the Russian truck to keep it on course over the pockmarked road.

"We'll make it, Howard."

"I like to assume the worst," Gilmore replied. "Then be pleasantly surprised when it doesn't happen."

A fist began pounding on the roof of the cab.

"Oh Jesus," Gilmore moaned. "Here it comes."

He steered to the shoulder and stood on the clutch and brake pedal with all his weight, bringing the truck to a jolting halt. They both jumped from the cab and ran out onto the road. The other trucks had stopped behind them, and men were pouring out the tailgates.

Rob was dismayed. Instead of following the plan to disperse and pull the trucks as far off the road and into the foliage as they could, they had parked all four vehicles nose to tail right on the highway.

Too late now. Most of the soldiers were already across the road and disappearing into the thick underbrush. With Gilmore he climbed into the back of the first truck to help the bodyguards lift Billy out.

He chanced a quick glance into the sky and saw the planes immediately. They looked like a flock of small blackbirds coasting on a current of wind.

The four of them lowered Billy over the tailgate and dashed with him across the road toward the protective cover of the jungle.

Rob crouched behind the trunk of a tree and looked up again. The foliage blocked his view of both the sky and the road. Over the noise of his own breath and the pounding of his heart, he heard the faint, jumbled whine of jet engines.

The discordant whine grew louder, then started to fade.

Relieved, Rob started to suck in his breath, then caught it. A series of powerful booms rocked the earth beneath him. An enormous puff of black smoke hissed into the sky, and the air was busy with a thousand birds disturbed from their jungle perches.

The planes circled back and unleashed a second salvo. After the explosions, a dense blanket of smoke spread out across the sky, turning the afternoon into a hazy, yellow-gray twilight.

Rob climbed dejectedly to his feet and pushed through the foliage to the edge of the roadway. Gilmore, Colonel Tieu, and the other soldiers filtered slowly out behind him.

All four of the Russian trucks were in flames.

Washington, D.C.

Walker rolled over on his back and coughed. He waited until the small spasm in his chest had subsided, then opened his eyes in the dark room. Something had awakened him. Not something obvious, like a nightmare, or a disturbance in the apartment. Something more profound. A psychic disturbance.

Walker turned on the computer terminal from the control panel next to his bed and watched as the green phosphor of the video display screen filled the dark room with a dim, lime-colored glow.

The news summary came first. He scrolled the screen through several pages of irrelevent items about Latin America and Africa and was halfway through the Asia report when he realized he had missed the crucial item. He scrolled backward. There it was, in a ten-line summary. Walker's eyes ran down it in a fraction of a second, catching a few words and phrases: "Ghislene Ferrer," "late millionaire William Grunwald," "two sons," and "MIA in Vietnam."

He punched up the complete text of the article. While waiting for it to appear on the screen, he reached for the medihaler by his bed, clamped his fishlike lips around the dispenser end, and pushed down with a finger on the small pressurized can of epinephrine bitartrate, sending a tickling mist of bronchial-dilating fluid down his throat.

The article alarmed him, as he knew it would. Some evil force was interfering with his plans. Monarch Eagle had been aborted. It was over and done with. It had been only a limited success, but if news of it managed to surface, that limited success would become an unlimited disaster. He believed he had done everything necessary to bring it to a secure termination, yet everything was going wrong. Captain Short had let him down abysmally.

When he had finished reading the article, he picked up the telephone and pressed a button on the console that would dial a preset number.

A curt male voice answered: "Captain Adams."

"Captain, this is Mr. Walker."

There was a pause while Adams digested this, then an alert, almost eager reply: "Yes, sir."

"I must travel today. Arrange for a private jet. I wish to leave for Bangkok this afternoon. Arrange my hotel and the special limousine."

"Bangor? In Maine, sir?"

"Bangkok. In Thailand. Sir."

"Yes, sir," Adams replied, contritely. "Who will be accompanying you, sir?"

"Just my chauffeur."

"How many days, sir?"

"I don't know."

"Very good, sir."

Laos

"Sounds like a spotter plane," Gilmore said.

Rob borrowed the binoculars back from Tieu and looked for himself. A single-engine plane was droning through the sky at low altitude, and it seemed headed straight for them. "But he's coming from the west," Rob replied.

"Savannakhet," Tieu explained. "The Laotians have a base there."

They watched the plane fly past overhead. It waggled its wings, then dipped around in a tight arc and came down so close alongside the highway that it seemed to pass almost abreast of them. The large, bright orange-and-red lettering on the side of the cockpit was easy to read.

" 'Chinaman Chin's Flying Dragons'?" Gilmore recited. "I think that guy's seriously lost."

Rob pounded Gilmore's shoulder and laughed. "It's McWhirter!" he shouted.

The aircraft swept around in another turn and lowered itself as lightly as a feather onto the road. It taxied to a stop ten feet from Rob.

McWhirter opened the door and strolled out as casually as if he was about to ask for directions to the area's best restaurant. Catching his style, Rob hid his own elation. "What took you so long, Harris?"

McWhirter shrugged. "You seemed to be doing all right without me."

Caroline appeared from around the other side of the plane, Lin Pao hopping gleefully at her side. She ran into Rob's arms and kissed him on the mouth until it hurt.

She pulled back, finally, and pointed at the row of burning trucks. "We were so afraid you'd been killed. What happened?"

"Air attack. We all got out, though."

"Ghislene Ferrer has already published the story of the mission," she exclaimed. "I can't believe what you've done!"

McWhirter knelt down by the stretcher. "This Billy?"

Rob nodded. Caroline turned and looked down at her husband for the first time. She caught her breath. Clad only in dirty shorts and the water-soaked shirt tucked under his neck, his nut-brown, emaciated body looked mummified—a worn relic of leather and bones, more dead than alive. Overwhelmed by the sight, she clapped her hands to her mouth and turned quickly away.

Rob pulled her against his shoulder. "He's still breathing, but he needs help fast."

"Let's get him on, then," McWhirter said.

The bodyguards hefted Billy's stretcher and carried him over to the plane. The Helio had originally contained six seats, but the back two had been removed to make room for cargo. Gingerly they maneuvered

Billy into the rear and laid him out on the floor. Lin Pao climbed in beside him.

"Can you get Billy to a hospital?" Rob asked.

"Sure. We'll fly him right into Bangkok."

"Take him. Get going."

McWhirter removed his sunglasses and stared at Rob, his eyes squinting in puzzlement. "You aren't coming?"

"No."

"What the hell do you plan to do? Walk back?"

Rob shook his head. "We'll commandeer some wheels in the next town. Or grab the next thing that comes down the road."

"You'll never make it. The Laotians'll set up roadblocks."

"We're a hundred men, Harris. We can get through a roadblock."

"They're not the only ones trying to stop you."

"I know. There's the Vietnamese air force."

"I'm not talking about the Vietnamese."

"Who else is after us?"

"The same people who blackmailed me. They don't want Billy back. Or you either. They're waiting to nail you at the Thai border."

"What's their problem?"

"They want to keep their secret war a secret."

"How many men do they have?"

McWhirter grinned. "Probably not enough to stop you," he admitted. "Caroline and the boy have wiped out two of them already."

Caroline had been listening to this exchange with growing apprehension. "For God's sake," she implored. "You've done everything. We've got Billy. You have to come with us!"

He gestured to the crowd of soldiers on the road behind them. "Those are Billy's men," he said. "They have to get out, too."

"Get out to where?" Caroline demanded.

"Thailand."

"Can't they do that without you?"

Rob didn't answer her. How could he explain it?

Gilmore intervened. "They expect Rob to lead them out."

Caroline's eyes widened in shock. She grasped Rob's sleeve. "I won't leave you again. If you stay, then I stay."

Rob pressed his hands on her shoulders. "No. Don't worry about me. Please. You have to see to Billy. We'll meet you in Bangkok tomorrow. If we get bogged down, then Harris can come back again and pick us up. But everything's going to work out. Make a reservation for all of us at that floating restaurant. We'll have one hell of a celebration."

McWhirter climbed into the pilot's seat. "We can't stay here all day!" he yelled. "What about you, Howard? You coming?"

Gilmore eyed the aircraft longingly and bit his lip. "I'll have to keep an eye on my friend here."

Rob helped Caroline in. "There wouldn't have been room for us all this trip, anyway," he said. "Isn't that so, Harris?"

"Be over my max gross," he admitted.

Rob hugged Caroline for a long, lingering moment, then pulled away.

"You better be there, damn it," she said, brushing back some tears. "I hate to be stood up."

Rob squeezed her hand. "I'll be there. Take care of Billy."

McWhirter leaned over to him. "Listen," he said. "Don't get complacent. You're going to be running a gauntlet all the way to Thailand. They'll try to bottle you up. And if those jets hit you once, they can hit you again."

Rob nodded impatiently. "Why don't you help us, then?"

McWhirter eyed him suspiciously. "How?"

"Aerial reconnaissance. Bring me back a radio and you can fly spotter for us."

"You want to get me shot down fast, don't you."

"I thought you were an ace pilot."

McWhirter laughed. "I'll be back in three hours. Don't get lost."

He fired the engine and the Helio's big prop spluttered a few times and then caught, its blades pulling water from the moisture-laden air and spraying a fine mist in a wide arc around the plane. Caroline leaned out the window and shouted above the roar: "I love you, Rob!"

"We gotta go!" McWhirter yelled. He latched his door closed, and the Helio rolled forward down the roadway and jumped into the air like an angry moth and buzzed away.

Grunwald and Gilmore stood next to each other on the highway, watching it grow smaller over the hills until it had diminished to a barely visible dot against the giant white pillars of thunderheads looming on the western horizon.

Rhinebeck, New York

James Safier, at the wheel of his Porsche, picked Sarah up at her apartment to take them to Greenwood for the weekend. He had been drinking heavily since lunch.

The news about Rob and Billy had put her in such a euphoric mood that she didn't even comment on the Porsche. She always hated to ride in it, complaining that it was uncomfortable and dangerous. As if to play on her dislike for the car, Safier raced up the East River Drive and across the Triboro Bridge.

"You've been drinking," she said, surprised. "You should have let Perry take us up in the limousine."

"Fuck Perry and the limousine," he muttered.

Sarah settled back into the bucket seat, forcing herself not to get angry. "I think we should postpone the wedding, Jim," she said, "until after Rob and Billy return."

Safier glanced sideways at her. "Why the hell should we do that?"

"Isn't the answer obvious? I want them at the wedding. They're family."

"They don't approve of me," Safier snapped. "Either one of them. They never have."

Sarah sighed. "We're not children anymore, Jim. They'll accept you if you give them the chance."

"It's no reason for putting off the wedding."

The argument continued all the way up the Taconic Parkway to Millbrook.

"It's Billy, isn't it," Sarah said, finally. "That's what's really bothering you. You can't bear the thought of him coming back."

"I can't bear the thought of him taking the company away from me," he retorted.

His remark infuriated her. "Taking it away from you? Since when was it yours to lose?"

Safier replied by pressing his foot on the accelerator and watching the RPM needle climb into the 4,000 zone.

"Slow down, Jim!" she pleaded.

"He hasn't earned it," Safier said, slurring his words. "*I've* earned it."

"He's not after your job, for God's sake. That's paranoid."

"He inherits controlling interest in the company."

"And if he didn't come home, you thought you were going to run the company through my sixty-percent share? Did it never occur to you that I might have some say about that?"

Safier pushed the RPM needle to 4,500. "I'm the chief executive officer of the company, god damn it," he snarled. "I've been working there all my adult life. I know the company down to the last goddamn paper clip. You don't know anything about it. You *or* your damned brothers. You're all just along for the ride. Extra baggage. Rich kids."

Safier glanced at the speedometer. The Porsche was rocketing along the narrow-laned parkway at 110 miles an hour. "That's all you are. Spoiled rich kids!"

He maneuvered the agile sports car through a series of tight winding turns, the tires screeching loudly as centrifugal force pulled the Porsche heavily from side to side. Sarah braced herself in the seat. "It's the damned company you really want to marry," she said. "Not me."

"If it wasn't for that damned company," Safier shouted, losing control of his temper completely, "you'd be a housewife in Queens!"

"You don't know me very well, Jim," Sarah said, her voice breaking, "if you assumed that I was going to let you make all the decisions in my life. You may be the next chief executive officer of Grunwald Industries, but I'm William Grunwald's daughter. Even if Billy never came home, I'd never have let you run Grunwald Industries without me. Never! You should have known that."

Safier blew his horn and flashed his lights at a motorist in the left lane ahead of him poking along at eighty miles an hour. He cursed him in a loud voice, then swept around and passed the car in the right lane.

"You hate my brothers," Sarah said, breaking into tears. "And you have contempt for me. I can never marry you."

"I've put my life into that company," Safier cried. "I've worked hard to get where I am. Much harder than you or your brothers. The company should be mine. I was more a son to your father than your brothers. Or even you. None of you care about the company. It's just the place where your money comes from. You've never lived with its problems, taken pride in its achievements. You don't understand it, and you certainly don't know how to run it. None of you. Spoiled rich kids. That's all you are!"

Safier hit a long, straight stretch, pressed the pedal to the floor, and watched the RPM meter climb. He saw it nudge 5,500. The red zone. He laughed. He had never had the courage to push it that far before.

"Slow down, you fool!" Sarah screamed.

The undimmed headlights of a car in one of the southbound lanes blinded him momentarily. Spitefully, he flicked his own beams to high and left them there. In the millisecond that his eyes were diverted, his peripheral vision failed to pick up the dark-brown form of a startled deer jumping out into the road from the wooded fringes of the parkway.

He swerved to miss it, but his coordination, compromised by rage and alcohol, and the car's excessive speed caused him to overcorrect.

The Porsche's front fender nicked the edge of the parkway's centerline divider, a four-foot-high metal guardrail. At the legal speed limit of fifty-five miles an hour, the car might have come away from the rail with little more than a badly scraped fender, but at 120 miles an hour the physics were entirely different. The Porsche kicked up sideways, did a complete cartwheel, and came down hard enough on its crash-resistant rubber bumpers to bounce it completely over the center divider and into the southbound lanes.

It rolled over several times and came to rest sideways in front of an oncoming van. Even though the van managed to slow down, it hit the passenger side of the Porsche hard enough to push it a hundred feet down the highway.

James Safier escaped with multiple bruises, a mild concussion, and several cracked ribs. Sarah was killed instantly.

48

Laos

As they flew westward toward Thailand, Caroline was beset with new apprehensions.

She looked at Lin Pao. He had crawled into the front passenger seat and was sitting with his face pressed to the side window, totally absorbed in watching the Laotian countryside roll past below him.

Rob should be with them, she thought. They should be safely on their way home at last. But he insisted on pushing his luck to the limit, on rewriting the meaning of his life overnight. It was a frightening compulsion that had seized him, and she couldn't understand it entirely. But how much like a Grunwald he was—determined that the world meet him on his own terms.

Gathering courage, she turned and looked down at the form stretched out in the narrow space behind her. Billy was lying on his back, his face just below her. She doubted that she would have known who he was, so dramatically had the twelve years aged him. He was thin, sinewy, his deeply tanned skin callused and scarred—a weathered, almost skeletal distillation of the husband she barely remembered. While his friends back home had grown soft and paunchy, Billy had grown lean and hard, forged in a crucible of experience that she could only guess at. His eyes were closed, but even in his comatose state, his gaunt features seemed tensed and wakeful, as if trapped in some endless vigil, some eternal watch from which he would never be relieved.

Poor Billy. She lowered her palm gently to his forehead and felt his hot, dry skin, dehydrated by fever. Here in her arms was the object of all those years of unanswered prayers, of all those nights of dreaming and waiting.

And the emotion she felt most powerfully was a numb, embarrassed guilt. She had worn out love itself with her love for him. But it was all a self-indulgent deception she had played on herself. They had never had much of a marriage at all; yet in the vast and silent stretches of his absence she had created a fantasy, the myth of an ideal lover who had never existed, and persuaded herself that it was Billy.

But of course it was not Billy. She had never really known Billy at all. Yet he was her husband. If he survived, she would still be married to him. To what? A collection of distant memories. A stranger who had shared some moments with her a long time ago.

Lin Pao jabbed a finger against the window. "Look there!" he cried. McWhirter dropped his right wing down and Caroline leaned across Lin Pao's seat.

They were passing over the village of Seno, where north-south Highway 13 intersected Highway 9 twenty-five miles east of Savannakhet and the Thai border. Several hundred trucks, jeeps, and tanks were massed at the intersection and backed up along the roadway in three directions.

"He'll never get through that," McWhirter said.

"We have to warn him!" Caroline replied, leaning forward to shout over the engine noise.

McWhirter nodded.

"I want to go back with you," she said.

McWhirter shook his head and pointed to the massive wall of cumulus clouds building on the horizon. "Too dangerous. I might have to fly in a storm."

Rob's army covered the two miles to Muong Phine at a jog. They entered the little village, a jumble of thatch-roofed huts and concrete-block houses attached to the edge of Highway 9 by three muddy streets, and looked around in vain for its inhabitants. Colonel Tieu found one toothless old crone on crutches in front of the town's outdoor market.

"Tell her we intend no harm. We need food, water, and transportation. We'll pay for everything."

Tieu translated this. The old woman spit some betel nut onto the ground and replied at length in a loud, cackling voice.

"She says they saw us coming and everybody ran into the woods. We can take what we want; she doesn't care. The only vehicles they have are two old buses, parked by the major's house."

While the soldiers helped themselves to the food in the abandoned market, Rob, Gilmore, Colonel Tieu, and Captain Deng found the major's house, the only place in the village with a fenced-in backyard and a garage—a low wood structure with barn-style doors locked with a padlock.

The two buses were parked beside the garage. They were of French manufacture and very old—high, huge-wheeled leviathans with open rear platforms, like train cabooses, and circular metal steps leading up to them. Someone had recently painted both vehicles with a hand brush—one bright orange with yellow trim, the other bright yellow with orange trim.

"Paris street buses," Gilmore said, staring at them in awe. "Look at this." He pointed to the faded lettering over the front windshield of the yellow one: INVALIDES—PTE. D'ORLEANS. "How the hell do you suppose—"

"All I care about is will they start," Rob replied. Captain Deng jumped into the driver's seat of the yellow one, found the starter button, and pushed it. The ancient autobus coughed, turned over, and caught with a wheezing roar and several loud backfires. Colonel Tieu tried the other one with equally good results.

"Can we load a hundred men and their gear into them?" Rob asked Gilmore.

"You going to hold out for a third bus if we can't?"

"Not funny," Rob muttered. "Let's check out the major's garage." He jammed the barrel of his rifle between the padlock's hasp and the doorpost and pried downward. The screws pulled easily out of the soft wood and the hasp fell off, freeing the door.

Rob whistled softly. Under a clear plastic cover, as spotless as the day it was rolled out of the showroom, sat a cream-colored late-thirties-model French Citroën sedan. He pulled off the cover, gazed reverently for a moment at the sleek clamshell fenders, then put a foot on the wide running board and turned the big door handle. The door opened backward. "Shades of Jean Gabin," he murmured, settling into the low mohair-covered seat. The key dangled from the ignition. He turned it, pulled out the choke, then pulled the starter next to it. The auto fired to life instantly with a pleasant deep-throated growl.

"We're not going to take it, are we?" Gilmore asked.

"You're damned right we're going to take it. We're leaving Laos in style, old buddy."

Rob drove the automobile out of the garage and checked the tires, fuel tank, and radiator. Everything was in perfect order. "Leave the major a note, Colonel," he said to Tieu. "Explain that we've had to borrow his car." Rob dictated the address of Greenwood, in Rhinebeck, New York. "He can write me there, and I'll send him a check for whatever amount he thinks fair."

"I suspect he will miss the Citroën very much," Tieu said, a sympathetic frown saddening his smooth tan features.

Rob smiled. "If he's a good Communist, he'll get over it. Property is theft, after all. Feel sorry for the French colonial he must have expropriated it from."

Captain Deng put a team of men to work rounding up extra gasoline and engine oil. Rob located a can of paint and a brush and quickly painted his initials, "RG," in big white letters on the tops of the three vehicles, to make certain that McWhirter could identify them.

"Gather the troops, Colonel," he said, sealing up the can of paint. "And let's get out of here."

Two of the officers drove the buses onto the roadway and assigned the seats, positioning crack riflemen at strategic locations on each vehicle—one by the open door and window on each side of the driver, two more on the back platform. After a conference with Rob, they added machine gunners fore and aft on the roofs. The rest of the troops squeezed into the seats and aisles.

Rob stationed the Citroën in front of the buses. Captain Deng rode shotgun beside him, and Colonel Tieu and Gilmore settled into the back. He pulled the long, spindly floor shift down into first gear and engaged the clutch. The Citroën rolled forward gracefully onto the rough surface of Highway 9, and the Army of the New Vietnam started west again, toward the Thai border, now just fifty miles distant.

Thailand

To the consternation of the control tower, McWhirter ignored instructions to land on Don Muang's runway 2-left, which would have put him several miles out from the main terminal. Instead he set the Helio down on a section of the taxiway dangerously close to the arrivals gate, maneuvered the craft under the wing of a departing Pan Am 747, and pulled up next to the ambulance he had radioed ahead to meet them.

The hospital crew quickly pulled Billy onto their special stretcher on wheels and loaded him into the back of the ambulance. Lin Pao jumped in behind. They held the door for Caroline.

"Keep a close watch on Billy," McWhirter told her, jumping back into the Helio. "He's got more than his injuries to worry about."

Caroline nodded. "Bring Rob back," she said.

McWhirter latched the door and touched his forehead in a little salute. "I never let anybody down twice."

She waved and climbed into the back of the ambulance. McWhirter keyed his mike and requested clearance for takeoff.

A squeaky voice from the tower came back at him: "That's negative, November-2-zero-5. Severe weather closing in."

"Shit!"

McWhirter taxied the small craft down past the terminal toward the private-plane hangars. He passed in front of Chinaman Chin's and swerved the plane around behind the hangar, across a swath of grass, and onto the service road that ran around the airport perimeter. The road saw only light traffic, and the section he had chosen was reasonably straight for at least five hundred feet. Heavy drops of rain began to spatter on the windshield.

He keyed the mike again and asked for a weather update. A female voice with an Asian accent read off a cryptic stream of letters and numbers in aviation-code shorthand that translated into a dismal forecast—cumulus clouds building to forty thousand feet, visibility approaching zero, a plunging barometer, a wind gusting to fifty knots, and a rapidly colliding temperature and dew point.

McWhirter looked down the stretch of service road and calculated his chances. He didn't need to calculate long. The spattering of rain turned abruptly into a crashing deluge, obliterating the sound of the Helio's engine and the sight of the airport around him. A bolt of lightning flashed nearby, followed instantly by a blast of thunder that rattled the Helio's limber joints.

He cursed, taxied back onto the grass verge, and killed the engine. There was no sense acting macho about it. There were times when it was impossible to fly, and this was one of them. He threw his legs over into the passenger seat, slid down against the side door, folded his arms across his chest, and closed his eyes. He'd just have to wait it out.

Laos

Rob lifted his eyes frequently from the road to the sky, anxiously watching the banks of clouds on the western horizon gradually thicken, then begin to glow red with the reflected light of the setting sun.

No sign of McWhirter.

Gilmore, in the back seat, read his mind. "He must have been grounded by bad weather."

Rob prayed that he was right. He could think of so many other things that might have gone wrong. He glanced down at the odometer and blinked to bring it into focus. They had traveled fifteen miles from Muong Phine without any problems. He wished they could move faster, but the buses were straining at thirty miles an hour, even on the flat. On the hills, their speed dropped to ten. He blinked his eyes again. Gravel seemed imbedded in the lids. The lack of sleep was making him light-headed.

"You notice there's no traffic?" Gilmore said.

"There never was much, anyway."

"They must have the road blocked up ahead."

"I think Mr. Gilmore is correct." It was Colonel Tieu.

"What should we do?" Rob demanded. "Stop?"

There was no answer from the back seat. He glanced across at Captain Deng. He was trying desperately to stay awake, but his eyes kept shutting and his head nodded forward.

"Maybe we should wait for McWhirter," Gilmore said. "He can tell us what's ahead."

"It'll be dark soon," Rob replied. "He won't be able to fly until tomorrow. We're only thirty-five miles from the border. Let's keep going."

They drove on in silence. The twilight thickened. Rob found the switch for the Citroën's headlights and turned them on. The total absence of other traffic on the road became increasingly ominous. He couldn't just go on ignoring it. But to wait overnight for McWhirter was out of the question. In the rearview mirror he noticed Tieu studying the map with a flashlight. He knew what he was thinking. "Where would you try to stop us," he asked, "if you were the Laotians?"

"At Seno," Tieu replied.

"Why there?"

"Highway 13 intersects 9 at that point. They can move men there quickly from Savannakhet to the west, and from the north and the south as well."

"Why not just wait for us at Savannakhet?"

"It would be a mistake. It would give us the opportunity to escape in either of two directions along Highway 13."

"There must be other roads we can escape on."

"No. The only other highway that crosses 9 is 23, back at Muong Phine. And they probably have that blocked by now also."

"How far are we from Seno?"

"Five kilometers—three miles."

Rob stopped the Citroën in the middle of the highway. He shook Captain Deng from his stupor. "Tell the buses we're taking a short rest stop."

Deng waited for Tieu to translate, then stumbled groggily from the car and walked back to the buses.

"We have to scout the roadblock," Rob said.

Gilmore and Tieu agreed. Captain Deng put together a recon team of four men and started immediately down the road toward Seno.

They never returned.

As the hours of waiting passed, Rob could no longer stay awake. He succumbed, finally, and lay out across the front seat of the Citroën and fell instantly into a deep sleep.

He was awakened by the hard rattle of rain on the car's roof. "What time is it?"

"Two in the morning," Gilmore answered, yawning powerfully.

Rob rubbed his eyes and shook his head. "They're not back?"

"No," Tieu replied. Rob felt the strain in the colonel's voice.

"You think they've been captured?"

"It is likely."

"They know we're here, then," Gilmore concluded.

For a long time no one spoke.

"How far's the border?" Rob asked.

"Twenty-five miles," Tieu said.

"Let me see the map."

Tieu handed the map and the flashlight across to Rob in the front seat. Rob studied the now mangled rectangle of paper for several minutes.

"As soon as it gets light, they'll move up the road," Gilmore said.

Rob nodded. "We still might be able to fight our way through. But we don't know what we'll meet."

"It won't be the Welcome Wagon," Gilmore replied. "They've already thrown the air force at us. They'll probably try tanks next."

They discussed their options. Gilmore and Tieu favored hiding off the road and setting up an ambush.

Rob disagreed. "The object is to escape. So far we've kept them off guard. If we stop, we lose our momentum. But the ambush plan gives me an idea. Why not take the men cross country, Colonel? It's light woods and field if you stay north of Seno. And if you keep straight west, the border is less than twenty miles. You can be there in five or six hours."

"You're not coming?"

"You'll need a decoy to make it work. With the two buses, Gilmore and I can make them believe we're dug in here. That'll give you time to get across."

"Then what will you do?"

"McWhirter will pick us up."

They discussed the details. Tieu agreed that it was a workable plan. The men would be happier off the road, he felt, because they were accustomed to traveling and fighting that way, and he believed they had a good chance of reaching the border. "But you must come with us," he insisted. "Your friend with the plane might not show up."

"He'll make it. We'll probably beat you across the border."

Tieu accepted his arguments.

"You should leave now," Rob said. "Once you're across into Thailand, you'll be political refugees. We'll wait to hear from you at the Oriental Hotel, in Bangkok. We'll alert the American ambassador and start the immigration stuff rolling for you. Then I'm going to rent the Oriental's banquet hall and throw the biggest party for you Bangkok has ever seen."

Colonel Tieu collected the men from the buses, organized them in small patrols of a dozen each, and gave them their new orders. Rob shook hands with each soldier and wished him well.

By three o'clock in the morning they were ready. Colonel Tieu cleared his throat, bowed his head slightly in his usual formal manner, and offered his hand to Rob to shake.

Rob took it. "We're almost home, Colonel."

"Yes, almost home," Tieu replied, without irony. "God be with you," he said in French.

Rob embraced him. Tieu then strode quickly over to the first party of soldiers and led them off into the heavy woods that bordered the highway.

He didn't even know the colonel's first name, he thought. He stood silently beside Gilmore in the rain and watched until the last man had disappeared into the dark.

Thailand

McWhirter woke at first light, his body plagued with aches from his contorted sleeping position in the back of the cabin. Someone was banging on the side of the plane. He groaned, then forced his stiff limbs to climb over the back seat and unlatch the door. It was Caroline, in clean pants and shirt, face washed and hair shampooed. "I knew it'd be you," he grumbled.

She held up a small canvas tote bag. "I brought you breakfast. Coffee, orange juice, and hard-boiled eggs."

McWhirter closed his eyes. Without waiting for an invitation, Caroline pulled herself into the cabin and dropped the bag in his lap. "I'm going with you," she declared.

"What about Billy?"

"He'll live."

"You're supposed to be watching him."

"He's registered under a false name. And I hired a guard to sit outside his room. And I made the hospital promise not to let in any visitors."

"I don't like it."

"Well, for God's sake," Caroline argued, "he's safer with an armed guard than he would be with just me there."

McWhirter gulped down the coffee and juice and closed the bag. "It makes me nervous flying with a woman," he complained.

"That's very old-fashioned, Mr. McWhirter. Just pretend I'm not here."

"Sure," he mimicked. " 'Just pretend I'm not here.' " He sighed in disgust, then busied himself with the preflight checkout list. As soon as that task was complete, he raised the tower and requested clearance for takeoff.

"You must think a hell of a lot of him," he said, taking the mike away from his lips. "To go through all this." He fired the engine and began the taxi to the runway. "If you were my woman, I'd be madder than hell at you."

"Why?"

McWhirter lined the Helio up at the takeoff point. Yesterday's storm front had cleared out and left the air dry and the dawn sky a brilliant, uncluttered blue from horizon to horizon. It was flying weather.

"One more thing to worry about," he replied.

"Didn't you ever have anyone to worry about?"

McWhirter waited until he had the plane airborne before he answered: "No, I guess I never did."

"Maybe you missed something."

"Maybe I did."

He nudged the Helio up to eight thousand feet, where he found a twenty-knot tail wind. He leaned the mixture control to preserve the optimum one part fuel to fourteen parts air, then eased the throttle forward as far as it would go and headed for Laos. Over the whine of the engine, neither tried to talk.

Approaching the Mekong, he took the Helio down to five hundred feet. Laotian radar was nonexistent and its air defenses primitive, but he wasn't taking any chances. In a Helio, it was both safer and easier to fly close to the ground. He flicked on the radio and scanned the channels. Nothing of interest.

Once across the Mekong, he flew a few miles into Laos and then banked sharply north, to intercept Highway 9. He found the strip of roadway and turned east to follow it.

Almost immediately he noticed a thin white contrail cutting across the eastern sky. It was high—about fifteen thousand feet—and headed directly west. He watched the plume of white zip past overhead, then flatten and dissipate, shredded by the teeth of the winds aloft. He scanned the radio channels again to see if he could pick up anything.

Nothing.

Five minutes later he looked up to see a new contrail, coming back east. This one was lower—ten thousand feet, he judged—and chewing up the sky at around Mach 1.

The contrail continued east across half the sky and then looped around, losing altitude fast. Near the bottom of its loop, it was low enough and close enough for him to get a good look at it: a thick, squared-off fuselage aft of the cockpit, and distinctive twin vertical tail fins mounted over a pair of turbojets.

It flattened out at about a thousand feet and closed fast in the direction of the Helio. Even at a distance of several miles, McWhirter could see the four wing pylons, loaded with missiles.

Caroline sensed his sudden agitation. "What is it?"

"Foxbat," McWhirter replied.

Caroline stared at the rapidly approaching MiG fighter. "What is he doing?"

"Getting ready to blast us to hell."

49

Laos

In the first light of morning Rob Grunwald and Howard Gilmore found a spot on Highway 9 where the road had been cut through a hill, creating a narrow pass with steep embankments on either side. They drove the buses to the spot and wedged them across the highway, stretching them out, one alongside the other, so that they blocked the pass completely, like a sliding door extended across an opening.

They punctured all the tires, then collected elephant leaves and branches from the nearby woods and arranged them in the seats as artfully as they could—a stick poking up here, like the tip of a rifle barrel, an elephant leaf carefully propped in the seat there, to look like the top of a helmet—to suggest that the buses were defended.

Finally, they drove the Citroën back about a mile, parked it on the shoulder with the doors open, and climbed to the top of a promontory over the road that gave them a view of their barricade.

"Now what?" Gilmore asked.

"We wait for McWhirter."

The sight of the MiG-25 closing toward them caused McWhirter to issue a stream of profanities to blunt the quaking sensations rippling across the floor of his stomach.

"You can evade him, can't you?" Caroline asked.

He glanced at her, incredulous. She looked anxious when she should have looked terrified. In her innocence, he realized, she had complete faith that he could save them. "Sure," he replied.

She nodded with relief and clutched her seat belt.

He ransacked his memory about the Foxbat: a top speed over Mach 3; a ceiling of eighty thousand feet. Its twin turbojet engines put it in a class with a guided missile, with enough power to leave the atmosphere altogether. It was usually armed with two radar and two infrared heat-seeking missiles, any of which was capable of destroying anything in the sky from a distance of fifty miles with even a near miss. Awesome.

But it had weaknesses, too. It carried no cannon. It was useless at close ranges and in normal air combat. It was a high-speed, high-altitude interceptor. What it did best was stand off and kill.

The craft had a short combat radius of seven hundred miles, so it must have flown out from Hue, the nearest base. Even that was a good two hundred miles away, McWhirter estimated, so he didn't have more than about fifteen minutes over his target. Russian pilot? Or Vietnamese? He scanned the radio channels. And this time he caught something. The pilot was calling his sighting back to base, and he was speaking Vietnamese.

That was a possible break. He wouldn't be as well trained as a Russian.

The MiG rocketed by them. The Helio shuddered and twisted under the impact of the shock wave, and McWhirter had his hands full keeping her from tumbling out of control.

Once steady again, he banked hard to the left, searching the sky around him. The MiG was climbing behind him, straight up, traveling like a rocket. He heard the radio crackle again: the pilot requested permission to intercept his target.

McWhirter licked his lips. It had been a long time since his mouth felt that dry. He dropped the Helio down as close to the surface of the highway as he dared, and looked for traffic. He had a wild impulse to land the craft and just jump out and run like hell, but he held her close to the highway, his brain working for some way to foil what was about to happen—the unleashing of one of those missiles in their direction.

The Foxbat had moved out in front of him again. He was several miles away and starting into a long, shallow turn.

"There's the roadblock," Caroline yelled, pointing down to the highway below.

McWhirter glanced down and saw the vehicles feeding onto Highway 9 from 13. A spearhead of four tanks was past the intersection and clanking east along 9.

The Foxbat completed its turn and headed toward him again. He knew it wouldn't fire, because it hadn't yet been given permission by the sluggish bureaucracy back at Hue. But McWhirter's eyes were clamped on the four pylons beneath the wings, mesmerized by them. The Foxbat's fangs.

The MiG shot by, this time at a safer distance. He heard the pilot acknowledge the okay to intercept target.

"Keep your eye on him for me!" he shouted to Caroline. "Follow him with your finger so I know where he is! Can you do that?"

"Of course!"

"Don't lose sight of him! Watch for a puff of white smoke by the wings. That's crucial. That means he's fired a missile. When you see that, yell!"

"Okay!"

McWhirter watched Caroline crane her head around, find the MiG out the side window, and point to the rear corner of the plane with her forefinger.

It had to be a heat seeker first, he decided. It was the most reliable, and the Vietnamese hated to waste expensive missiles.

He slammed the stick over hard and brought the Helio through a sharp 180-degree turn, putting the Foxbat in front of him again. Caroline scrambled in her seat to keep the MiG in sight. Her finger swung around to the front and pointed straight out the windshield between them. Just where he wanted it.

McWhirter pressed his face against the side window and looked down. He was just coming up behind the long column of military vehicles starting to move east on Highway 9. When he saw the tanks at the head of the column, he eased out the flaps until he was just keeping pace with them. He was dangerously near stall speed and prayed the tanks didn't slow down on him. He stole a glance at his airspeed indicator. The MiG might be able to fly at 2,100 miles an hour, but it damn well couldn't fly at thirty-five.

The hatch on the lead tank was open and the crewman in the turret was trying frantically to bring his machine gun to bear on the Helio, now cruising twenty feet behind and one hundred feet above him.

"Now!" Caroline yelled.

McWhirter held the Helio on course, hovering over the tanks as closely as he dared. In his mind's eye he saw the missile carving a contrail across the sky, sniffing for the heat of its victim.

He counted out four seconds, then pushed the stick hard to the right, jammed the throttle forward, stood the Helio on its wings, and pulled away from the line of tanks at a near right angle.

The infrared missile, suddenly presented with a choice of two heat sources, picked the one closest to its trajectory—the lead tank.

The explosion nearly knocked the Helio out of the sky.

"Educational software," Gilmore said, rubbing the fatigue from his eyes.

Rob steadied the binoculars on the two buses barricading the highway a mile to the west. "What did you say?"

"When we get back home, that's what I'm going into," Gilmore replied. "Educational software. I've thought a lot about it. With the money from this venture, I can start my own company."

Rob leaned back against the ledge of stone and squinted up into the sky. It was eight o'clock and the sun was well up.

"What are *you* going to do?" Gilmore asked.

Rob guessed his friend was simply talking to keep his courage up. He didn't feel the same need, for some reason. His mind was totally focused on their present predicament. "I haven't thought about it, to tell you the truth."

"You'll be a celebrity. You know that, don't you?"

Rob put the binoculars to his eyes again and scanned the western horizon, looking for McWhirter. "No, I don't know that."

"Sure. Ferrer's already started it: Son of millionaire industrialist rescues MIA brother from Vietnam, leads a guerrilla movement to safety, and ends a clandestine U.S. operation in Vietnam. What a story! They'll be waiting for you in Bangkok—the news magazines, the networks, the talk shows. You'll get the treatment, believe me. I know how these things work. There'll be publishers and movie producers climbing all over each other for your story. You'll be an overnight sensation. I'm not kidding."

"There're a few holes in your scenario, Howard. Billy may not live, and we're still in Laos."

Gilmore removed his spectacles and wiped them nervously with the tail of his shirt. "No, no. I see a happy ending. I see you and Caroline and Lin Pao living happy and famous ever after."

Rob rested the binoculars in his lap. "Don't talk like that. You're making me nervous. And if I don't see McWhirter's airplane in another five minutes, I'm *really* going to get nervous."

Gilmore ignored him. "The only thing I'm jealous about is Caroline.

If you hadn't gotten there ahead of me, I'd be panting after her like a lovesick puppy. She does things to me. But if I can't have her, I'm glad it's you. You're a lucky son of a bitch, Robbie."

Rob laughed. It was a reaction to nerves more than anything else, a sudden release of tensions that had been held in tight check for a long time.

"Something funny?"

Rob shook his head. "Not really. Just absurd. Everything you were telling me about what my life is going to be like. You may be right, but it sounds so unreal. And you know why? Because of these last few weeks—these last few days. So much has happened. Bad and good together. Whatever's in store for us after we get out of here— *if* we get out of here—it's got to be a big anticlimax."

Rob held the binoculars up again and trained them on their barricade. "To tell you the truth, Howard, I feel as if I've already lived my life."

Severomorsk

Koenig appeared early. Even with no way of telling the time, Grunwald knew that the German's visits occurred with an established and predictable daily rhythm. This one seemed only a few hours since the last. Koenig walked in as he usually did, his back straight, his watery eyes flashing aggressively at their target. But this time he didn't sit down. The guard remained by the door but didn't close it. Koenig's manner was formal.

Grunwald sensed that an important moment was at hand. He steeled himself against the pathetic mixture of anxiety and hope that churned in his guts.

"In a few hours we will dock at the port of Severomorsk, Herr Gruen," Koenig said, his voice flat. "You'll be given some additional clothing, and your personal effects will be returned to you. Please be prepared to depart at that time."

"Is this the truth?"

The German ignored his question. "The guard here will see to your needs. He will take you to another part of the ship, where you will be fed. Then you'll be able to change, shower and shave, and walk around for a while. The light and exercise and the fresh faces, after all these days down here, will do you good." Koenig turned to leave. "When we have docked," he said, "I will join you on deck to give you your final instructions."

Laos

Rob saw the contrail high overhead and trained the binoculars on the silver pinpoint at its tip. "Another fighter," he said. "Like the ones that attacked our trucks."

"He seems to be circling a target over there somewhere," Gilmore muttered, shading his eyes and squinting up into the sky.

Minutes later they heard a distant rumble in the west. Rob held the glasses on the horizon. "A column of smoke," he said, finally. "Looks like he bombed something on the road. I wonder what's going on."

"What if McWhirter doesn't show up?" Gilmore said, voicing the unspoken possibility that had been on their minds all morning.

"We'll walk out, I guess," Rob replied evenly. "Like Tieu and the others."

"You think they made it?"

"They've had six hours."

Gilmore suddenly pressed his face into his hands. Rob had noticed him doing it with increasing frequency. He was hiding another upsurge of tears. His nerves were betraying him. "It's damned tough, just sitting here," he said, uncovering his face after a pause. "I feel like I'm waiting for my own execution."

Rob handed him the binoculars. "Here. Do something, then."

Gratefully, Gilmore pushed his spectacles up onto his bald head and pressed the binoculars against his eyes.

Rob stood up and paced the few short steps the ledge allowed. It was nearly ten o'clock and getting hot. After a few minutes he sat down again, covered in a film of sweat. "I keep thinking about Wyler," he said.

"Don't think about him," Gilmore warned. "You didn't have any choice. He would have killed Billy."

"I did have a choice. I shouldn't have taken him on the mission."

"Why not? He was qualified. And he lied to you about his reasons. How could you know what was going on in his head?"

"I did know," Rob said. "At least I had some idea. Little hints from things he said now and then. The way he acted. Inside, I knew."

"Why *did* you take him, then?"

Rob rested his head against the stone ledge. "I don't know. Some part of me couldn't resist setting him against Billy. I couldn't resist giving Wyler his chance. Of course, I thought his reasons were better than they turned out to be. I thought he had a legitimate grievance against Billy. I never dreamed that he was covering up his role in a massacre. And I didn't imagine that he'd try to kill him." Rob looked up at the sky and then started pacing the ledge again. "I wanted to find Billy, but I didn't want to find a hero. I wanted to bring him home in disgrace. Wyler fit into that. Not very noble of me."

Gilmore didn't reply.

"It was part of my fantasy of revenge against the old man. That's really what motivated me—at least in the beginning. Otherwise I wouldn't have had the guts or determination to see it through. It was revenge. The whole rescue mission was revenge."

"You're being too hard on yourself," Gilmore said.

"My father's dead, Howard."

Gilmore removed the binoculars from his eyes and looked at Rob. "How do you know?"

"Billy heard it on the shortwave. It happened when we were on our way in here. His plane crashed."

"I'm sorry."

"He was in the SS."

Gilmore squinted at his friend in confusion. "What did you say?"

The turmoil that had raged within Rob since first learning of his father's death overwhelmed him momentarily, leaving him too choked to get out the words. Finally he swallowed hard and tried again, delivering his revelations in a terse and swift monotone: "My father was in the SS. He wasn't a prisoner at Dachau—he was a guard. He wasn't a Jew—he was a Nazi. He killed an inmate and stole his identity. That's how he escaped."

The words out, Rob sat down hard, pulled his knees up, and buried his face against them.

Gilmore's astonishment was complete. He dropped the binoculars against his chest as if someone had struck him a blow. "Are you sure of all that?"

"Billy found out," Rob whispered. "It's true. It fits."

Gilmore kept shaking his head.

"I'm half Jew and half Nazi, Howard. How do you like that for an inheritance? Half victim and half oppressor. No wonder my life has been so fucked up."

"That's not a parallel construction," Gilmore replied, weakly. "You're half German and half Jewish. Nothing wrong with that."

Rob ignored his friend's reply. "I wish he hadn't died, Howard. I want to talk to him. For the first time in my life. He made a terrible mistake—once a long time ago—and he spent the rest of his life trying never to make another one. But he did make that one mistake. He's human to me, at last."

RICHES AND HONOR / **423**

Rob picked up a stone lying beside him and heaved it with all his strength out over the ledge. "Imagine how he must have felt," he said. "The awful fear he must have lived with every day of his life, knowing that everything he had built could be destroyed overnight if his secret got out. No wonder he needed to control us, to control everything around him. He was afraid. He needed power, authority in great doses, just to keep his fear at bay. He needed to be invincible—and he damned near was. I hated him because I couldn't understand why he had to be that way. But at least now there's an explanation. I could talk to him now. We'd have something to say to each other."

Gilmore tensed suddenly. Wordlessly, he passed the binoculars to Rob. Rob held them up and rewound the focus knob in the center to adjust them to his eyesight.

The field of view sharpened. In a hazy wriggle of heat on the far side of the buses, their shapes foreshortened by the high-powered magnification of the lenses, a column of tanks was moving toward them.

The Helio was blown into a tailspin. Barely above the treetops, the cockpit reeling around him like an out-of-control carnival ride, McWhirter battled desperately, his hands and feet moving in response to the ingrained lessons of thousands of hours of hazardous flying, to bring the Helio back into level flight.

He succeeded partly because the impact of the blast carried the plane out over the edge of a drop-off, giving him a precious additional fifty feet of airspace to wrestle the battered craft back into trim.

McWhirter found a long slope of open pastureland below him and made an instant decision to land. He pulled around into the wind and landed the plane uphill, using less than a hundred feet of the rock-strewn field to bounce to a stop. He choked off the gas, jumped from the plane, ran around to the passenger side, and pulled Caroline out.

She fell to the grass and vomited. He flopped down near her and lay motionless on his back, listening to his ragged breath and booming heartbeat.

When he felt calmer, he sat up. Caroline was already back on her feet, wiping her face with her shirt. He was aware suddenly how peaceful it seemed. The pasture was empty and the Helio was still sitting where he had parked it, innocent and whole.

He stood up and searched the sky. Nothing in view but the hot morning sun.

"That was close," he said.

Caroline nodded. "You got us through it."

"Just barely," he admitted. He inspected the Helio's fuselage and control surfaces. No damage. He walked to the rear of the craft, hoisted the tail in his arms, and hauled it around until the plane was facing down the slope.

"You game for another shot?" he asked.

Caroline climbed back into the plane. McWhirter climbed in after her, fired the ignition, taxied rapidly downhill, and popped back into the sky.

He leveled out at a hundred feet over Highway 9. The column of tanks had moved around the smoldering derelict in the middle of the road and were racing eastward. He leaned on the throttle, curved swiftly past the tanks, and steadied the craft directly over the roadway, his eyes shifting nervously around the sky for signs of another MiG.

Caroline saw the buses and pointed excitedly. "They've barricaded the highway!" she yelled.

They flew over the Citroën. McWhirter saw the open doors. "He wants us to land," he said. "But where the hell *is* everybody?"

Bangkok, Thailand

Walker depressed the intercom button as soon as his chauffeur had seated himself in the front.

"He's on the fourth floor," the chauffeur said. "Room 412."

Walker looked across the parking lot at the hospital. Even through the heavily tinted glass the deadly glare of the midday sun was obvious, its wounding shafts ricocheting from the car tops and the hospital windows. "How did you find out?" he demanded.

"The Press. They're all over the lobby, trying to get up to see him."

"What about Mrs. Grunwald?"

"No one knows where she is."

Walker nodded, glancing distastefully out at the sunlight. "Drive up to the side entrance, over there. I'd like to do this without my umbrella."

Laos

Grunwald and Gilmore sat and watched the pair of ancient autobuses take round after round from the turret guns of the lead tank. Each hit caused them to quake like some enormous trapped beasts in terror of their own destruction. Holes gaped along their flanks. The roof of one lay blasted open, and smoke billowed out in dirty black clouds.

The first tank reached the barricade and stopped. At that same moment a small single-engine aircraft popped into view, skimming the treetops along the south edge of the highway.

"Here he is!" Rob yelled.

They snatched up their rifles and began the difficult scramble down the steep face of the ledge.

The lead tank backed up, accelerated to about thirty miles an hour, and crashed into the corner of the left bus, its treads chewing into the skin of the huge vehicle with a screech of tearing metal. The bus shuddered and bounced backward, opening a gap between it and its sister.

The Helio circled overhead. Rob and Gilmore staggered out onto the roadway near the Citroën and waved. McWhirter waggled his wings in response.

They jumped into the Citroën. Rob started it, accelerated into a skidding U-turn, and raced away from the barricade just as the lead tank burst through.

50

Laos

McWhirter banked around over the breached wall of buses. Four tanks had pushed through the gap opened by the lead tank and were now rumbling down the open highway. Behind the tanks came the trucks of soldiers, one by one squeezing through the narrow space between the two burning vehicles and chasing to catch up to the tanks. McWhirter estimated the distance between the lead tank and the Citroën to be about half a mile. The tank fired a shell that exploded in the roadway about a hundred feet short of its target.

McWhirter leaned on the throttle to catch up to the Citroën. When he had it directly under his left wing, he checked his airspeed. Eighty knots. The Citroën, he guessed, was doing seventy miles an hour and rapidly increasing its distance from the tanks.

He turned to Caroline. "It looks like there's only Rob and Howard left down there!" he yelled over the whine of the engine. "I'm going to try and pick them up!"

She nodded. If she feared for her own safety, she no longer showed it. She strained forward in her seat, clutching the support under her side window, her concentration totally fixed on the drama beneath them.

McWhirter climbed to two hundred feet and raced east above Highway 9 at full throttle. The road weaved through several low hills, then rose to a wide, flat plateau where it ran straight and level for nearly a mile. The perfect place to land and wait for Rob to catch up to him.

Except that somebody else was already there.

A long line of military trucks, some hauling light-artillery carriages, was rolling westward, to close with the tank convoy from Seno. In the lead was a half-track with a machine gun mounted up front.

The Citroën was now trapped on a rapidly shrinking stretch of highway.

McWhirter banked around. He saw the Citroën just appearing over the rise onto the plateau.

"The plane is back!" Caroline yelled, jabbing her finger against the windshield. McWhirter saw it. Another MiG-25, just leveling out of a steep dive and headed directly at them.

A gigantic red-brown flower of smoke and dirt blossomed suddenly out of the highway twenty feet in front of the Citroën.

"Jesus Christ," McWhirter whispered. "He missed."

The MiG exploded past with a trembling concussion of air, fired its afterburners, and shot into a vertical climb to set up for another pass. McWhirter worked the controls to keep the Helio on course in the wake of the Foxbat's turbulent slipstream. He banked around to approach the Citroën. Rob had probably been saved by the sight of the second convoy in front of him. He had slammed on the car's brakes just in time to miss the Foxbat's missile. Luck was still with him.

The Citroën was turning around slowly, to head back in the other direction.

"Get out of the car, Grunwald!" McWhirter implored, between clenched teeth. "Get out of the fucking car!"

The Citroën had been badly battered by the missile's near miss. The driver's side was blackened and at least one tire was flat.

The tank column reached the far edge of the plateau. About a mile separated it from the truck convoy approaching from the other direction. The Foxbat was out of sight somewhere at the top of its arc in the sky above them.

He put the Helio in a wide circling approach, losing altitude until he was barely ten feet above the ground. He lined up with the highway to land.

The Citroën's big back-hinged doors opened at last and Rob and Gilmore scrambled out onto the road.

McWhirter hit Caroline's arm. "Unhook your door!" he yelled. "Then climb into the back! This'll be our only shot!"

Severomorsk

William Grunwald hoisted himself slowly up the metal rungs of the conning-tower ladder and emerged through the open hatchway into the daylight for the first time in many days, his legs trembling beneath him.

He was still in shock from the memory of his reflection in the mirror over the sink where he had shaved. A gaunt, sallow-faced old man had stared back at him, his jaw slack, his cheeks sunken, his eyes hollow and rimmed with shadow. He had lost nearly twenty pounds, and his flesh was still covered with yellow and black bruises and the crusts of healing scabs from the beating he had taken.

He walked carefully down the steel steps to the railing on the old submarine's aft deck. It was a bright, chilly day, with a biting wind. June in the Arctic Circle. He pulled the brown quilted cotton coat he had been given tightly around his neck and gazed out at the incredible panorama of the Russian Northern Fleet at anchor.

Ships of all sizes, from aircraft carriers to small coastal minesweepers, crowded the flat waters of the White Sea in all directions, their gray hulks swinging at anchor in rows that seemed to extend clear to the horizon. To the south, enormous submarine sheds and repair docks crowded the harbor. The long necks of loading cranes clanked and swung above them, like giant mechanical birds.

Koenig appeared at his side. The German was wearing a luxurious leather greatcoat with a high collar. The supple sheen of the material contrasted vividly with the ruined face of its wearer. Koenig reached into an inside pocket and withdrew a thick document and unfolded it. The pages crackled in the wind and he was forced to grasp them tightly with both hands. "A transcript of your trial, Herr Gruen," he said.

"My trial?"

"You were tried in absentia by the People's Court of the German Democratic Republic in Karl-Marx-Stadt, in the province of Saxony, in August of 1949."

"I don't understand."

Koenig grinned, exposing his bad teeth. "War crimes, Herr Gruen. War crimes." The German turned several pages of the document and stretched them flat in his hands. "Specifically, you were tried on two charges: membership in a criminal organization—the Waffen SS; and for the murder of one Simon Grunwald, in the infirmary of Dachau Concentration Camp, on the night of April 29, 1945."

Grunwald stared at the pages in Koenig's hands. They were yellowed and brittle, as if someone had left them out in the sun. He started to ask to inspect them but changed his mind. He didn't doubt their authenticity.

"You were found guilty on both counts," Koenig continued. "I was the chief state witness against you. You were sentenced to twenty years at hard labor."

Grunwald shook his head slowly, as if to dismiss the whole matter. "That was a long time ago. Most sentences were shortened to three or four years. I would have been released by the early fifties."

"You are wrong, Herr Gruen. Only in the Western-controlled sectors were the sentences shortened. War criminals in the DDR served their time—to the day."

"Why are you telling me this now?"

"Haven't you guessed? There is no statute of limitations for war criminals in the DDR. You are guilty, Willi Gruen, and you must serve your time. And you will serve it in the same place as most of the other war criminals who came within our jurisdiction—in a Soviet labor camp."

Grunwald felt light-headed.

"I stuck with your case single-mindedly," Koenig said, allowing himself to boast a little. "Getting you tried and convicted was relatively easy. Getting you to take your punishment has been far more of a challenge. But I have been patient, and at last I have succeeded."

Grunwald squeezed his fingers around the cold metal railing, afraid that he was about to pass out. "You are a monster," he murmured.

Koenig laughed. "In a way you are right. I was forced to become one—to catch the monster I was after."

"I have been punished enough."

"You murdered a man who had been punished enough—far more than you will ever be. A poor Jew, an angelic human being who suffered every grief and humiliation the Nazis were capable of inflicting on a man. Think of him, the helpless victim whom you suffocated to death with a blanket on the eve of his rescue, whose name you then appropriated and defiled. I think that you can never be punished enough, Herr Gruen."

"You can't get away with this. The United States government will discover what you have done."

"You forget that you are a citizen of the German Democratic Republic, not the United States. Your fraudulent career as William Grunwald will hardly help you now. You have come full circle. You have lost your capitalist wings and become a caterpillar again. William

Grunwald is dead. And you are your true self once more, the Aryan son of Berta and Klaus Gruen, from Chemnitz, Saxony—the Hitler Youth, the Waffen-SS corporal, the concentration-camp guard."

Grunwald saw a motor launch approaching across the blue harbor water. A small Russian pennant fluttered from the bow. Several Russian police officers stood on the deck.

"Since you have no living relatives as Willi Gruen, you will not be permitted any contact with the outside world during your imprisonment. No doubt you will entertain fantasies of somehow smuggling your story out to the West. But nothing escapes easily from a Soviet labor camp, not even news. And even if you were to reach someone in the United States government, he would be disinclined to believe your story. A dead William Grunwald suits the purposes of the United States far better than the live one would, given the inevitable embarrassment that the truth about him would cause to his former family, his former business associates, and, of course, the present administration in Washington."

Koenig folded the document he had been holding all this time and handed it to Grunwald. "If you survive your sentence," he said, "and you might—you're only in your fifties, after all—you will be allowed to return to the Democratic Republic. You will be well past retirement by then, so you will become a ward of the state. Despite your crimes, Herr Gruen, our Socialist society is still willing to undertake the responsibility of your welfare."

The motor launch came alongside, and three Russians in uniform stepped onto the deck of the submarine. Papers were produced and signed by both sides, and the exchange of the prisoner was officially consummated.

Willi Gruen was handcuffed and escorted onto the motor launch and taken to a dock in the harbor. He was then transferred to a police van and driven to the municipal jail in Murmansk. There he would await a special train that would take him to his final destination—a labor camp in Kolyma, in the remote Yakut Republic in northeastern Siberia.

Laos

McWhirter touched the Helio down in a powered landing and gunned it eastward along the highway. With the tail of the plane settled on the ground, he was forced to lean out the side window to see the road ahead of him. Grunwald and Gilmore were running toward him. Behind them, the Citroën stood with its doors open, partially blocking the path of the approaching half-track, now less than a hundred yards away. McWhirter could see the machine gunner standing in the lead half-track, swinging his weapon back and forth in a narrow arc on its pivot post. Two bullet holes blossomed suddenly in the lower right corner of the windshield, inches from where Caroline had just been sitting.

The Citroën exploded with a flash and a boom, and McWhirter heard the shrieking whine of the MiG as it pulled out of its dive. Fifty feet from Grunwald and Gilmore he banged the flaps full open, swung the craft around 180 degrees, and braked to a stop.

Gilmore was at the door. He scrambled in and dove into the back beside Caroline to leave room up front for Rob. McWhirter watched the open door, but Grunwald didn't appear. Seconds thundered by. Still the doorway gaped empty before his eyes. Then Gilmore was yelling and scrambling back out of the plane.

McWhirter fell across the seats to look out behind him. The half-track had stopped just past the burning Citroën, and the machine gunner was firing intently, kicking up puffs of tar and dirt all over the road around Rob. Gilmore reached him, knelt down, and lifted him into his arms. He staggered to his feet and came running back toward the Helio. McWhirter heard the rounds ripping into the tail section of the plane with little pinging pops. How they were failing to hit Gilmore he couldn't understand.

Gilmore shoved Rob's inert and sagging form through the doorway, and Caroline pulled him into the back. McWhirter pushed the throttle hard and the plane lurched forward, the unlatched passenger door banging in the air.

Several soldiers had leaped from the half-track and were now running alongside the plane, shouting and firing wildly. One round shattered the window beside him, showering him with pebbles of Plexiglas. He pulled back on the stick and the plane nosed into the air. Several more rounds blew small holes in the wings, but in seconds he was out of range. He stayed low over the column of tanks until he reached the west edge of the plateau and was able to disappear over it.

The Foxbat, its time over target exhausted, had gone home.

McWhirter didn't look at his passengers until he was across the Mekong River and safely inside Thailand. Gilmore was sitting heavily in the seat beside him, still breathing hard, his face turned away to the side window. Rob Grunwald was lying across the back seat, his head in Caroline's lap. His eyes were closed and Caroline was cradling him like a baby. The cabin, front and back, was spattered with blood.

"Is he bad?"

Gilmore nodded, unable to speak.

"You all right?"

Another nod.

McWhirter turned back to the instrument panel. He coaxed the engine to its maximum output, watching the RPMs hover into the red as the airspeed indicator grudgingly granted him another couple of knots. "The hospital in Bangkok has a parking lot," he said. "I'm going to land in it, somehow."

Bangkok, Thailand

The hospital official was cordial and eager to please, but he stubbornly refused to permit anyone into Billy's room.

Walker nodded calmly and produced a document, signed by the highest U.S. military authority, that specifically identified Walker as Billy's superior officer. Still the hospital head hesitated. Finally a telephone call to the U.S. ambassador broke the impasse. Apologizing all the way, the official personally escorted Walker and his chauffeur to Billy Grunwald's room, bringing them up via a service elevator to avoid the prying eyes of the media camped in the lobby. The guard Caroline had hired was allowed to remain at his post outside the door.

Walker was made comfortable in a chair next to Billy's bed, and the official pressed a lengthy medical report on Billy's condition into Walker's hands. "You can rest assured," he said, in his elaborately effusive manner, "that everything is being done. We are bringing the best of medical knowledge and technological innovation to bear on this most important case. Nothing within the scope of the healing arts—"

Walker laid his white-gloved hand on the man's narrow shoulder. "Doctor, the United States government is grateful for your efforts. And we have complete trust in your wisdom."

"Thank you," the official said, making a small bow. "Thank you. . . ."

Walker pushed the man's shoulder gently in the direction of the door. "Now, it is important that you give me a few moments alone with our patient."

"Of course, sir. Whatever you require, I am at your service." The official backed out, still smiling.

Walker turned to his chauffeur. "Close the door and wait outside," he ordered.

When the chauffeur had gone, Walker pulled off his gloves and removed his hat. His face was flushed pink from the walk from the limousine. He was grateful that the room was air-conditioned, but there was much too much light. He moved to the window and pulled the venetian blind tightly closed.

He sat down, flipped briefly through the medical report, then rested it in his lap and looked over at Billy Grunwald. He lay with his head propped up on two big pillows, his arms at his sides. An I.V. tube ran from one wrist to a plastic bottle hanging from a pole. Another tube ran from his nostrils to an oxygen-supply valve in the wall behind the bed. He had been washed and shaved, and his hair was combed.

"Well, your medical prognosis seems quite favorable," Walker said, tapping a long-nailed finger on the top page of the report. "Unfortunately," he added, with a wheezing sigh, "the political prognosis is not."

Walker removed the handkerchief from the breast pocket of his linen suit and dabbed his brow delicately. "I don't suppose you can hear me, so I won't bother to explain."

Billy's legs moved slightly under the bedclothes. Walker flinched in surprise, and waited to see if he moved again. He didn't.

"Right at this moment you're a hero," Walker said, like a proud mentor congratulating his best student. "A genuine hero. That's such a rare and privileged thing, isn't it? How many of us, in our entire lifetimes, can ever claim such status? Yet you have achieved it. The fact that your cause is lost in no way detracts from your glory. In fact, it really makes you more attractive."

Walker patted the handkerchief on the wattles of flesh around his neck. He saw the pitcher of ice water on the bed table and poured himself a glass. It tasted sulphuric. He sat down again. "But tomorrow, or several months from now, you will fall from grace. Today's hero will become tomorrow's villain. You will have to face all the ugliness of a court-martial. And the Press, who wait for you downstairs, eager today to make you a legend, will tomorrow, without a trace of regret, tear you apart."

Walker burped from the water. "You weren't supposed to get this far, you know. You and that extraordinary brother of yours certainly defied the odds. A remarkable performance, truly."

Walker's voice grew stern. "But you shouldn't have done it, you see. You should never have come out. Don't you understand that? My God, the inquiries, the inquisitions you would have to endure. The rumors, the scandals, the disgrace. The harm to our government. The questions that would be asked—thousands of questions—by the media, by this committee and that committee. It would be ruthless, unfair. You don't want that. You don't want to see your life broken open and trampled on, your family disgraced."

Walker took a deep breath, pushed himself up out of the chair, and waddled the two steps to Billy's bedside. He squeezed Billy's wrist between his thumb and forefinger. The pulse was strong. "Can you hear me, Billy?"

Billy gave no indication that he could.

Walker lifted Billy's head gently and slipped one of the pillows out from under it. "It's a tribute to your stature that you caused me to come all the way out here, just to settle your case."

Walker placed the pillow over Billy's face and pressed down on it with both hands, leaning as much of his considerable weight into the effort as he could. He felt no resistance.

"You'd have wanted it this way," he whispered. "Believe me, you would."

He held the pillow in place for nearly five minutes, then removed it, raised Billy's head, and tucked it back under his neck. He felt for the pulse again. There was none.

A thin sheen of perspiration covered Walker's glowing pink flesh. He washed his hands at the sink in the corner of the room, then mopped around his face and neck with a towel. "After all," he said, folding the towel and hanging it back on its rack, "nobody wants to live in disgrace."

He recovered the medical report from the chair, folded it and tucked it into his side jacket pocket, and left the room.

The hospital parking lot spun into sight below him. There was some space near the back, if he could get low enough soon enough. "Strap Rob into the seat beside you," he yelled without looking back, "and buckle yourself in tight! This may turn into a crash landing!"

McWhirter came down to fifty feet, banked around behind an office building and a pagoda, and straightened the Helio out for the approach to the parking lot. There were obstacles everywhere—trees, walls, utility poles. The only space clear of cars was a ridiculously small area at the far end of the lot about fifty feet long, bracketed on one end by a ten-foot-high Cyclone fence, and on the other, by a wall of the hospital. He was confident he could float the plane into it, but there was no room at all for a rollout. He had one stunt up his sleeve to solve that problem, but he had done it only once before and that was unintentionally—trying to land in a windstorm on the Plane of Jars, many years ago. He had survived, but the plane, a Pilatus Porter, had not.

He drifted the Helio over the Cyclone fence, his wings just squeezing between the trunks of two large trees, hit the tarmac about forty feet from the hospital wall, and slammed the ailerons to full extension and the rudder full right, causing the plane's tail to sweep around like the rear of a car spinning out of control. A millisecond before the tail reached the 180-degree point of its swing, facing him back the way he had come, he jabbed the throttle forward, giving the propeller a quick boost of RPMs, timing it so that the sudden acceleration acted as a brake, slowing the plane's backward dash. It still crashed into the hospital wall, the tail collapsing against the solid façade of concrete block like a flimsy toy.

McWhirter shut the throttle and jumped out to open the passenger-side door. He helped Gilmore pull Rob out of the plane. Caroline climbed out after them. The front of her shirt and pants were soaked with blood.

For the first time he saw Rob's true condition.

Gilmore took Rob up in his arms. McWhirter started to tell him that there was no point in hurrying, but Gilmore shoved past him and headed toward the hospital's emergency entrance at the other end of the parking lot. Caroline ran along beside him, one of her hands clutching Rob's shoulder.

McWhirter started after them but quickly gave up. He returned to the crumpled plane and rested his arms on the top of the open door, feeling too numb to move. Some gawking onlookers crowded around him, but he barely noticed their presence.

Across the lot, McWhirter saw a chauffeur leaning against a limousine with dark back windows. He looked familiar.

Of course. Walker's chauffeur. McWhirter guessed what was happening. Or had already happened.

His eyes went back to Caroline and Gilmore. She was in front of him now, pulling him along. His ponderous, football-player-size body was doing its best to follow, threading itself awkwardly through the lines of parked cars, a lifeless package of limbs bouncing in his arms.

Later, when McWhirter had time to think about it, he decided that this was the saddest thing he had ever seen.

EPILOGUE

Ghislene Ferrer, in her best-selling autobiography, *Targets of Opportunity,* devoted many pages to Rob Grunwald's ill-fated mission to rescue his brother. In the intervening years, numerous other articles and books had explored the story exhaustively, but Ferrer's account stood apart from the others in several significant respects. As both an eyewitness and a participant in many of the key events, she had the advantage of knowing where to look and who to ask, and her thorough follow-up of the story and the subsequent lives of the survivors shed more light on the remaining unresolved questions than all the other accounts combined.

Her chronicle of the extraordinary metamorphosis of Caroline Grunwald, for example, was particularly thorough.

As Billy's widow, Caroline became the sole living heir to the Grunwald fortune. When the estate was eventually settled, all its vast holdings, save for Cornelia Grunwald's personal trust, passed directly into Caroline's hands, and she set about immediately to transform it.

James Safier, whom she had allowed to stay on as chief executive officer of Grunwald Industries, was summoned to Greenwood one morning and given an assignment unique in the annals of big business: He was offered the choice of either resigning immediately or, in return for a large cash settlement, presiding over the liquidation of the entire corporation. Safier tried desperately to dissuade Caroline, to stall her, to outmaneuver her, and, finally, to block her legally. But nothing worked.

Ultimately, Safier accepted Caroline's offer. It took him several years, but he eventually dismantled Grunwald Industries totally, selling off each of the major divisions one at a time for the best price he could negotiate, until nothing was left but the shell of the parent company, which he then simply put of of business. A rich man, he went on to establish his own management-consulting firm, Ferrer reported, and lead the life of a bachelor playboy. He became a fixture on the New York party circuit, with a reputation for dating models and actresses and drinking too much.

With the enormous pool of capital created by the liquidation, Caroline established, with the blessing of Cornelia Grunwald, the Robert Grunwald Foundation, a nonprofit organization dedicated to the assistance of refugees and victims of oppression worldwide. She appointed herself Chairman of the Board, and through her foundation, went on to become a powerful national voice in diplomatic and political matters, and the darling of the media, who chronicled her every public appearance with the slavish attention normally reserved only for movie celebrities and heads of state.

She reverted to her maiden name, Caroline Appleton, and after she had legally adopted the Laotian orphan Lin Pao, she rechristened him "Lindsay Paul Appleton," and established a fifty-million-dollar trust for him. She hired the best tutors to educate him, and after two years of diligent academic effort, he was accepted at Groton, where he quickly rose to the top of his class.

Howard Gilmore established his software company and prospered. He saw Caroline through the worst days immediately after the tragic end of the mission, and continued to see her, frequently, for many years afterward. He also tried hard to persuade her to marry him. But the very thing that had brought them close, Ferrer speculated, was their memory of Rob Grunwald, and for Caroline, marrying Gilmore would inevitably keep alive her bitter sense of sorrow and loss.

So they remained close friends, even after Gilmore married someone else. And Lin Pao always thought of "Uncle Howard" as his second father.

Caroline herself never remarried.

It was ironic that, as thorough as Ghislene Ferrer's account was, it never penetrated to many of the deeper mysteries beneath the surface of the story. She never discovered, for example, the truth about William Grunwald's past, a secret shared only by Howard Gilmore and

Caroline, and the chief reason, of course, for Caroline's decision to liquidate Grunwald Industries.

And neither did Ferrer ever unearth the real story behind the bizarre accident that nearly took Harris McWhirter's life.

McWhirter, who had dropped out of sight after the Grunwald funeral in Rhinebeck, New York, reappeared dramatically one morning about a year later, flying a single-engine aircraft of exotic manufacture over the Virginia suburbs of Washington, D.C. The plane, apparently out of fuel, crashed into a government limousine traveling southwest on Dolley Madison Boulevard. The aircraft struck the roof of the car in a near-vertical dive and lodged itself there. McWhirter suffered burns over much of his body, multiple fractures, and severe damage to both knees.

At Caroline's insistence, he was moved to the Dutchess County Hospital in Rhinebeck, where he spent a year, at her expense, recovering from his injuries. When he was released, she helped him get a job flying again, this time as an instructor at a local airport. His first student, Lindsay Paul Appleton, he took great delight in turning into a first-class pilot.

The back-seat occupant of the limousine McWhirter crashed into was not so fortunate. He was squashed so thoroughly between the nose of the aircraft and the reinforced-steel floor of the limousine that it took a team of men with acetylene torches all day to cut the wreck apart and scrape out his flattened remains.

No one, including Ferrer, ever guessed that the crash was anything but an accident, because no one, outside McWhirter and a handful in military intelligence, knew the identity of the obscure Pentagon official in the limousine—Alvin Payne Walker—or anything of his relationship with McWhirter.

Some matters that Ferrer did know about she chose to leave untouched—the Long Ba massacre and Billy's role in it, for example, and the circumstances of Frank Wyler's death in Vietnam.

Behind the main house at Greenwood, on a high bluff of land overlooking the Hudson River, Cornelia Grunwald created a small family cemetery and placed four gravestones in a row, bearing the names and dates of Sarah, Billy, Rob, and William Grunwald. She visited the spot every day, sometimes sitting for hours on the wooden bench she had placed under the shade of a giant elm tree. The markers, and the graves under them, were, save for Cornelia herself, all that remained of the Grunwald name. And the earth under the last stone, a beautiful rectangle of Carrara marble with a large Star of David carved over the inscription, contained only an empty coffin.

And there the last, untouched mystery remained, the final secret that Ghislene Ferrer's diligent research never uncovered.

Willi Gruen, the man who had lived for so many years under the name William Grunwald, was of course still alive in a labor camp in Soviet Siberia, unaware of the fate of his family and his fortune. Occasionally a report—usually a rumor overheard by a prisoner somewhere in the Russian Gulag—would surface in the international press about an old man in one of the camps who spoke perfect English and claimed to be William Grunwald. But such stories were simply too incredible for anyone to believe.